THE MESSENGERS OF DEATH

Pierre Magnan was born in Manosque in 1922 and has rarely left his native Provence. In 1943, during the Occupation, he fought with the Resistance in the Isère, and in 1946 he published his first novel *L'Aube insolite*. Since then he has devoted himself to his fiction.

PIERRE MAGNAN

The Messengers
of Death

TRANSLATED BY
Patricia Clancy

VINTAGE BOOKS
London

Published by Vintage 2007

2 4 6 8 10 9 7 5 3

Copyright © Editions Denoël 1986
English translation copyright © Patricia Clancy 2006

Pierre Magnan has asserted his right under the Copyright,
Designs and Patents Act 1988 to be identified as the author
of this work

First published in Great Britain in 2006 by
Harvill Secker
Random House, 20 Vauxhall Bridge Road,
London SW1V 2SA

www.vintage-books.co.uk

Addresses for companies within The Random House Group Limited
can be found at: www.randomhouse.co.uk/offices.htm

The Random House Group Limited Reg. No. 954009

A CIP catalogue record for this book
is available from the British Library

ISBN 9780099470199

The Random House Group Limited makes every effort to ensure
that the papers used in its books are made from trees that have been
legally sourced from well-managed and credibly certified forests.
Our paper procurement policy can be found at:
www.randomhouse.co.uk/paper.htm

Printed in the UK by CPI Bookmarque, Croydon, CR0 4TD

For Domnine Pico,
my ideal reader

I have smelt them, the death-bringers!
T. S. Eliot, *Murder in the Cathedral*

I

ON THE GATE OF THE CEMETERY AT BARLES, THERE'S A POSTBOX. When you climb up the pebble-paved road, you can see the slot from quite a distance away. The right-hand half of the gate is lit up like a smile by this carefully delineated mouth with a drip channel at each end for the rain to run off.

Many burials have passed through when the two sides of the gates are wide open, without anyone giving a thought to this slot. It looks out of place, although it's perfectly natural when you come to think of it. Actually, the thing itself – a postbox – is so ordinary that no one notices it.

During the 1960s, however, the murderer with the fine handwriting sometimes used this letterbox. It was very old even then, the bottom had fallen out and the door was loose. On blustery days, when the mistral whips around the Couar Peak as if it were the sails on a ship, this little door would gently rattle on its hinges. But there were so many rheumatic skeletons under this old cemetery who still predicted rain by the creaking of their bones, just as they did when they were alive, that this muted weathervane was not noticed either.

It was at the time when Émile Pencenat was digging his own burial plot, Sunday after Sunday. He had obtained permission, although there was no precedent for this kind of thing. The town council was not impressed by this whim, but could find nothing that formally forbade it. Moreover, there was a lack of men willing to do the low-paid work of looking after the field of the dead. Finally, to clinch the decision, Émile Pencenat had declared:

'I'll sweep your cemetery myself; I'll throw out the dead bouquets; I'll weed the grass around the graves, and I'll even pick up the pots of chrysanthemums blown over by the wind.'

How could they resist the offer of so much free work? They didn't even ask him why he insisted on a separate burial place, when there was a spacious and resoundingly empty family vault, because everyone was only too aware of the reply to that question: it was to avoid sharing eternity with his wife Prudence, with whom he did not get on.

Besides, he didn't like that plot. It looked like a Protestant mausoleum in the middle of the Catholic cemetery. It was sharp-edged, forbidding, and to makes matters worse, it had a mean and parsimonious view of eternity that made the afterlife seem quite unattractive. As it happened, Émile Pencenat was fortunate enough to imagine the realm of the departed in a happier light – when one has gloomy thoughts, all the more reason for them to be flowery: if it were possible, his tomb would be a small-scale copy of an eastern potentate's ceremonial tester bed swathed in gold-fringed theatre drapes. The whole thing would be dominated by an opulent canopy and surrounded by a festooned balustrade with columns.

'You're out of your mind,' Monsieur Régulus, the atheistic primary teacher, used to say to him, 'thinking of sullying such beautiful things with the excretions of your decaying carcass! It's just macabre hedonism!'

But Émile Pencenat took no notice of these sarcastic comments. On rainy days he spent his time in his shed sculpting cherubs' heads, with which he hoped to enliven the pink marble columns around his master-piece. Not that he had reached that point. He didn't know yet where he could get pink marble, nor how he was going to pay for it. But he'd only been thinking about digging his tomb for a few months; in fact it was since his retirement, when he was wondering anxiously what he could do to lessen his boredom. And so he had plenty of time to make enquiries, he thought.

One fine autumn evening when he was digging in the cemetery – the earth was warm to the depth of a whole metre – Émile Pencenat heard five o'clock striking and emerged from his hole to avoid being caught unawares by the evening dew.

He had scarcely climbed up the two steps of the stool he used to get out when he noticed at eye level a white rectangle on the vault of the Pourcin du Charmel family. This permanent plot was just below the broken letterbox that no one ever thought about. It had flowers in profusion, which were put there to last for ever: those vivid plastic chrysanthemums in colours that never fade.

Pencenat peered at this rectangle of paper. He came closer, bent down, and pricked his fingers on the sharp edges of the uninviting flowers. When he straightened up again, he found he was holding an envelope in his grimy fingers. An envelope . . .

Apart from anything related to decorating his final resting-place, the former postal employee Émile Pencenat had no imagination. The unexpected use of this letterbox didn't startle him in the least, despite the fact that until now it had been purely ornamental. It was, after all, quite logical. Indeed, what could be more normal than slipping an envelope into a letterbox, even though this one had no bottom? There was only one thing he found a little strange, and that was the address on the envelope:

Mademoiselle Véronique Champourcieux
4, rue des Carmes
Digne (Basses-Alpes)

It was written in a fine, free, even aristocratic hand, as far as Pencenat could judge. The word *Mademoiselle* spelled out in full showed off both the upstrokes and downstrokes of the pen. The word makes one think of a bird taking flight, and Pencenat thought he could hear it being said. The person of this unknown young lady was suddenly endowed with every wickedness. He imagined her tantalisingly undressed, like a model on the cover of those naughty magazines he sometimes leafed through furtively at the newspaper shop, on the days when he went into Digne.

The letter suddenly seemed to burn his fingers at the thought of this resemblance. He most certainly should not take it home. The very sight of the word *Mademoiselle* on an envelope that had sat snugly in Pencenat's pocket would make Prudence baulk like a horse at an obstacle. (The very fact that Prudence was his wife's first name had made him dislike the virtue it symbolised.)

Not that she was jealous. Heaven forbid! But she never missed a chance to make her husband's life a misery. One day, a long time earlier, she had caught him pawing Rose Roche, the tobacconist. Rose, a buxom war widow, seemed to have chosen that trade especially to meet as many men as possible. You should have seen her offer her breasts to their gaze as she leaned over the counter. Prudence took advantage of this indiscretion to deprive Pencenat of her body; not that it cost her anything, having always disliked sharing it with him, and wanted for some time to be the only occupant of the marital bed.

In five seconds flat she had set up a little bedroom in the draughty north-facing fruit storeroom, which smelled of withered fruit both summer and winter. Pencenat had no option but to put up with it.

Since then it was Prudence (always popularly known as 'the mother of security', after the proverb) who went every other day to get the packet of tobacco needed for Pencenat's mental equilibrium.

In the beginning she put on a thin smile for Rose as she placed her three francs on the counter. 'As if she was making me go without dessert,' Rose thought. She had intended adding Pencenat to her collection of men, as simply and casually as others might pin a missing specimen to their collection of butterflies. In the end, she could stand it no longer. 'I'll bring this arrogant female to heel. Just see if I don't.' So, one stormy day when the rain was falling so heavily that Prudence hesitated crossing back over the road for fear of getting the tobacco wet, Rose came out from behind the counter, hips swaying, and brought her voluptuous person over to thin Prudence on the doorstep.

4

'You know,' she said quietly, as a clap of thunder made the windows rattle, 'you were wrong not to let me seduce your man. I'd have taught him things you might have enjoyed, if he'd done them to you later . . .'

Prudence slowly turned and looked her square in the face. Rose noticed then that she had very pretty almond-coloured eyes and full lips that must never have been used for much else than tasting soup. It was from these lips that came the following indelible words:

'Perhaps you could teach these things to me directly?' Prudence said.

Rose's mouth fell open and stayed open. As it happened, for quite some time now she had regretted the fact that her enriching experiences still lacked an essential spice. It made her rather melancholy, so this was a ray of light. Prudence had scarcely finished speaking before Rose was hastily fastening the catch on the handle of the glass door. On that day she realised that behind Prudence's forehead were thirty-odd years of repressed unsatisfied desire. Prudence's tongue was so insistent that she nearly asphyxiated Rose, while she gripped her fiercely with thighs like a strong, thin goat. She was the one who dragged her, pushed her, willing and eager, towards the little bedroom behind the shop. And there, both of them had their first and definitive lesbian experience. After that it was nothing more than a habit dependent on the whim of the moment.

That's how you fight boredom in these sleepy villages. For here, as elsewhere, all that is needed is a little daring. Sometimes, deceived by appearances, you may spend ten years not daring. But once you've taken the plunge, you throw yourself into banishing anxiety with cries of joy.

Hardly anyone but gravediggers finds fault with that, even though they certainly get up to other tricks. Nevertheless, as he looked at the puzzling envelope that fate had just stuck into his hand, Émile Pencenat was far from finding it entertaining. He wondered how he could get rid of it before Prudence discovered it. Throw it away? The thought of that worried his ex-postman's conscience, just as he could not bring himself to stuff it down the nearest drainpipe. He finally decided that the simplest, wisest and most logical thing to do was to send the letter through the post, even though it naturally had no stamp.

'Why did I think "naturally"?' Pencenat said to himself. 'The natural thing would be quite the opposite: it *should* have a stamp . . . What the hell does it matter to me anyway? If Prudence gets hold of it, I'll be making my own bed for a week. I should just tear it up . . . If I decide to do that, I can read what's in it first . . . find out what's in it . . . A letter slipped into the cemetery postbox must contain something fascinating . . .'

But this fine word, *Mademoiselle*, written in full, kept his couldn't-care-less attitude at bay. Not certain what to do, with the envelope held carefully by the tips of his fingers as if he were carrying the Holy Sacrament, he suddenly realised that he had gone down the steep path from the cemetery, crossed the square dedicated to the Heroic First World War Soldier, and was now standing in front of the post office. He went in.

Félicie Battarel said later, when she'd had time to turn her original thoughts to her own advantage, that this time Pencenat had slipped through the door like a thief.

'Like someone who is feeling guilty . . .' she said.

He asked for a stamp, stuck it on, went off to put it into the box, the box outside, and went home with a light heart.

All ears as usual, Félicie Battarel dashed over to the basket. The only really enjoyable part of her work was trying to figure out the customers' little secrets by carefully examining the letters they entrusted to the post. All the more reason for her to do so, as the collections were small and the evenings long in Barles, which gave plenty of time to ponder each case.

This estimable postmistress, who weighed 80 kilograms for a height of 1 metre 54, racked her brains for some time, her rubber stamp in mid-air, guessing what Pencenat with his grubby fingernails could have to say to this Mademoiselle Véronique Champourcieux, 4, rue des Carmes in Digne. And where did he pick up this flowing, aristocratic handwriting? And . . . now she came to think of it: was Prudence aware of this correspondence, which Félicie immediately took to be secret?

A young lady in the postal service racking her brains can invest the dramatic potential of the most insignificant event with some very wild

6

views. Feeling the envelope with her plump fingers, in less than two minutes Félicie Battarel had imagined a whole human comedy of complex intrigues she hoped to explore in instalments over the approaching winter nights.

Félicie gave a little sigh. The only thing, alas, she was not permitted to do was to open the letter. But she hung on to it as long as possible, propping it up in a prominent position on her desk, against the green shade of the Carcel lamp, which was only used now as an ornament.

That evening, before Big Magne the bus-driver arrived in his Saurer mountain truck, she held the letter up to the bulb in the ceiling lamp, but she still could not see the contents. There was nothing for it but to put it into the jute sack with all the others, the ordinary ones that did not invite one to unseal them: their regrettable banality was so obvious at first sight.

But Félicie didn't really need the envelope anyway. It remained engraved in her memory. It wasn't business correspondence, nor anything pretentious, neither mauve, nor blue, nor even the pale pink that inspires all kinds of conjectures. It was entirely and austerely white, but a disturbing kind of white, like marble on a grave. This elegantly fine pen dipped into very black Indian ink – Félicie's experience convinced her of that – was not the only thing that gave all this whiteness a funereal undertone. From a slight creasing on the glued edge, she went so far as to deduce that the flap had been folded down and sealed by an angry fist.

Could one take intuitive speculation any further? In any event, the postmistress was ready to swear that neither the writing, the ink, nor the envelope came from the Pencenat household.

That evening, Félicie's imagination focused on that special letter until she fell asleep. As far as imagination was concerned, she flattered herself that hers was fertile, brimful and extremely colourful. Later, much later, when she found out, however, she had to admit that there are more things under the sun than can be conjured up by the brain of a solitary postmistress, deep in the valley of the River Bès, in that harsh countryside between Barles and Verdaches.

II

IN THE EVENING, THE MISTRAL WAS BLOWING THROUGH THE *clues*.[*] It rarely comes as far as that, but when it does venture there, you hear it like a hunting horn through the gorges of the Bès. The gorges are too narrow for such a blast, but the mistral never stops trying to force its way in with squalls.

Émile Pencenat walked down beside the dark playground where streams of dust made a whispering sound in the dim light of the street lamps. They chased after the thin whirling dervishes draped in dead leaves that swirled into the walls, vainly looking for a way out.

Pencenat opened the creaking iron grille gate and walked under the tricolour flag flapping in the wind. He looked up. A light was shining on the first floor, above the high classroom windows. Thin shadows were gesticulating in front of the low ceiling lamp.

It was one of those solid schools built in Jules Ferry's time, with its sturdy brick groins and window mouldings. One of those schools that had formerly been thought ugly, but through the nostalgia they still inspired now seemed to have a rather touching beauty.

Pencenat went down the corridor where a few forgotten scarves still

[*] The *clues* are narrow traverse valleys or canyons.

8

hung on their pegs. He went up the stairs. The door at the end was half open. He hesitated. Since he had posted *that* letter, then drunk his soup in silence sitting opposite Prudence, who was watching him intently, he felt a tremendous desire to tell his story. His head was full of: 'Would you believe it . . . Listen to this . . .' A while ago when he was with Prudence, he had taken a breath, and had even opened his mouth, then closed it again hastily before saying something he might regret. That was an indication of how much his strange experience preoccupied him. However, he was not very keen on the idea of telling it to the Wednesday card-players. They were all educated people who would purse their lips, give him a stealthy glance and by their silence make him feel how silly and insignificant they thought him.

'What could I do? If you were in my shoes, what would you have done?'

No one here this evening would answer these two questions.

Deep in thought, Pencenat automatically pushed the door open. He entered a large, well-scrubbed, old-fashioned kitchen furnished with a round table covered with oilcloth and a familiar wood stove. It dominated the room like a real person, and you felt that it was the most important occupant of the household: nothing could get done here without it. The cast-iron plaque, burnished with emery paper, gleamed like a dark mirror.

'There you are, Émile! What the devil were you doing? It's past eight o'clock! We weren't going to wait much longer!'

Wearing an alpaca jacket buttoned up to the neck and big, silent, clerical shoes designed to creep up on people, Monsieur Régulus was the last relic of an extinct breed of primary teachers. Every morning he put on a pair of shiny oversleeves and surveyed his class of twelve pupils with an Olympian gaze.

He was bald to the top of his slightly pear-shaped skull. His eyebrows bristled like ears of wheat, and the pince-nez his pupils thought he didn't really need gave him that glare he thought appropriate to assert his authority. He was so attached to the ideals of old-style secular primary school that he lit the stove in the classroom himself every morning, deploring the fact that it was now oil-fired.

The punctilious rigidity of his bachelor existence, which could hide the real person, whatever that might be, allowed Monsieur Régulus to disguise his real passion.

No one knew what it was. The only visible part of his secret was a fancy key, kept separate from the bunch hanging on the watch chain across his old-fashioned waistcoat. Hardly an hour in the day would go by when he wasn't fiddling with this key. Sometimes it would slip down the watch chain from its usual place. (For example, during the sweeping gestures he made when cleaning the blackboard.) Then suddenly his hands would frantically search his waistcoat and a look of anxiety would temper his glare.

Afraid that they might get him talking, he avoided open, jovial people whose cordiality could have induced him to confide in them. But one cannot live in complete solitude, especially in Barles, when the students have gone off down the street shouting to each other, and only the sound of the Bès fills the silence again. Consequently, Monsieur Régulus had resigned himself to making a few concessions to relieve his isolation. That was the reason for the three strange companions he had persuaded to play cards with him on Wednesday and Saturday evenings.

In his presence, Émile Pencenat found himself reacting like a schoolboy again. He hurried over to his chair at the round table and guiltily sat down on it. The mushroom-hunter shot him a severe look.

'Well, Émile? You certainly took your time! Were you making love to "the mother of security", by any chance?'

'Not at all, not at all, Monsieur Fondère. But . . .'

He didn't finish his sentence, pretending to catch his breath like a man who has been hurrying to avoid inconveniencing others.

The mushroom-hunter's lips curled with self-satisfied mirth at his own joke. On the rare occasions when he laughed it was noiseless; he looked like a skeleton with long yellow teeth. Besides, he normally never laughed freely. When faced with anything the slightest bit unusual, he was as resistant and touchy as a mule.

Esprit Fondère. This impressive, reassuring, well-to-do name graced a man with a strangely spotty, purplish nose and the round red eyes of a frightened rabbit under a brow that was brown and bumpy like a cottage loaf. He lived on the Digne road in a decaying villa overgrown with lilacs, comprising only two rooms, one above the other, under a four-sided roof where the rusty flag of a weathervane creaked in the wind.

When the postman had reported what the villa contained – a camp bed, a table, three chairs, a gas ring, four saucepans and two suitcases – the locals christened the morel hunter 'Ready-to-Run'.

He lived on a mysterious pension which must have been paid every three months, in cash, at some secret location. At least that was what the residents of the valley had been able to work out from his regular absences.

Big Magne, the driver of the Seyne bus, said that he had often come across Fondère beyond Selonnet, sometimes on the other side of Verdaches, or climbing the path up to Le Vernet and jumping into the ditch to hide as soon as he saw him coming. Once, Magne said, he thought, but couldn't be certain, that he even surprised him disappearing behind the tall thuja trees at the Chateau des Pautrelles, which looked down on some fine open country near Seyne.

When Fondère came back from these short absences, he paid his tab at Grimaude's bar and Gardon's grocery shop with crisp notes, sometimes brand-new ones; in any case, they were carefully folded and had a slight smell of that old lavender that people who lead quiet lives keep in their tidy wardrobes.

The pupils of the mushroom-hunter's eyes were always at the extreme edge of his eyes, as if he were on the lookout for something, as if he expected blows to suddenly rain down on his back. It also seemed to those who watched him from day to day that fear made his ears grow strange, pointy and quivering like a hare's.

Every three months or so a police van would park for more than an hour in front of Fondère's villa. The locals would watch those gendarmes, and as they were leaving would just happen to find themselves in their way; they'd work out little ruses to keep the policemen there: talk about stolen chickens, two-legged foxes, strange noises in the ruins of farmhouses. In short, they did what they could to find out what was going on.

Grimaude, standing at the entrance to her lair like a big-bellied spider, tried to lure them into the pleasant shade of her café with glasses of icy-cold pastis. Sometimes they accepted. When she thought she had them well in hand, Grimaude would stand up on her short legs, lean over the counter and say, full of anticipation, 'Well then?' as if she was expecting them to make love to her. But they just looked amused, winked, slapped each other on the back, said thanks and went on their way. Impervious to everything, they left with a smile for all, as if they didn't know that the locals were all hanging on their words like an Indian beggar at the heels of a lady colonel from the Salvation Army. (The expression came from the mayor, who wasn't from these parts.) Gendarmes wouldn't do you a good turn if they could.

Félicie Battarel said that they came to see if he was still there, if he hadn't run off. She said that he was ostensibly a free man, but that the country from the Barles valleys to those at Verdaches was actually his prison and he wasn't permitted to leave it. She had constructed a marvellous past for Monsieur Fondère, which fascinated her whenever she happened to meet him.

But what offended people most about him, and made them dislike him, was the fact that he took all the mushrooms. Some families had been been living here for nigh on a hundred generations, and yes, they found some morels every year, but only ten or twelve, sometimes fifteen, and not every family found some. He taunted them with the full baskets he carried through the village, left ostentatiously uncovered.

Some of the villagers tried to track him every spring, to no avail. He left in the direction of the Blayeul and came back down via the Montagne de Chine right opposite the valley. He began by doing two hours' extra walking just to put them off the trail. It was no good following him through binoculars either: he would suddenly disappear, swallowed up by the shadows on the edge of a wood, and sometimes even in the middle of a meadow, apparently sunk out of sight into the bowels of the earth.

And those morels: he ate the lot, on his own, without giving away a single one and without even selling any. He made huge omelettes, always to the same recipe (one egg per mushroom). People would say to each other, 'That must kill him in the end.' They pinned some hope on a type of morel that was very common in the area, and poisonous. But no, they didn't kill him. Besides, he looked so cadaverous that nobody was sure that he wasn't more or less dead already.

On the subject of Monsieur Fondère, Prudence had urged Émile Pencenat in no uncertain terms to try and find out something about him by whatever means he could. She was spurred on by Rose, who was just as intensely curious as all the rest, and who would not have been at all reluctant to enhance her erotic album by adding a person of mystery.

'Find out something!' Pencenat muttered. 'She's a laugh, she really is. What do you want to find out? And what is there to find out? The man's a poor devil, no more no less, just like the rest of us . . .'

However, compared with the master mariner, the morel-hunter seemed quite ordinary. When the old salt arrived here three years ago, a woman from the village was the first to bump into him – literally. She cried out in fright when her breasts hit his bony body as she was coming round the corner of a barn. The primary schoolteacher, remembering a picture in his old Mallet and Isaac history primer, nicknamed him 'Ramses II'.

You could say that he looked like a variety of kipper. He had the same nasty yellow colour, and sunken eye-sockets like flattened gills. Whisky had consumed his fat, muscles and nerves. The small amount of flesh remaining between skin and bone made a noise like scales when he moved.

The man always wore a navy blue wool overcoat that caught all the dandruff on its worn cloth. He walked in fits and starts, with a rolling gait, always looking around him for something to hang on to. At the slightest alarm he would bend over as if a huge wave was about to come crashing down on him.

He arrived without luggage one Wednesday on the Verdaches bus, and had received very little since then: a strange mixture of more or less useful things as might have been piled on to a makeshift raft in a sudden shipwreck.

The first person he went to see was the teacher. That was the beginning of their friendship.

'They tell me,' the captain began, 'that you know this area well.'

'I've been here for fourteen years, monsieur, and what's more, I was born at the foot of the Cheval Blanc, in Archail, to be precise.'

'Then you can give me some information. Can you see the sea from here?'

'The sea?'

'Yes. The sea.'

They were walking in the school yard at the time. Beyond the small plain where the village stood – the only possible place for it – all that could be seen was rock, collapsed ravines, high meadows cut off by landslides, rock faces outlining steep forests, and high above, very high up, the Blayeul on one side and the Montagne de Chine on the other. Whether you looked towards Digne, where a light mist always indicated the valleys, or towards Verdaches, with its glittering golden birches always blowing in the wind, the valley was locked in a V with both sides closed off. Boxed in: this sinister expression reminiscent of a coffin was the only one that was appropriate to the Barles valley.

'Where on earth do you imagine you can see the sea from here?' Monsieur Régulus exclaimed.

'No doubt you can't from here, but what about up there? From the top of that mountain? Or the one over there?'

'No, monsieur! You can't even see it from the summit of the Estrop!'

'What's the Estrop?'

'The highest mountain in the region: two thousand nine hundred and sixty-one metres, monsieur! No, I'm very sorry . . . If you want to see the sea, you need to go elsewhere.'

'No, but . . . You guarantee it?'

'I'm not guaranteeing anything. Really! What are you talking about?' Monsieur Régulus retorted, quick to fly off the handle. 'I'm telling you that you can't see the sea, full stop, end of question!'

Then the sea captain told him that his name was Horace Combaluzier; that he had been wedded to the sea for forty years; that he had eaten, drunk and slept the sea, its splendours and its siren call, its romance, its vast empty spaces. And he never wanted to see or hear of it again.

He raised his sleeve, showed his skin, his veins, his jowls, and his sunken eye-sockets.

'I was caught by the sea, monsieur, like a smelt between the metal bands round a package of stockfish. Salt got into my pores, my membranes, my bones. I'm salted to the core. I'll last for a thousand years in my coffin, monsieur, like a cod in its crate.'

He decided to stay. He bought an Anglo-Norman-style villa built on a rise by an eccentric man from Marseilles just before he died. He got it for a song. The house was half-timbered and made of solid stone – that shiny stone the colour of weathered moraine, the colour erosion paints on all the rocks in this part of the world. In it he had a bedroom facing north, looking out at three thirty-metre-tall pine trees that bent over dangerously at the back of a steep field.

Jealous because they hadn't been able to sell him some nice plot of land on the bank of the Bès at a good price, some of his neighbours thought they could annoy him by pretending to feel sorry for him.

'My dear fellow! Didn't you notice? The field behind the house is sliding down on it. It's bracing itself against it. No one knows how long it will last. We don't even know if it will last at all. Now, if you had spoken to us earlier . . . One day the mountain will cover that house! Plop! Just like that! You'll find yourself under forty metres of earth before you can say the Lord's Prayer!'

He replied that as far as the Lord's Prayer was concerned, there would always be enough time for the little he knew of it. As for the forty metres of earth, in his view that would scarcely be enough.

'On the subject of earth above me,' he said, 'I can't get enough of it.'

Sometimes at night, when the wind hurled itself against the narrow ends of the valleys, he would suddenly sit bolt upright in bed, his forehead damp with sweat. The sea sprang up at him through all kinds of intermediaries, keeping his fear alive. He detested it like an expert, as a man who really knows what hate means.

Sometimes when they were playing cards, he would shuffle and forget to deal. His obsession came over him like a rising tide. He didn't tell stories. Suddenly, with no warning, he would spew out what was eating him in words. Without catching his breath, he would start reeling off pages of a story he was writing in his mind, and which sometimes rose to the surface and emerged into speech.

'. . . And then . . .' he would suddenly say out of nowhere.

And the three others would stop and listen to him open-mouthed.

'And then . . . Calm the waves, just after the eye of the storm, with barrels of oil. It was the freight. I poured that oil out through the hole in the latrines. I must have poured a thousand tons! The bridge: a waste-land! No more mast, no more antenna, no more funnel, no more rails! The sea at eye level. Or thirty metres above us . . . Just enough rudder – it was buckled – to avoid putting us beam on. Three days and three nights. And you think the sea's nothing much at all!'

'Come now, Horace!' Monsieur Régulus said to him sternly. 'You're raving.'

'You'll see. She'll swallow you up! It's already started . . . Your Blayeul, your Montagne de Chine, the top of your Estrop. They're molehills! She'll swallow all that in five seconds flat. She's like a quivering, starving cat. She'll raze all the earth, drawing it under her, into her with sexual frenzy. She'll cover everything. You'll become just like sea monsters! You'll see, you'll see . . . I lived with her for forty years. When I tell you she's a bitch . . .'

So there you have the companions at the card table Monsieur Alcide Régulus had found to fill his winter evenings. (In summer he worked in the garden.) They were men who had retreated to Barles to lie low. In any event, they were punctilious, polite, quick to doff their hats, and agreeable enough company in their own strange way, despite their cadaverous coldness. If, in the past, they had played other things but fish, there was no sign of it now.

They needed a fourth player. All the taciturn mule-drivers, all the mistrustful goat-herders and all the canny wizards of well-kept gardens – that is to say, everyone else – had disclaimed competence to get out of accepting the teacher's proposals. He had been obliged to fall back on Émile Pencenat, who had reluctantly agreed.

As for Pencenat, there was nothing to tell about him apart from his gravedigging: no sea pursuing him, no mysterious income from beyond the deep woods, no little key hanging on a watch chain.

That evening he made some lame excuses for his lateness, which they grudgingly accepted before offering limp hands for him to shake.

'You realise,' he said, 'that I don't notice the time passing when I'm in my hole.'

'Spare us the details, please, Émile,' groaned Monsieur Fondère.

'I'm sorry, Monsieur Fondère, and you too Monsieur Combaluzier.'

When he was wedged between those two gentlemen, Pencenat would keep a low profile. In their company, he felt a barely controlled cold fear flowing around his toes. When they were all gathering their things to leave, he was always careful not to even brush against them. The school-teacher – yes, the schoolteacher himself – scared him stiff. In the same way as a hare senses the hunter, he felt he was dealing with clear-headed men who were always alert, while his own head was idle and empty.

And they looked as if they were thinking that he should have lain down long ago of his own accord in that wretched grave, useless as he was, and paid some hired hand to throw back over him all the earth he had dug up.

'Come on, Émile! What are you thinking about? I'm leading with diamonds and you follow with spades!'

'I was thinking . . .' Pencenat began.

He didn't finish the sentence. He meant to say, 'I was thinking about that letter. The more I think about it, the more it seems incredible that . . .'

But fear of their ridicule stopped him from confiding in them. He thought in his humility that he was dealing with people who were level-headed, impervious to anxiety, people who would laugh at his naivety; that's if they didn't accuse him of having drunk too much.

If the truth be known, they all had their thoughts elsewhere. Did they even see the colour of their cards as they slowly sipped Monsieur Régulus's

17

walnut wine? Sometimes a victorious trump card ready to be played was held suspended in the air while they listened to heaven knows what going on in the valley, around the school: the dismal howl of the wind, a fox yapping, an embankment collapsing into the swollen bed of the Bès, or the sudden outburst of a voice berating the wife or the cattle.

In fact, they were just as caught up as Pencenat in the spell of the poor land where they had found refuge, but which was inexorably burying them while they ceaselessly plotted and planned.

'You need to be well occupied,' Captain Combaluzier thought, 'to withstand the type of solitude in these places. The noise of torrents, streams and winds fills the silence and eats away at the earth, draining it towards the sea.' At least that was what he always heard.

At each round, Monsieur Régulus simply licked his thumb and dealt the card in silence, no doubt to allow his guests to appreciate the mystery of the countryside around him to the full. He did, however, observe Pencenat out of the corner of his eye. He saw on his face that secretive look of a child hiding a freshly caught toad in the bottom of his desk. It's a look that doesn't fool an old chalkie.

'It seems to me, Pencenat,' he said gently, 'that you want to tell us something.'

Pencenat, caught unawares, lied as one does under the gaze of a schoolmaster, without much hope of being believed.

'Oh no!' he said. 'Not at all. Nothing at all. I was simply counting. I was thinking that I've dug down for a metre and a half and, believe it or not, the earth is still dry. With the rain we had in September, it should be sodden . . . But no, it's dry, it's crumbly, it's easy to dig, it's light! It's just a bit damp at the edge of the hole – no more than a depth of twenty centimetres. Let me tell you, the bodies in there should stay dry for five hundred years. It would need a flood for *them* to get wet!'

He was very pleased with this improvisation, during which he had allowed himself to gloat a little.

'Well,' muttered Monsieur Fondère, 'it looks as if you at least are looking forward to exhilarating future prospects!'

'Why?' Pencenat replied. 'Death's natural, isn't it?'

'Not always,' grumbled Combaluzier. 'I could easily name some that were far from it.'

'Why?' Régulus asked calmly, as he took a trick. 'How does the fact that they were violent and unexpected, as you seem to be suggesting, prevent those deaths from being natural? And besides, what do you call . . .'

He stopped short. His watchful eyes turned upwards to the rim of his lids, then he raised his head to look at the ceiling.

'Sh!' he said, as if giving an order.

He had the impression that in his bedroom, or under the eaves, or – who knows – in the woodshed, some mouse was causing irreparable damage. And whenever he heard that, or thought he heard it, his blood ran cold.

This 'Sh!', meant as much for himself as for the others, was the explosion of anxiety that always brought his life to a standstill.

What wore him down was not the slow work of the Bès and the lulling wind acting together on the Barles valley during the night; it was the barely audible gnawing, there, quite close, in the shelter of the solid roof and school walls. That relentless, familiar gnawing that could have . . . that could . . .

In these anxious moments he always thought that he really should get a cat. And then he forgot about it. He half rose out of his chair and, with a gesture that looked as if he were about to kill a fly, quickly put his hand flat over the key on his watch chain.

'Well?' barked Monsieur Fondère, pressing his cards against his chest. 'Be my guest! Look at my hand now, why don't you?'

'Oh,' Monsieur Régulus whispered. 'I swear my mind was a hundred miles from the cards.'

'You're not feeling well?' enquired Pencenat with concern.

'Oh no! Nothing. Nothing at all.'

Régulus turned to Combaluzier with a wry smile.

'I too, you know,' he said, 'sometimes I too have my own oceans to contend with . . .'

*　*　*

'Tell me, Monsieur Combaluzier, I've wanted to ask you something for some time . . .'

'What is it, Monsieur Fondère?'

They were going out through the narrow school gate, which seemed to throw them into the street, or rather they shot out as if avoiding a hand of justice ready to descend on their shoulders. Once out, they usually went their own way, making off towards their various lairs at a strange, uneven pace, as if hurried along by invisible kicks in the rear.

Once again they had just been relieved of two or three francs by Monsieur Régulus, which happened more often than it should. And the strange thing was that Pencenat, with his timorous air and bad eyesight, always just managed not to lose, and even won sometimes.

Oh! In the beginning they had certainly tried to cheat, but they were dealing with a sharp-eyed, grasping man, wise in the scheming ways of schoolboys. The first time they tried some kind of dirty trick, Monsieur Régulus took a steel ruler out from under the table and smartly tapped the cloth with it.

'Tell me, gentlemen,' he asked gently, 'will I have to rap *you* over the knuckles too?'

They left it at that.

'Well? What did you want to say that was urgent enough to make you accompany me without asking me first?'

Walking along the path, they trampled wild oats and late citronella. They forged on through the autumn stars in the dark sky. Their clothes gave off a stale odour of cheap cafés. Their faces looked withered and they smelled musty, like men who had long been deprived of women's company. But this is the very state in which the most extravagant hopes can arise in sluggish hearts.

'I've had an idea . . .' Monsieur Fondère announced. 'To tell the truth, it's been niggling at me for some time, but . . . I hesitated to share it with you, as we scarcely know each other . . .'

'Is it so useful for us to know each other better, Monsieur Fondère?'

'Well, if we want to increase our meagre incomes a little, I should certainly think so.'

'Our meagre incomes! You might well say that. Especially in my case, Monsieur Fondère.'

'I have actually wondered whether you might have had some unfortunate adventures at sea.'

'That's hardly the word for it. Much worse than unfortunate. But I see that you've made enquiries.'

'I have a few old acquaintances . . . One of them met you in Malacca, when you were both rotting on the same wet straw, a situation from which you only just managed to extricate yourselves, it seems . . .'

'Indeed. But in my case, with only the clothes I stood up in. I had to start from scratch again.'

'Thank you for being so frank with me. But perhaps I should now explain to you . . .'

'No need. I have no old acquaintances, but I do have a surprisingly sharp sense of smell. You should stop keeping your clothes in those cardboard cases: they have a very strong whiff of prison about them.'

'All right,' Monsieur Fondère conceded. 'Let's just say that we have a lot in common.'

'Which goes to show,' the captain said ruefully, 'that crime doesn't pay.'

'I know a bit about that,' the morel-hunter sighed. 'I've hardly got enough left to live on now. And not anywhere else but here! But . . . who knows? Perhaps we went about it the wrong way. Who knows if today, with maturity and experience . . .'

The captain gave a wry smile in the dark and shook his dead man's head, from which the parchment skin had not dared fall.

'You've stayed very young, Monsieur Fondère . . . But tell me, I haven't quite understood how you fell from the love of God – you were a seminarian, I believe? – into the love of money?'

'Gambling, monsieur. I've always been fascinated by those double-headed cards, those red and black mysteries . . . They cost me, first off, a large farm in the Isère, in Le Grésivaudan, which my father inherited. As for the rest, I won't bore you with the minor details. My mother was a Bayard . . . In less than three years I went through a three-centuries-old flourishing paper mill in Pontcharra-sur-Bréda ... I ended up hanging around high-school gates. Yes, monsieur! As sure as you see me now, I hung around high-school gates!'

The captain took a step backwards, like someone deeply shocked.

'No, no!' Fondère exclaimed. 'What are you thinking? My job was selling drugs. My past is full of mothers on their knees, monsieur! Coke, heroin, hemp, magic mushrooms. That was my speciality! I picked them from the railway sleepers along the track.'

He gave a big sigh.

'What a life! I changed schools every day and regions every Sunday. I jumped night trains, scared they'd catch me . . .'

'My poor Fondère, your high-school stories hardly raise a laugh,' the captain burst out, having contained himself with difficulty. 'Here in Barles, standing beside you – by some miracle – my feet planted on this goddamn . . . well, on this ground . . .'

And he struck it with his heel to be sure that it was still there, real, firm and solid.

'I, monsieur, I was the guardian angel of ship-owners in desperate straits – naive ones at that – whom I alone could save. They thought they were big-time crooks dealing with the insurance companies. Poor things! In short, I wrecked maybe thirty ships, each of them repainted fifteen times. Only the rust was holding them together . . . Ships, monsieur, on the brink of collapse. They already had six hundred cubic metres of water in the hold when they'd scarcely passed the jetty. And at every pitch of the ship, the movement of that mass of water made it go astern like a stubborn horse . . .'

'And probably with a cargo of quarry stone?' Fondère asked, to be quite sure.

'Correct! Jealous nations began to imitate us. We were exporting a lot of copies of France's village war memorials. Have you got second sight?'

'It was fairly obvious . . .' Fondère grinned.

'Just think of it! Three hundred war memorials, dragging down a leaky ship. And me on board as boatswain, dragged out of the grog shops by invitations to crime . . . To christen them, I chose Force Nine winds likely to get even stronger. I had enough oil and coal to travel three hundred miles, no more.'

'No minor savings there!' Fondère chuckled.

A sepulchral laugh rose up from Combaluzier's hollow chest.

'Master mariners are captains for the long haul. I was a captain for the short haul!'

His laughter made him choke, so to calm it he lit a cigarette.

'The whole sea,' he continued, 'was nothing but a trap. I spent my time evading the setbacks my employers had strewn in my path. My inflatable lifeboat, for example. Well, I always kept it with me in a huge suitcase. Why? Because one night I found myself madly blowing into the valve of an air chamber that my ship-owner had slashed with a razor.'

Monsieur Fondère threw his arms in the air.

'That's hardly surprising,' he muttered.

'Why is it hardly surprising?' the captain asked sharply. 'Have you ever owned a ship?'

'No, unfortunately. But I can put myself in the ship-owners' shoes. A dying captain clinging to the railing looks more believable, don't you think?'

Combaluzier looked him up and down.

'You have a very practical mind,' he said. 'You'd have made a good ship-owner.'

'Ah, yes,' Fondère sighed. 'But . . . I can see that being a captain has hardly made *you* rich . . . judging by the cloth of your overcoat.'

'Decide for yourself. I worked on percentage: when my employers got ten years, I copped five, or three . . . Sometimes, if I could afford a good barrister, I got off with a suspended sentence.'

'We have both been unlucky!' Fondère groaned.

Carried by the wind, the night noises of the Barles woods – which had heard many a story – emphasised the dreadful whispered confessions of these two puny men and their oft-repeated refrain:

'Oh! We're unlucky. Oh! You're right: crime doesn't pay.'

Commiserating with each other in this way, they arrived at the captain's villa.

'But,' the captain said suddenly, 'one thing strikes me: you surely haven't followed me this far just to hear me tell you my life story?'

'No, not at all,' Fondère exclaimed. 'Although I must say, that has been a great help. You see, it seems to me that in the situation we're in, if we joined forces we could recoup a bit . . .'

'Where? Here? In Barles? You must be joking!'

'Unfortunately, I gave up joking long ago. But . . . have you been watching our host?'

'Who? Monsieur Régulus? An obsessive old bachelor.'

'No, but . . . Have you observed him really closely?'

'A secretive worrier. He's always playing with his watch chain.'

'Indeed. But it's not through anxiety. I've rarely seen a man more in control of himself.'

'On the surface . . . One day I saw him give a terrible kick to a dog that was pissing on the school gate. When he realised that he'd been seen doing it, he gave me a filthy look . . .'

'I didn't say that he couldn't be nasty. I said that if he fiddled with his watch chain, it wasn't because he was anxious. It's because of the little key that's always hanging from it. And it must fit something.'

'A lock.'

'Agreed. But what could be behind that lock?'

'No doubt a miser's obsession with nothing of any great importance.'

'Indeed? I've made some calculations. Régulus has been a teacher for more that twenty-five years. He's a vegetarian. The school boasts a big garden where he gets all his food. When I've been passing by, I've sometimes seen a student digging there on the pretext of doing practical work. There's a henhouse where he gets his eggs – enough over to sell! He doesn't have a car. He doesn't take holidays. If he has a woman somewhere round about, she can't cost him much, maybe nothing if she's bored . . . And finally, let me tell you: one evening I arrived early. He was rummaging through something in his bedroom and had unintentionally left his chequebook open.'

'Unintentionally? I didn't think our host was capable of acting carelessly.'

'Well, let's say he wanted to show me how poor he was. In any case, the balance on the last stub was ridiculously small.'

'Well, there you are! A primary schoolteacher, with the starvation wages they get . . . it's no wonder he's a vegetarian, given the price of meat these days.'

'Starvation wages they may be, but that doesn't stop me thinking this one could be putting away at least half. And half of a teacher's salary over twenty-five years, converted into whatever that key is keeping safe, and which must have increased in value . . .'

'Pure speculation. From too much time on your hands. How do you know that our host doesn't gamble? Just like you? And, like you, loses his shirt?'

'A miser like him? Not on your life! See how easily he fleeces us. He'd never risk playing anything where he could lose. Have you noticed, for example, that his walnut wine has so much sediment in the bottom of the glass that we always leave half?'

'Which he puts back into the bottle. I know. I've noticed him doing it.'

'Have you noticed that he always roasts the same number of chestnuts for each person? And he even fishes out the tobacco from his already tiny fag ends to fill his pipe.'

'He even uses ours and Pencenat's, and they're soggy with saliva. Oh, yes! As far as that's concerned, he's not squeamish at all.'

'And you'd have me believe that a man like that could gamble or lose? No, no! Believe me, Combaluzier, that man has a passion and it can only be a miser's passion. And it can only be something very valuable.'

'All right. Let's assume that's the case. How can we get this thing from him then? And first of all, how can we find out what it is?'

'Exactly!' Fondère said, panting slightly. 'Through the attic window of the toilet in the villa I have a view of the whole front of the school, with its high windows – without curtains, I might add. I can see everything: the classroom, the kitchen, the bedroom, the storeroom, the little window in the attic. Absolutely everything, I tell you. Only,' he ended pathetically, 'it's too far away. I can't make things out well at all . . .'

'Well then. There you are. Give up this utopian scheme. It's likely to get us five years anyway.'

He was already jingling the keys in the pocket of his overcoat, and was about to take them out to open his door. Monsieur Fondère was rocking from one foot to the other.

'I've been wondering . . .' he said hesitantly, 'I'm no doubt quite wrong . . . whether from all your shipwrecks, you might have been able to save one of those pairs of seaman's binoculars. It seems they're very expensive but very good.'

'Who told you that?'

'Oh, I don't know. Rumours going round. They even say that you lent them to Grimaude's daughter to spy on me when I go looking for mushrooms.'

'Rubbish! Why the devil to Grimaude's daughter?'

'Why . . . Perhaps in the hope of getting her into bed . . . as a foot-warmer . . .'

'You're joking! She's got a terrible hunchback.'

'They're the best in bed, or so I'm told. Anyway, can we be choosy, with all the skinny creatures around? I can tell you that . . .'

'She promised she'd come across if I told her where you find your morels,' Combaluzier said soberly. 'In other words, she was having me on.'

Monsieur Fondère thought more than twice before he spoke.

'Well,' he said at last, 'if we bring this off – once you've lent me your binoculars, of course – I'll show you two of the places where I find my morels.'

'You'd do that?'

'It's a deal.'

'Wait here!' Combaluzier exclaimed.

He rushed to the door, opened it, and went inside. When he reappeared, Monsieur Fondère hadn't moved.

'There you are,' he said, handing him the binoculars. 'But I'm warning you, that's all. Don't ask me for anything else. Steal whatever it is you're excited about, but don't talk to me about it again. I've found a spot with no sea and, if you don't mind, I'm not about to risk losing it.'

'Are you scared?'

'Call it what you like. But Monsieur Régulus said something this evening that should make you think twice.'

'What was it? What did he say?'

Combaluzier's bloodshot eyes in his pickled-herring face looked intently at Monsieur Fondère's spotty nose.

'Didn't you notice?'

'I don't know. He didn't say much, as usual.'

'Not like you, of course! You need a lot of words!'

'Not as many as all that!' Fondère retorted. 'And to prove it: I'm off home. The devil take your riddles. Anyway, thanks for the binoculars. I might soon know what it's all about. In the mean time, good night to you.'

'Good night?' the captain said wryly. 'How could it be good? Don't you hear the wind blowing over the breakers?'

All you could hear was the wind brushing against the bitter bark of the ash wood down near Verdaches. It was a sad sound.

'Look!' Monsieur Fondère whispered.

He squeezed his companion's arm as he pointed through the branches to the school, where the light had just gone out in one window and another lit up.

'Look!' Fondère said again, highly excited. 'I bet he's counting his treasure!'

'Or his oceans . . .' the captain murmured.

He closed the front door on his companion, who was still standing there transfixed, staring at the school.

III

AT A VERY QUICK TEMPO, WHICH SHE INVARIABLY ADOPTED WHEN filled with emotion, Mademoiselle Véronique Champourcieux was murdering a Brahms sonata at her out-of-tune piano. She always stumbled over the same phrase and, on the pretext of wanting to perfect it, repeated it over and over again so that she could be moved by it to her heart's content.

And indeed this music, sobbing with so much unexpressed love, went straight to Véronique's lonely heart. Her angular body had faded without ageing, the dark lines under her eyes an indication that she had had dry skin all her life. That did not prevent her, however, from having a tender heart and sighing with regret.

When the winds of lost years are blowing through the trees, a Brahms sonata is not much of a defence against profound loneliness, and yet Véronique Champourcieux came back to it time and time again, threw herself into it like a fly against a window pane, sensing perhaps that hidden somewhere in this mystery was a way to find love.

She lived in an austere grey house on the rue des Carmes, behind casements with open shutters and dirty windows leading to dark bedrooms. The autumnal meditations of Brahms rustled through the empty rooms, where bygone families – so large, so noisy, so real – were now a distant, mouldering memory.

Each separate note hung in the permanent silence of the long corridors and the staircase with the steps worn down by so many feet. The stucco angels' heads supporting the mouldings of the Gothic arches in the ceiling seemed to be listening to this German music with a look of surprise, as if they had never heard anything like it.

The fragile lace of the railing itself, with its twenty-metre spiral forged in one piece, vibrated up and down its length like an iron harp. Although the house had been peaceful for fifty years, it had not yet completely freed itself of the busy hubbub that Monsieur Champourcieux, Véronique's father ('the man of iron'), had imposed during his lifetime through his business in leather and cobblers' tools, carried on from father to son since 1830. It was as though a host of factory lads, jobbers and metal-trimmers were scandalised to hear this music and, afraid of being caught listening to it, were scuttling off in all directions through the empty stables, the lofts and the lattice-walled drying areas under the highest roof in Digne. Sometimes an ox skin left hanging on a wire for half a century would still flap in the night wind.

In this way the hollow depths of this ugly house were slowly filled with a long procession of ghosts haunted by bitter regrets. Véronique had only to press the keys lightly with her thin, ringless fingers roughened by the housework that took up all her time, and this ghostly population would sigh.

She was certainly fanatical about order and cleanliness, but the size of the house had a correspondingly discouraging effect on her willingness to do the necessary work. She never got to the end of tidying, dusting, and washing windows, floors and tiles. Some fireplaces – in her mother's sewing room and her father's billiard room – had never had their ash removed. It had been there for years under a thick layer of dust, like the bulls with square-cut beards that decorated the fire dogs. There were some rooms, cellars and lofts Véronique had not visited since she was a child, when she played hide-and-seek with her cousins.

In particular, five or six abandoned fulling mills that stood in deep shade, below the field of nettles that sloped down from the north side of the house. After the last stiff turn of their indestructible wooden arms, the machines had frozen three quarters of a century ago. The unbearable smells that used to hang over the tanning leather still lingered on the ground or in the stained stone troughs, but having lost their sting, they only gave off a mild whiff of green Spanish leather.

These basement of these mills led to the gaping tunnel of a water supply canal which had dried up long ago. And even here, in the deepest shadows, under vaults eaten away by saltpetre, the notes played up there in the formal drawing room still trembled in the stale air.

These were the only beings Véronique Champourcieux had had around her since the death a few years ago of the father to whom she had devoted her whole life.

Outside, the October night swept along the garden paths lined with hardy saxifrage, under the plane trees moaning in the rising wind.

All around her, the town of Digne, sleepy and secretive Digne, was taking stock of the day behind closed shutters. You could go out for a walk at eleven o'clock at night in any guise at all: carnival costume, golden-spurred horsemen, girls in see-through underwear and harlots' corsets, stern monks in wooden sandals, magicians in top hats and evening capes, carrion-coloured ghosts, Tibetan lamas in shimmering black, sailing down the footpaths of the boulevard Gassendi as if over water, wearing shoes with huge points curved around like horns. Yes, you could wander about through Digne dressed as any of these if you liked without causing the slightest stir.

To prove the point: two people passed by unnoticed. The first was a widow in full mourning, whose high-heeled patent shoes clicked smartly on the footpath. The second was even stranger: a moped rider of indeterminate shape on a colourless machine, probably with buckled wheels and a light that went out with every turn of the wheel. It was impossible to make out the night rider's face as it was so wan, even with the street lighting, and what he was wearing looked so strange and ragged that it defied description.

Both of them crossed the esplanade below the statue of Gassendi, albeit an hour apart, without anyone being aware of them or reacting to their presence.

After being twirled around by the wind, the dead leaves blown from the plane trees sometimes stuck their spread fingers on to the extraordinary outfits of these furtive passers-by, as if they were part of an invisible force intent on holding them back.

Both of them were heading towards the rue des Carmes and the former Champourcieux tannery. They calmly made their way along the courtyard of the police station, where the man on duty was crouched over the oil stove reading *The Red Inn*.[*] They went past the last café still open without quickening their pace. The waitress, professionally sensual, was dreamily drying a saucer between the curves of her breasts. In front of her, three tired, limp, unsteady men were propping up the counter over their last coffee laced with kirsch. They lusted after her like a promised land, and dared not go home to bed for fear of the night, loneliness and their wandering thoughts.

Neither the men, nor the waitress, nor even the owner, Pernelle Fabre, frowning as she calculated the takings in front of the cash register, noticed the two figures who slipped past them on the footpath, an hour apart.

The unusual moped rider, almost hunchbacked in appearance, with a very pale face, had got off the moped and was pushing it. In the distance the River Bléone flowed mournfully over its unstable bed. Close to the boulevard Gassendi, the big trees blown by the wind obscured the street lamps. The wind also carried the sound of the Brahms sonata, which could be heard from the beginning of the path, just through the gateway to the tannery.

'Oh, damn!' the woman in widow's clothes exclaimed softly as she hurried along on her spike heels. 'There's Véronique attacking her piano again!'

The front of the Champourcieux tannery still had its faded name painted in *trompe l'œil* on a scroll. The building hit you in the face,

---

[*] This spine-chilling tale, reminiscent of that of Sweeney Todd, is based on fact. Guests at the Auberge de Peyrebelle in the Ardèche were robbed of their valuables, killed, and disposed of in the oven.

31

appearing out of the shadows at the end of the path, as soon as you moved towards it. It presented the stubborn features of a human being who had decided its future a long time ago. The former factory received you full on, with all its cantankerous heart and its plain, graceless exterior. Surprisingly enough, during the fifty years it had been disused, the distress of the things that had mouldered there had endowed it with a kind of soul.

Three high windows on the first floor were the only ones lit. The two sides of the door beneath the fanlight were wide open to the hall.

'Always without a care in the world!' the widow thought. 'How many times have I advised her to close her door. If she knew what I know . . .'

She went in. A small lamp dimmed by a layer of greasy dust hung in a corner at the end of a long bare wire. It was the only beacon lighting the scrolls of the grand staircase with its fragile banister decorated with wrought-iron flowers.

'How mean!' the widow thought. 'At least I have a chandelier. I'll admit it's dirty – but at five metres above the ground, what can you do? But at least it's a chandelier.'

She had never liked this dim staircase much. It went up the three storeys in a single curve to the almost invisible landings, and at the top it continued directly up to the roof, as if Monsieur Champourcieux had intended to add yet another floor to his factory.

Through the sighs of Brahms's music, Véronique heard the imperious clacking of very high heels on the stairs. Both sides of the doors to the red drawing room were wide open too, and she could also hear the soughing of the tall trees outside.

'Blow!' she thought. 'It's Ambroisine!'

The peremptory clacking of the heels was now accompanied by the determined swishing of several layers of silk.

'Véronique!' Ambroisine called out. 'Véronique! Are you there?'

'I'm here,' Véronique replied in measured tones. 'No need to shout . . .'

'Véronique!' Ambroisine called out again, taking no notice of the reply.

Through the doors with carved foliage, she burst into the cheerful light of several chandeliers. There was Véronique all in black, a stark contrast to the sumptuous red surroundings.

Ambroisine was a very attractive woman of about forty; the kind that connoisseurs of female flesh dream about. She had a few unexpected imperfections, of the sort that excite perceptive males not particularly drawn to flawless beauty. They only made her seem more enticing.

She collapsed into the nearest red chair.

'Phew!' she breathed. 'I've been running. Excuse me.'

Véronique slowly turned round towards her.

'You really don't change, do you?' Ambroisine continued. 'Here you are still acting out your unrequited love for that big, beer-sodden man! And don't tell me: "If he'd drunk less, he'd have been liked more!"'

'No doubt,' Véronique replied sharply. 'But then who would have consoled us?'

'Ah! Yes indeed. Consolation. That's it. To be consoled by a third-rate musician is a fine excuse for not living! Do I need consoling?'

'No doubt, judging by your get-up . . .' Véronique said. 'But come to think about it . . . You've been a widow for two years now. And really, if I may say so, you don't look so very inconsolable.'

'Don't call it a get-up, please! If you only knew what it cost . . . But you've no idea how it captivates the men. Without all this black – well chosen, I might add – I'd only be one sensual woman among many others, which, even at my age . . .'

'But you've no need to envy my age, my dear Ambroisine . . .'

'True. I do forget we're both approaching forty-three.'

'Knocking at the door, more like it . . .' Véronique said sadly.

'But look at me. And look at you. Don't you see a big difference between your forty-three years and mine?'

'Yours are more showy,' Véronique conceded.

'Perhaps. But if you like, we can have a contest. Let's go out one evening, you in the check suit that looks so good on you, and me in my widow's silks. You'll see if they don't . . .'

'Oh, but . . . it's not necessary. I'll take your word for it.'

'Pity. We'd have caused a sensation. Mind you, it's not as simple as that. You have to do the rounds of the cafés at closing time, and not worry about hanging around the bar.'

'And what do you get out of all that?'

'I get laid! Yes, my dear. You'll have to get used to it. That's the word these days. Anyone who's afraid of it doesn't make love. Oh, I know: you have a good reputation and I have a bad one. I don't deny it. But in the mean time, I make love. Nearly every night. Well . . . one night in four, or five . . . You should try it. Believe me, it banishes fear.'

'Fear?' Véronique exclaimed. 'You're afraid . . .'

She bit her tongue. She was about to say 'you too'.

The widow got out of her red armchair as if pricked by a thorn. She began to walk around the piano and the sofas, wringing her hands.

'Yes, afraid! Absolutely! Scared witless. Oh, of course, as someone who leaves her front door wide open, you can well make fun of me!'

'Why would I do that?' Véronique said gently. 'Fear's a natural reaction . . .'

'Oh, I don't know,' Ambroisine replied. 'I don't know if the fear I feel is natural . . . Or rather, I don't know if I'm afraid of something that's really natural . . .'

She stopped beside her cousin and knelt in front of her where she sat. Véronique saw Ambroisine's slightly veined chubby cheeks, her nose that was more comic than sensual and the outline of her pouting lips enlarged with a lipstick brush in a red that clashed with the rest of her face and made it look cheap.

'But,' Véronique thought, 'she probably does it on purpose.'

'Do you have an attic?' Ambroisine asked out of the blue, almost in a whisper.

'What a question! Of course I have an attic. And lots of other outbuildings.'

Véronique patted her hair with a certain self-satisfaction.

'My place is at least as good as yours . . .'

'Indeed!' Ambroisine replied. 'Have you ever had cedars around your house?'

'I have my plane trees!'

'No doubt! I can hear them. But the music they make is nothing compared with the symphony of my cedars. To prove my point: he always chooses the time when the wind rocks their branches. He thinks they'll muffle the noise he makes.'

'Who is this "he"?'

'The person who walks in my attic at night.'

'Why . . .' Véronique began.

She hesitated for a moment. Her dear cousin was being too forthcoming. Fear increases tenfold once it is put into words. Ambroisine should have known that.

'Why are you telling me this?' she continued. 'And why this particular evening?'

'Because I'm afraid!' Ambroisine said again.

She hammered her small fist on the piano lid in time with her words.

'I don't dare go home alone. I had a lover but he's left me. Besides, you know what it's like: even if they're unattached, they never stay all night. At some time or other you get too keen . . . And then the man, the other one, waits . . . He waits until I'm alone. Oh, he never shows himself. But sometimes, as well as the footsteps, I hear his heavy breathing. He stops. Everything is quiet. But I know he's there, that he's watching me and waiting.'

'And . . . what do you think he's looking for?' Véronique asked.

'How can I tell? You know what attics are like. There are things in there that must be a hundred years old!'

She began nervously walking about on the carpet, wringing her hands and gesticulating as she talked.

'In any case,' she said, 'he doesn't make a mess. I know. I went up there to look.'

'Attics are very dusty places. Haven't you . . . seen any footprints?'

'Lots of them! Down the middle of the room. For instance. Among my grandparents' furniture. Um . . . I mean *our* grandparents.'

She thought that her cousin was quietly smirking.

'Oh yes, I know,' she said. 'My mother was favoured in the will. But she had cared for them in their old age, after all.'

'What's past is past,' Véronique said. 'I don't hold that against you.'

'No? It did seem to me, though . . . Besides, how can I put it . . . If you want this furniture, you only have to send someone to pick it up, you know.'

'Heaven forbid!' Véronique exclaimed. 'Don't you think all this is enough?'

With a wide sweep of her arm she indicated the room full of ornate but solid imitation Louis-Philippe furniture, made around 1900. Just the right furniture for the set of a Meyerbeer opera, she always thought.

'You're right to refuse,' Ambroisine sighed. 'It's all so ugly. I really wonder . . .'

'You wonder what "he" is looking for? But why do you say "he"?'

'Ah! If you heard those steps, you wouldn't need to ask a question like that. They're the steps of a fireman, a roughneck soldier, a boor. And besides, I've seen his footprints. He wears hobnailed shoes. Big, thick shoes. Shoes . . . how can I describe them. Like a navvy's shoes!'

'Lace-up boots?' Véronique suggested.

'Yes. That's it! Boots . . .'

She clapped her hands over her ears.

'I still hear them now,' she groaned.

'Well,' Véronique said, 'we know one thing. A while ago you told me, "I don't know if I'm afraid of something natural . . ." It seems to me that hobnailed shoes . . .'

Ambroisine looked her up and down.

'As if you don't know that most of the horrors that abound in this world are capable of putting on hobnailed boots just to allay our suspicions.'

'You're saying some very strange things this evening.'

'I'm afraid!' Ambroisine said for the second time.

'Then lock yourself in.'

'That's easier said than done. The cellar door is completely worm-eaten. What's more, it gets stuck. A panel's missing from the one in the laundry; not to mention the hothouse that my husband had the weird idea of joining to the house with a glass door. What can you lock? And besides . . . One of my former lovers sometimes arrives unannounced and unexpected at three in the morning, either because he hasn't found anyone else, or he wants to cry in my arms because his wife's cheating on him.'

'You certainly lead a complicated life.'

'Probably. But it *is* exciting! I never have a moment to myself.'

Then she suddenly placed herself in front of her cousin so that she could look her straight in the eye. She no longer seemed distressed.

'I'm wondering,' she said quietly, 'why you haven't advised me to go to the police?'

It was Véronique's turn to look away to the score of the Brahms sonata.

'I imagine,' she said, 'that if you haven't done it, you have your reasons.'

'Oh! An excellent reply,' Ambroisine said sarcastically. 'And so well chosen. Of course I have my reasons. First of all, the police and the tax department work hand in glove. If you don't want a visit from one of them, it's advisable to keep your distance from the other. No one,' she maintained forcefully, 'is proof against a piece of paper that may be left lying about . . . And besides . . .'

She was walking around the room, apparently less anxious, having recovered her composure. She was also listening, waiting to catch anything that might come from the echoing depths of the house that was three times bigger than hers. But, contrary to all her expectations, nothing was happening there.

'And besides, to avoid further argument,' she continued, 'I've collected a number of those objects of pleasure that one can indulge in when living alone. I never know where to put them, because of the house-keeper, so you can imagine that I wouldn't want the police in the house.'

'You're talking to me as though you were in the confessional,' Véronique said. 'I'm discovering a whole new side of you. You were always much more reticent.'

'I told you. I'm afraid.'

Véronique was exasperated by this stage and stood up. She too began to walk around the room, looking up at the funereal paintings that hung around the crimson walls.

'You've told me that three times!' she exclaimed. 'What can I do about it?'

'By the way,' Ambroisine remarked, 'what have you been sitting on? What's happened to your piano stool?'

Véronique hesitated for a few seconds before answering. She felt as if she were blushing to the roots of her hair, although she had no way of knowing whether it showed. She thought she saw a glint of triumph in her cousin's eyes.

'It was falling to pieces,' she said, 'and I sent it to be repaired. I've had to use an old pouf . . .'

'That's no reason to cover it with a black shawl. My goodness! It looks as sombre as I do.'

Ambroisine gave this strange seat in front of the piano a disdainful little kick with her pointed shoe. When she made contact, a booming sound came out of it and echoed from one room to the next through the depths of the Champourcieux house, like a distant but threatening avalanche.

Ambroisine stood there astounded for some moments, her eyes fixed on the heavy black shawl of Spanish lace concealing the makeshift seat in front of the piano.

'It can't be very comfortable to sit on, can it?' she said slowly.

Véronique remained tight-lipped as she anxiously twiddled her fingers.

'Why ask me,' she said finally, 'since you know everything?'

'Everything?' Ambroisine exclaimed. 'Surely not!'

She took out a handkerchief covered with black flowers and dabbed the fine perspiration where her make-up had been touched up.

'Goodbye!' she said abruptly.

She had just realised that all in all, plane trees or cedars, she was no less frightened here than at home.

'Goodbye!' she said again. 'I can see that I'll get no comfort or advice from you tonight. You're away with Brahms. I hope,' she added tartly, 'he brings you to a good climax!'

She turned on her high heels and ran out of the room in a rustle of black silk.

Véronique listened to the fading sound of steps hurrying down the stairs and into the drive, where every few yards Ambroisine twisted an ankle on the uneven gravel. She remained standing beside the piano, uncertain what to do, looking around the room as if she had never seen it before. A kind of irrational impulse made her rush into the corridor and down the stairs after her cousin.

'Ambroisine! Ambroisine!'

Now she was the one shouting. A panic-stricken curse she wanted to hurl came to her lips with an irrepressible need to talk, to give shape to everything that haunted her disorientated thoughts like a nightmare.

She went out under the plane trees, right up to the gateway. The wind had grown stronger.

'Ambroisine! Ambroisine!'

She ventured out on to the footpath on the boulevard. She thought that she could still make out the widow's black silhouette in the distance on the deserted road. She was about to run after her, but then it occurred to her that she had rushed out of the house leaving the door wide open. Normally this never worried her, but this evening it pulled her back with the same speed as her panic had sent her rushing out.

She went up the stairs three steps at a time and burst into the empty drawing room. Once inside, she went to the piano and sat down again, cautiously and deliberately, on her makeshift stool.

She drew a long, deep breath and felt her jaw tighten. Her heart was pounding in her chest as she listened to the silence inside and the wind outside. Its irregular beat seemed to emphasise the murmur of the tall trees in the garden.

Véronique felt it unnecessary for all four chandeliers to be on in the empty drawing room. She got up and switched off three, leaving on the one above the door.

This sensible action calmed her. Before sitting down again, she opened the front of the writing desk, pulled out one of the many drawers and took out an object which she weighed in her hand. She put the object on the last keys of the piano, the ones she avoided as much as possible as they were so out of tune.

It was one of those tiny pistols with a mother-of-pearl handle and a blue barrel that ladies around 1900 used to hide in their muff, just in case it might be needed.

Véronique settled her bottom – which was still quite attractive – on her makeshift stool like a mother hen. With her head slightly to one side to catch the sound, she began playing again softly at the point where she had left off. That melody made her fingers stumble but her heart melt with gratitude for their efforts.

Since her cousin's unexpected arrival, however, Brahms no longer seemed to convey the same soothing magic. For that matter, a vague irritation had arisen between Véronique and her mystic lover during the last few days.

The fact was that fond, romantic Véronique became a she-wolf as soon as anyone wanted any of her possessions. There wasn't a single hundred-franc note, a single pot of aspidistra, a single crumpled circular at the bottom of a basket, a single word written on an old piece of paper lying around the house that she would willingly give up to someone else. What was more, that was the reason why she was so reluctant to confide in Ambroisine: it was avarice. To her, even anxiety was an inaccessible asset. If fear is a remarkable antidote to boredom, avarice is just as good against fear. Since she realised that her possessions were under threat, Véronique looked ten years younger.

When her cousin had burst in, she had hurriedly closed the album of Brahms sonatas. Now she opened it again with a quick, if slightly trembling hand, as if apprehensive that the letter it contained would no longer be there. That letter had been there for three days, opened out and clipped to the book. Tidy and thrifty as usual, she had joined it to its envelope.

It was a page of very old, yellowed music manuscript with a watermark that was no longer in circulation. Three quarters of the staves were blank; only the last two had been used to write this maxim in a flowing, florid hand:

The measure you give will be the measure you get.

Véronique reread these words for perhaps the twentieth time. She looked long and hard at the envelope that bore her address:

Mademoiselle Véronique Champourcieux
4, rue des Carmes
Digne (Basses-Alpes)

The postmark was quite visible. The letter had been posted in Barles six days earlier. It was the logical outcome of everything she had dreaded for some time.

'He hasn't a hope!' she muttered.

She automatically began playing the Brahms piece again. It seemed to her that she had at last found the ideal tempo she was seeking, as well as the lightness of touch needed for this melody of such gentle, resigned melancholy.

Was it because of the silence that reigned once more? The murmur of the plane trees had ceased. The chill of nightfall had suddenly laid the wind. The little that lingered over the grass and along the paths was soft and silent.

It was then that Véronique heard another noise beyond the muted music. It came from deep within the house, on a level with the milling area or the tannin vats; perhaps a tool hitting the earthen floor.

Véronique sat there with her hands poised above the keyboard. She listened. Nothing. The church clock at St Jérôme's solemnly struck the half-hour. She began to play again, still convinced that for the first time she would get right to the heart of this sonata. But it gave her no pleasure. There was an anger in her heart that distanced her from Brahms.

Then the muted sound was heard again, coming from the basement. Véronique's quick ears identified it immediately as footsteps coming up the wide stone staircase that jointed the vats of the Champourcieux factory to the milling area. One would have called them unhurried, nonchalant steps, as if the person had a right to be there. That thought made Véronique very angry indeed.

The mildewed door to the wine cellar groaned as it turned on its hinges. Véronique was shocked; her hands stumbled on the keyboard. The wine cellar! It was her father's pride. Very occasionally, for special guests, he would triumphantly take out certain bottles as if he were producing the Holy Sacrament. But since his death no one – Véronique never entertained, and drank only water – had gone near the racks, and they were covered in dust. The thought that someone could help himself to one of those bottles was intolerable to Véronique. She stood up, seized the revolver and walked resolutely towards the landing.

But then the creaking of the door that always stuck, on the ground floor opposite the entrance, indicated to her that the intruder had not lingered in the cellar, but had only passed through it.

She quickly came back to her seat at the piano and began playing again, although it was only a ruse. She was just playing one note after another as she listened intently. She even had time to vigorously rub the raised piano lid with the sleeve of her blouse, making sure that the mahogany was highly polished enough for the doorway and the figure that would be framed in it to be reflected in the light from the chandelier. She worked out that there was a distance of about six metres between that door and the piano. She would have to calculate her moves and only confront him when she couldn't miss.

Sometimes the pianist would glance at the little gun balanced on the end of the keyboard. Meanwhile the footsteps were coming up the stairs. Now they sounded quite loud. They were the footsteps of a man breathing hard, climbing with difficulty, not sure of being able to make it – a heavy, common man.

'She was right,' Véronique thought. 'He walks like a bricklayer or a navvy . . .'

Suddenly she couldn't hear him any more, but thought she could make out heavy breathing. She stumbled over a low note. She looked at the keyboard lid and realised that it was too small for her to see what was happening behind her back. She closed the music, took it off the stand and laid it on the lid. Now that there was nothing obscuring it, the front of the piano was just like a mirror. The chandelier, the carpet, the door wide open to the dimly lit landing could all be seen in it.

Véronique was not afraid. The knowledge that her property was under threat bolstered her courage. Besides, she felt a strange curiosity about this person who would sooner or later loom up behind her. Would he be like her?

The sound of footsteps began again, as weary and unconcerned as before. The intruder was now climbing the second flight of stairs towards the floors of unused bedrooms stuffed with objects stopped in the course of their lives, which would take ages before they no longer meant anything to anybody.

The feet kept climbing, sometimes stumbling against a step that was too high. They had now reached the second floor. A switch clicked. The footsteps advanced down the corridor. The ceiling creaked under a fairly heavy weight.

The syncopated rhythm of this uncertain progress amazed Véronique. She heard doors opening to empty rooms that had been closed for thirty years, as the shoes of the stranger with the heavy tread clomped across the parquet floor.

Véronique was appalled by this search, this patient quest. She was several times on the point of standing up, climbing the stairs herself and confronting the intruder with the little gun she found so reassuring. But she resisted the temptation, knowing that the safest way of keeping the best of her belongings was to stay there, seated at the piano, calmly and studiously playing the piece she knew by heart.

'He's got no hope!' she muttered, almost choking with rage.

She was sufficiently in control of herself, however, for the tempo of the sonata (*poco sostenuto*) to be unaffected by her fury. The footsteps could echo, the doors be pulled open on their greaseless hinges,

Véronique played on, squarely seated at the piano, with her mouth twisted in a joyless smile.

The stranger walking about the house came back from the end of the corridor, always at the same pace, then suddenly stopped. Véronique held her breath. The irregular rhythm of her heart travelled down to her fingertips and made them stumble over an appoggiatura. She went on again immediately.

The hesitant steps stopped and started again twice, but Véronique didn't flinch and the Brahms meditation continued serenely filling the silent intervals.

Then, with more creaking and stubbing of toes, the footsteps began climbing again. This time he was going up steps that were in worse condition than those of the first two flights. A few loose tiles rose under his weight.

'The attics . . .' Véronique thought. 'Whatever Ambroisine says, they're bigger than hers. He's not finished with them yet! Go on, look, you stupid idiot! Wear yourself out! You've got no hope!'

The clock in the tower at St Jérôme's close by gave a single chime. From upstairs, under the exposed larchwood beams that had been supporting the roof for 150 years, came the muffled sound of furniture being pushed about, the deep sigh of compressed air issuing from marriage trunks as their lids were opened, objects falling on the floor, apparently disarranged by someone annoyed and impatient.

A cat, probably flushed out from its hiding place, let out a shrill howl of protest, rushed down the stairs miaowing angrily, and fled into the garden. After a louder dull thud, someone up there seemed to begin quietly crying.

'My mother's harp!' Véronique thought. 'The brute must have kicked it!'

This harp used to be in the sewing room, and when his wife died, Monsieur Champourcieux had relegated it to the attic with the loom and the nest of tables. When his daughter expressed her surprise, he replied, 'Familiar things bring ghosts. Your mother has already made my ears suffer enough with her harp. I wouldn't like to find her shade sitting in front of . . .'

Véronique's keen ear registered and identified all the noises that came from above, as if they were the instruments of an orchestra accompanying her sonata. She thought the moment would never come when the intruder would give up at last, come out of the attics and down the stairs again to her.

After more than an hour's calm, she was almost startled by a sudden change in the direction of the wind. It was a wind that tried all the points of the compass, blew the leaves on the plane trees the wrong way, then pulled them off by the handful; a wind that slapped the face of the building with its own loose shutters. The racket made by the wind helped the stranger up above when he came out of the attic by covering the slow creak of the warped door as it closed behind him.

Then the heavy steps immediately began coming down the stairs with as much difficulty as when they went up.

Véronique was doubly alert. She needed to judge the approach of those steps and prepare herself well. The intruder had only this floor left to search, only this floor where the first door he had to pass was wide open, showing Véronique at her piano. He could not avoid it.

With her eyes trained on the reflection of the door in the polished mahogany of the piano, Véronique only permitted herself a quick sideways glance at her weapon. Even so, she didn't immediately make out what suddenly darkened the reflection of the space in the doorway and blocked out the gleam of the chandelier. It took her by surprise; she wasn't expecting it so soon. Nevertheless, her courage had built up so much as the minutes went by that she didn't flinch.

She went on playing with her left hand, as her right slid to the end of the keyboard and her fingers closed around the miniature gun. But there was something she hadn't foreseen that disturbed her: the reflection was too blurred for her to tell whether the person was standing still or moving towards her. She was worried that now the familiar sound of those footsteps would be muffled by the huge carpet with David's *Oath of the Three Horatii* in the centre. Six metres . . . not a very great distance. The intruder must not be allowed to cross it without hindrance.

Véronique swung round on her seat, the gun held in both hands so that she could aim without trembling.

No, the intruder had not moved. He was standing there blocking the doorway, squat, heavy, awkward, as his footsteps had indicated. But the resemblance stopped there.

He was a ridiculous-looking *sapeur* from a picture-book Napoleonic army, wearing a kind of busby that came down over the tops of his ears, and a big, stiff, dull white apron down to his knees, hiding his trousers. And he did indeed have those big navvy's boots that Véronique had identified. At the end of his short arms, he was wearing a pair of wide-fingered gloves with high cuffs of the same dull white as the apron. They were clutching a Chassepot rifle that dated from 1871, the terrible year of the Franco-Prussian war. Véronique immediately recognised Grandfather Melliflore's outfit, which had frightened her so much as a little girl scarcely five years old, when he used to dress himself up in it. It came from the attic. She had seen it only the day before yesterday during her search for the object that temporarily replaced her piano stool. The uniform had actually been piled on top of it, forgotten under the dust. She had had to remove it and put it on the marble top of a bedside table nearby.

As for the rifle, it had always hung by its sling from a low roof beam, and would swing with the draughts of air that blew through the attic. Véronique had hit her head against it as a child playing hide-and-seek. The frightening thought struck her that at least the bayonet at the end of it should have been removed. If he ever wounded her with that, she would get tetanus.

This thought flashed through her mind as she stared at her attacker's slack features. It was a kind of ruddy face but powdered frosty white, even over his wide moustache, where the snow of a previous winter seemed to have faded. The fact that death should have presented itself in such a ridiculous guise did not make it any less real under the high ceiling of that room, in the muted light of the chandelier, on that carpet where three Roman men were raising their three swords bound together.

But there must be someone hiding under this carnival figure of a *sapeur* of the Grande Armée. Someone real, with the head and body of a man. Someone she had to unmask.

It was this desire to know, as much as the sight of the horrible bayonet, that decided Véronique to almost instinctively press the trigger.

A ridiculous little sound like a strangled chicken was the only result of her action. A miniature lady's gun, unused for fifty years, sometimes plays this trick on you: its last one.

Véronique, panic-stricken, looked at it with horror. Without hesitating, she hurled it with all her strength at the vaudeville *sapeur*'s head, but missed. The gun flew through the door, along the corridor and over the wrought-iron banister. It plunged down to the ground floor, hitting the tiles in the entrance hall.

The *sapeur* let out the growl of an enraged bear as he charged at Véronique with the bayonet. He nailed her against the name *Laharpe* written in gold letters on the mahogany of the piano. When Véronique's arm fell back limply on the keyboard, the low notes sounded all at once.

Now that the cafés were closed and the duty officer in the police station kept nodding off over *The Red Inn*, it was even easier than two hours ago to go about in Digne looking like a murderer without disturbing a soul. The indistinct bulky shape comprising a moped, someone who looked vaguely like a tramp, and a large parcel jammed against the bike frame could go on its way undisturbed.

The moped, with its unreliable headlight and regulation red taillight, shot furtively down the boulevard Victor Hugo, the one and only person on the road under the chestnut trees. Without passing another car, or a lover coming home from visiting his mistress, nor even a dog knocking over dustbins, he went the length of the boulevard, turned sharp right, along the rippling Bléone, over the Bailey bridge and down the road to Barles.

Sometimes an indistinct rumble, like the growl of a caged animal, came from the black object on the handlebars.

IV

HE HAD AGED. HE HAD INHERITED SOME MONEY. HE HAD BOUGHT a house where he could peacefully mull over regrets at things done and left undone. It was a villa built in an extraordinary style of architecture and called Popocatepetl.[*] The doors were always left unlocked, in the hope no doubt that someone might try to murder him.

He had his lair in there on the ground floor, west side, looking out on to the garden through four high windows. As he grew older he had come to love the long twilight evenings painted against the autumn sky. He would stay there, not moving hand or foot, until the last gleam of light went out in the trees.

All the rest of the house – a large empty space still resounding with the tragic words of the former occupants – was only used to house his cats and feed his dreams. At his age he had no need of happy dreams; sad ones suited him perfectly.

At sixty he still had great difficulty in sorting out true from false, separating good from evil, choosing between strong and weak, whole-heartedly siding with someone not just to please them, discerning the superiority of one opinion over another, even deciding once and for

---

[*] See *Le Sang des Atrides (The Blood of the Atrides)* by the same author.

all if he believed in God or not, and sticking to it. He called this wavering indecision in his character – which spared him suffering – being a contemplative.

He had planned to settle in Courbons, to retire to Piégut where he had a house, apples, junipers and thrushes. But in the end he'd said to himself, 'Where better than Digne?' Everyone knew him here. They called him Superintendent, although he had given that up five years ago. He could go out without an umbrella, and someone would hand him one; without his wallet, and they'd give him credit, even at the tobacconist's or the post office. He could take for granted the friendliness of a whole population, which was so like him in so many respects, and he shamelessly took advantage of it.

There was also the friendliness of the climate, the enchantment of mountains, hills and valleys where the slowness of life was such a good imitation of eternity. It kept him in a state of divine well-being and deep satisfaction, knowing that he was part of it, could blend anonymously into its background and merge with all that landscape of the soul.

He put his patriotism into action, even taking an annual cure at the delightfully designed spa, although he didn't need it. On his return he would proclaim the great benefit he felt from it to anyone who would listen.

During his reign, Popocatepetl's unkempt garden had become the refuge of all the starving cats that the dustbins of Digne could not feed. They were looked after by old Madame Chabassut, who cooked and cleaned for him, fattened them up, killed the litters with chloroform, had the males desexed and the females spayed, when they could be caught. On the nights when the moon shone clear there were, nonetheless, the finest feline concerts you could imagine. He liked listening to them. He liked cats. He always had one or two of the biggest sitting on his lap, paddling their paws into his stomach, preferably after a meal.

In short, if happiness exists, Laviolette in retirement was a happy man.

One evening, it must have been around 10 October, he heard car tyres crunching down the gravel drive, and soon after, the banging of a disillusioned car door. Of course it wasn't the car door that was disillusioned, but the person who had shut it. There are a hundred ways of shutting a car door, and Laviolette had heard so many that he prided himself on being able to give a particular meaning to each one.

'The person who closes his car door like that,' he thought, 'must be down in the mouth.'

He waited. Someone was approaching through the fallen leaves. He slowly and almost unwillingly climbed the six steps that went along the side of the house with the four casements to what he called his 'lair'. A silhouette broken up by the lattice panes could be seen behind the French window. It was tall and thin, and looked rather old-fashioned, pensive. It stood there, quite still, like someone meditating beside a grave. The stranger finally decided to take a step forward and knock lightly on the glass.

'Come in!' Laviolette called from the fireplace, where he was roasting the first chestnuts in a perforated pan.

When he turned round, he saw a tall, thin man with a yellowish complexion and eyes hidden by thick glasses, although he was considerably younger than Laviolette. He had an air of condescension, but his face also expressed an incorruptibility that always goes with a certain melancholy.

Laviolette quickly recognised Judge Chabrand.

'He hasn't changed,' he thought.

Especially as he had thrown over his shoulders the forest-green carrick coat * that was so much a part of him. It had now reached the venerable age when garments begin to have a character of their own. It was shiny through noble wear, although scarcely halfway through its life, which made one suspect that there were still many years of intimacy left between it and its owner.

'To what do I owe the pleasure?' Laviolette called, delighted.

They hadn't seen each other for years. Laviolette had, of course, heard that against all odds and not a few complications Chabrand, through

---

* A nineteenth-century-style overcoat with a short cape over the shoulders.

hard work and good reports, had managed to get himself reappointed to Digne. However, Laviolette had never tried to see him again, and even discreetly avoided him, not knowing whether the judge would be pleased to meet him again, even by chance.[†]

'I come like Henri IV to Canossa[‡] . . .' the judge said in a rather doleful tone of voice.

'Ah!' Laviolette exclaimed, continuing to roast his chestnuts. 'I don't know what you mean by that, but there's a welcoming settee here, a coffee table, an ashtray and a footwarmer. Take off your shoes and put your feet in it. A chill wind is blowing off the Bléone this evening, and colds start through the feet. Besides, I've noticed that the first snow has fallen on the Estrop . . .'

As the chestnuts were cooked, he straightened up and shook hands with his visitor.

'Actually,' he said, 'you've come at a good time. I was wondering why I'd roasted so many chestnuts and especially why I'd taken the cork out of this bottle of Sancerre.'

'You'll recall,' Chabrand complained, 'that my stomach . . .'

'Ah! That's right. You had a stomach problem.'

'Unfortunately, I still have it . . .'

He took off his coat and laid it over the back of an ottoman. He looked comfortable in a tweed jacket that was too big on the shoulders. Over the last seven years he must have lost another three or four kilos. He sank down into the seat Laviolette offered him.

'Well,' he sighed, 'I'll let myself be tempted by a drop or two of Sancerre . . .'

He put his hand out towards the pan.

'And just a few of those chestnuts,' he added.

He began peeling them cautiously, as they were extremely hot, throwing the skins into the fire.

[†] Laviolette's house, Popocatepetl, belonged to Irene, a woman Chabrand fell in love with during the investigation of a series of murders when he was thirty. He blamed the police in general for not preventing her son's death, which turned her against him and soured his outlook on life.
[‡] To go to Canossa is to undergo humiliation, as Henri IV was obliged to do when he went there seeking help from Pope Gregory VII.

'You could at least,' he grumbled, 'have refrained from making your home in this particular room . . . in Irene's room. You really have no imagination.'

'Why? I'll be damned if I didn't do everything possible to make it unrecognisable. Really! Look what I've managed to make out of that temple of good taste. Something really awful,' he burst out laughing, 'but supremely comfortable.'

'The surroundings are the same,' Chabrand replied. 'And if I turn round, I can see the same trees . . . You haven't even got rid of the satrap's tomb . . .'

'A person's last resting-place is sacred. And it's in the title specifications. Besides, what a sun trap! I spend hours there lounging in the sun.'

'How do you manage to be so happy?' Chabrand sighed. 'You're alone, after all.'

'What of it? Do you think one must always have company to be happy?'

Laviolette got up, stretched, went and opened the French window for a cat that was discreetly scratching to be let in. It walked in majestically, tail held in an enquiring curl. It looked Chabrand up and down, sniffed the cuff of his trousers, remained unmoved by Laviolette's advances, and finally jumped on to Chabrand's coat, which it proceeded to trample with claws extended.

'Ah!' Laviolette sighed. 'You have to live with an open house . . . Don't you hear the magnificent wind in the trees tonight?'

'Yes,' Chabrand replied, 'I can hear it. And by the way, since we're on that subject . . .' He held out his empty glass. 'Let me taste a little more of that Sancerre. You may have tried to make this room ugly, but there's still something here that won't go away . . . something that still draws me to it. Alceste was right: time doesn't change things.'

Laviolette half filled his glass and stood waiting for him to continue.

'You can well imagine,' Chabrand said, 'that if I've come here this evening – taking it upon myself to do so, make no mistake about that – it's not to talk with you about the wind.'

He was silent for a few seconds, enough time to empty his glass and hold it out again expectantly.

'And even less,' he added, 'to bring up the past.'

'What's all this about Canossa?'

'A problem. An . . . insoluble problem.'

'Come on. That's probably because it's right under your nose . . .'

'There's been a murder,' Chabrand said.

'I know. I read the paper every morning, and more and more I find myself beginning with the death notices. So I knew that Mademoiselle Champourcieux had been called to God before hearing that she had been murdered.'

'Yes indeed. With a rusty bayonet.'

'Good Lord!' Laviolette murmured.

'Yes! At night, with no sign of burglary, all the doors unlocked! I ask you! Would you, in an isolated house, think of leaving your doors unlocked? At least at night!'

'Well, as far as I know,' Laviolette retorted, 'you had no difficulty in opening mine.'

'Ah! That's right. As I was passing, I even saw the front door banging against a big stone.'

'Yes. To stop it shutting. Because of the cats, you know . . . The rest of the house belongs to them and they can't turn keys in locks.'

Chabrand laughed to himself.

'You certainly are from these parts,' he said. 'You're a real man of the Basses-Alpes! Mademoiselle Champourcieux was very Basses-Alpine too. And look what it got her: thirty centimetres of rusty steel in the belly. That's what comes of leaving your doors wide open.'

Laviolette did not reply. He was peeling a chestnut and could see an image of Véronique between himself and the glowing hearth. He knew her, just as everyone in the area did.

A spinster . . . having devoted her life to the late Augustin Champourcieux (known as 'the man of iron'), officer of the Legion of Honour, an industrialist who retired about thirty-five years ago. He left a gentle daughter, whom everyone was sorry for, but no one loved well enough to do anything about her isolation.

Occasionally, when he came across her at the market, Laviolette had thought of going up to her and talking to her, trying to communicate. As she was rich, the only thing that could be wrong with her was loneliness. But there you are: life is made up of separate, fleeting moments, as strictly defined as a pack of tarot cards, and making these moments fit together takes a will of iron. And when one is essentially a waverer . . .

Laviolette sighed.

But now she was dead. He would no longer be able to give her that vaguely encouraging smile whenever they met. She was dead . . . Killed by a rusty bayonet. He tried to imagine it.

'And we have no idea,' Chabrand lamented, 'not only *who*, but also *why*. Nothing was taken; no cheques, bank books, money, deeds, jewellery – it may have been unfashionable, but there was a lot of it, all jumbled together in an old sewing box. Nor,' he added, finger raised, 'any of the fifteen gold ingots, each in a drawer in the old Empire writing desk.'

'Raped?' Laviolette asked.

'No. *Intacta virgina*! Nothing, I tell you. No sign of violence.'

'Apart from the rusty bayonet.'

'We found it. At the end of a rifle, 1871 model, undetachable, rusted to the gun. It was in the same room, lying on the carpet. The murderer had pulled it out of the victim's body.'

'Why?'

'Why?' Chabrand repeated, dumbfounded. 'How would I know?'

'I'm sorry. I didn't express myself properly. Generally, when a murderer removes the weapon from his victim's body, he intends to take it away. Or else he wants to use it again, even though it could help identify him. But removing it and leaving it there is very unusual.'

'Oh! If you react to everything that's bizarre in what I have to tell you, you'll never stop being surprised.'

'Come now, you're saying that to get me interested. You know I love cases that are very unusual.'

'Believe me, if this one wasn't, I certainly wouldn't have come. If you think I'm happy to find myself in Irene's room again . . .'

He threw a chestnut husk into the fire and drank the Sancerre in one gulp.

'And with you,' he added.

'Oh, come on!' Laviolette grumbled. 'You have a sneaking liking for me. Admit it.'

'Believe me, I don't know why.'

'That's very simple. Because you hope to be like me one day.'

Chabrand stood up. He was about to unceremoniously remove the cat that was ensconced in his coat.

'Wait!' Laviolette exclaimed. 'Cats have weak stomachs. If you're rough with it, it may throw up on your coat.'

He lifted the animal off as if it were a Sèvres vase and, with endless 'puss pusses', placed it gently on the armchair he had just vacated.

'Do you know the Champourcieux tannery?' Chabrand asked.

'Never had occasion to go there.'

'Pity. It's just the sort of place you like. Especially at midnight.'

When he had finished adjusting his coat around his shoulders, he suddenly opened his hand containing a large key that he had just taken out of his pocket. He held it up under the nose of his host, who was eyeing it like a delicacy.

'Wait a minute!' Laviolette exclaimed.

He disappeared in the shadows at the back of his messy room. Chabrand heard him there puffing and panting over something that seemed to take a lot of effort. When Laviolette came back into the light, he was covered from head to foot in a thick overcoat, muffler and fur hat, and was just putting on a pair of gloves.

'I imagine that's where we're going?' he said.

'Why not? I'll hardly need explanations at the scene of the crime. It will speak for itself. And you'll see that I certainly haven't made up any of these very peculiar circumstances.'

With that wind and that moon, the Champourcieux house seemed to have gone out of its way to show itself to Laviolette in the worst possible light. Now in complete darkness, it gave an impression of definite hostility. It had the closed face of someone miserly and mistrustful.

As soon as it rose up from behind the plane trees, Laviolette clapped his right hand over his mouth, as if witnessing a disaster. He was overjoyed.

'Good God!' he exclaimed. 'What a pity I already have Popocatepetl. This is even worse.'

The shutters creaking on their hinges began to slap hard against the front of the house. A downpipe rattled in its loose brackets. The leaves of a Virginia creeper on the wrought-iron arbour were spewing on to the ground. High up, at the top of the four storeys, under the four rows of Roman tiles that were a sign of indestructible houses in these parts, huge galleries with bare timbers were full of the raucous wind, which sounded even more deep-throated after blowing through them.

'A house where anything can happen,' Laviolette concluded. 'There's a real tension in the air.'

In front of the door with the fanlight, Chabrand was trying to turn the big key in the unwilling, unused lock.

'Remember that this door was wide open,' he said. 'It always was, according to people who knew her.'

He had succeeded in turning the lock and pushing the door. The empty space of the stairwell echoed with the sound of the two men entering the hall. Chabrand put out his arm to stop Laviolette.

'Before going any further,' he said, 'note that between this earthenware jar and that piece of pillar, on the tiles . . .'

'You don't see tiles like that any more,' Laviolette sighed. 'Wide, faded, and laid in a herringbone pattern . . .'

'That may be. But they're also not very solid. The gun lying there broke off a piece of the pottery. Oh, look! The chip is still there.'

'A gun!' Laviolette muttered scornfully.

Vulgar weapons of that sort usually made him lose interest.

'At least wait a while before you treat it with disdain,' Chabrand grumbled.

He took a labelled bag from the deep pocket of his coat, and dropped something out of it into his open hand.

'That's it!', he said.

'A miniature ladies' gun!' Laviolette exclaimed. 'That's a bit more imaginative. Did you know that Madame Caillaux killed Calmette with a weapon like that?'

'Imaginative it may be, but still pitifully unreliable. There are six bullets in it and one is engaged in the barrel and had been fired. Everything points to the gun having jammed in the victim's hand. All she could do was throw it at her attacker.'

'Was she killed here?'

'No. Upstairs in the drawing room . . . where the door was open. Let's go up there.'

The judge had turned the switch for the small lamp over the staircase. The two men climbed the stairs in the gloom. On the first floor, everything was dark and yawning in front of them. Chabrand cautiously moved across the landing. He pressed the light switch. A drawing room as crimson as a theatre curtain suddenly appeared before Laviolette.

'Good God!' he exclaimed. 'The whole thing is imitation Louis-Philippe!'

He looked around the walls.

'And three paintings by Meissonnier,' he added. 'They must have cost a bundle at the time, even if they're not worth anything today.'

'Nothing's been touched. Except the rifle and the bayonet, of course. They've been taken to the clerk of the court's office. If you want to see them . . .'

Laviolette did not reply. Standing in front of the still-open piano, he was quite enthralled looking at the evidence of the murder: a hole right in the middle of the gold plaque where the maker's name, Laharpe, was engraved. A rough hole surrounded by tiny splinters of rosewood or mahogany. The blow must have been made with uncommon fury to pierce such hard wood after running through a human body. A trail of blood, now turned black, had run across the keyboard, fusing the keys, as if forbidding them to ever play again.

'She fell in front of it,' Chabrand said. 'The housekeeper found her at eight o'clock the next morning. She had her back to the piano. She must have thrown the gun at her attacker's head, and missed. The weapon went out into the corridor, over the banister and crashed on to the floor below, where we found it.'

'That's probably how it happened . . .' Laviolette murmured.

He was mentally saying a prayer for the poor woman whose only consolation in life was the empty memory of that enormous house and the dour company of a stiff, rigid, upright piano which was so prim and proper that it seemed imprisoned in an orthopaedic corset.

Laviolette stood there, quite still, quite alone – he had forgotten Chabrand – listening to the sound of the banging shutters and the wind in the plane trees. He was Mademoiselle Véronique Champourcieux five minutes before her death.

'One thing is certain,' he murmured. 'Since she was armed, she was expecting to be attacked.'

He could see her hunched silhouette in the polished wood of the piano and the dim perspective of the drawing room under the chandelier.

'There . . .' he said. 'She must have followed the murderer approaching her in this reflection.'

Without moving from where he was standing, he called to the judge.

'Tell me, Chabrand . . . Nothing has been touched, you say?'

'No. Everything is just as it was.'

Laviolette leaned over the carpet with the scene by David. He was looking closely at a small wooden slatted crate about twenty centimetres high, forty wide and a metre long, standing parallel to the piano and looking out of place in those surroundings. He finally sat down on it with an effort.

'Do you play the piano, Chabrand?' he said out of the blue.

'Heaven forbid!' the judge replied.

He looked down on his companion from his considerable skinny height. Laviolette's chin was on the same level as his knees.

'So,' Laviolette sighed, 'you can't give me any information.'

'About what?' Chabrand asked somewhat haughtily.

'Look! You're tall. Come and sit next to me. No! Not like that. Turn towards the keyboard.'

'What's all this nonsense?' Chabrand complained.

He nevertheless got rid of his coat, which he tossed on a couch. (Oh, what a terrible combination, that forest green with the crimson velvet.) He then settled his bony behind on the crate next to Laviolette.

'Well,' he growled, 'a lot of good that does.'

'Wait! Let's suppose that you can play this instrument. Could you do it sitting here like this?'

'Of course not. How could I? My knees stop me from reaching the keyboard. What's more, I'd have to put my hands over them. What are you getting at?'

'I don't know. I'm trying to work something out.'

He stood up again, groaning all the while.

Chabrand did the same.

'Do you know any pianists who can play standing up?'

'Yes! Jazz pianists can when they feel like it: Ray Charles and The King himself!'

'Fine! Do you think Mademoiselle Champourcieux could do a blues number, or ragtime?'

'No!' Chabrand replied, in all seriousness.

'Right. Yet you've assured me that you found the victim in front of the piano. You've assured me that nothing has been touched since then.'

'Nothing at all.'

'Well, that only leaves two possibilities: either the victim was playing standing up, or else she was sitting on this crate.'

'The devil take you and your nonsense! She was obviously sitting at the right height. The position of the bayonet wound through the body and the point of impact in the piano prove that she was sitting down.'

'Well then . . . the investigators must have moved the seat.'

'No! I have the plan of the room. I came that morning with the deputy public prosecutor. Everything was as you see it now.'

Laviolette trained his big expressionless eyes on Chabrand for some time. After which he lit a cigarette and, with his hands behind his back, began to walk slowly and deliberately across the room. He looked through two of the high windows at the dark drive and the wind-blown plane trees. The red curtain was drawn, however, in front of the third. Laviolette stopped suddenly and looked at it in silence. Chabrand watched these comings and goings with interest.

'You're certain that the curtains weren't touched either?'

'No,' Chabrand sighed, beginning to regret having come to Canossa.

Laviolette felt behind the curtains. He caught hold of the cords that worked them and gave them a tug. They gave a tearing sound and parted.

'I suppose the investigators must have done as I did and closed them again, because they found nothing special behind them . . . Apart from this piece of furniture . . .'

'No,' Chabrand said. 'The reports don't mention anything of that kind. They can't have opened those curtains, otherwise they would have remained open.'

He went up to Laviolette, who was pointing to the space between the curtains and the casement window. Right in the middle stood a stool in Louis-Philippe style covered in red velvet like the rest of the furniture; its very presence there a puzzle.

Laviolette picked it up and put it on the duckboard.

'It was there . . . no doubt about it,' he muttered, 'despite your reports and plans. They can't have told you.'

'No again! The investigators had been working for scarcely half an hour when I arrived. The body and the murder weapon were still there. And those curtains were closed!'

He shrugged his shoulders.

'An oversight! As if you've never come across them in the course of your enquiries.'

'Good Lord! I certainly have,' Laviolette agreed.

He was awkwardly balanced on the stool placed on top of the wooden crate.

'It's not possible,' he muttered. 'I don't know anything about the piano, but after lowering the stool as far as it will go, it still feels as though you're almost standing. You're right. This seat wasn't in front of the keyboard.'

'I keep telling you that!'

'But what then? Can you see the poor woman playing while sitting on the wooden crate? No! Do you see her playing standing up? No!'

He noticed a closed album on the top of the piano. He picked it up, opened it and put it on the music stand.

'And Brahms, what's more! A Brahms sonata played standing up? No!'

'No!' Chabrand echoed.

At that moment, Laviolette noticed a paperclip sticking out of the music. He automatically turned to the page indicated. The letter and envelope held by the clip then appeared.

Neither Laviolette nor Chabrand, who was looking over his shoulder, reached out to touch this revelation. They both knew how much care they should take with a clue of this kind. Laviolette just let out a whistle, while Chabrand read the address on the envelope out loud:

Mademoiselle Véronique Champourcieux
4, rue des Carmes
Digne (Basses-Alpes)

and this maxim on the last staves of the otherwise unused music manuscript sheet:

The measure you give will be the measure you get.

'Isn't there an envelope of some kind around here to put this in and keep it safe?' Laviolette asked. 'Look on the table . . . I saw a pile of magazines on it a while ago. It would be surprising if there wasn't something we could use.'

Chabrand went over and rummaged around, but came back empty-handed.

'If we close the music album,' he said, 'we'll be protecting both the sheet of paper and the envelope.'

'A letter . . .' Laviolette said pensively. 'So, she had received a warning before she died. And she found it important enough to keep the envelope . . .'

'And was obsessed enough,' Chabrand pointed out, 'to keep it in front of her while she was playing Brahms . . . And by the way, I know a few people who'll be hearing from me for not having opened the music book . . .' he said, clearly annoyed.

'Come on, don't talk nonsense! Would you have thought of it? What's a piece of music? I only picked it up more or less without thinking. But tell me, before we put it away safely . . . The light is bad . . . You have your glasses. What can you read on the postmark?'

Chabrand leaned closer.

'Barles, the fourth of October.'

Laviolette started walking around the big carpet again, trampling the three Horatii underfoot. He went towards the windows and looked outside. The light from the street lamps outlined the rhythmically moaning trees against the dark sky. But Laviolette was gazing beyond those waving branches.

'Barles . . .' he said. 'That's where my mother came from . . . When she married my father, who was a railway worker, she had never seen a train in her life . . . And when I say Barles, that's a euphemism. She was actually born in Esclangon. Do you know where Esclangon is?'

'Not the faintest idea,' Chabrand muttered.

'We'll go there. You'll see . . . So this letter really does come from Barles?'

After searching about in the drawing room and opening cupboards, Chabrand finally came across a large plastic bag. His gloved hands reached over for the music to put it in the bag.

'Wait!' Laviolette said. 'Let me take a closer look at that beautiful handwriting; it looks as if it could have been stencilled . . .'

He studied the music manuscript with the blank staves until he came to the last two lines that contained the writing.

'*The measure you give will be the measure you get,*' he recited slowly and deliberately. 'You know, Chabrand, as far as getting something from a handwriting expert, nothing doing! He chose ruled paper for a reason.

Every letter takes up a whole space. It's not written; it's drawn. And the same goes for the address on the envelope.'

'Yeah . . .' Chabrand muttered. 'And as for fingerprints . . .'

'Don't expect much there either.'

'All the same, thanks to the various methods at our disposal, we'll get something.'

Still looking out of the windows at Digne by night, Laviolette slowly shook his head.

'What could poor Véronique have miscalculated?' he asked, thinking out loud.

'Who knows? Her virtue, perhaps,' Chabrand said. 'These days, and in Digne, being *intacta virgina* at forty-three is something of an achievement.'

'Anyway, it's not true that nothing was stolen! Someone stole the seat the victim was sitting on; that's for certain! What do you think it could have been? And why did she take the stool away?'

'When I think that I came looking for you in the hope that you'd throw some light on this for me,' Chabrand remarked sarcastically. 'But you show up, then after you've left, it's just the opposite: I'm more in the dark about everything than before!'

Laviolette raised his arms in a comic gesture of helplessness. Chabrand looked him up and down from his great height as if Laviolette were a schoolboy being admonished.

'Thanks to your contribution,' he repeated, 'I'll have to do two things: send the investigators to track down some sort of seat, and find the author of a letter written with a stencil.'

'And who comes from Barles. Don't forget that.'

'Good Lord! Where anyone, from anywhere, could have gone to post it without attracting attention! Oh! You really haven't changed. You're still trying to play the oracle, but without a leg to stand on.'

'An any rate, an oracle with frozen feet,' Laviolette groaned. 'The atmosphere in this house makes me rigid with cold. Get me out of here if you don't want to have my death on your conscience.'

'I ask you,' Chabrand retorted. 'As if it was any more cheerful at your place, at Popocatepetl.'

But Laviolette wouldn't listen. Waving both hands in denial, he turned his back on the scene of the crime, went down the stairs and shot outside as fast as he could. He didn't want to spend any more time here. Chabrand had enough official bodies available to complete the enquiry.

'Reading about the case in the newspapers will be quite enough for me,' he grumbled.

'Thanks!' Chabrand said, having caught up with him. 'Just like your comradeship of old!'

They both leaned over the recalcitrant lock. Laviolette braced himself to keep the door tightly shut while Chabrand tried the key.

When they turned round, puffing a little from their exertions, they could hardly believe their eyes. There in front of them in the windy moonlight night was a fashion illustration that could have advertised a pre-war Paris–St Raphaël car rally. They were looking at a lady draped in a long coat with cassowary boas standing elegantly in front of a 1930 white Delage.

'Tell me I'm not dreaming!' Laviolette whispered to Chabrand. 'I'm looking at my ideal woman! That was my dream ever since I was twelve!'

'A nightmare more like it,' Chabrand muttered. 'I know your tastes. This lady is very thin, with prominent collar bones and a flat chest. Come on, wake up!'

They walked towards her. Despite the fact that it was two in the morning, and very chilly, the lady resolutely barred their way. She was impatiently slapping the palm of her left hand with the gloves she had taken off, and you could feel that her large handbag was ready to swing at the first alarm.

'Well,' she exclaimed, 'make yourselves at home! Go through dead people's property, why don't you!'

Chabrand looked the woman up and down with deliberate arrogance, allowing a magisterial silence to hang in the air before asking:

'Who are you?'

'And who are *you*?' the lady retorted aggressively.

'I'm the examining magistrate.'

'You're expecting me to congratulate you, perhaps?'

She turned towards Laviolette, who was trying to make himself inconspicuous. He saw a face carefully made up with foundation, each eyelash brushed and separated, eyelids with blue eye shadow, a cherry-red mouth, and to top it all, salon-set bright blonde hair à la Mary Pickford. But despite this strange costume, there was fear in her eyes. It was fear that made her aggressive and unnecessarily prickly.

'And this . . . gentleman,' she said, 'is no doubt your clerk?'

'Not at all,' Chabrand replied. 'He's just a friend.'

The lady raised her eyebrows.

'Am I to understand that you search people's places without legal authority?'

'I was only checking something,' Chabrand explained patiently.

'Nevertheless, you're carrying a suspicious-looking parcel under your arm. Where did you get it and what does it contain?'

Despite the moonlight, it was fortunately difficult to see the judge's wan complexion grow even paler. Laviolette knew that it was never a good idea to be a witness when the great and powerful of this world got caught red-handed abusing their authority. Chabrand was not, of course, one of the great, but he shared their easily provoked vanity; consequently, Laviolette tried not to listen to him answering the lady's accusation. Standing a little to the side, he whistled as he gazed at the clear night sky.

'It's not at all suspicious,' Chabrand said with restraint. 'I had it with me when I came. They are personal items I brought myself.'

This ability to tell bare-faced lies with aplomb had remained with him from the time when he was keen on dialectics.

'What is more,' he added, 'you still haven't identified yourself, or explained what you are doing here at two o'clock in the morning. Don't forget,' he exclaimed, raising an admonishing finger, 'a murderer always returns to the scene of the crime.'

He had to deflect the woman's attention from the parcel under his arm by any means possible. 'In complete defiance of the law,' Laviolette was thinking, in grudging admiration of the judge's dishonesty.

'I can't believe it,' the astounded woman exclaimed. 'You suspect me! You dare to question me!'

'Yes indeed. I'm questioning you. What are you doing in the private driveway in front of this poor woman's house at two in the morning?'

'This poor woman!' the lady retorted. 'My sister, a poor woman! When she's the one who robbed me! She got everything except . . . well . . . a trinket.'

'Your sister?' Chabrand said. 'I didn't see you at the funeral.'

'After what she did to me? You must be joking. She wouldn't give me the time of day. So you don't imagine I'd be going to the funeral. I'd never forgive myself.'

She took a step towards Chabrand and gripped the lapel of his overcoat.

'Don't you know,' she said, 'that if I had the strength, I'd have committed that murder myself long ago? You have no idea what a bitch my sister was! Do you think she stayed an old maid by chance? No! It was avarice! Give nothing. Let nothing go. Nothing! I never saw our old parents again until they were laid in their graves. All the furniture . . . except . . . but that was just a souvenir.'

Chabrand pulled her hand away from his coat, which she was still clutching.

'You still haven't told me what you are doing here at this ungodly hour.'

'I was coming home from the nightclub. I saw the light on and I wanted to know what was happening. After all, the house is *mine* now. And besides, I'm not just anyone. I have a name that's well known. Because I've been married. I'm Madame Maillard! Violaine Maillard. Yes, you heard me: Violaine. My mother was a great admirer of Claudel. My sister, who was born three years after me, never forgave me for it, as she was only called Véronique, a very ordinary name.'

'Only called . . .' Chabrand said. 'She's dead. Have you forgotten?'

'There's no chance of that. I can hardly contain my joy! She had enough happiness living the way she did, with her old father to coddle for so long . . . and this beautiful house!'

She waved her arm at the whole of the Champourcieux tannery, a pompous gesture emphasised by the trailing arc of the gloves still in her hand. Chabrand looked at the building, and pursed his lips.

'Oh, I know what you're thinking,' the lady exclaimed. 'But there are degrees of beauty. Come to my home and you'll understand. No more questions?'

'Not for the moment,' Chabrand muttered after giving it an appropriate moment's thought. 'It's possible that later . . .'

She turned on her heel, swaying her narrow hips, then opened the car door and sat herself at the wheel. During this operation she made sure that she exposed her legs in their flesh-coloured silk stockings. Chabrand looked away, but Laviolette savoured the nostalgia of his early longings in this act of old-fashioned eroticism, which revealed the complicated bits and pieces of a lacy suspender belt.

'The nightclub!' Chabrand declared scornfully.

The lady wound down the window and put her head out.

'And you know,' she said, 'you'll never understand a thing about this affair. Never. No matter how hard you look.'

She turned on the ignition, then the headlights, and gave Chabrand a smile he saw as maternal.

'You're too young!' she added, shaking her head.

The Delage made a sweeping, majestic turn, driving silently over the dead leaves, cushioned by its magnificent springs.

'She threw that at you,' Laviolette obligingly commented, 'as if you had suggested making love to her . . .'

'I'll summon her . . .' Chabrand growled between his teeth.

'Yes! Summon her. If you can . . . And when you've got her there, do please ask her what that *trinket* she managed to snatch from her sister's grasp might be . . .'

They both began walking, calmly reviewing all the disconcerting aspects of the puzzle, which seemed to comprise nothing but inexplicable questions.

Behind their backs a deathly silence descended on the Champourcieux tannery.

V

'I'LL FOLLOW THE CASE IN THE NEWSPAPERS,' HE HAD STATED. Slowly but surely and day by day, however, Véronique's ghost came between himself and the fine weather that was lasting so late in the season.

He imagined her walking around Digne, always classically and tastefully dressed, her real self discreetly hidden behind a modest smile. He heard her gentle, slightly drawling voice. He had always found something charming about her, despite her being called 'an old maid', which was not an apt description of her at all.

On certain afternoons, when he lay in the sun, a cat curled up on his stomach and only an old horse blanket between himself and the satrap's tomb, Laviolette caught himself muttering these words, which were not a good sign for his peace of mind:

'No. You can't put up with that . . . You're not going to risk being repeatedly kicked in the backside by your conscience . . . We must look and see if there might be a way of getting into this story . . . Without making waves, of course! Remember how touchy you were with amateurs when you were still in the service . . .'

He could see himself in the noble role of the ex-cop getting back in harness to make up for the supposed shortage of police in the younger generations. If the truth be known, he looked at this mystery as covetously as a drooling child looks at a cake-shop window. There were times, which he quite enjoyed, when he didn't sleep for repeating, 'The measure you give will be the measure you get.' He could see the piano, the drawing room, the Champourcieux tannery. On several evenings he went and roamed around it in the dark.

Judge Chabrand had telephoned him the laboratory test results.

'The letter itself,' he explained, 'only contains the fingerprints of the victim, as you might suspect. On the envelope, however, we traced six different sets.'

'You didn't expect any fewer, I suppose?'

'As well as those of the victim, four others have been identified: the postman, two letter-sorters and the postmistress in Barles. As for the sixth: unknown. It should be noted, however, that the fingers have earth on them and clearly visible dirty prints. Naturally, the Barles postmistress could not tell us who put the envelope into her letterbox.'

'Naturally,' Laviolette said sarcastically.

'As for the sister with the Delage, who seemed to heartily detest the victim, she has a good alibi for the night of the murder: she spent the evening at the Le Picrocole nightclub, where several regulars said they danced with her and saw her leave, a little unsteady on her feet, under the influence of four large gin fizzes. This is not an unusual occurrence, it seems.'

'Gin fizz – the fashionable drink of her youth and mine,' Laviolette thought. 'A thing that went out of fashion at the same time as we did – so much so that you can't find a single barman who can make one properly.'

Leaving the heat on the satrap's tomb, he got into his venerable apple-green Vedette and slammed the door. The car was fifteen years old and looked after like an old dog by its devoted owner.

The October sun was kind to his rheumatism as he drove along at his usual speed of forty kilometres per hour. He crossed the Bailey bridge and on to the narrow, bumpy, winding road that disappeared under the crimson foliage of the maples and beech trees at every turn: the road to Barles. The further you progress along its twenty-kilometre length, the more aspects of disturbing beauty it reveals. The Bès accompanies it, intertwining with it under all sorts of oddly shaped bridges, as the crystal-clear waters flow in an anthracite-coloured bed ten times too big for it. The air that travels over these prodigious deposits of gravel and alluvium has the hollow resonance of a deep cave; the wind that moans over them, the funereal sound of the dark forests weaving through the valley. The valley is as one with the river. It has just one season: autumn. It has its spring when the leaves are ready to die. It smiles when all the rest weeps.

To properly enjoy the charm of the Bès valley, you have to be from the Basses-Alpes, which Laviolette was passionate about it. Everything spoke to him of love from the depths of this poor, harsh countryside: four gnarled apple trees in an abandoned garden, old hay spilling out of a barn, which no longer had a flock to feed. Sometimes it would be a hillside farm still being worked, with a large wash hung out to catch the afternoon sun. Sometimes he would also feel it going through a hamlet already plunged in deep shadows, where he smelled wood burning under vats of pigs' mash.

They were the feeble signs of life in a land that had slowly got the better of its inhabitants one after the other – it may have taken a thousand years – through bad harvests, bad treatment, landslides, flooding of the usually small River Bès, which could become a hundred metres wide in a short time. A land that tried to get rid of the most obstinate of them like unwelcome lice, through misfortune, death, too many children; that took unexpected swipes at the survivors which they couldn't deflect; that did them in with treachery which was always sly, always inconceivable.

Yet despite all that, some were still there. And as he progressed along this road in the middle of nowhere, Laviolette knew that they always would be. For love of the land is not measured by the favours it hands out, nor the consolation it offers, above all the country around Barles, where an ordinary stone – and God knows there are enough of them – can without warning turn into something magical. There are some standing among the juniper bushes that seem to make signs of friendship to you from afar. They are pale as ghosts and vaguely still, but they disappear, slip away as soon as you try to approach them. Do you think that a land lapped only by the sky is unremarkable? It's not easy to capture. It slips through your fingers like an adder still soapy after shedding its skin. Ten writers and sixty poets have never succeeded in opening its belly to have it at the mercy of their imagination.

In short, it was one of those places that made Laviolette so proud of being Basses-Alpine. When he was there, he felt how unsurpassed the people of his race had always been in the face of isolation, permanent poverty and endless adversity.

Ragged valleys, the *clues de Barles*, branched off to left and right, draped in tattered fields like an ancient Greek cloak torn to shreds by giant brambles. Their sparse trees were bidding summer goodbye by bursting into colour for the last time.

Up above stood the bare peaks waiting for snow: the Cloche de Barles and, higher still, the Blayeul, whose name always evokes the lime tree, *le tilleul*. Its crest is so close that it looks huge when seen from below, although it is actually only two thousand metres high.

Using the need to take a piss as an excuse (for modern men need an excuse to indulge in contemplation), Laviolette got out of his car at the Pierre Pass, the narrow exit of the *clue*, which is part of the road to Barles. The Pierre Pass, rising vertically for two hundred metres, looks down on the Bès like a stern forehead. It's a continuous curvilinear wall hardly pierced by this ten-metre-wide fault through which the Bès and the road thread their way. At its base, a scree of debris bears eloquent witness to the fact that sometimes, every hundred years or so, the wall shakes its head to get rid of the surplus weight caused by erosion.

But this threat has no effect on people devoid of imagination. A person who died long ago, seeing this sheer wall as nothing but an ideal sun trap, built a little house snug against the rock, with blue shutters, two deckchairs and four heads of celery. His descendants have lived there after him with no more fear or apprehension than he had. And indeed it's true that the wind whistling through the narrow opening of the *clue* never stirs the trees in that place. To these people, the cliff is a providential shelter, until one day it crushes them all.

During the many years he had been exploring this countryside, Laviolette had never tired of contemplating the extraordinarily hostile things that nature had produced here. Since he was quite young, he had come to immerse himself in the atmosphere of the place whenever he felt melancholy.

He began walking into this dark and echoing fissure where hammers had been used to widen the narrow parts and build tunnels through the rock sparkling with veins of quartz. It is chiselled in such a convoluted and oddly jagged way that you have the impression of making your way through a keyhole.

When nature took the trouble in a place like this to create a geological knot that exemplifies its mystery, you can be sure that she didn't stop there, but for man's edification continued down to the smallest detail. Who can deny, for example, that scarcely a hundred years ago, the goats in the Barles valley still had three horns? Far from considering this curiosity simply as one of nature's marvels, people of the Basses-Alpes passing through the area used to interpret it as an alarm signal. If they had to come to these parts for any reason, they whipped up their horses and carts or carriages at the entrance to the *clues* and didn't stop harrying them until they reached the environs of Verdaches where suddenly, miraculously, the countryside stopped being so unusual.

Until about the 1860s, those who passed the valleys often reported that somewhere between earth and sky – they couldn't say exactly where – a fire for burning heretics at the stake was blazing away, with crackles, muffled explosions and sudden showers of sparks they couldn't locate. And when they were asked how they had come by the absurd conviction that it was a heretics' fire, they replied that the name had come into their heads the moment they heard it.

They were mostly horse-traders with florid faces who described the thing with an eye half closed to see how far they would be believed; illiterate road-workers brought up in the state orphanage; gypsy couples on foot, dragging their poor show around from hamlet to hamlet at the dead-slow pace of their skinny nag; or wily pedlars with uneasy consciences; in short, those who saw these wonders tended to be people who were untrustworthy or unintelligent.

Nevertheless there was also, and on several occasions, a pale, thin tax-collector coming back from some investigation on his knock-kneed mount, and a bailiff scarred with sticking plaster after a turbulent seizure of goods and chattels. And there was even, but only once, a priest taking the sacrament to someone who was ill (that shows how much he agreed with this rumour about the fire that filled the valley). This priest never breathed a word of it to anyone, but his acolyte could not contain himself. As soon as they reached the quiet spot where there was nothing more unusual than a man dying, he confided at length to them all, with teeth still chattering.

Of course, since then the very real and explainable horrors of modern times have dispelled these imaginative fears which so easily deluded the simple-minded folk of yesteryear, but the fact that things are not spoken about does not mean that they no longer exist.

Laviolette spent some time contemplating the elements of this stone enigma where sounds, colours and shapes combined with the noise of the river to make man understand what cold eternity might be like. He had gazed at it from the bottom to the top, and now his back was aching. It had made him forget the reason why he had come there.

The fading light colouring the rock with ochre tints like seashells, and the sudden cold wrapping itself around the canyon finally made him leave this lonely place. He hurried to the car, settling himself inside with all the windows up. He set off again and came out of the *clues* into a watercolour landscape where the autumn foliage of thin sumacs bronzed deep hollows and mounds of scree. A few farms with Lombardy poplars took advantage of the rare plots of earth bounded by black-thorns.

Beneath the Blayeul came a succession of round hillocks that had been pushed, jostled, then frozen in extraordinary attitudes, either rearing up or rolling back. They had been at the threatening edge of a whirlwind suddenly stopped by cold and suspended in time, for beyond that point the land, torn between two opposing geological folds, retracts back on itself; it curls up. It has the sour look that comes over a child's face when he bites into a unripe fruit. And in the winter months, the sky above is scarcely more friendly. This explains the inhabitants' love of extraordinary possessions: building an opulent tomb for oneself; loving too intensely; thirsting for a little blood or a little mystery; acquiring perishable goods in this world. After all, it has taken a lot of imagination to keep hanging on in this place.

Laviolette arrived in Barles at about half past four. He immediately found himself encircled by a cyclone of a dozen children who had all just surged out of the school gate shouting and laughing as they kicked through the dead leaves. A smell of chestnut husks being burned and sometimes exploding with a dull bang rose with the smoke from behind the railings of the school yard. Alone in the dust and wind, a primary teacher of a bygone age was carrying – triumphantly, one is tempted to say – a squirming mass of field mice caught in traps, which he was no doubt going to throw on the fire, perhaps specially lit for that purpose.

Smells of jam and quinces cooked in the oven were lingering in the air. Nothing in the world could be more peaceful than Barles on that October evening.

Under its wrought-iron arch covered in Virginia creeper losing its leaves, the green bistro advertised itself as a hotel with four rooms overlooking an arbour. It looked appealing to Laviolette, but he resisted. He had just learned that the post office was still open, so headed in that direction.

For the whole week since she found out, Félicie Battarel's ample form had been trembling like calf's-foot jelly. Every morning *Le Provençal* newspaper arrived by post in its wrapper to be delivered to Colonel Moutiers, who prided himself on his left-wing views. Félicie was in the habit of taking it out of its wrapper and casting a quick eye over it before the postman left on his round. And that was how, a week earlier, she had been devastated by the following headline, which covered four columns: *Mlle Véronique Champourcieux bayoneted to death.*

She hadn't stopped shivering since, for she hadn't forgotten the letter with the fine handwriting posted by Émile Pencenat. First of all she tried to see reason, telling herself that there was probably no link between the letter and the murder, and that she had too vivid an imagination. But she had scarcely begun to feel reassured when two huge gendarmes pushed open the post-office door and shoved that envelope in her face; the very one she had taken out of the basket, stamped and examined so carefully; the envelope she knew Émile had slipped into the box.

Since then, another pair of gendarmes had arrived, then two plain-clothes inspectors, all repeating the same question:

'Didn't you notice anything on that particular day? Couldn't you see? Can't you describe to us the person who posted the letter?'

'How could I?' Félicie had retorted indignantly. 'With all the work I have to do! All alone in this office that should have at least three people working in it.'

'Yes, but sometimes without thinking, without being aware of seeing anything . . .'

'Without thinking? You're saying that maybe I'd take the time to look at everything that falls into the box and who puts it there. Of course not! Don't you think I have enough to worry about? And why on earth would I look at them?'

She moved towards them menacingly, hands on hips and red in the face. She literally pushed them outside with all the power of her aggressive bosom. They beat a retreat before this force of nature.

But after they left, how that well-padded heart pounded. Félicie had been blatantly lying for a week. Being unmarried, she was not used to lies and lying made her feel sick. Yet she had to do it. The administration were sticklers for postal confidentiality, and even under duress by the judicial authorities, an employee who had been too observant of a client, even a murderer, would not have been looked on kindly. A postmistress is like Caesar's wife: the least suspicion and she will lose the public's trust.

And yet . . . that obligatory lie was not the worst of Félicie's worries by far. Towards five o'clock on the previous Wednesday, as the sun was setting, she had raised her head and seen a pale, haggard Émile Pencenat standing there before her. A Pencenat who had turned the door handle like a sleepwalker, silently sidled up to the window holding an envelope in his hand, asked for a stamp in a toneless voice, and left again with the same strange sluggish walk of a man half drugged.

Then Félicie had heard the soft swish of a letter slipping into the box, and had rushed to the basket to take out the letter that had just fallen into it. She held it away from her between finger and thumb. She put it down on her desk. She examined it without touching anything. Naturally, as she had expected, it was the same large, beautifully formed handwriting that one only sees painted on hairdressers' or milliners' windows, and always very black, like a death notice. The only difference was the name and address:

Madame Ambroisine Larchet
Villa des Cèdres
Route de Gaubert
Digne (Basses-Alpes)

As Félicie franked the stamp, put the letter in the sack that would be taken to Digne that evening in Big Magne's bus, she could not suppress a feeling of dread. She felt she was thrusting the rusty bayonet the newspaper described into this Ambroisine Larchet's breast herself, although she was a perfect stranger.

Every morning since then her hands shook as she took Colonel Moutiers' copy of *Le Provençal* from its wrapper. Nothing had happened yet, but the trembling of Félicie's flesh had not disappeared, not even in the arms of Big Magne, who tried to corner her in the back room without success, but who had become more hopeful over the last few days, mistaking this frisson for awakening desire.

It was in this state of internal tremor, punctuated from time to time by an anxious sigh, that Félicie saw a person enter, rugged up and as solid-looking as a tree trunk. He took an age wrestling with the door and then, taking off his silly hat, he came towards her.

'Another one,' she thought.

Although she didn't leaf through many illustrated weeklies, she had still seen pictures of all kinds of heavies, which confirmed her opinion that the man who had just come in was one of them. And in fact he hadn't taken any trouble to appear different. He looked like your average man in the street, but with a slightly more melancholy look in his eyes.

'I've already been questioned three times,' she pointed out to him.

Laviolette had always had a weakness for big women. He leaned good-naturedly over Félicie's voluminous breasts. He even risked paying her an oblique compliment in which one could interpret a subtle allusion to their firmness and roundness.

'He's not a policeman,' she decided.

He bought a stamp and asked for the phone box. She thought he would never fit inside it with his overcoat, fur hat and tree-trunk figure. She began to warm to him.

Laviolette called Villa Popocatepetl. Old Chabassut's lyric soprano voice vibrated through the glass in the phone box and reached Félicie's ears.

'I won't be back today,' Laviolette announced to his housekeeper. 'Would you leave Rodilard's dish on the refrigerator and make sure that the kitchen door stays open so that he can get in.'

He had just decided that he would spend the night in Barles.

Old Chabassut's piercing voice was still coming through loud and clear from the other end of the line. Rodilard's name made her hit the ceiling. He was a cat weighing almost seven kilos that was nice to people only when hungry, and had Laviolette dancing attendance on him as if he was a mistress who didn't love him. Rodilard was a cat that could go away for ten days then scratch at the door and walk over his master's feet without a glance, making straight for the kitchen, shrilly demanding all the meals he had missed, thrashing his tail and pissing if, by chance, one was missing.

Of course Laviolette was very fond of this fat scrounger as round as a barrel and with balls as big as walnuts. He stooped to giving him tender words that went unheeded and pats rewarded with scratches. Love is as unfailingly attracted to scorn as a magnetised needle to the north.

Chabassut held forth for three full minutes on the subject of Rodilard. This was just what Laviolette wanted. During that time he could stand with the receiver to his ear and observe big Félicie through the glass furiously stamping the small amount of daily mail. Sometimes a nervous spasm went through her like a horse annoyed by a fly.

'She's cold,' Laviolette thought. 'My word! I wouldn't mind warming her up!'

His old libido was slowly getting his imagination going at the sight of all that abundant, rounded flesh, which would be so nice to cling to. Desire is always unpredictable; it makes itself felt at the wrong time, just when the mind should be focused on something entirely different and more important. For if Laviolette hadn't felt an erotic charge for Félicie, he would have noticed immediately that she was trembling with fear and not with cold. And this strange attitude of hers would perhaps have made him see the whole affair in a different light.

He went out of the phone box and the post office a little light-headed with desire, for he had never expected to be aroused in as unlikely a place as Barles. He shook himself, took a deep breath, and looked around him at the Blayeul and the Cloche de Barles high above him, sparkling in the sunset. The air was heavy with the smell of burning leaves, but with a nasty undertone of scorched rat. The teacher had left the school yard. He must have finished his auto-da-fé.

Whenever Laviolette arrived in a town, his first stop was always the cemetery. As far as he was concerned, there were no places where he would like to live; there were only places where he would like to die. Especially on one of those fine evenings bathed in Italian light, when billowing lilac clouds float over the cypresses.

He therefore climbed up the steep steps leading to the cemetery in Barles. Like everyone else, he passed by the rustic postbox on the left side of the gate without batting an eyelid. Dull thuds echoed around the small space within the walls. Laviolette felt great pleasure seeing the gravestones in the rosy glow of the setting sun and the peaceful names hidden behind the vases of plastic flowers. The brown photos from another time spoke to him of well-earned and dearly bought rest.

He noticed a mound that someone was very actively increasing with large shovelfuls of earth. He heard the sound of a pick down below at the bottom. He went over to it.

When he stopped digging for a moment, the burden of his worries sometimes made Émile Pencenat jump like a startled goat. For a week now he had been through all shades of panic. He had opened the newspaper one morning at Grimaude's, where he went for his morning coffee, and felt as if he had been struck by a thunderbolt.

One may well be digging one's grave, but it's purely a figure of speech coupled with an ordinary hole in the ground, until the day when some particular threat to your well-being warns you that you already have a foot in it. It's only then that the hole becomes a grave. That is what happened to poor, trembling Pencenat. Like everyone else, he had seen the two pairs of gendarmes and the inspectors arriving at Félicie's office. He had finally worked out that they were looking for the person who had posted the letter. It was then that he began to feel the cold steel of the guillotine on the back of his already wrinkled neck, and his grave began to seem like one. For if Félicie revealed to the gendarmes what he was sure she had seen, knowing her habits, he was well and truly done for. Who would believe his story?

His teeth chattered for the whole of the next three days. Suspicious as ever, Prudence asked him why he was making that curious sound like clicking castanets so often, especially in the evening. He said he was cold in the apple store, which was where he slept, and that if she wanted to keep him and above all his pension, she'd do well to slip a bedwarmer into the bottom of his bed. But this explanation did not satisfy Prudence, who continued to watch him closely.

However, seeing that the gendarmes were not making another appearance, he thought that Félicie mustn't have said anything, either because she didn't know or because she was being cautious. He felt reassured and set to work again.

Little by little an idea that was slowly taking shape in his mind transformed his fear into a burning desire. Now Pencenat was not a quick thinker, but he had all the time in the world to marshal his wandering thoughts, get them into order, trim them into shape, polish them up, and finally draw a dazzling, obvious conclusion from them.

'If I could find out the identity of the pilgrim who is getting me to post his letters,' he thought, 'perhaps I'd be able to order my pink marble columns straight away.'

The thought of that cheered him up and he forgot his worries. He began to build castles in the air. Blackmailing the sender of the letter as soon as he discovered who he was seemed like child's play. There are always potential rogues who, seeing an opportunity, will flirt with death and then, at the very last moment, will be surprised to have met with it so easily.

It was at this time, when he climbed out of his hole one windy night exactly a fortnight after finding the first letter, that he found the second. The envelope, stuck sideways in the prickly petals of an artificial aster, seemed to be waving at him as it trembled like a dead leaf. He went over to it, hardly believing his eyes, hypnotised, drawn to it as to a magnet. He wiped his dirty hand carefully on his trousers. When he picked up the letter with two fingers and read the address, he felt as if he were holding a death notice. He was seized with fear once again despite all his plans. This was the Pencenat Félicie saw standing pale and shaken before her, asking for a stamp. His hands were trembling so much that it took him three tries to put the envelope into the slot. He was overwhelmed by the ghastly thought that with this simple gesture he was condemning the recipient of the letter to death.

And yet he didn't tell anyone of the terror he felt, as the prospect of the pink marble columns suppressed all of his scruples. He had to admit that he was not really anxious to see the murderer arrested, which would mean the end of the marvellous prospects he had been dreaming about. But it still caused some jolts to the conscience of a person who was usually a decent enough fellow.

And he had other worries on his mind . . . The large excavation he was digging would soon be finished and he would have to get the sand and cement to build the tomb up there using just a wheelbarrow. He would need the old pair of postman's boots he only wore to save his other shoes when he was making mortar. The fact was that those boots had disappeared. Normally they sat there big and dusty, with their rusty nails, on the uneven shelf among the dirt-covered tools and tattered beehives in a lean-to open to the elements on the lane side of the garden. He knew the spot they occupied by heart, so much so that the other day when he wanted to scrape some mud off them, he reached out his hand to the shelf without looking and, to his great surprise, found an empty space. As he didn't use them very often, he couldn't be sure how long they had been missing. He was so astonished that someone had stolen two objects of such little value that he had dared to question Prudence. That gave her the opportunity to berate him once again.

'Me? Your postman's boots? What would I want with them? I'm glad they've been taken! Tell me if I'm wrong, but it seems to me that I've been at you for ten years to buy a padlock for that shed.'

Having mentally run through all his worries, Pencenat heaved a deep sigh as he stood at the bottom of his hole. He put down his spade, wiped his forehead, spat into his hands and looked up at the sky to see what time of day it was. It was then he saw the man above him, standing there solidly with legs apart. He was dressed in an overcoat that was too long for him and swathed in a huge hand-knitted scarf.

The stranger was wearing one of those heavy fur hats sometimes seen in the newspaper on the heads of important people as they hoist the coffin of one of them on to their shoulders. All the people in this world who are a real pain in the neck have the same strange bland appearance. Pencenat immediately thought that Félicie had talked and they were coming to arrest him.

'Work going well?' the man asked.

'Well . . .' Pencenat said in a quavering voice. 'It's a bit dry . . . You wouldn't have the time, by any chance?'

'A quarter to five,' Laviolette replied.

'Oh, shit!' Pencenat exclaimed. 'And my wife's expecting me at five to get the apples in from the garden.'

He climbed up the stepladder that he always left there. The man wanted to help him.

'Oh, no thank you,' Pencenat said, refusing his offer. 'I'm used to it.'

He feared that if he gave his hand to this stranger, the man would never give it back to him. He was up on the edge of the grave in a moment, going from one foot to the other, wondering whether he should get away or linger.

'What's wrong with him?' Laviolette wondered. 'Here's someone who's really scared! Of what? Why? But careful, don't ask him anything. He'll clam up straight away. Let's just look casual. And come to that, it just occurs to me that it's a long time since I had a cigarette.'

He took out the makings and stuck a rice paper on his tongue. That gesture would reassure a startled rabbit. It had the desired effect on Pencenat, who decided to act naturally. He even rolled a cigarette too and they lit them from the same lighter.

'I'm from Digne,' Laviolette informed him.

'Ah,' Pencenat said, 'I go down there sometimes.'

'Is it quiet here?' Laviolette asked.

'Um, pretty much . . . as you can see.'

Laviolette wasn't one for asking a lot of questions. Pencenat wasn't very talkative to start with, and although reassured by the cigarette that his companion had hand-rolled, he was still being cautious. As they walked down into the town, their conversation was limited to those four utterances. They parted company at the soldiers' memorial.

The sun had disappeared. The presence of the Bès was now apparent as the sound of its waters rose up from the low ground. An alder tree over the hut by the public weighbridge was losing its leaves in a wind that seemed to blow for it alone, since none of the other trees around it moved at all.

Laviolette hurried towards the café-hotel. As he passed, he glanced through the dim window of the post office, but could only vaguely make out Félicie moving about inside.

He opened the door of the café, which was almost empty, apart from three or four old men. They had exhausted all their topics of conversation and were whistling to kill time. They watched him enter, hoping that he was someone unexpected, not local.

There were two other people standing at the counter drinking pastis and talking secretively to each other. They were nervous as hares and so skinny that their worn-out clothes hung on them. Laviolette noticed their sour expressions, their worried foreheads, the dark circles under the eyes of one, and the network of little veins on the nose of the other. The looked like people whom good fortune had abandoned, despite their various attempts to capture it. What's more, they gave out a smell that Laviolette knew well: it came from the gowns of poor lawyers who rinsed them in vinegar and coffee to make them black and shiny. These lawyers are only consulted by pathetic offenders, who become impregnated with this smell of vinegar and sugarless coffee in the cramped offices where they invariably get a poor reception.

'Criminal court fodder,' Laviolette thought.

Besides, when he entered they both turned towards him in unison and, having spotted him, finished off their drinks in one gulp before bolting for the door. Laviolette always exuded the odour of the police station, another smell that never goes away.

Grimaude watched him come in while nonchalantly wiping a cup. He greeted her politely and pleasantly, gave his name and humbly asked for a room for the night. She nodded as if to agree to this request, but replied with a curt no.

'The room isn't made up and I've only got enough food for Françoise and myself.'

'Ah well,' Laviolette sighed, 'in that case . . . Give me a coffee with a shot of rum before I go back to Digne.'

'Oh?' Grimaude said. 'You're from Digne?'

'Why? Doesn't it show?'

She pursed her lips.

'Not as much as all that . . .' she said. 'But if you are, that's different. I might have a portion of baked kidney beans and some thick vegetable soup. Will that do?'

'Good Lord!' Laviolette gasped. 'I didn't think that existed since my grandmother's day!'

'Why? Do I look as old as all that?' Grimaude muttered, coming out from behind her counter.

She set about reminding the old men that their wives were waiting for them to have supper.

'I don't want any trouble from them. God forbid! And given the small amount you lot drink . . .'

She pushed them out with the same gestures she used to sweep the sawdust around the stove and put down fresh.

'So, you're from Digne?' she said, looking at him attentively.

'Yes, and as far as the room not being made up, it wouldn't be the first time that . . .'

'Oh! Don't worry about that,' Grimaude said. 'Françoise will see to it.'

In no time he was seated, supplied with a paper napkin and was being poured a glass from a litre of wine, bluish tinged and of indeterminate origin.

'People from the same neighbourhood should lend each other a hand, don't you think?'

She too had recognised Laviolette's previous history. Besides, it wasn't difficult. He was dressed up like a heavy, as others dress up as Harlequin or Pierrot.

She sat herself down opposite her customer and looked at him for a few seconds in silence. A strange tic left over from the convulsions she had had as a baby came back when she felt a strong emotion or intense curiosity, which was precisely what was happening now. Without warning she suddenly sent him a real come-hither look and, at the same time, nodded her head three times to the left, as if in the direction of some bedroom where they could go for a while.

Laviolette, who knew nothing of this, was about to politely decline her offer when a shrill voice suddenly yelled from the back of the room.

'Take no notice! It's just a tic that comes over her!'

Laviolette turned round. He saw two big feet in red shoes with stiletto heels standing out in the dim light. One of the legs, which were resting almost vertically against a walnut table, had an anklet with silver bells. Sunk deep into an armchair, the owner of these wonders was engrossed in reading an interminable serial in a newspaper she was holding.

'What tic?' Grimaude growled. 'And what about you? You haven't got one? You haven't got a tic, eh? Well! Instead of criticising others, why don't you go to the pork butcher, the "love" butcher, and see if he has two rounds of black pudding!'

'He never has anything,' the girl complained without moving. 'And besides, he's always closed!'

'You only have to knock and he'll open up for you! Anyway, come on, Françoise! Put down that wretched paper and do what I say. The customer is waiting.'

The girl hauled herself out of the armchair, grumbling all the while. The colours in her dress were as bright as the shoes led one to suspect. Despite being twenty-five, she wore a bow in her tow-coloured hair, which hung loose over her shoulders. The charm of her long fair face was spoiled by two black teeth that showed when she smiled.

It would be exaggerating to say that she was hunchbacked. Her left side was just a little higher than the other, as if she had swum out of her mother's womb and this swimmer's stroke had become permanent. She walked slightly sideways, moving through the air as if moving through the sea with her shoulder as the prow. This unusual gait nevertheless had a certain grace about it.

'Well then?' Grimaude asked. 'Are you going to the butcher?'

'Please!' Françoise whined. 'Every time he sees me coming, he licks his lips as he sharpens his knife on the steel hanging from his belt.'

'Are you going, or do you want to feel my boot on your backside!'

'All right, all right. I'm going. Only . . . if he rapes me one day, it'll serve you right!'

'Oh, that. We'll see about that when it happens. In the mean time, get going! My foot's fairly itching.'

Françoise disappeared through the jute curtain. Grimaude rushed after her, shouting, 'And if he hasn't any black pudding, get him to give you two quail. I must have something to feed this poor man.'

She came back towards the kitchen slapping one hand against the other.

'Rape her!' she exclaimed, raising her eyes to the ceiling. 'Rape her! I ask you!'

Laviolette stood up and followed her.

'What's the story about this "love" butcher? Is that his name?'

Grimaude burst out laughing.

'Heavens, no! His name is Crépin Enjolras.'

She leaned forward and was lifting the pot of soup to heat it gently on an asbestos mat. Her head was under the big hood over the commercial-sized oven and her voice was rather muffled when it reached Laviolette below.

'You want to know why he's called the "love" butcher?'

'Well,' Laviolette said, 'I suppose it's because he's a Casanova?'

'Him! He's as faithful as a pigeon! Yet, I have to say . . . it's not because he isn't handsome!'

She extricated herself from the hood and looked intently at Laviolette to judge if he was worthy of hearing what she was going to say.

'One fine day,' she began, 'this Crépin . . . he comes up to my counter. He drinks two pastis without saying anything . . . Of course I'd seen him coming and going, but being discreet, I ask no questions. He's the one, after two pastis, who suddenly comes out with this question, point blank: "How old are you?" he asks me. "Hey, is that any of your business?" "A bit," he replies. "How old were you when Ange Philibert still had his delicatessen?" "About twelve," I say, clasping my hands. "It smelled so good when you passed by!" "Exactly," he says. "How long has it been since you smelled a delicatessen like that?" "I've never smelled it since," I reply with feeling. "There you are! That's it!" he says to me. "I'm sick of it. You see, I love the smells that come from a delicatessen in autumn. And I'm forty-five! And I haven't smelt it since I was ten! So . . . I've bought Philibert's shop. I've bought a boar and a sow from a place near Chauffayer, in the Champsaur – a place where they still do things the right way – and I'm going to set up shop. But listen! I won't serve everyone. Those who want ham on the bone without the bone can get lost." "But you won't make a go of it with an attitude like that! Ange didn't make enough to keep going, and he had a pension and couldn't afford to be fussy about who he'd serve and who he wouldn't." He stops me. "Don't you worry about that," he says. "When they're here on holidays or coming back from skiing and get a whiff of that smell, they'll come, even from Paris." That's what Crépin Enjolras said to me. There, just where you're standing now. Five or six years ago.'

'And was he true to his word?'

'More or less. He's always closed. Those in the know – and it's true, there are some who come all the way from Paris – they knock at the door. He appears. And hey, he's not very friendly! He has a real *mouro dé toulo*,[*] let me tell you. If you have the misfortune to ask for two hundred grams of sliced sausage, he won't even reply. Sometimes you don't even have to speak. He looks you up and down, and just by looking at you he knows that you have no taste. He shuts the door in your face before you have time to explain.'

'Really!' Laviolette exclaimed in admiration.

'That's the way it is,' Grimaude said. 'He's an oddity. He only works for the love of it. And you know, we're proud to have a pork butcher like that here in Barles.'

The little bells around Françoise's ankle could be heard tinkling outside. She opened the door and hurried in.

[*] The face of a killjoy or a wet blanket.

'Ooh! It's cold!' she exclaimed.

It wasn't exactly cold, but the wind had risen over the Bès and threatened to become fresher. Whirls of dead leaves danced around on the terrace like children playing 'ring-a-roses'.

'There you are,' Grimaude said. 'He hasn't raped you yet!'

'Oh, but he'd like to.'

'My poor Françoise, really! Well now, have you got those two rounds of black pudding?'

'I've got three, and freshly made.'

When she opened the pink paper parcel, the smell of the black pudding rose up into Laviolette's nostrils. He immediately felt a rush of longing for his childhood, so long ago it seemed lost in the mists of time. He dined with the evening wind blowing outside, intoxicated by this nostalgic food for the soul rather than the wine of doubtful provenance, which he hardly touched. Finally, sure that now he would tell all, Grimaude brought him a glass of hyssop to wash down the black pudding, she said, and leaning so close that their hair was almost touching, enquired:

'Now then. What about this murder? You know something about it, I imagine?'

'Well! What can I say? It's a murder . . .'

Grimaude drew herself up to her full height and narrowed her lips.

'I needn't have bothered going to the trouble of letting you taste Enjolras's black pudding!'

'Please don't take offence. I haven't found out anything, but who knows? I may discover something. I promise you, if one day I do, I'll come here especially to tell you about it.'

He licked along the edge of his cigarette paper.

'But tell me,' he went on, 'have you had a death here too?'

'No!' exclaimed Grimaude, looking worried. 'Who could have died?'

'No? I only ask because a while ago I saw someone digging a grave.'

Grimaude heaved a sigh of relief.

'Oh, you gave me a fright! No. He's digging his own.'

'Oh!' Laviolette said.

'Yes. It's Émile Pencenat. He has his own weird ideas. What can you do?'

'Oh, nothing, naturally,' Laviolette agreed.

Then, from the corner of the fireplace, Françoise's shrill voice rang out again.

'His wife's a dyke,' she proclaimed. 'That's why he's digging his grave.'

'Ah, I see,' Laviolette said, as if this explanation was really illuminating.

Françoise closed her newspaper and stood up with ankle tinkling.

'Yes indeed!' she exclaimed. 'That's the way it is. Do you think it's easy living here? He's digging his grave and the other one only thinks of making black puddings that remind him of those he ate in the 1940s. And that's not all. I'm sure my mother hasn't told you everything: he cries every time he kills a pig. Can you imagine that? It takes him three days to get over it. And you haven't seen everything yet: we have two strangers. One looks like a pickled herring and the other like Dracula. And apart from them, there are twelve trendy young men who go off to Digne to have a good time. Oh, I nearly forget. There's Big Magne too, but Félicie's got him . . .'

Grimaude shrugged.

'You're talking nonsense. Félicie's so fat that there's no chance of anyone wanting to get her.'

'Félicie?' Laviolette asked in a small, innocent voice. 'That wouldn't be the lady in the post office, by any chance?'

'Lady!' Françoise said with a sneer. 'Hardly! But that's not important. Just take a look at the countryside around here!'

She gave a tragic wave of her arm, indicating what lay beyond the closed shutters and thick walls.

'Just listen to that wind! And I'm alone, always alone. Alone in all of that! Surrounded by all these lusts and desires!'

She bore down on the table where Laviolette was quietly sipping his hyssop and, slapping the marble top with the flat of her hand, stared at him full in the face with a look like Cassandra predicting the fall of Troy.

'No, really! Have you taken a good look at the country around here? Picturesque they call it. I'd like to get them down here for a while, I tell you. For three days, just three days. No, I ask you! Why wouldn't we be digging our own graves?'

Laviolette, of course, felt so at home in these big valley corridors where the earth jealously pushes everyone aside to ensure it's alone to brood over the dangers of its rugged landscape. He almost asked her what she was complaining about. But he understood straight away that she was bewailing her lack of love in every word she said, and that there was no remedy for that emptiness.

'You're getting on my nerves!' cried Grimaude, who had been wringing out a floor cloth from a bucket during all of this. 'You're getting on my nerves! Why don't you settle for the primary school-teacher? He's still not bad-looking, and he's been hanging around you after all.'

'The primary schoolteacher!' Françoise wailed.

As she had already been spending Sunday afternoons with this methodical man, she had to at least appear insulted.

'It's degrading!' she hissed. 'The teacher! My own mother! You'd give me to anyone. Well, I prefer to go to bed.'

With a few agile strides, her asymmetrical body reached the stair-case.

'Phew!' her mother sighed after she had left. 'She'll be the death of me, that girl. She wanted to be an actress. Really! But I can't tell her,' she sighed again, 'that with the body she has, she'd do well to be satisfied with those men who want it.'

'No, you can't . . .' Laviolette conceded. 'You can't tell her that.'

Grimaude jostled him a little as she was putting a huge wooden bar across the two sides of the door. She did the same thing with the shutters, over the windows, remembering to carefully fasten the catches.

'Ah!' Laviolette exclaimed. 'That should make thieves behave themselves.'

Grimaude shrugged her shoulders.

'Thieves! Do you think I go to all that trouble for a few stupid prats?

I have two hunting rifles loaded with buckshot next to my bed. And – now don't tell this to anyone – two good grenades that my poor husband brought back from the Resistance. He showed me how to pull the pin.'

'Wow!' Laviolette exclaimed. 'But then . . . who or what are you keeping out with those bars?'

'Nothing,' she replied curtly. 'My mother before me used to put them up. She would say to me, "When you live in a strange part of the country like this one, you can't let the night come into the house. My own mother used to pile up chairs and tables behind the doors! Remember, remember," she said, "what happened to your grandfather!"'

Laviolette pricked up his ears.

'What *did* happen to your grandfather?' he asked.

'Ah, well,' Grimaude replied, 'it's a terrible story.'

'Sit yourself down,' Laviolette suggested. 'Let's have something strong to drink. I love stories.'

Grimaude went to the counter and fetched a bottle of kümmel and two small glasses, which she filled to the brim.

'Thanks,' she said, 'I won't say no. As I only drink when someone buys me one, it doesn't happen often.'

'So? Your grandfather?' Laviolette asked, eager to hear what she had to say.

'My grandfather was a good-looking man, tall, well-built, with terrific legs. At least that's what I've been told, as I never knew him: my mother was forty-three when I was born. My mother called me "my fibroma". I was a menopause child. My grandfather was the postmaster here in this house that I shut up every evening, and you'll soon understand why.'

She settled her behind into the chair like someone intending to make herself comfortable for quite some time.

'My grandfather,' she continued, 'had only one failing. When he had a row with his wife – about once a month – he would sleepwalk. And when that happened, do you know what he did? He got all dressed up in his big red jacket with the frogging, the nickel-plated boots with spurs, the riding crop, the red riding cap on his head, and at his side he slung his father's post horn. It was his best outfit, the one he put on only to honour a visiting postmaster-general.

'On those nights he would go down to the stable, which is still down below, and saddle up his horse, Bijou. Dr Pardigon had said that, in situations like these, you mustn't cross him . . . So, they let him go. What else could they do? Oh, he didn't go very far. One night my uncle followed him to see what he did. Nothing extraordinary, really. He went down to the valleys. He set his horse off at a gallop, blowing his horn as loudly as he could as he rode through them, as if warning people that a stagecoach was coming through.

'And then, believe it or not, when he'd given his horn a good blow, he'd come back, put the horse back in the stable, the saddle back on the nail, the costume in the wardrobe, and climb back to bed. My grandmother said that he sometimes began snoring just where he left off when he got up. "As if," she used to say with finger raised to frighten us even more, "as if he wasn't the man who had got up, dressed and left; as if not a minute had passed between the time he got out of bed and when he climbed back into it. Ah, children! They say that you shouldn't worry about this world. But when you're trapped in it . . . !"

'She was right, that grandmother of mine, because this'll just give you an idea of how one thing can sometimes lead to another. One night my grandmother wakes up with a start. She doesn't know why. She reaches over and feels the bed cold beside her. At that moment she hears a horse neighing outside. She gets up, goes to the window and sees Bijou below, all white, saddled, tossing its head, wanting to get back into the stable.

'That sets everyone into a flurry. The whole of Barles is woken up. Groups of twenty or thirty almost run down to the valleys. My grandfather is found dressed in his good red outfit, lying on the ground at the end of a tunnel. He says, "I don't know . . . The horse was frightened by something. What am I doing here?"

'They put him on a stretcher, take him home and put him back to bed. Dr Pardigon, the father of the one at the old people's home, arrives and says, "He's damaged something in his spine. He'll never walk again."

'He never did walk again. He was pushed around in a wheelchair. I still have that chair in the attic. As for him, eloquent as he was before the accident, after it he hardly spoke at all . . . But then, after a certain amount of time of course, what's bred in the bone comes out in the flesh: he starts having rows with my grandmother again. And then suddenly one night, the whole family, my mother, her two brothers, Aunt Claire who lived with my grandmother, her sister, the girl from the orphanage we found work for, everyone was woken by a frightful *de profundis*! It was being sung very loudly with cries, groans, curses, howls of pain. And all of it in . . . can you guess? In Latin! And the poor thing didn't know a word of it!

'So everyone rushes to my grandfather's bedroom. There he is, arms stretched out to the sides, eyes closed, a serene look on his face, but talking. And in Latin! And in a voice that was different from his own. A preacher's voice, my mother told me, an educated voice, the voice of someone who had studied, an accent that wasn't ours. "May I be struck down on the spot," she said, "if I'm not speaking the truth: there was smoke coming out of his mouth. And with these moans he would sometimes imitate the sound of a crackling fire." Dr Pardigon shrugged it off. "It's natural," he said. "He can't walk any more so his somnambulism comes out through his mouth. There's no need for anyone to carry on about evil spells!"

'"All the same," my mother said, "we may not have been great believers, but one night, without telling Dr Pardigon, we asked the priest to come, just to make sure." Well, my dear! No sooner does he hear all that than he falls on his knees. "Good Lord!" he says. "Let us pray! There are souls in Purgatory who need help. Let us all kneel and pray to the Lord." "Well," my mother said, "you know how it is. We prayed once but then we got used to it . . . There was only one good thing about it," she said. "After that my mother avoided having arguments with him as far as she could. But sometimes it got too much for her, and afterwards we would have a performance." That's what my mother told me . . .'

Grimaude stood up. She walked over behind the stove pipe, and from its place over a school photo she took down a kind of ancient yellow trumpet with a long leather strap and a red pompom.

'Look!' she said to Laviolette. 'This is his post horn. After that incident, Grandfather lived for another twenty-eight years. He was certainly raving during the last few days of his life, but my mother said that it was never again the way he was during those bouts of sleepwalking. And never again in Latin.'

She went over and hung the post horn back on the wall, then came back to Laviolette, making sure it was securely fastened as she passed.

'No one has ever known the truth about that whole scene,' she said, 'nor what was going on under the surface, but it just goes to show you: when a place can deal you a blow like that, it's best to shut up your house at night.'

Grimaude fell silent. She was wary of the world of Barles at midnight.

'Especially,' she said, wagging her forefinger, 'when on top of everything else, you have an idiot digging his own grave!'

He was about to reply that bars are no use against fears of this kind, but he thought that she no doubt enjoyed these fears, and that at night she hugged them to her bosom instead of a lover. He therefore contented himself with bidding her good night.

He went into a bedroom that had borne the brunt of the leather goods lugged there for more than a hundred years by a half-starved army of commercial travellers on foot or on horseback. The wallpaper had often been renewed, but on the parquet floor composed of thick blocks badly joined, the black wounds of a century of service still showed through the wax.

The bed was a whole country in itself. It was set up to allow the person occupying it, lying still but very much alive, still but watching, to resist the strange and supernatural spirits of the mountain that prowled about out there. It was a double bed with pillows and an eiderdown that were so huge you'd swear someone was already in it. The head of the bed naturally faced north.

Laviolette eyed it warily and walked around it slowly before jumping in. He was well acquainted with beds like these in mountain hotels in October. Nevertheless, when he did get in he almost cried out, for the sheets were as cold as if they had been recently soaked in water from a well. It took a long time for the eiderdown to respond and give back a hundredth of the heat it had first taken away from him. This left him ample time to think of the more-than-plump postmistress, the gravedigger, the love butcher, Grimaude's grandfather who sounded his horn in the middle of the night from deep in the valleys. And the saying from the Gospel: *the measure you give will be the measure you get*; time and time again he heard the sands of that unstoppable hourglass running out. He also had time to hear all the ordinary sounds of life in the house and the village fade into silence. Soon, as he lay there shivering between the sheets, the only sounds that came under the uneven door were the snores that afflicted his hostesses, amplified by the long, echoing corridors. Françoise's version was a virginal cooing, murmuring softly like a trickling fountain. On the other hand, the expansive, exhausted breathing of a woman who has been worked hard simmered away under Grimaude's double chin. Laviolette fell asleep rocked by this curious dialogue that seemed to continue the mother and daughter's daytime arguments.

A little while later, he awoke with a start. He was hot but dared not move for fear of the cold around his body just waiting to close in on him. The wind, a very noisy wind, carried away the last vestiges of an interminable hour striking in the clock tower nearby.

It also carried away the small amount of exhaust from a moped going by on the road; its backfiring drowned out by a sudden squall.

If Laviolette had taken it into his head to look out of the window while this vehicle passed in front of the hotel, perhaps he might have immediately understood something about the Barles mystery.

But on that cold night, why would his suspicions be aroused by a sound which was so familiar, and which emphasised the quiet without disturbing it?

VI

AMBROISINE SAT WITH HER HANDS CROSSED BETWEEN HER breasts, listening to the wind moaning in the trees. The house was encircled, almost eaten alive by their possessive branches. As they swayed in the wind, they seemed to be doing a sinister dance around it. The family had planted some cedars for fun one morning on St Catherine's Day a long time ago, because that was the fashion in 1860. Standing at the top of the double flight of steps, the children at that time liked to see how much they had grown.

On that evening more than a hundred years later, there were thirty cedars, each twenty metres high. Their waving tops stroked each other in the light of the lamp posts nearby, soughing with that deep, desolate lament. They were a battalion of gloomy, solemn cedars, like judges frozen on their feet by death and cold; a last square of mould-green trees moaning together like a flock confined between the rusty iron railings around a would-be park, but bursting out into the street.

If plane trees in the wind play with a merry, disorderly commotion that spreads a feeling of hope, cedars, on the other hand, spread an atmosphere of hostility and disapproval. They reach out after us, they chase us away, with great slow sweeps of their ghostly branches.

Ambroisine nervously followed their desperate signals from behind the windows. What were they saying now? 'Don't stay here! Go! Get out of this house! Leave it all behind! Go!'

She turned away from them, wringing her hands. The light in the large drawing room was growing dim. It was already difficult to make out the shape of the tea things on the low tables, from which her now-departed friends had been sipping earlier while they enjoyed the vicarious terror of the world's catastrophes.

The drawing room and those adjoining had never seemed so gloomy to Ambroisine as they did now. When the villa had been renovated in the late twenties, her parents had given the fashionable decorator carte blanche; consequently there was nothing but art deco motifs of apples and oranges everywhere, on the walls and the furniture, or profiles of mannish women with urchin-cut hair. Light fittings, clocks, jardinieres and vases were all weighed down with plaster mouldings like funerary urns. Even Ambroisine's bed was imprisoned by an iron lattice between marble columns dotted with peach flowers, like the tomb of some high-born lady.

One could not take a step without being confronted by one's own image in smoked-glass mirrors surrounded by solid iron frames, either wrought, beaten or open-work. Since her cousin was murdered, Ambroisine could not bear to be always seeing herself in her bedroom mirrors dressed in full mourning. She had had a crimson ensemble made which she had just worn for the first time for her admiring friends. The corners of her mouth still retained a trace of her delighted smile.

But now the wind was rising and the heavy branches of the cedars were creaking. It was on a windy night like this, scarcely two weeks ago, that Véronique had met her death sitting at the piano, no doubt after receiving this same letter, which no one but the two cousins would understand.

She anxiously scanned the darkening sky. The shadows had already spread and deepened under the trees. The cedars weighed down on the house and the house weighed down on Ambroisine. She knew that if she didn't think of something, she would be there alone that evening. Oh, yes! She'd had a lover lately, but lovers are like crows: fiercely attached to their comfort. The moment any obstacle appears, they zoom off in seconds. Véronique's death was enough for Ambroisine's to take flight.

Alone . . . with the letter that crackled against her chest, which she dared not show to anyone. She knew this biblical precept by heart, an inflexible precept that did not admit any attenuating circumstances:

The measure you give will be the measure you get.

Ambroisine went upstairs. It was large and comfortably furnished in cherry red. There was ample space for the seven or eight people who used to live there. The vast empty space seemed to be impatiently waiting for them to return – even though they were dead or scattered throughout the wide world – to capture the sound of their voices and their self-confident opinions.

Ambroisine stopped on the landing. She looked up towards the ceiling. Above it an echoing attic stretched for the full length of the building under its boat-shaped framework.

'Just as vast as yours,' she had said to Véronique, who had smiled condescendingly. No, it wasn't as big as the Champourcieux attic, but did it need to be to contain what was at the heart of the mystery?

Up here the cedars sounded different. They no longer surrounded the house; they soared above it, swishing through the air like wings. Sometimes, quite often in fact, one of their branches brushed or beat against the roof, then across the tiles, like a wide, caressing arm. However, this sometimes interminable slither was more horrible than the shrill wailing that Ambroisine had heard earlier through the big drawing room windows.

That was enough. She ran off to her bedroom. Opening the wardrobe, she took down the coat that matched the ruby dress she was wearing. It slid into place over her shoulders, and for a moment the smell of the new material banished fearful thoughts from her frivolous mind. Standing in front of the mirror, but not daring to look into her own eyes, she hastily redid make-up and hair, then, with handbag slung across her shoulder and almost running, she went back along the wide corridor, down the staircase and out on to the front steps, leaving all the lights on.

She fumbled as she tried to put the key into the lock of the wrought-iron door. The car was there in the moonlight in front of the open gate. She jumped in, slammed the door and shot off, forcing the gears.

The peaceful autumn night lay softly over Digne. The statue of the philosopher-mathematician Gassendi looking benevolent on his high pedestal on one side of the esplanade was in poetic dialogue with the band rotunda on the other, but there was no one to hear it.

A sad, caressing wind was gathering force as it glided down from beyond La Bléone near the cliffs of Les Dourbes village, which are Digne's crown. But the sadness and tenderness of the winds here are never muted. There are too many empty chimneys caused by erosion along the overhanging rock faces sucking in the air in their path for their sound to be discreet. Too many imposing trees ostentatiously welcome them into their branches. In this part of the world, when the wind sighs it sounds more like the desolate bellow of an animal deep in the woods.

When Ambroisine shut the car door in the nightclub car park, once again she heard the mournful sound she naively hoped to have left behind under the cedars. As in all towns born to highlight the inevitable work of time and fate, Digne sits there surrounded by nature, which seems to breathe all around you, wherever you may shelter.

The concrete car park, the ugly, vulgar red cube of a building, the bright neon lights accentuating the glowing artificial roses around the door, the posters of musicians bent back, hips erotically thrust forward, and girls with accentuated bums in tight jeans, all of that could not keep out the night, silence the wind or take the taste of death from her mouth. For someone who was afraid, all that gave no more defence than a shield made of cardboard.

She went in. Le Picrocole was like a jewel box in which to shut away one's cares. With soft blue padding everywhere, including the ceiling, its confined atmosphere deadened pain. The shady businessmen who had planned it were clever psychologists: they had made an inventory of all the troubles that could afflict the public they needed to attract, and worked out the particular way to ease each one of them. From the moment the customer entered the vestibule, the heady unreality of erotic dreams hung in the air like perfume, already comforting souls in distress. The cloakroom was attended by a sickly-looking, unattractive girl, so that all the women customers would think they were beautiful in comparison.

Ambroisine, feeling light and rejuvenated, took off her coat and handed it to the plain check-in girl. She stopped for just a moment as she passed the mirror panel in the passage to smoothe her eyebrows and try out – if she could still do it – her famous secret smile that was so appealing to men. She went confidently into the room, swinging her hips under the soft material of her dress.

A banjo solo was encouraging four couples who were gauging their erotic affinities on the dance floor. Three saxophones sobbing the blues backed it up, raising, lowering and crossing their gleaming chrome instruments around it. Their deep voices inhibited the laughter of two or three groups seated around the ritual champagne for some celebration or other. Sometimes the piano in the background gave out an impertinent riff that made fun of the melancholy saxophones.

Stuck at the bar smoking or looking slightly desperate, a few men and women who were perfect strangers to each other played with drinks that the revolving lights turned lilac or methylene blue. As debris from an old shipwreck one day comes together in the backwaters of a gulf, so the wrecks of a day's existence in Digne gathered at that bar. Ambroisine got up on a stool between two drinkers who made room for her. She ordered a greenish concoction made of gin, absinthe and pale vervain liqueur, which had its effect in two minutes, went right down to her heels and straight away made her ready for anything. Her broad shoulders – she was the descendant of a roadworker, after all – leaned casually against her neighbour's, as if by chance. He asked her if she'd like to dance. She climbed down from her stool without saying anything and stood facing him. The three saxophones, the bass and the banjo immediately became her accomplices to love. Digne, the cedars, the art deco villa quickly faded far away.

Going against the tide of the dance, which was two people isolated from the rest of the world, her partner realised from the beginning that he had to seize Ambroisine tightly round the waist and not worry about appearing indecent. The letter between the widow's full breasts crackled in his embrace and kept reminding her that it was there.

The measure you give will be the measure you get. That hypnotic refrain went through Ambroisine's mind once again. Intoxicated with alcohol and vague feelings of desire, she scornfully dismissed it.

The dance came to an end for the banjo, the three breathless saxophonists and the pianist slyly plagiarising Chopin. Ambroisine and her partner went back to their bar stools and looked each other full in the face at last. Of course each of them knew who the other was – in fact they knew who their fathers and grandfathers were – and had come across each other several times in Digne.

They went back to her villa, The Cedars, together. With the help of her fertile imagination and exaggerated sighs, Ambroisine managed to prolong their interlude until well after midnight. But that was all. The lover was not willing to stay for the crucial hours in the dead of night, the hours to be navigated between two inaccessible havens. Besides, a quarter of an hour earlier, despite the pleasure he thought he was giving, this assiduous partner suddenly stopped, raised his head, said, 'Ssh,' and listened.

It was because the wind and the cedars together were making a dreadful noise. The dark house had already made a bad impression on the man from the moment he began walking down the path under the trees. They made him think of his grandmother, who always used to tell him that a cedar less than a hundred metres from a dwelling was a jealous man turned into a tree who was intent on finding a home again, sitting at a table somewhere, lying on some woman; if he could not actually get into the house, he would try to empty it of its inhabitants through some patiently induced misfortune, making it dark and cold so that he could raise it up on his roots, encircle it with his caressing limbs, and finally assimilate it by turning it into a ruin under the darkness of his branches.

It is impossible to say by what means the nonsense repeated years ago by an old woman can somehow return and combine with the alarming reality of the present. In addition to that, there was something wrong in that house; something that the wind in the cedars was trying to stifle; something like someone holding their breath; something surreptitious, muffled.

The man gave a start as he was listening. Far away, far up above the bed, came the sound of something soft collapsing, like a kitten with velvet paws hitting a ball of wool.

'What's the matter?' Ambroisine asked, stopped short in her pursuit of pleasure.

He looked closely at her in the opaline light of the small rose-coloured lamp she had left on to smoothe over the few imperfections of her body while emphasising its tantalising shadows. Her face looked too red to him, like a vampire in a film. She was part of the mystery he sensed around him, which unsettled him. Despite the forty years of age Ambroisine happily admitted to, the skin over her cheeks was taut and smooth. Her eyes were bright to the depths of the iris where the sharply defined pupil shone with glints of green. Years, decades later, the anguished expression of that look would haunt the life of this very ordinary man. It would pursue him, hound him, feed his remorse for not having heard or not wanting to hear; its call for help would demolish the good reasons he would keep putting up to justify himself.

But for the moment, he felt there was a hint of magic in their love-making. The only thing he wanted now was to get away as fast as possible from this partner who was capable of keeping him there longer with her tenderly daring caresses. He opportunely thought of wife and children. He stood up, preparing to make his escape, and walked quickly around the furniture looking for his clothes, which had been impatiently flung to the four corners of the room. His search began with a full erection, but it lessened and soon subsided in a wave of fear. He had to ferret around for some time. The socks especially gave him a lot of trouble before turning up on top of the mantel clock.

Ambroisine scornfully watched the silhouette scurrying from place to place, looking ridiculous now that it was devoid of all mutual desire. The body of the so-called intelligent ape: black hairs at the top of the divide between buttocks shaped like drops of oil, balls hanging between parentheses . . . In short, everything that contributes to the fact that, seen from behind, the male of the species has nothing to crow about.

He mumbled some excuse about the time, what people might say, the conjugal bed deserted for too long. Once again (there are several moments like that in every woman's life), Ambroisine saw the male as he really is: always ready to cut off your hands so that you don't cling to his boat. Although he was possibly abandoning her on the night of her death, she knew that with the perfect logic of public opinion, he had every good reason in the world to leave her to her fate.

He left the room naked, holding his clothes in a bundle against his stomach, intending to get dressed later, far away from the howling wind in the cedars. On second thoughts, he didn't even bother to put his clothes on. He threw everything into the car, slammed the door and sped off with fear at his back.

The silence had been contained for as long as the panting couple filled it with their pleasure. Now it closed in on the house once more, and vague rustling sounds could immediately be heard again within it.

'What am I doing, staying here like this?' Ambroisine exclaimed.

Like this meant flat on her back in the double bed, hands clasped on her chest, lying there like a sacrificial lamb, her mouth dry with fear, having already forgotten the recent embraces that had been so reassuring.

She leaped out from between the sheets and got fully dressed again, including her tights and the shoes with stiletto heels that gave her the alluring bottom she felt was such an essential part of her charm. Then she listened.

Was it the branches of the cedars, surging like waves on the ocean? Was it the plaintive moan of the weathervane turned this way and that on its hinges by the wind? Was it the creaking sounds of a ship in distress that echoed every autumn through the attic of the huge, uncomfortable, pretentious villa? No, it wasn't. Ambroisine had been used to all that since she was a child. No. The only sound her ears retained was underneath all that noise: the indefinable rustling down below to the north, at the back of the villa, somewhere in the vicinity of the worm-eaten laundry door that had become mouldy in the shade of the big trees, and which Ambroisine always put off replacing through unacknowledged miserliness.

A semblance of intoxication from all the alcohol consumed at Le Picrocole still clouded her brain despite the vigorous lovemaking. It gave her the false impression that she was still quite lucid and knew what she was doing, and that it was going to be easy to counter the menace slowly moving in on her. This was her frame of mind as she stretched out her arm towards the telephone to ring the police. She guessed that the best way to calm one's fears, if need be, was to transfer them to the gendarmes. She confidently picked up the receiver but then dropped it immediately, as if it had been red-hot. She had just remembered what she said to her cousin on the very night she died. She could still hear herself advising Véronique: 'The police and the tax department work hand in glove. If you don't want a visit from one of them, it's advisable to keep your distance from the other. No one is proof against a piece of paper that may be left lying about.'

No, definitely not that! You mustn't involve any official body in this affair; you mustn't raise the alarm; fight it in your own way. No one must know.

She stood there undecided, surrounded by her own image in the bedroom mirrors, which she thought looked out of fashion. She shrugged. Hardly the time to think of such nonsense.

It was then that she heard the distinct sound of footsteps through the noise in the cedars. Regular, slightly dragging footsteps; the footsteps of someone walking where he had a right to be; footsteps that echoed around the empty wash troughs that had not been used for years. Yes, it was down far below in the laundry so badly secured by its rickety door. Ambroisine bit her lip, reproaching herself for having been unwilling so long to spend the derisory sum to replace it. It was too late now. The intruder only had to cross the winter garden (and Ambroisine thought she heard someone trying to force the iron door at that moment). Oh, the attacker would certainly have trouble extricating himself from there. For the fifty years that it had been neglected, a casualty of changing tastes and the expense of gardeners, this winter garden had undergone the law of the transformation of species. The few tenacious plants that had resisted the torrid summers and harsh winters had spilled over and out of their tubs. Two glass panes smashed by a hailstorm had given them enough rain water to just survive. They had resown themselves and mutually subsisted, living off each other and themselves, becoming entwined and choked. A tap that had been dripping for half a century had attracted a few thirsty wandering roots. Then the soil had burst open. Under the concrete, plants had slowly found their way to the old pit of the septic tank and had gone through the top.

As the decades went by, tentacle rootlets had reached the surface of the water. Life had been crippled for a while, then postponed, protecting itself to slowly build up huge swellings ready to burst at the right time. Now it began to surge again, more luxuriant and threatening for having been restrained for so long. An elder tree from heaven knows where had burst out of this greenish magma. Their energies intensified by the struggle for existence, all these aberrant forms had inevitably reached the dome of the winter garden and covered it from top to bottom like a jar. Sometimes in spring, one or other of the glass panes still intact could be heard breaking under the pressure of their slow, regular growth, and through this new opening some branch sprouting black umbels would shoot out towards the sun.

Yes indeed, the intruder would take quite a while getting out of that virgin forest, but after that he would only have to raise the latch on a rattly lock to come out directly on the cellar landing, opposite the pantry, then go up the stairs and down the corridor to finally confront Ambroisine and reveal who he was.

Wild panic seized her once more. She thought that she hadn't planned properly, that the thing she wanted to protect from the stranger's greed was not in a safe place. Without a moment's hesitation she quickly climbed the two flights of stairs that led to the attic.

Her run was stopped short by the closed door ahead of her. She stood there panting for almost a minute, aware of the mysterious object she had to fetch from the room on the other side of the door. In her genetic make-up there were fortunately four generations of women who had made money supporting her with their down-to-earth outlook that had no time for fantasies. She lifted the latch and gave the door a good push. At the sight of the dark space before her shrouded in heavy silence, her spirits fell.

A smell, a scent almost of sweetness, floated in the air above this cemetery of objects. They were useless now, but indispensable to the living in days gone by. The smell came from the beams and joists made from larch trees that still remembered the forest, even after being dead for a hundred and fifty years. Sometimes in the summer this wood still wept drops of honey-coloured resin.

Ambroisine felt around for the light switch. It was pre-1914 and the button had long ago lost its insulation. Whenever it was handled, it gave out an unpleasant little electric shock. As in all well-run houses where they counted the pennies (it was by counting the pennies that one grew rich), two low-wattage bulbs dimly lit this unoccupied room. Unable to banish the shadows from a space that measured fifteen metres long by nine metres wide, this lighting was just sufficient to bring to life everything a quite terrified woman had only imagined until then.

Attics are the holds of ships on land. They accommodate everything necessary for a successful journey across time, just as real holds are full of everything needed for a successful journey across the sea. However, you couldn't say that this one contained wrecks. The dark, disparate collection, where the odd sharp edge of a clock, light fitting or heavy wardrobe stood out against the mass, was nothing less than the museum of a dynasty built up through the ages.

Neither Ambroisine nor any member of her family had ever made an inventory of this shambles, but even without making a note of it, she knew the place of everything there. Just one object, which dominated the whole thing, encapsulated the character of the people who had lived beneath this attic: it was an old, elaborate business sign. On the death of his mother, after the building in the boulevard Gassendi that housed the shop was sold, Ambroisine's father had insisted that it be taken down from the wall and brought here with great ceremony. It was made of iron, heavy, and difficult to handle. It had taken four workmen to haul it up to its last resting-place here in the gloom, leaning against the main wall, wedged under the framework of the roof against a complicated tenon and mortise join.

It was a huge, almond-shaped convex shield, like a mandorla.[*] The fine, light letters of a confident signature stood out against the austere dark-brown background. They were written diagonally across the sign like swallows taking flight. They announced:

> *Madame Scholastique Melliflore*
> *née Rosans*
> *Milliner*
> *from mother to daughter since 1845*
> *Hats made to order*

For more than a hundred years, the Misses Rosans as they were called, even though they were wives and mothers, worked in the shadow of that sign. They earned enough, first of all, to build that huge villa, buy the building that contained the shop and a few other assets that were nothing to boast about but made a good profit. This evening, however, there was something out of place at the foot of the sign. A whole lot of unidentifiable objects were piled up in front of it so that it was impossible to read the last line, which had been so important in those days: *Very competitive prices.*

[*] An almond-shaped aureole enclosing a holy figure in medieval art and architecture.

Intrigued by this, Ambroisine took several steps across the parquet floor. All the boards creaked under her weight. She was so surprised that she let out a cry, which she quickly tried to stifle by clapping her hand across her mouth.

There before her the large black cupboard – the pride of the Misses Rosans' shop, the main feature for their talent, the receptacle of all their milliners' secrets – stood with both its doors flung wide open. All the boxes it contained had been knocked off the plundered shelves. They had opened or burst, spilling their masterpieces around them. There they were, strewn on the floor like a ludicrous parade, fallen on their sides or gallantly tilted on their framework as if heads of yesteryear were still under them.

In the indistinct light from the two bulbs, all that remained of the Rosans' creations now lay quivering in the draughts of air outside the empty cupboard: audacious creations that a certain number of clients had not wanted or dared to wear through timidity or changed circumstances.

Vieux rose, leaf green or parma violet, they conjured up the flowerbeds of an old-fashioned garden. All the whims of fashion were there, released from their light boxes which had cracked open like eggs: a bittern with wings outstretched and beak wide open showing its red tongue was still defending its nest against an intruder in the front of a floppy Italian straw hat. It was next to felt hunting hats with bustard feathers, pink cloches trimmed with a simple wild rose on one side, English-style caps, spring boaters for Impressionist painters. But they were all outdone by a huge grieving widow's headdress, square with a long veil, which had emerged from a box twice as big as the others. It must have made the men of the day shiver with horror at the thought of the face that could be hidden under that rampart raised against envy by unassailable and henceforth useless fidelity. This symbol of death sitting arrogantly on the top of a charming profusion of frippery spoke so eloquently to Ambroisine that she stood there stiffly in front of it for a moment.

So, he had come again, the faceless enemy who sometimes made such a noise in the house, the enemy who had made himself known to

Véronique and to herself, whose last letter wrinkled the front of her dress. It fascinated her so much that she had stuck it down there when she was hardly dressed.

She put her hand on it as if on a talisman that could exorcise what threatened her. But that was not going to be enough, for it seemed to Ambroisine that beyond the hats strewn on the floor, beyond the sign, the shadows at the end of the attic were slowly becoming lighter. She saw a shape down there in the dull moonbeam that struggled through the dirt on the small circular window with its lacy cobwebs; a shape without a distinct outline or identity, but which still had a somewhat human appearance. A shifting mist seemed to rise up around this marshy half-light.

God, how awful this fine attic was now. It used to be golden with sunlight. She had played hide-and-seek among the old things here so often in her childhood. Suddenly it refused to be recognised and seemed to be showing itself in its true light, exposed for what it was, a place full of unexpected deceit and hostility.

She drew back, and at that same moment the disembodied light in the distance moved, multiplied, spread, became distorted then went back to what it was, stiff and still, shimmering and vaguely iridescent. While this was happening, the cedars rhythmically swept their caressing branches over the roof.

Ambroisine wanted to run. She turned on her heel ready to rush to the door. But within the slim figure that made her look like a weak woman there lay the determination of all the grasping Melliflores, ever ready to defend their inheritance, come what may, against magic spells, plague, cholera or simply the wrath of God, all the things that the people of this region were used to living with.

The idea that she was abandoning all her goods and property to someone else's greed without a fight rooted her to the spot. A rebellious sense of injustice overcame her panic, giving her the strength to confidently retrace her steps towards the solid shelves where memories of the past slumbered for ever.

These sets of shelves were level with the first light bulb, and

Ambroisine knew exactly what she would find there. It was a large, handsome square package wrapped in brown paper and carefully tied with string. The words *My mother's hat* were written on it in felt pen.

It sat next to a postman's leather satchel, lid raised as if being carried on its rounds. Obviously happy rounds, as post-office calendars were spilling out of it. And to Ambroisine's right on a footless shop dummy, a complete uniform of a postal employee hung pensively suspended between roof and floor. It was an ancient uniform made up of a jacket with gilt buttons, sky-blue trousers with a navy stripe down the seam, and a kepi with rosette. The whole ensemble with its empty sleeves and trousers, and hat held up by a wire-mesh dummy head, turned around slowly in the draught and seemed to be whispering something to Ambroisine as she stood there before it.

Then, acting on a sudden intuition, she took the big parcel and held it tightly in her arms. She made straight for the door, opened it, closed it again behind her, turned the key and, with a wildly beating heart, sank on to the top step of the staircase. But while she was running across the attic, she had had time to catch a last glimmer down at the end under the round window, a glimmer that moved as quickly as she did. Once the door was closed again and she was sitting on the step, she realised at last that, partly due to alcohol, she had been the victim of an illusion. The only thing at the end of the attic under the round window was an old cheval mirror, and all this time the fly-specked oblong glass with its peeling mirror coating had been reflecting her own wild image distorted by the reddish gloom from the dim lights. She took a deep breath of relief and rested her arms on the square box.

But almost immediately a new anxiety had her shivering and up on her feet again. It had just occurred to her that although she had only imagined an intruder in the attic, the one she had heard a while ago in the old echoing laundry was real, and in that case there wasn't a moment to lose.

She opened wide the heavy front door (coloured glass panes and wrought-iron bars), holding the parcel against her knee, and after putting it down on the balustrade, she double-locked the door behind her. Under the misleading impression of having safely locked her fear inside the villa, she heaved a sigh of relief.

She had forgotten the noise the cedars were making, but now it was there all around her once again. She shivered in her crimson dress, whipped up by the wind, and looked frantically around her. Was there no help she could call on? Not a sign of anyone in the whole vast estate. The villa was well protected behind its iron railings and its garden, and the quiet cul-de-sac where it had been built for peace and quiet fulfilled its promise. The villa was so isolated that no cry or call for help could cross the space that separated it from anything inhabited in the vicinity. However, from the platform at the top of the curved flight of steps on each side, which commanded a view down the avenue bordered by the cedars, Ambroisine could survey the town where she was born, so charming and so close, inviting her to come and enjoy its pleasures again.

The moon had suddenly risen into the wind-swept sky. The crown of Les Dourbes had never looked more familiar up above, or the St Jérôme's steeple more reassuring down below. Tomorrow, under the benign gaze of Gassendi in bronze, the Saturday market would be held amidst the fresh smells of the vegetable stalls and the sweet ripeness of the autumn fruits.

Ambroisine felt an impulse to dash into the car gleaming under the trees and flee the place, sleep anywhere, even on the esplanade, where the street lamps threw light into every corner between Gassendi and the band rotunda.

No! Why should she? A rebellious reflex made her straighten her back. First of all she had to find a safe place for this precious possession that the intruder was so intent on taking. No one would think of looking for it in the place where she intended to hide it. After that she would be free; after that she would get away.

There is no lack of poor shipwrecked souls lost in the night who have gone under because they would not let go of a heavy case containing all their possessions, except their lives.

Ambroisine put her arms around her box once more. She hesitated in deciding which flight of stairs she should take, as had all the generations who had lived here. They had all finally chosen the same one, for if one side was clean and worn, the other disappeared under the fallen leaves of the Virginia creeper on the front of the house.

That evening, perhaps for the first time in her life, Ambroisine in her agitated state chose the other side. She felt her way down because of the package that blocked her view of the steps. And it was while she was holding it tightly against her cheek that she realised why the person who wanted it chose those very windy nights, why Véronique had been killed on such a night, and why she herself was at that moment in very great danger. This was because, whenever it was lightly touched or accidentally bumped, the large cube that was so awkward to carry emitted a kind of angry grumble; a sustained, unnerving trembling note that struck the ears and even the heart; a kind of prolonged avalanche of sounds, dull but deep. Once provoked, it seemed capable of travelling through space and causing alarm for an infinite distance. Hence the need to take advantage of noisy winds to hide the sound.

For the moment it was saying strange things to Ambroisine; the same as all the cedars, which were swishing their branches as if to send her away, make her flee the place. No, no! She held firm. And yet . . .

And yet this central path between herself and the place she wanted to reach was full of danger. Someone could suddenly appear from behind any of the eighteen cedars planted ten metres apart, nine on each side. Someone could rush out and bar her way or steal up behind her, knock her to the ground and stab her, yes, stab her with that horrible rusty bayonet that had been found next to Véronique.

The same sensation of hostility she had felt a while ago in the familiar attic came over her in the presence of those trees. To think that when she was twelve years old and her father had talked of having them cut down because they made too much shade, she had prevented him doing it with her tears, her pleading and three days of fever from all the vows she made from her bed. It was because as a girl she had known so many moments of delightful apprehension in their shadows, hoping that some fresh-faced cousin would jump on her from behind one of the trunks and only regretfully let her go after many half-hearted cries and languid contortions on her part. Where had these cousins gone? They were now either indifferent or old. Why weren't they here to accompany her, reassure her, protect her? We become children again when it's death that has us playing hide-and-seek.

But the greedy obstinacy of the Melliflores rose up in her again. That rock battered by the wind of fear, but basically unshakeable, was the foundation of her life: the love of lucre mocked her instinct for preservation and urged her on. She must reach the summerhouse deep in the garden at the end of the path. In the old days the whole family would go there on Sunday to see the three o'clock train leave, for the wall of this miniature fake-medieval folly with its pointed roof looked out over Digne station.

A well beneath a rose arbour added its charm to this place of former delights, where the families of yesteryear came and cooed with pleasure to see themselves so well-off and settled compared with so many mediocre souls on foot down there at the station.

Because of the children, the well had been closed off with a heavy round metal cover. One half of it was hinged and could be raised so that a basket of bottles could be lowered on a chain to keep the drinks cool. The chain was attached to a solid ring set into the inside wall between the stones. That ring was what Ambroisine had in mind. She hoped to entrust her precious possession to the well – it seemed even more precious to her now that someone else was after it – since she thought that neither the house nor the attic was safe. But . . . she still had to reach it.

She began walking down the middle of the path, darting fearful glances to each side as she went. It seemed to her that the tunnel under the branches was endless, that the cedars were increasing their alarming noise, and that someone was taking advantage of it, following her, drawing nearer. Stumbling along under the weight of her package, she turned round several times to make sure. But the further she went, the more the path seemed to narrow behind her and close up with the slow beating of the branches in the dark. The only thing that she could call familiar or at all reassuring was the sullen boom in her ears from the parcel, sounding like a solid heartbeat, but ten times louder.

Suddenly there was light from the moon above and from the ground below, as the area around the station was brilliantly lit. She had reached the end of the path unhindered. There, rising up from the grass they called a lawn strewn with cedar needles rose the graceful ensemble: the summerhouse and its well under the rose arbour, where a few flowers were still battling the wind and resisting the autumn.

Ambroisine, with great relief, put her large parcel down on the rim of the well. She took off the key that she had hung on her bracelet and bent over the well to pick up the padlock that held the cover in place. The key creaked as it turned in the rusty lock, but the padlock sprang open with no difficulty. Ambroisine put it next to the package.

She was a strong woman. She had good hard muscles in her arms as in her buttocks. A silky firmness that delighted her lovers. And so she managed to lift the heavy, rusty iron half-circle without too much effort, and attach its handle to the hook on the arbour.

She leaned over the side of the well. Scarcely a few metres below, a circle of water shone in the light of the full moon, fluttering like a dazzled eye. Ambroisine had no time to waste admiring it. She felt about, making sure that the iron ring fixed to the wall which held the chain was still there. She tried to rattle it to see how solid it was. Then she quickly took the package and hung it on the ring by its thick string. When it hit against the wall, the dull, seemingly angry grumbling sound came from it for the last time. It suddenly sounded menacing when echoed by the well, like a rumble of distant thunder.

She was about to straighten up again when she noticed that the calm eye of the water below was now obscured, as if a cloud had come between herself and the moon. That shadow made her freeze. She held her breath

Then, a strange perfume seemed to float in the air all around her. Was it chrysanthemums from the pots in front of the summerhouse waiting to decorate the graves on All Souls' Day? No, of course not! How stupid she was! Despite their sombre significance, chrysanthemums had a cheerful smell which somehow held the promise of good times to come.

No, what Ambroisine detected was what one might smell around a sickly old man: the smell of chamomile tea.

That was the last sensation of her life. There was a huge crash: it was the iron cover falling back into place and encountering the bones in Ambroisine's neck, as she had not stood up quickly enough.

For a fraction of a second, the moaning of the wind in the cedars gave precedence to this sound like a falling guillotine blade, then continued its monotonous wail through the ghostly branches as if nothing had happened.

From then on it calmly occupied the whole space of the night, alone and unchallenged.

VII

THE OCTOBER RAIN WAS SLOWLY EATING AWAY AT THE LAST TRACES of summer around Digne. But falling on gardens that were dying like forgotten flowers in a vase, it finished everything off as quickly as possible: the sunflowers drooped, the horse chestnuts fell and rotted on the ground, bringing the dead leaves down with them.

With his feet up against an armchair and a cat lying across his stomach, Laviolette in retirement was savouring the pleasures of autumn with the greatest delight. He was rereading Proust for the fifth time in his life. He was up to the pear trees at Combourg and his lazy mind was taking its time, slowly relishing every sentence. He was shamelessly enjoying the privilege of wandering alone through an art gallery where all the Sisleys, Pissarros, Renoirs and Manets in the world had been brought together especially for him. In just ten lines, Proust's art blended them all together and, through the magic of his words alone, distilled the fascinating imprecision, the mysterious haziness of dying colours.

At least that was the interpretation given to it by Superintendent Laviolette (retired), and after all, wasn't that the most important thing? He gave a sigh of satisfaction at regular intervals, and the smile of delight never left his good-natured face.

Someone knocked on the glass panel in the door.

He turned round. It was Judge Chabrand's outline in the dark behind the glass, still rugged up in his bulky old-fashioned overcoat, looking like the coachman of death. Laviolette called out to him to come in. Despite the invitation, the judge stood in front of the door thinking about it before putting his hand on the latch, as this gesture in itself brought back so many bitter memories. The limited amount of optimism that had been given to him at birth had died in Popocatepetl, so that he always had to force himself to go in.

He bade Laviolette a gruff, cursory good evening. He was morose, as was his custom. On his face, around his big glasses, there were still some of those unhealthy yellowish patches left by his viral hepatitis, which showed that it was still a worry. In addition, slight traces of juvenile acne remained on his cheeks and chin, the after-effects of a long and difficult adolescence.

He picked up the book that Laviolette had just put down on the table to greet him. He picked it up, opened it to see the title and, once he had read it, tossed it back irritably.

'Quite incompatible!'

'What? What's incompatible?'

'You! You and this snob, this decadent with his sick imagination and sick view of the world. To think that ninety per cent of today's writers still chase after his genius.'

'Ah well,' Laviolette sighed. 'If you don't like him, you don't like me.'

Chabrand made a face.

'Oh, I like him in spite of myself . . . But that's enough of Proust. I didn't come to talk to you about him.'

'So? To what do I owe the pleasure of seeing you again?'

'You get on my nerves with your "to what do I owe the pleasure"! You know very well that pleasure never comes into it.'

'Yes, I know. I was trying to forget it, but that's hardly possible where you're concerned.'

'If you like, I can . . .'

Chabrand indicated the door and began to take a step backwards.

'No, no! Of course not! Stay. Sit down . . . Take off your cape.'

'It's a carrick coat,' the judge muttered.

'All right! But take it off all the same. And then pour yourself a glass of this organic apple juice I've just opened to celebrate the occasion.'

'Apple juice?' Chabrand asked, looking amazed. 'But . . . you never drink it.'

'Let's just say that I was expecting you,' Laviolette sighed.

Chabrand sat down in an armchair.

'Madame Ambroisine Larchet has been murdered,' he announced, 'some time during last Friday night, probably between three and four o'clock in the morning, according to the forensic pathologist. As your newspaper would have informed you, her death was caused by a heavy blow on the neck from the metal cover over the well. For the moment, as your newspaper also reports, it is still a complete mystery.'

'The paper also says,' Laviolette remarked, 'that she was a first cousin of Mademoiselle Véronique Champourcieux, also murdered in very nasty circumstances scarcely a fortnight ago.'

'Of course! And the press is starting to prick up its ears.'

'Anyway, at least the police have arrested a suspect,' Laviolette said with some satisfaction.

'Oh, please! That's enough! Yes, the night before, Madame Larchet was seen dancing with someone at Le Picrocole. They were seen leaving together, but it's not known which of them took the lead. There were lots of his fingerprints in the villa: on the door knobs, the bedposts and the bathroom. There's no doubt that he was the last person to see the victim alive. How could you not arrest him? At the moment, the lover is in police custody. His wife is asking for a divorce. His children are with his parents-in-law. In short: it's a disaster. A family torn apart. And I'm the one who brought scandal down on their heads!'

'Well,' Laviolette said philosophically, 'it's your job, after all.'

'No doubt. But I should never have chosen it. I'm just not cut out for it.'

'I wasn't meant to be a policeman either. The delight I feel in no longer being one is proof of that. Still . . . I suppose you'll be letting him go?'

'Tomorrow probably. But the harm's been done. He'll never recover from it.'

'Are you sure that he's not involved in any way?'

'I had made up my mind from the first moment. And anyway, the investigators discovered a vital clue: they heard – and these are their own words – "something rustling in the well-filled bodice of the *corpus delicti*." They put a hand inside and pulled out . . . this!'

He produced a plastic bag containing a letter and an envelope from his pocket and waved it under Laviolette's nose.

'The same as the one found in the Brahms album in Mademoiselle Champourcieux's house,' Laviolette noted.

'The same! And sent from Barles. And, make a note of this, bearing the same series of fingerprints. All identifiable except one: the earthy fingers.'

'Just like the other one,' Laviolette said. 'And . . . what does it say?'

'"The measure you give will be the measure you get",' Chabrand intoned in a lugubrious voice.

'And naturally, just as with Mademoiselle Champourcieux, nothing was stolen?'

'Yes it was. Something *was* stolen.'

'What was it?' Laviolette asked, showing great interest.

'I wish I knew.'

'What! You say that something was stolen, but you don't know what?'

Just as he had done on his first visit, Chabrand suddenly opened his right hand and produced a key. He tossed it in the palm of his hand as one shows the tip that's coming to a errand boy. Unable to resist a mystery, Laviolette looked covetously at the key.

'We'll go there if you like,' the judge suggested. 'It's less than a kilometre from here. And, if you don't mind, we'll go on foot so as not to attract attention. For of course all this is quite illegal.'

'Of course.' Laviolette agreed, not taking his eyes off the key.

'The gendarmes and the police already have their eye on me . . . because of course they know that I came to you . . . as to Canossa!' he said ruefully.

'Oh, that word!' Laviolette groaned. 'Is it so hard to imagine that we might have some sorrows to share?'

'What can you expect,' Chabrand sighed, 'when you're dealing with pragmatists? It's raining,' he added. 'That doesn't worry you?'

'On the contrary. Just wait a moment. It's not every day that I need to get out my big brolly. You can hold it. It'll do for both of us. That will bring back old memories.'

The cedars were now completely still, standing in the steady rain like a battalion at attention. Thrown together and struggling along, one built like Sancho Panza and the other like Don Quixote, the judge and the retired policeman climbed one of the curved flights of stairs under Laviolette's big blue umbrella. The leaves from the Virginia creeper were already starting to rot against the door closed on the abandoned house.

The judge put the key in the lock and pushed the door open. When a house has just lost its soul, a stricken silence falls over the sudden emptiness that no one will fill again. And all the noises that may be made later in that house will be like a scandalous din, ugly echoes from one room to another, from one corridor to another, sharp and discordant as if the walls are no longer able to absorb any music once the source of harmony has been taken away. But this strange detail about the power of death can only be picked up by ears that are very attentive to the smallest murmurs of life. Rational people go through these empty spaces with the serenity of a lawyer, and their indulgent smiles categorise you if you decide to point out in their presence that there is something lacking in the atmosphere.

'Let's speak quietly . . .' Laviolette murmured, for he knew this secret about houses.

Chabrand looked at him askance, shining the torch on him to examine him more closely, but did as he was asked.

'It's better not to turn on the lights,' he whispered. 'Given the fact that this operation is illegal, the less we make waves, the better. Stay with me. I'll light the way.'

He began by going upstairs to the first-floor corridor. Ambroisine's subtle perfume was still floating in the air around the ornaments and fragile furniture.

'Do you want to see . . . her bedroom?' Chabrand offered.

'I suppose your men have searched everywhere?'

'Everywhere! The wardrobes, desks, rubbish bins, toilet and cisterns. The backs of paintings, mediocre for the most part, but lots of them. You should have seen the dust and cobwebs! The insides of light sockets,' he said, pointing his finger. 'Every facet of the light fittings. They even unscrewed the counterweights of the ceiling lamps, opened the doors of clocks. They swept the chimneys. To sum up: I have three hundred photos on my desk that will be of no use whatsoever. If there was something to be found, believe me . . .'

'In that case . . . there's no point,' Laviolette said.

He was not anxious to see that scene of devastation: the crumpled bed of a pretty woman who would never make love there again; the wardrobe with all its dresses; the chest of drawers he imagined in bow-front Louis XV style, with drawers full of white, coloured, but always transparent lingerie she must have liked to slip on, to see in the mirror or in her lovers' eyes that she was not yet getting old.

'What I want to show you is up there . . . in the attic.'

Chabrand went lightly up the flight of stairs two steps at a time, which was easy for him as he was so thin. Laviolette followed as best he could. The air whistled in his bronchial tubes as if through the holes in a sieve.

'You should have more regard for a retiree!' he panted.

But Chabrand didn't hear him; he was already opening the door at the top of the stairs and signalling to Laviolette to go in first.

'Here we can allow ourselves to put on the light,' he said, turning the switch. 'The round window is so dusty that no one will notice.'

Under the light of the two twenty-five-watt bulbs, Laviolette had already made his way to the centre of the room.

'But you didn't tell me,' he said joyfully, 'that this house has the greatest attic in the world!'

He literally moaned with pleasure as he gazed at his patchy reflection in the oval cheval mirror where spots of the silver backing had come away. It stood under the round window near a solid dressing table with Moustiers* china utensils that Laviolette suspected were from the best period. When he caught sight of the charming avalanche of all the old-fashioned hats spilled out of their cupboard, he stopped in his tracks, obviously entranced. The investigators had plunged into them looking for clues, scattering them even further. But above all, he stood for some time in front of the sign: *Scholastique Melliflore . . . Milliner*. Fifty years ago, he had waited under that sign on the boulevard Gassendi when his mother had gone to choose the only hat she had ever worn in her life.

Chabrand watched this childlike wonderment, this old man's almost voyeuristic enthusiasm for someone else's past.

'A pile of old rubbish!' he hissed. 'Leave that and come over here.'

He pointed imperiously to the empty place on the large set of shelves.

'That's what was taken,' he said. 'The thing I told you about. It was there. Thanks to the outline made by the dust, our investigators have been able to calculate its size: sixty centimetres on all sides, a perfect square. As for the height, of course we don't know that, nor the nature of the object in question.'

'It could have been taken earlier,' Laviolette objected.

'Not at all. When the search took place, the light layer of dust that has formed since didn't even exist where the object was sitting in the middle of the very old thick layer, as you can see. Therefore the . . . package had only just been taken away. Do you follow me?'

'Oh. Perfectly.'

He replied without really paying attention, as he was fascinated by the disembodied postman hanging from the beams, which he had just discovered. It kept twisting in the draught, and its kepi rather roguishly tilted on the wire dummy head seemed to be looking at something over the judge's shoulder.

---

* China from Moustiers-Sainte-Marie near Digne, a large manufacturer in the seventeenth and eighteenth centuries.

'My word!' he whispered. 'You'd swear he was just about to go out on his round!'

Chabrand turned to face him.

'Ah, him? What a strange idea to keep that. But for your information, we were so professional that we even searched the pockets of his uniform.'

'Oh, I don't doubt it,' Laviolette protested deferentially.

His gaze had slipped from the uniform to the shelves and the postman's leather box satchel, which also looked ready to be slung over the dummy's shoulder for a Christmas round when there would be tips aplenty.

'Calendars!' Laviolette exclaimed.

They were literally bursting out of the satchel. There must have been more than a hundred of them.

'May I look?' he asked apprehensively.

'Yes, don't worry! There were no prints on them. However, the dust had been disturbed, which proves that they had been touched.'

'Why and by whom?'

'I'm not a fortune-teller, you know! I was informed of the fact, that's all.'

'And only the fact. . .' Laviolette muttered.

He had taken the packet of stiff cardboard sheets out of the satchel with infinite care, anxious to examine them. Some still had that loop of red string knotted through the eyelet, which was used to hang them on a nail in the kitchen.

These large cards on various subjects surrounded by the calendar had been obligatory companions in the lives of the French people for a long time. They were distributed even to farmhouses in the furthest depths of the countryside, where perhaps no one could read except the child going to school, and it was given to him to consult for the dates of the new moon.

For a long time it had been the only luxury item, the only printed matter that a lot of poor people ever had. They were never thrown away. They were piled one on top of the others and always hung up on the same nail. Sometimes in the summer they were used to block the outlet of the stove pipe to keep hornets and rats out. Nothing was surer than the ritual of the post-office calendar: its arrival around Christmas time sounded the death knell for the year.

In the dim light from the electric bulbs those stereotyped pictures, nearly always naive, passed before Laviolette's eyes: the joyful scene of the postman on his bicycle arriving at a flower-covered cottage, where a housewife in white apron carrying a child in her arms is waiting for him; the Cathedral of Saint-Pol-de-Léon surrounded by a garland of roses; a donkey at a level crossing refusing to move despite being beaten, while a train comes smoking over the horizon and the guard raises his arms to heaven. In the years of suffering, the war, there was the letter from the man at the front, the parcel for the soldier: 'All my thoughts fly to you,' says a young woman smelling a tricolour rose; the soldier is welcomed home, the crossed flags; the French troops entering Strasbourg and the return to the peaceful countryside of ploughed fields, forests and mountains, where the Gallic soul of the French loved to totally reimmerse itself. All of that – from 1870 to 1940, when the series stopped – passed before Laviolette's eyes.

The person who put the collection together must have had some difficulty in procuring certain examples, for many were blackened or fly-speckled, and one had obviously even been folded in four, and later fixed up to make it presentable. All the years represented were in strict chronological order, with the last one, 1940, placed on the top.

'The year 1912 is missing,' Laviolette observed.

Chabrand shrugged his shoulders.

'Well, it's a collection . . . Who knows if it was originally complete?'

'No doubt . . . But why would only one year be missing? Look at the trouble that's been taken to put it all together. Some of the calendars have been retrieved from smoky chimney pieces, mouldering behind damp cupboard doors. Look at 1909; it's aged in plaster and saltpetre. I'd swear it was snatched from the ruins of some cellar. Besides, you pointed out to me yourself that the postman's satchel had been touched, as the dust covering had been dispersed.'

'All right! The year 1912 is missing. That gets us a long way, I must say!'

'So, not only an unidentified object with a square base, but also the 1912 post-office calendar has been stolen,' Laviolette said, calmly summing up the situation.

He looked slowly around the space that went from the round window to the door. It was crowded with all the flotsam and jetsam left by a succession of families, but there was a certain order in the untidiness.

'Families,' he thought, 'who never wanted to let anything go. The sign and the uniform are proof of that. Families where the cries of the dying expressed the pain of losing their possessions rather than their lives.'

Ambroisine's death, however, affected him more than Véronique's. Like the rest of Digne, he knew the temperament of that vivacious widow, and it seemed to him an unspeakable waste that she should have died so miserably, robbed of living out her destiny as a sensual woman. 'She loved life,' he thought, 'which, all things considered, is not such a common thing.' It seemed hard to believe that she would no longer be there to enjoy it.

There are certain people – rare beings – who are good players in life and it does one's heart good to see them perform. When they leave us, boredom descends on the scene of their exploits, and the days drag miserably by. Ambroisine was one of those. She had given a virtuoso performance in her role as a freewheeling widow, in full view of the whole town. It would be a long time before another like her came along.

All around him in that heavy, sad silence, in the perfume still floating through the house, Laviolette could feel the lament of the things she had left behind and which no longer had any purpose without her.

'Show me the place where she died,' he asked.

'By the way,' Chabrand said, 'I forgot one detail: there were no finger-prints, but we did find numerous traces of those hobnail boots. Similar to those we found at her cousin's house.'

The judge was already going down one of the curved flights of steps leading to the garden, with Laviolette behind him, and like Ambroisine on the last evening of her life, he had chosen the side that no one ever used. The basic independence of some people comes through even in details like this.

It had stopped raining. The light from the last quarter of the moon was playing on the tall, still trees. The path had lost its forbidding look. The cedars that said so many things during the storm the other evening were now enigmatically silent. Their horizontal, mould-green branches looked like gags placed over mouths, concealing the truth.

It seemed hardly possible that this charming well, framed with climbing roses, could have become a guillotine. Under the petals from the last roses slowly drifting around the coping of the well, the murder weapon – the iron cover – had turned pink in the moonlight.

'No need to lift it up,' Chabrand said. 'It wouldn't tell us anything. We've already searched the well. All you need to know is that the water is five metres below the coping and there's a ring set in the wall. The victim was probably trying to hang something from it.

'Something that someone took after killing her,' Laviolette observed.

'Very likely.'

Laviolette looked intently at the coping, the rose arch and the short grass. He pointed to the summerhouse with its smart pepperpot top and coloured tiles, like something from an operetta. The tiles were an elongated diamond shape, and glistened in the moonlight.

'Do you have the key to the pavilion?' Laviolette asked.

Chabrand gave a knowing smile.

'Ah! You're an old romantic. I thought that you'd be attracted to this rococo folly like a wasp to a honey-cake. Don't worry. I've brought the key, although in my opinion . . . We didn't find any prints there; not on the door or inside. It's been years since anyone set foot in there.'

Chabrand went in and shone his torch around the interior. It was just one room of seven sides and no windows. The big door with glass panels and fanlight took the place of windows. There were very few furnishings in this useless piece of architecture, except a fireplace that was out of proportion with the dimensions of the building, taking up a quarter of the space. A deep armchair stood in the corner by the cold fireplace.

'We even sifted the ash,' Chabrand said.

An elegant chair with open back featuring a treble clef sat beside a spindly legged table. There was an inkwell with a reed pen stuck in it on a green desk blotter. Who would ever have used it?

'You see,' Chabrand said, 'I told you there was nothing here.'

'Just a moment!' Laviolette exclaimed.

It was the half-portrait of a nineteenth-century man, who had tried to look as innocuous as possible to escape the painter's eagle eye. An anonymous portrait is always a mystery. You would swear that this one was a good likeness, as the artist was good but not brilliant. He could not have imagined the thin-lipped mouth shut tight like a purse; the watchful, acquisitive eyes, trained no doubt on some purely material object: counting money or cutting a cake into portions; the hair of economical cut with a triangle coming down in the middle of his forehead like the chevron on a coat of arms. A low, wide, domed forehead like the lid of a soup tureen. A forehead that must have made his mother groan giving birth to this character . . . A forehead . . .

'It's curious . . .' Laviolette murmured.

'A moron's head, if ever I saw one.' Chabrand commented.

'No. An archetype. It's very rare to come across one that hasn't degenerated. This one is the result of a pure hereditary line. All the hollows, all the scars on a skin constantly eroded by the wind and battered by the mountains, the eyes set deep in their sockets, everything screams at you that he's from around here. And yes, marked by a certain hereditary ugliness that we from these parts happily accept . . . even, I agree, down to facial features that could be classified as somewhat cretinous . . .'

'Especially the ears. Look at them. They stand right out from his head,' Chabrand insisted.

'That may be. But the look in his eyes belies all that. It's unwavering, perverse, fierce, greedy, whatever you will, but it's not moronic.'

Chabrand sighed.

'Perhaps, but a lot of good all that will do for the matter in hand.'

Laviolette was silent for a few seconds.

'I don't know . . .' he said at last. 'But what I do know is that this portrait, I've seen this portrait somewhere before.'

'Oh! How could you?'

'No. I expressed myself badly. What I've seen in fact is someone . . . a man or a woman . . . I can't say . . . who is like the man in the portrait. But when did I see this person? Three months ago? Last week? And when I say "I've seen", can I be sure? I just caught sight of him perhaps and it was gone in a flash . . .'

'Since you claim he's an archetype, there must be lots of Basses-Alpine people around here who look like him.'

'Oh, no. Not as many as all that. Because here, as everywhere else, there's been a lot of intermarriage in the last few centuries.'

'So you've seen a ghost,' Chabrand said, having a dig at him.

'Don't laugh. There are all sorts of ways of being a ghost. "Death has a hundred hands and walks by a thousand ways." Don't worry, it's a quotation. Would it be too much to ask to have a good photo of that portrait?'

'You'll have it tomorrow.'

Chabrand closed the door of the pavilion and set off slowly down the path. Laviolette stood in front of the summerhouse that still gave out the pleasant smell of walls warmed by the sun. He felt the poignant call of this folly from another age, a call like the appeal you sometimes see in the eyes of a lost dog as you pass it too quickly to feel guilty. The look that says, 'What will become of me if you don't take me?' Laviolette felt the sadness of the situation, standing in front of walls that were said to have no soul and which would soon be demolished, as they were in the middle of a prime development site.

'I really can't buy all the old things in Digne on the pretext of saving them,' he muttered. 'And besides, I'll also die one day, and before that I'll be a ruin too . . .'

'What are you mumbling about now?' Judge Chabrand asked sourly.

'Oh, nothing . . .' Laviolette sighed. 'If I told you, you'd have a good laugh. We don't feel the same way about things,' he added.

They walked on under the cedars. In the distance, at the foot of the double staircase, they saw shining in the moonlight the apparition that had intrigued them so much on the night they had first encountered it in front of the Champourcieux tannery.

The woman was leaning against the white mudguard of her luxury sports car. Under her glistening fur coat she was wearing a navy blazer with gold buttons over a white pleated skirt; white stockings and tennis shoes completed the outfit. She looked tiny against her enormous car, and very thin, without boobs or bum. A large charm, probably gold, on the end of a thick chain sat on her bony chest. Her face was powdered as white as a ghost in a play, and two flat raven locks of hair curved down from her cloche hat, starkly emphasising her hollow, deliberately livid cheeks. At the time when the coat, the clothes and the car were the height of fashion, she would only have been a child.

'It's not possible!' Laviolette moaned. 'I'm going to touch her to make sure she's not a ghost.'

'I wouldn't if I were you,' Chabrand whispered. 'Although she hasn't much of it, she's flesh and blood all right! We made enquiries. She's the grieving widow of a head militiaman executed after the Liberation. He owned two small sawmills in the area and a power station that was nationalised at the same time . . .'

She was determinedly barring their way, a cigarette holder clenched in her teeth as she blew smoke in their direction with each breath she exhaled. Traces of gin and the stale smell of some nightclub where she had gone to finish off her evening floated in the air around this strange fashion-plate from another era.

'She's as pale as a hungry vampire,' Laviolette whispered.

'She's looking at us like Circe,' Chabrand joked under his breath. 'Don't you feel as if we're changing into swine?'

'Really!' she said when they were within earshot. 'Illegally entering private houses seems to be a tradition with you two.'

'The explanation of the truth . . .' Chabrand began.

'The explanation of the truth, my arse! You're here again to pinch something.'

'Madame! Mind what you say.'

'All this is mine. Do you hear me? Everything! I'm her only relative, just as I was to my sister. The drug addict who calls herself my cousin doesn't count.'

'Don't shout, please. It's never good to inherit from two people who have just been murdered, one after the other.'

She clapped a hand with turquoise fingernails to her chest.

'What! You don't still suspect me?'

Laviolette was quietly rolling a cigarette. He began speaking to her without raising his voice.

'Madame,' he said, 'no doubt no one would dare suspect you. Moreover, I'm not in a position to do so, but if you're not guilty, there's a strong chance that you may be the next victim. And you'd find that prospect even less comfortable, believe me.'

He ran his tongue along the edge of the finished cigarette and added, 'Because . . . and I don't presume to tell *you* this . . . the whole thing is a family affair. And you could perhaps save your life by giving me the answer to one question.'

She smiled disdainfully.

'Oh yes. And what would that be?'

'What valuable object do you possess that could be contained in a square package with sides measuring sixty centimetres?'

She seemed stunned for a few seconds before bursting out laughing.

'Oh, no! A square package! It's too ridiculous! That's all you've discovered!'

'No, it's not. Do you know what was the subject of the illustration on the 1912 post-office calendar?'

Her laughter choked.

'You're insulting me!' she shrieked. 'I was born in 1922! Under the sign of Taurus, with Virgo in the ascendant. And if you think you can frighten me . . .'

She heaped insults upon Laviolette, talking volubly as though hastily trying to cover up, with incoherent words, the shock that had so disconcerted her. Still gesticulating, she turned her back on them and walked towards her car. Once there, she swung round and flung at them, 'Save my life! Do you think I care about that? My dearest wish is to leave you all.'

She slammed her car door and suddenly blinded them with her headlights. Like the ghost of a bygone age, she and her sports car disappeared swiftly through the gate.

'Apropos of ghosts,' Laviolette said, 'that portrait in the summer-house . . . The Basses-Alpine with the low forehead . . .'

'Well?'

'Well, you can see here and there in that woman's face some of the elements – disparate elements, I'll grant you – that went into the original in that painting.'

'What's surprising about that? It's probably the portrait of some common ancestor, since the victim was the cousin of this extraordinary woman.'

'Oh, I'm well aware of that,' Laviolette agreed tersely. 'I'm not referring to a look that shows they're related.'

'What is it then?'

'Let's say that there's a constant in their propensity for misfortune, to put it in a nutshell. That's why,' he added, 'I see in her a future victim rather than a possible suspect . . . Yes, the more I think about it, the more essential it is to have a copy of that portrait. I must . . .'

He hesitated for a moment.

'I must reflect on that. At length,' he added. 'At length.'

He walked past Chabrand and on towards the gate, gesticulating all the while.

'Family affairs,' he muttered. 'Family affairs! Is there anything in the world more complicated and less rational than a family affair?'

He suddenly turned round towards Chabrand.

'But what family? Where should we go looking for it? Do *you* know how we should go about it? It all sounds like the dusty past to me. Some sordid old story. A motive which probably isn't one. In the eyes of the law, at any rate. Well . . . in your eyes.'

'You say that condescendingly,' Judge Chabrand remarked, somewhat put out.

'No, no. Not at all. Ruefully at most.'

At that moment a cold breeze arose, setting the cedars whispering among themselves.

'Ssh!' Laviolette insisted. 'Listen!'

'Listen to what?' Chabrand asked with surprise.

'The wind in the trees. It's trying to tell us something.'

'Come on!' Chabrand said, quietly admonishing him. 'At your age. And from you. Such nonsense! What if someone heard you?'

'Ah, my friend . . . Unless you take account of this "nonsense" and others like it, you'll never understand anything of the tricks this land can play.'

While he was talking, he kept on walking ahead towards the deserted streets of Digne, where nevertheless there was light shining everywhere, from the street lamps, from the neon in the shop windows with their cadaverous-looking dummies. So much light for nothing, as if all the actors in this theatre had suddenly been whisked away by fate, and the play was continuing with its invisible plot regardless, acted by their ghosts.

'A family affair,' Laviolette raged under his breath. 'A simple family affair! A *big* family affair, more like it!'

He walked, he gesticulated, he muttered to himself. His silhouette could be seen advancing noisily towards the deserted town that had been his delight for the whole of his life. He couldn't see that his companion kept nodding his head as a sign of commiseration.

The mysterious pathos that weighed on his words, and probably his thoughts as well, revealed in fact that Laviolette had a regrettably off-hand attitude towards the rationalists who darken this world. Chabrand was unable to accept it. The judge never revealed to a living soul the way his companion had acted in this case; he was so dismayed that a man for whom he felt some admiration could possibly have even one foot anywhere but on the ground.

VIII

BURIED UNDER THE NOISY PARADE OF ITS TALL TREES IN THEIR
October garb, crowned by Les Dourbes, coloured like the undergrowth,
Digne curled itself up peacefully in its mantle as a russet and gold
autumn town.

A few of the best restaurants were offering the first braised wild boar
of the season. Judge Chabrand came across Laviolette standing in the
street gazing at one of their menus.

'You're lucky not to have a bad stomach,' he said.

'Come on now,' Laviolette sighed. 'You have plenty of other pleasures. Every age has its own. But what have you got there? The X-ray of
your liver?'

'That's no joking matter!' Chabrand muttered. 'I was actually coming
to see you to show you the photos of the portrait you found so intriguing.
I've had six copies made, from every angle and in every possible light.'

'Give them to me quickly. I'm really anxious to get home and study
them.'

'You were on your way home then?'

'No, not at all. I intended going to look at the archives.'

'The archives? But they're close to . . . well . . . close to your place.
You're hardly going in that direction.'

'I didn't explain myself properly: it's not archives on paper that I want. I need living archives. So I was on my way to the old people's home . . .'

'I don't follow you, as usual.'

'Let me put it this way: I'm looking for stored memories . . . I must find some old men, do you follow? Old men who know the history of the valleys – the history of Barles, for example – and who still have all their wits about them. And where would one find a wider choice than in the old people's home? That's where they've all been stored,' he said ironically, with a bitter twist at the corners of his mouth.

'Much good may it do you!' Chabrand replied. 'Surprise me. Bring me the truth from the mouths of your old men.'

It was both a word and a subject the judge did not like to hear. In that way he could keep some aspects of life conveniently veiled, so as not to disturb any of his firmly held beliefs.

When Laviolette began climbing the path under the pines leading to the hospital, he came across one of the nurses who had helped him when he had his hernia operation.

'My dear,' he said, 'I need to find a man who is from these parts, and not too uncouth, if that's possible. Someone well past eighty who still has all his wits about him. In short . . . who is still interested in the nurses and women visitors, if you see what I mean.'

'Oh yes, perfectly.'

She turned and looked around her at the paths and clumps of trees where the pensioners usually strolled. They were all on the terraces warming themselves in the morning sun.

'There you are,' she said. 'You're in luck. I think I have the one you need. See up there? The green seat between the laurels? The thin man sitting by himself, taking up the whole bench.'

'The tall one? Dressed all in black? With a hat like Verdi? And a leather shoelace for a tie?'

'That's right. Your sight's still good.'

She laughed.

'Anyway, go to it! He still has good sight too. As for the women visitors, there's no one like him! He should have his hands tied down.'

'What's he called?'

'He's Dr Pardigon.'

He was an old man indeed. An old man of more than ninety, with the word 'venerable' written all over him. A fellow who smoked a pipe, although tobacco is supposed to shorten one's life. There are people like that who have luck with them, constantly watching over them to the end. He was the ideal old man, the one that we would all secretly like to become: straight, tall, neat, clean-shaven, the cane held nonchalantly between his legs, more like a sceptre than a crutch. He also had the pride and self-assurance of the ideal old man. 'I'm a winner,' he seemed to be proclaiming. 'Just look at all those I've passed on the way.' There comes a time when living becomes something like a competition, when one shamelessly rejoices over the death of one's neighbour, as if he were a rival who has been eliminated. And one felt that this nonagenarian took this fantasy, this stroke of fate, as a personal victory.

The man deliberately watched Laviolette come up the path towards him. He gave the impression that while he was observing him, he was calculating the time his visitor still had to live. It's true that Laviolette was puffing a bit as he sat down on the green bench beside Dr Pardigon, who was blowing smoke in his face.

'Well!' the old man exclaimed. 'It took you a time to get here.'

'It's steep,' Laviolette said as an excuse.

'Oh, I don't mean that. I'm talking about the murders: first Véronique and now Ambroisine. I said to myself, "One or other of them will end up coming to ask for your help." What have you got there under your arm? The X-ray of your lungs?'

'That?' Laviolette said with surprise. 'No, not at all. They're portraits, family portraits.'

'Ah! They won't be of much use to you. You smoke too much,' he added, drawing on his pipe with great enjoyment.

Laviolette had caught his breath while all this was being said.

135

'So you knew them?' he asked. 'Véronique and Ambroisine?'

'Of course. I brought them into the world. They were cousins. Véronique was the younger: no trouble at all. But Ambroisine: that was another story. It was her mother's first child and she was closed as tight as an oyster. They lived in the villa, The Cedars, and you could hear her yelling as far away as the Bléone bridge. That's just to give you some idea.'

He burst out laughing, coughing a bit at the same time.

'As if she didn't want to produce the girl. Just keep her . . . for ever . . . inside her. What can you expect? All those Melliflores, they're like a family of rats. It's not for nothing that they grew rich.'

'As rich as all that?'

'Well . . . it's obvious: the girls married well and never worked. At one stage these Melliflores had some fine building sites around Digne. They sold them at the right time. Ah! It's not for nothing that they came from Barles. People from over that way . . .'

'They were from Barles?'

'The grandfather was, and the whole family before him. Ah! If I told you everything I know! . . .'

'Exactly! That's just what I want to know: everything.'

The old man took his pipe out of his mouth and traced several arabesques in the air, which were to give some idea of the infinite possibilities of this *everything* demanded of him.

'Everything! Everything!' he repeated. 'You're brave. If I told you everything, we'd be here for a year!'

Laviolette took the Valda pastilles tin he used as a tobacco pouch, and deliberately began to roll a cigarette

'It'll take as much time as is necessary,' he said.

Pardigon looked at him with narrowed eyes

'It may take several sessions,' he ventured.

'That doesn't matter,' Laviolette said. 'I'm retired. And since I have you here, and you're an old inhabitant of Digne, and you were a doctor as well . . .'

'Yes,' Pardigon said, 'for more than fifty years. That's an age. And my father was before me. My father treated people as far away as Seyne. There were only two doctors in those days. And,' he added, 'my son would have been one too, only he decided to join up and get killed in the war. My wife slowly died of grief ten years later. As for me, when I turned ninety-five, I said to my housekeeper, "Marie-Rose," I said to her, "I've always lived among the people of Digne; I want to go and die among them." "But . . . you are among them here!" she told me. "No! No!" I said. "I don't know anyone here any more. The real people of Digne, those I've always known, are up there – in the home." "In the old people's home!" she shrieked. "That's right! In the old people's home. They're fine up there, aren't they? Why not me?" Well, she carried on for a while, begging me not to go, but she's a reasonable woman. I told her that the house and everything in it would be hers alone, and consequently . . .'

'You're a good man,' Laviolette said.

'You know . . . I'm not really grateful to hear that. Being a good man has never been my ideal. And besides, there have been several occasions when . . . Anyway! It's not my story that you've come for. So? You want me to talk to you about the Melliflores?'

'If you can,' Laviolette said.

'I'll give you the relatively short version: cut the family off at the beginning of the century; begin with the grandfather because . . . if I go further back, there's enough for a whole year.'

'Who was this grandfather?'

'He was called Gaétan Melliflore. From Barles, as I said. And the family goes back in Barles to Protestant times. His grandfathers had been mayors and knew everything about that region. Barles is a wonderful place. Do you know it?'

'I think,' Laviolette said, 'I think I'm going to know it pretty well.'

He leaned comfortably against the back of the seat, extending his arm behind the old man, and it was in this relaxed position that he listened, with eyes closed.

'This Gaétan Melliflore,' Pardigon said, 'was the lady's man of the family. His brother wore himself out on land that was on such a slope that they had to put a little bag on the hens' tails if they wanted to keep the eggs; otherwise they'd roll down as far as the Bès! Well . . . that's to give you some idea . . . There would never have been enough land there for two, so Gaétan became an assistant postman. He was no slacker. He quickly got himself noticed, was transferred to Digne and given tenure.

'A postman's uniform is not very impressive, but it's a uniform nonetheless. This postman we're talking about was tall, thin, hard, with bushy eyebrows like a prehistoric man and the face of someone who looked as if he would be without refinements in his private life. You know . . . At that time men wore handlebar moustaches, and Melliflore wore his better than anyone else. Then, with these assets, he sets out to conquer the Mesdemoiselles Rosans, who sold hats and umbrellas in the place du Mitan. These demoiselles were really the mother, widow of a sheep-seller, and the daughter, who was slowly going to seed. She'd have been twenty-five or twenty-six. Virtue is necessary, but it shouldn't be allowed to moulder away. A dark shadow was beginning to grow under her nose and a blotchiness to appear on her cheeks. Melliflore arrived just in time. To cut a long story short, they shook hands for the first time beneath a pile of millinery ribbons that cluttered the counter . . . With the mother two metres away. Afterwards, it was an endless stream of "my love" here and "my love" there. He used to come and jump over the iron fence around the villa. It was very romantic.'

'The Cedars . . .' Laviolette murmured.

'The Cedars?' Pardigon repeated, rather puzzled. 'Ah, yes, The Cedars . . . I understand what you mean. It's true: I'm telling you a story that goes back to the 1860s, and those cedars that witnessed it are scarcely much bigger today, while those who larked around beneath them are all dead. All of them dead!'

He sighed.

'Oh dear. A hundred years is too little. We should live for five hundred years to understand everything. I'll die as sorry to leave at a hundred as I would at forty.'

He fell silent, looking around sadly at the glowing autumn landscape.

'You were up to the fence that Grandfather Melliflore used to jump,' Laviolette reminded him gently.

'Ah, yes. The mother was a bit standoffish with him, naturally. She watched him coming through her lorgnette, as if she had a whole heap of nobility behind her. "He has nothing! " she said disdainfully. It was then that the daughter realised that she would have to force her hand. So, one evening, when she and her Melliflore had to take shelter in the summerhouse because of a storm, she takes off her camisole . . . ostensibly to dry it. And there and then, dripping wet as they were, with the basque and the stockings giving them no end of trouble . . . and the taffeta roses on the garters that prickled . . . and the girl's cries, which she knew would be drowned out by the thunder, and the trouble she had in saying no and yes at the same time . . . because . . . she'd had time to sum up her Melliflore. She knew he was quite capable, if it was all too difficult, of dropping both her and her virginity!'

'Now here I think you're embroidering . . .'

'I'm embroidering!' Pardigon exclaimed. 'Embroidering!' he repeated quite outraged. 'It was Grandfather Melliflore himself who told it to me on the grandmother's deathbed. Probably forty years ago now.

'When families are down in the dumps, you know, especially the men, when they're driving you home . . . knowing that there was no hope for the mother who held all the money . . . They tell you some ripe old tales. And in unimaginable detail. And besides, you seem to forget that my father had already looked after these people for fifty years. That's a hundred years we'd been in charge of that valley; a hundred years to track down the constants in their characters through the generations. Why would I need to embroider? I knew them like the back of my hand. A hundred years. That makes a lot of secrets. A hundred years,' he repeated.

By now he was panting a little. As the doctor recalled his memories of the nineteenth century, he gave Laviolette the impression that he was crushing it between his teeth as he spoke. But he was a man who had plenty to tell. He drew an angry zigzag in the dust in front of the bench, then continued.

'In short, the girl falls pregnant. She goes and tells her mother, who yells and screams and raises her hand to her daughter. Her daughter says to her, "That's right! Scream away. Send me to the hospital. If you don't want people to know, that's just the way to go about it." "But I don't want people to know. I don't want any of this, full stop." "He wants to make amends." "Amends? With what, may I ask? A postman, for heaven's sake! And a country postman at that." Then the daughter retorts, "I've had to take what I can find. If you'd made me a bit better-looking I could have had a choice." She throws that in her face just like that! "With what I have! With what we have!" the mother wails, wringing her hands. "But wait! Wait a moment! Isn't that miserable fellow of yours from Barles? Didn't his father have some land? Why, he must have something! There's no one in Barles with nothing, unless they've been dead for a long time. No! No! He must have something, however small. We'll see. I'll go there myself, to Barles."

'Off she goes, so tightly corseted that she can hardly breathe once a minute, wearing the moiré dress that makes her look twice as rich as she really is, and a solid gold necklace to hold her lorgnette, which bounces on her vast bosom, enhanced by the corset squeezing her stomach. And with it a hat that would silence crows for miles around. Of course it was all a bit white with dust: it had travelled down the valleys in the old carriage that had a good inch gap between each panel. Nevertheless, she was still a very impressive figure.

'Anyway, she finally gets there, puffing and perspiring. The brother was waiting for her, watching out of the corner of his eye. Up comes her lorgnette and she gives him the once-over from head to foot. Incidentally, he was putting manure into his wheelbarrow at the time, and not inclined to stop for something so unimportant. "Well," she shouts at him. "He's a fine one, that brother of yours!" "Oh, excuse me," he says. "Let's get this straight. I'm not my brother!"

'There was no point in acting surprised, because then, as now, news travels across our lonely countryside with the speed of an arrow. Added to that, there's so little of it. And it's usually so trivial. News of this calibre does the twenty kilometres from Digne to Barles in no time at all: "The Rosans girl has got herself made pregnant by the postman!"

'"No, but he's your brother all the same," she retorts. "And do you know who I am? You don't really think that I'll accept him, that brother of yours, with nothing? With only his postman's wages? There must be something of his up here. Surely your parents left you something?" "This farm," the brother replies, pointing his chin at the land around him. "Well then, you can see that there is something!" says she triumphantly. The brother shakes his head. "Nothing," he replies. "For him; I have everything and he has nothing. That's the way it is." "What! How do you mean, that's the way it is? Come now, it has to be shared. The law of the eldest getting everything no longer exists." "Oh no," he says to her. "And what about shotguns? Perhaps they don't exist either?"

'And upon my life, their conversation ended with this appalling question. Madame Rosans later told it to the whole of Digne. "My son-in-law," she would say, "was done out of an excellent property in Barles by his brother." Within ten years, the wretched Melliflore farm had blossomed like a chateau with lawns and an ornamental lake.

'She came back to Digne in a fine state: her jewellery was tarnished, her lorgnette dull, her hat as flat as a soufflé in a draught. "He has nothing! He has nothing!" she cried. "Unnatural child! Presenting me with the child of a pauper." "He has his two good hands!" the daughter retorted.

'But the mother was a woman who could gauge a situation quickly and well. No sooner has she smartened herself up again than she summons the postman and says to him, "Well now! You must act like a man. You must go up to Barles and speak to your brother. The law of the eldest inheriting everything no longer exists. He must give you what you're entitled to." She thought that there were only two possibilities: either his brother kills the postman and they'll be rid of him, or else he kills his brother in self-defence and then, as he has no children yet, he'll inherit. "And look," she says, "to prove my goodwill, we'll celebrate the marriage first."

'Because, of course, if the child wasn't first legitimised by marriage, there was no question of it getting back the Melliflore inheritance, should the need arise. Younger brother he may have been, but this fellow

141

didn't come down in the last shower. "Oh dear!" Gaétan said to her. "Did you get a good look at my brother?" "Sure," she said. "Probably for half an hour. What of it?" "Did he listen to you? Didn't start talking shotguns?" "Vaguely . . . But you know how it is. People say these things and . . ." "Oh, people say things! People say things! Where I come from, they don't just say them, they do them. My brother first and foremost. And tell me this . . . I have responsibilities now. You wouldn't want me to leave my son without a father, would you?"

'She just couldn't make him budge. He said it was always like that with the Melliflores. It was a tacit agreement; the law didn't enter into it. And moreover there had been an earlier example: one younger Melliflore had objected and his brother had set him straight in no uncertain fashion.'

Pardigon stopped short at that point. He seemed to be reflecting for a few moments. Then he continued.

'By the way, remind me to tell you about him too . . . Anyway, Madame Rosans had to avoid scandal at any cost. The shop would have gone under. But you can well believe that it made her sick at heart. It actually killed her, but slowly enough for her to explain to the whole of Digne why she was dying.'

At that moment Pardigon noticed that his pipe wasn't drawing well. He stopped once again. He loved to have people hanging on his words and so, like the consummate bad actor he was, he took advantage of his pipe, which he kept on relighting.

'Anyway, the marriage took place well before the mother died. With so much white you'd have thought it was snowing outside. And on the daughter's head was a hat which was a good advertisement for the shop, and which must have taken the two women a good month's work to complete.

'Well, on the wedding night . . . they had other things on their mind than sex. She had just been struggling for a quarter of an hour to get herself out of her corset. Proof that it was a real love match, because the first time, in the summerhouse, he was the one who undid her laces as best he could.

'Then she goes back into the bedroom and finds him, braces down, calmly seated at the little table, writing. "What are you doing?" she asks him casually. "As you can see, I'm writing my letter of resignation." "Oh, and what do you intend doing?" "Why . . . helping you!"

'Because he saw himself doing accounts, chatting with commercial travellers, writing bills . . . even flattering important clients to get business. But above all, above all, keeping an eye on the till. Just think! Generations of Melliflores in their native Barles had been dreaming of a till for the last hundred years. Oh, not to steal it. Heaven forbid! Stealing a till profits you only once, while owning a till is like a siphon. You empty it and it fills up again. And every day! Melliflore was thinking that a till is too important a thing to be left to the discretion of women.

'Oh la la! Madame Rosans's daughter was not the little woman Melliflore naively thought her to be. That's it! It's coming back to me now. Her name was Scholastique. Perhaps that's why she hadn't found a suitor. Anyway, she walks around him for a good minute, shaking her head and saying, "Tsk, tsk, tsk, tsk," and then she takes the letter from under his elbow and deliberately tears it into four pieces, and says to him, "No, no, no! You stay with the postal service, darling. It gives us security. After all, there's no dishonour in being a postman. Until Mama dies – which can't be too long – we'll live from the shop and your wages will go into my account. It will be for our little girl!" As she says that, she pats her stomach, which was already starting to show a little, head thrown back the way pregnant women do. "Little girl!" says Melliflore. "You mean little boy." "No, it'll be a little girl." And naturally, it was.'

Pardigon sent a spurt of saliva and nicotine some distance from their feet. He glanced at Laviolette, who was gazing at the horizon.

'Perhaps all that doesn't interest you? Because, you know, if it doesn't interest you . . .'

'Yes, it does! It does! Actually, I find it fascinating. I'm just picturing it in my mind. I can see those two as if I were there.'

'With lives like those, you know – and I've seen so many like that – it's always the same afterwards. If it's the protagonists themselves who are telling you the story, they always end up saying to you, "I stored

that away in the bottom of my pocket with my handkerchief on top."
And in this case there were two things that Melliflore had to bury deep
down in his: "keeping an eye on the till" and "our little girl", when he
wanted a boy.

'There was another one, actually, another girl, scarcely two years later.
But I think it must have been a mistake. Misers rarely have two children, or it's nature getting the better of them. Anyway, these two girls:
one married the tanner Champourcieux and the other the almond
merchant Raffin. One was the mother of Véronique, and the other of
Ambroisine, the two victims. Do you want me to tell you about them?'

Laviolette didn't reply straight away.

'No,' he said after a moment. 'Keep on telling me about the grandfather. He was from Barles, and it's Barles that interests me.'

'Fine! Let's talk about this Gaétan Melliflore then. He's about to
become very interesting, because he goes from one disappointment to
another. First of all he realises that if he's mean, well his wife's a real
miser! There's never a sou left lying about on the counter. Sometimes
a small coin slips out of a customer's purse and she says, "Leave it. The
apprentice can have it." Not likely! Every Sunday evening Scholastique
runs a ruler down the cracks in the parquet floor, and the two or three
sous she sometimes prises out go straight into the till. That'll give you
some idea.

'That should really have brought them together, the both of them
being so penny-pinching. But no. Because avarice is a solitary passion.
You can't be a miser with someone else. Avarice needs secrecy, and naturally, a secret can't be shared.

'And the worst of it is that Scholastique, no doubt bewitched by her
own name, had zero libido! She gives a sigh during the conjugal act,
turning it into something of a cross she has to bear. Melliflore is left
dangling, in more ways than one, but he begins to lose interest fairly
soon. Avarice doesn't favour love either. So here's this couple embarked
on the sea of life. Oh, Lord!'

Dr Pardigon has another bout of spitting. There was more and more
nicotine and less and less saliva each time.

'They make money. They grow rich. The till is never empty. It's the time when widows' hats sell like hot cakes. There are so many widows: the war, the Spanish flu, cirrhosis of the liver after celebrating the victory too long and too hard. But! Melliflore makes his life a misery. He becomes a collector . . . He starts to read a big biography of Napoleon in twelve volumes, which he found in the attic of the villa . . .'

'What did he collect?' Laviolette said, interrupting him.

'Post-office calendars. They were the cheapest thing for a postman to collect. Also, and most importantly, he develops a passion for Bonaparte, especially the period when he was on the island of Elba. Trying to get away from it all, he goes out sniffing for any traces of him he can find around that area, on all the so-called *routes Napoléon*. According to him, he even found a new one that went via Le Corobin. In short, I know that in a second-hand shop in Manosque he discovers a moth-eaten old uniform of a sapper in the Grande Armée, complete with gaiters, fur cap and pigskin apron. He snaffles it. Sorry. I mean he acquires it. And then, as soon as he retires – which happens early with postmen – to shame his family and get his own back for having been kept away from the till, every Sunday he goes off on foot, dressed as a mendicant, to solicit alms at church doors!'

Dr Pardigon stopped speaking. He used very learned words for these expressions which he was confident would floor his listener and fill him with admiration.

Laviolette let the silence descend, using it to roll another cigarette. The withered lives of these two people in conflict filled him with sadness. The trees around the hospital rustled and their yellow leaves trembled, only holding on by a thread. Laviolette watched them, taking what consolation he could.

'He went begging at church doors disguised as a vagrant,' he translated with a sigh.

Pardigon looked him up and down with a rather wary respect.

'In short, yes,' he said curtly. 'But what I haven't told you is that long before this retirement, the brother in Barles falls gravely ill. Before he dies he does his accounts. He calls for his son and tells him, "Your uncle is richer than I am. Don't forget that. You should always be on good terms with rich uncles. A guarantee sometimes costs nothing and can be very useful. Who knows who'll be exempt? With this shitty land? With these lambs that keep getting harder and harder to sell? So go and find your uncle. Tell him that I've acted badly, I'm sorry, and I really regret that he's not here at my deathbed. Well, you'll say it the best you can in your own way . . . and you'll find enough old things to fill a cart down there in the sheds. Your uncle loves all that old stuff."

'That's exactly what the son does. "Uncle, I've come to do justice to you." "Good heavens, my boy, I don't ask for anything." "Yes, yes! My father wronged you. He's sorry for it. I promised him on his deathbed that I would make amends." "Ah, yes indeed," says Scholastique, "a deathbed wish is sacred."

'She and the two daughters, who are already growing up, crane their necks to look past the nephew at this cart full of all kinds of things that defy description.

'When the nephew leaves after having drunk a glass of walnut wine as a sign of general reconciliation, the three of them throw themselves at the load that he has left at the foot of the steps. They spread it out, dissect it, examine it in detail. "Bah! You've been conned! There's nothing here worth a thing! You reconciled with your brother's memory for peanuts." "Things to remind me of the family, that's all I asked!" Gaétan said, trying to save face.

'The two daughters had pulled a portrait out of the pile of junk and were exclaiming over it. "Look how distinguished he was! Papa, who was this fine-looking man painted in colour?" "How should I know? Some grandfather, or uncle. What's it to you? You tell me that it's all worthless!" "We want this," they tell him. They go and hang it in the summerhouse, over the mantelpiece. I must have seen it a hundred times when they invited me there for coffee.'

Laviolette gave a sigh and picked up the envelope he had put on the bench beside him. He took out one of the copies that Judge Chabrand had obtained for him and stuck it under Pardigon's nose.

'This wouldn't be it, by any chance?' he asked.

'Why, yes it is!' Pardigon exclaimed. 'Well, well, well! And how do you come to be interested in this man who probably died a hundred years ago?'

Laviolette shook his head.

'When you have nothing,' he said, 'you take an interest in anything and everything.'

'Maybe,' Pardigon insisted, 'but for you to take an interest in this portrait . . . it must have said something to you.'

He looked his companion up and down with the same suspicious, reproving look he had given fifty years ago to a quack who was claiming to cure juvenile acne. He took his time weighing up the pros and cons. He made several cabalistic gestures with his pipe, which he was brandishing vengefully at some image from the past that had come into his mind. He opened his mouth, closed it again, clamped his pipe between his teeth, and when he began speaking again, Laviolette had the impression that he had decided not to divulge some important secret.

'Oh, that family!' he sighed. 'They were enough to make you wish you'd never had one. In any case, they made me glad I no longer had any. They spied on each other. They nicked things they thought were essential. They harboured terrible secrets about each other.

'Aided and abetted by her daughters, Scholastique pampered him to death. She tried to eliminate him little by little, serving him nice small dishes of food that was too rich for lunch and dinner and inciting him to alcoholism with a cellar that was too well stocked. By the way, here's a piece of advice: when you notice nice cooking smells in the house of an ill-matched couple, don't rule out the possibility that the woman is killing the man. But, to get back to what I was say, it was also by hurling dreadful words at him, while she laughed uproariously and the girls joined the chorus, as if they were the funniest jokes in the world. But, there you are. Nature goes its own way, and in the end it was Scholastique who died first – from a cancer of avarice, a cancer of the soul. Because it's all very well to turn your back on love, which wastes time for the till, but in the end the parts of the body that are designed for that take their revenge. It struck her in the breast. It wasn't nice, I can tell you.

For six months the poor woman paid a hundredfold for the emptiness of her wretched life. I must add that a few years earlier, Gaétan Melliflore had played a really reprehensible trick on her to kill her faster.

'At that time Digne still had a town crier. Well, the man who did it died and Melliflore offers to do the job on the pretext that he's a good walker, having been a postman who delivered on foot. He's accepted out of maybe ten other more worthy candidates. Why? The Misses Rosans, as they were still called – all three of them, Scholastique and her daughters – because they were fashionable, mean and rich, were not universally liked. It amused certain people to make them feel uncomfortable.

'Every evening before he went out on his rounds of the crossroads, Melliflore would put on that moth-eaten old uniform of a sapper in Napoleon's army. And when he passed by the villa, he played his instrument twice as loudly. What was that instrument now? A bugle? A trumpet? A post horn, or something else? What a dreadful thing memory is! I can remember incredible details, but that one's gone to the devil. I've forgotten it.'

That annoyed him. The idea that he wasn't all-knowing, infallible, that his brilliance could suffer any loss made him scowl.

'It's not important,' Laviolette reassured him. 'It's only a small detail . . .'

'You're right. It's not important.'

And indeed, it wasn't important. Only later, much later, when Laviolette was unhappy with himself, he had to admit that on that particular morning, that happy, warm autumn morning, the truth had tried to make itself heard through those words, and he had only been half listening to it.

Pardigon, however, noticed that his pipe was definitely blocked. It gurgled like a clogged sink. He emptied it out completely, scraped it conscientiously, filled it again, lit it and had two puffs, which he blew some distance, making a great show of it. Then he took up his story again.

'Meanwhile . . . one day I see this Melliflore arrive when I'm in the middle of a consultation. Oh, it must have already been quite late in the 1890s . . . the two girls were already married, one to the tanner Champourcieux and the other to the almond merchant Raffin . . . of course they hadn't given up the hat business for a small thing like that. The dead woman had kept her grip on the two still living. Melliflore was kept away from the till for ever. The two of them already had two beautiful little girls – see what heredity can do. Melliflore fumed to see all this multiplication of girls and not a single boy.

'As I was saying, one afternoon I see him arrive, obviously in very high spirits. You do realise, I've told you, how miserable, miserly and hard-hearted he was? Yet he had one of those beaten-up faces of a generous, outgoing bon vivant that the mischievous nature of our valleys can imitate to fool everyone. He looked as pleased as Punch. So much so that saliva was running from his thin lips under the handlebar moustache he still wore.

'I'd already noticed him looking so joyful in the waiting room that I said to him, "What are you doing here? You don't look sick." "I'm not," he tells me. "I've only come to see you to find out how much more time I still have to live!" "Are you making fun of me, or do you take me for God the Father?" "Oh!" he says to me. "I know you're confident enough to calculate that for me to within a year or so." "Why do you want to know?" "Ah," he say, looking mysterious, "I've hit the jackpot." The local expression he used means the best discovery you could make: a lord of the manor for a daughter, a crock of gold for an inheritor. "So," I say to him with the greatest indifference, "you've found a treasure, have you?"

'He stands there speechless, with his mouth open, looking at me as if I were Nostradamus. "That's it!" he whispers at last. "How did you guess?" I reply without thinking, "You're very gullible." "Maybe," he replies. "All the same, they thought they'd conned me, but I've done them!" He bursts out laughing. "When I think that my brother sent me that cartful of old stuff as a settlement for all our accounts! What it is to be ignorant! It's incredible what stupid things they can do!" "Oh," I say to him somewhat disdainfully, "what can you possibly have found?"

"I've found . . ." He stops short. "You don't really think I'm stupid enough to tell you?" "Why not? I'm a doctor. What patients tell me is confidential." Then he tells me in so many words, "The day Jansselin caught you-know-what at the House of Dazzling Dreams, his wife knew about it within twenty-four hours." "Excuse me! It wasn't the same thing. That was just taking precautions." "Maybe, but in the mean time she asked for a divorce. Mind you, it wasn't as bad as all that: she was also deceiving him for all she was worth . . . But in my case, it's different. It's serious. It's about money." "A lot?" I ask him, my voice a bit strained all the same. "More than you think," he says craftily. "In gold?" I ask him. "You haven't a hope if you think you're going to worm that out of me," he says.

'I tell him to piss off. He turns to leave. But I was so annoyed that he wouldn't confide in me that I decided to tell him just how much time he had to live. Whatever people say, even if you're told forty years more than you thought, you're never pleased to hear the fact that there's a limit. "Wait!" I tell him. "You wanted to know, so I'm going to tell you: you smoke, you drink, you eat wild boar, you have a siesta every afternoon. The arch of your aorta must be as opaline as a hairdresser's whitened window. You're sixty-five, am I right? Well, taking heredity into account, I'd say eighty at the most; and let that be an end to it!" "Fine," he replies. "By that time my granddaughters will be more than twenty years old. They can inherit. Because my daughters are a couple of bitches! I don't want them to have anything. Nothing!" he says. "Nothing!" As he says this, he slices the air with his hand as if he were mowing something.

'So he made a will?' Laviolette asked hopefully.

'A will? You must be joking. If you'd known Melliflore, you wouldn't ask a question like that. If he could have had his two houses, his four sunny fields at Le Cousson, his vines and even his bicycle buried with him, he'd have done it. As he was dying, he still made the gesture of gathering everything together like a bouquet in his hands, in the same way as one checks one's luggage. And he looked anxiously into all the corners of his bedroom, for fear of having forgotten some trifle. I know.

I was there when he died. At seventy-five. Taken by surprise. When he had strength enough to speak, he said to me, "You told me eighty." And I said to him, "I told you eighty at the most." When the daughters weren't there eavesdropping, I whispered to him, because the secret he'd told me still stuck in my throat, "Gaétan, get it off your conscience. What about that treasure?" "You haven't a hope," he replied. "And your granddaughters?" "They haven't a hope either."'

'So what did he die of?'

'Oh, nothing really. A bout of pneumonia that was hardly more serious than the flu. But you should have seen what happened later with the daughters and the loot. They glared at each other with eyebrows raised, visibly suspicious. If looks could kill!'

'I was told that one of them played the harp . . .'

'What of it?' Pardigon asked in amazement. 'Do you think something like that prevents greed? The ceremony where everything was shared out lasted for four days. The notary was worn out. It was as if they were playing chess. It's yours, it's mine: a coffee pot . . . a glazed cooking pot with handle; another one glazed but without its handle . . . a painting of a sunset on Berre Pond signed by Durand took two hours of suspicious bargaining. And as for the furniture! It almost came to sawing the various items in two: half for you and half for me. What's more, they examined them, every one.

'In short, obstacles were raised every step of the way. The notary told me about it himself. It was "Just a moment! Show me that silver spoon which is supposed to be the same as the one I've just been given. Here you are, monsieur. Just put them on the scales. Separately. Ah! You see! Yours is a gram heavier. You see that I'm right. You see that I'm right not to trust anyone."

'I'm giving you quite a bit of detail here,' Pardigon admitted, 'but it's to let you really understand the dominant gene, the motivating force in the Melliflores. And if you've been following my story, you should know now that looting was a tradition with these people, and that these two sisters had every reason to be suspicious of each other.

'In the end they were disappointed. "But that can't be right. Is that all? There's nothing else?" "What else were you expecting?" the notary asked. "He used to talk about a treasure." "Ah! And when did he talk about that?" "When he'd been drinking." "And when did he drink?" the notary enquired. And then both of them replied as one, "Every time my sister invited him."

'They never spoke to each other from that day on. They died on hopelessly bad terms with each other. They never spoke to the notary again either. They even forced their husbands to take all their business away from him. And every time they came across him in church or elsewhere, they'd look him up and down with a scorn that would have made a more resolute soul than he want the earth to swallow him up. Fortunately the notaries round our way are indestructible . . .

'In short, they even suspected me. They came separately to see me. They tried all the approaches they could think of. One of them – it was Véronique's mother – jingled the cash in her purse; the other – Ambroisine's mother – deliberately put her pussy within reach of my hand and mouth on the pretext of a medical examination. It was very plump, by the way. You could close your hand around it like an apple, and it had a triangle of tightly curled hairs that looked like chain mail. Damn it!' he exclaimed. 'I've never seen anything like it, and in fifty years of practice, how many would I have seen!

'In short, both of them then tried the direct approach. "But look! He came to consult you. Several times. He must have said something to you?" In the end I'd had enough and replied, "Yes! He said, 'I've found a treasure. I don't want to leave it to my daughters because they're a couple of bitches!' That's what he said to me, full stop!" They went off squawking like angry turkeys and they never darkened my doorstep again.

'As you can imagine, I wasn't going to let them know that Gaétan Melliflore originally intended leaving this treasure to his granddaughters. All wound up as they were, they'd have been quite capable of stripping them, upending them and shaking them by the ankles! The poor little things – they were in their teens at the time – it would have been torture for them. Their mothers would have questioned them to death.

And between you and me, despite what he told me on his deathbed – though he was no longer lucid – I don't think Melliflore had time to leave it to anyone. Just enough,' he added with finger raised, 'to hide it away for good.'

'So it's lost, is it?' Laviolette asked.

'Not for everyone, perhaps . . . because I . . . I have . . . a slight idea . . . of what . . . of what . . .'

Having stammered out these few disjointed words while sneezing, Dr Pardigon choked in a false fit of coughing, cleared his throat and spat, into his handkerchief this time, looking slightly panicky.

Laviolette had had time to thoroughly sum up the old man, or at least as much of him as he allowed to show. Laviolette didn't say a word, didn't ask a question. He sat there whistling a cheerful little tune. With eyebrows raised, Pardigon looked at his companion, who was vainly trying to seem unconcerned. He was well aware that Laviolette had pricked up his ears, and that if they could have grown longer, they would have beaten King Midas's.

At that moment a little bell sounded from the depths of the park. Dr Pardigon leaped to his feet as if he had heard the death knell.

'Well?' Laviolette asked, giving in. 'What slight idea?'

The old man had already started to move, replying to the call of the bell.

'Didn't you hear that?' he said. 'It's meal time. The best moment of the day!'

He was making his escape, striding down the path strewn with dead leaves.

'But after that?' Laviolette asked. 'You should tell me everything.'

'Later!'

'This afternoon?'

'No, no. Never in the afternoon. That's visiting time. There are some women visitors . . . who have behinds on them . . . if you only knew what they were like!'

Laviolette gave up. He watched the old man gaily rushing off for his lunch. He could hardly believe his eyes.

IX

MEANWHILE IN BARLES, THINGS WERE PROGRESSING AT A STRANGE rate.

The idea of getting the voluntary postman who sealed a victim's fate through the cemetery letterbox to pay for his pink marble columns kept going round and round in Pencenat's head. Every Wednesday and Saturday he would be in a hurry to leave the schoolteacher's card game to go and lie in wait behind the honeysuckle that lined the road. He had to make sure he played more or less correctly, as the new game that occupied him overshadowed all other distractions as far as he was concerned.

What is more, something had changed around that table. It did seem that for the last few evenings there had been an inner elation buoying up the usually sad and timorous Fondère. His glasses sparkled with it every time he threw down an ace. He made more silly mistakes than usual, and his bad-tempered companions didn't hesitate to point them out, lecturing him unmercifully. Somehow, the sight of a light-hearted man always seems to annoy his fellows.

Autumn was advancing. The teacher had replaced the walnuts from his tree with chestnuts that a toadying pupil brought for him, and which he roasted in the oven. There was always the same number of them as there had been of the walnuts: never more than eight per person.

It had been very windy for the last few nights. Pencenat had not forgotten that he had found the first two letters the day after just such an evening when the wind had been blowing like that. And that about a fortnight had elapsed between each discovery, which was roughly the time that had now just passed. The two murders had been committed in the interval.

Pencenat's mind worked according to three or four very simple rules. 'If this person who uses a strange way of posting letters is consistent, it shouldn't be long before he puts another missive in the letterbox and then commits another murder. Unless the first two were enough . . .'

But Pencenat didn't believe that possibility. 'A man who has drunk will drink again,' he thought. 'All the more likely because, according to the newspaper, they haven't discovered a motive. Therefore he must be a madman. And if he's a madman, he must do it again. Yes, but in that case . . .' he thought anxiously, 'if he's a madman, how can he realise that he should buy my silence?' No matter. It was worth a try.

He had plenty of elbow room on the evenings when he didn't play cards, for now that the weather was colder, Prudence and Rose were meeting more frequently. Leaving his icy little room with its smell of apples, he could quite easily walk past the door of the conjugal bedroom: it was often empty or, if Prudence was there, she was fast asleep after the preceding late nights.

For several mornings he came back empty-handed and down in the mouth, with stiff legs and back, freezing-cold feet. He had to break off digging his tomb and take siestas to recover.

On this particular evening, which was no different from any other for the inhabitants of Barles, Pencenat left his house by the garden gate. He stopped for a few seconds in front of the storeroom on the porch where he kept all his old things. With his chin in his hand he gazed at the empty space on the shelf from where someone had taken that pair of old boots he used for heavy work. Then he continued on his way, shaking his head.

Because of the wind, it was one of those striking moonlit nights peculiar to the valley, where the bright, harrowing light outlined everything normally left strange and shadowy. Pencenat was not the least of these. He was carrying a rolled-up horse blanket across his shoulders, which was his sole provision for his night watches, and thus equipped he made his way towards the burial ground. His shadowy figure first took the direction where there were houses that hid him in their shadows, but he had no protection at all from the indiscreet moonlight as he climbed the path to the cemetery. It consisted of wide, sloping steps which wound without protection from one narrow, abrupt turn to the next, finishing over a sheer drop.

There was a harsh note to the wind as it blew through the valley. The Lombardy poplars lining the banks of the Bès had long since been stripped of their leaves. Now it was the turn of the birches and aspens to lose theirs with the sound of slow, heavy rain whispering through the night behind the wind.

Pencenat climbed up the familiar steps. He was puffing a little, thinking of the dead he had helped to carry. The coffins weighed heavily on the pallbearers' shoulders, and they began to tilt at a dangerous angle on these steep steps, drifting like unmanageable ships with the twists in the path, to the accompaniment of the patient puffing and panting of the bearers hauling them up to eternity. One day he, Pencenat, would be hauled up like that on the shoulders of the living. He would have to finish his tomb before then!

This idea renewed his energy and spurred him on. If he succeeded in blackmailing this person who took him for a postman permanently on duty, it would not be long before it was complete. He was almost running when he reached the little bower of honeysuckle and clematis where he had made a comfortable hideaway to lie low and wait during the long hours on watch. He rolled out the horse blanket, drew his sheepskin-lined jacket around him and pulled on his hunting gloves. Even with these, he knew that when the night was coldest, he would feel as exposed as a worm coming out of the earth on a rainy day.

Naturally he could not allow himself to smoke, spit or do anything at all to arouse suspicion, as he certainly didn't think that the person who would come was a fool, mad though he may be.

The moon rose in the sky. The wind clattered around inside the roofless chapel where the dead were put in times gone by. Large leaves from the plane trees sometimes fluttered down through the gloom like bats. The wreaths of beads and bouquets of plastic flowers scratched against stone and marble behind the cemetery gates.

Before Pencenat the sloping steps of the path wound their way up from the last turn, where there was a wayside chapel with a niche closed off by an iron grille. That was where the person he was waiting for would appear.

He did appear, but at first Pencenat didn't think it was a human form. He thought it was a dog sniffing, growling or following the path at ground level; at least some kind of animal on four legs with a coat that looked pale and woolly like stiff badger hair.

This vagueness of outline lasted for a long time. The shape didn't move much, didn't advance any further, crouched down on a level with the steps, turning this way and that. Pencenat only realised that it was a man when he suddenly heard from that direction the sound of a hammer or a stone breaking something or driving something into the ground. The noise stopped and started for several minutes, then ceased. Then the shape stood up to its full height and began laboriously climbing the steps towards the cemetery gate.

Pencenat hid deep in his wallow like a wild boar, and gulped. Now he would know. At that moment he couldn't think of any human pleasure that was more exciting. There was not even a thought of pink columns in his mind any more. He took a good swig from the flask of brandy he had brought just in case. That was his first mouthful, and from that moment on his Adam's apple kept going up and down. The shape, however, was slowly coming towards him, becoming clearer and brighter in the moonlight.

It was an old man with a cane, who puffed and cursed as he climbed the stiff slope. Sometimes he halted and glanced up to the cemetery, as if he feared he might never reach it.

Pencenat didn't realise straight away that what was running down the lines in his neck and along his shirt collar was cold sweat, for the old man climbing the steps, mumbling to himself, coughing and spitting, was Gaétan Melliflore, who had died in 1929. Now this person by rights had been buried there, only thirty metres away, in the imposing family tomb of the Melliflores for more than forty years!

Pencenat had grown up in Digne, and the sight of that old man had frightened him enough since childhood for him to recognise him immediately.

'He died in '29! Bloody hell!'

Pencenat tried to disappear into the grass, to plant his body among the flattened daisies and cornflowers. He felt much more flattened than they did. A dead man who dared to come back to life would paradoxically never be well received by mortals, despite the great hope that this anomaly should inspire in simple hearts. On that night, Pencenat was an ideal example of this. His teeth began chattering, but it wasn't from cold.

'He died in '29! Bloody hell!' he repeated.

He could only just stop himself from shouting this alarming fact into the night, the resemblance was so striking between this apparently living person and the real living person from the past.

Gaétan Melliflore had been a town crier for twenty-five years until his death, and the proof was that he was still wearing the strange get-up that had earned him an equally strange nickname. The children called him 'Soapy', for at that time there was a brand of soap powder which had a sapper as its trademark, and Melliflore had taken it as a model to make up his outfit, the fur cap included.

This outfit gleamed in the moonlight, paler than a ghostly shroud. Pencenat was fascinated by the whiteness of the leather gloves, which still looked so new. He couldn't take his eyes off them, for the right one was holding a flat oblong object, obviously an envelope, between its thick fingers.

As for the face, now visible less than five metres away, it was broad, with big cheeks like an angry tiger. It even had the jealous moustache and the irate eyebrows. It certainly was a carnival face with the frosty white of the powder and the exaggerated pink of the cheeks, but a lugubrious, merciless one. Pencenat could never express more clearly to himself the thought that crossed his mind when he saw that figure – mainly because he didn't have the chance – but it stayed in his mind for the rest of the time he still had to live: 'He acts as if he's doing the right thing!' he thought.

The apparition went past him, so close that he could hear him breathing. It passed beneath the bare elder tree which bowed down to the cemetery wall with each gust of wind. Its heavy, trudging steps kicked up the winged maple seeds strewn over the flattened grass on the path.

'He died in '29! Bloody hell!'

The so-called Gaétan Melliflore stopped before the gates, lifted his gloved hand up to the slot in the letterbox and dropped the envelope into it.

Then he turned round. Once again he passed within scarcely a metre of Pencenat's hideaway. And this time the particular smell of this person was carried on the wind to Pencenat's nose.

Like boars, birds, water and stones, every living being in these valleys becomes impregnated by an odour of its own. An odour that comes not only from these places, but also in time through the daily perform-ance of favourite occupations. In short, an odour which may not be a scent, but at the same time is not necessarily unpleasant.

Now the odour that wafted under Pencenat's nose as the apparition passed by smelled of chrysanthemums or, more exactly, of infused chamomile. And Pencenat knew that there was only one man in Barles who would always have that odour about him. And that knowledge sent him into a state of shock as the person went down the steps, for it was scarcely more believable than if the stranger had really been the ghost of Gaétan Melliflore, who had died in 1929.

Pencenat watched him with passionate intensity, shivering with both terror and astonishment. He saw him stop when he reached the chapel, but this time he remained standing, looked at his feet, then plodded on again, his cane regularly striking the ground, until he finally dis-appeared.

Then Pencenat came out of his hollow, rolled up his blanket, which he slung across his back, and drank a last, badly needed swig of brandy.

He rushed up to the cemetery and carefully pushed open the gates, trying to stop them from creaking. The letter was there in front of the impressive tomb of the Pourcin family, stuck vertically on some unprepossessing ranunculi, among the eternal regrets so easily and cheaply bought with plastic flowers. It trembled in the wind. Pencenat lunged at it as if he feared it might fly away like a butterfly. He even creased it a little in his haste. He immediately began looking for the writing on the envelope. But although it was sealed, the letter had no address.

Pencenat could hardly believe his eyes. He struck a light to see if the moonlight may not have been bright enough for him to read. But no: seen by the flame of his cigarette lighter, as by the light of the moon, the envelope was blank.

The possible threat of this immaculate letter should have made alarm bells ring in Pencenat's mind, but he was too intrigued by it to think. Without hesitating for a moment, he rushed down the steps waving the envelope in pursuit of the fake Melliflore. He wanted to catch up with him, put a hand on his shoulder, turn him round towards him, show him the unaddressed envelope, and say, 'Well then?' For now his intense curiosity overcame his desire for money. He little cared whether his pink marble columns were erected quickly on his mausoleum or not. What he had to know, and right away, was the name of the next victim.

At that moment he found out, just as he went down the step in front of the wayside chapel. As he lunged forward, he realised what had tripped him: it was a simple piece of cord set up across the step.

He cried out. But a cry in the Barles night, when the wind is blowing and the sound of the Bès echoes from one side of the valley to the other, is a waste of breath for the person who utters it.

There was a drop of hardly ten metres between the grassy edge of that step and the trees that screened a dump for building rubble. It was far enough, however, for Pencenat to plunge into space like a high diver, and break his neck when he landed on his head. There had been talk for some time in Barles of installing a guard rail at that spot, but as there had never been an accident, the demand for it had slowly disappeared.

The sound of that fall made a hole of stunned silence in the noise of the wind, drowning the hissing of a wildly startled cat.

Then, emerging from the thicket where he had been hiding, the person dressed as a sapper showed himself in full light. Puffing and grunting, he climbed the steps up to the chapel again. Once there, he leaned over the cliff for a moment to make sure that Pencenat was not moving. He sighed, shook his head and, without stopping his puffing and grunting, began to undo the fatal string, which he wound into a neat ball. Pulling out the stakes that he had solidly hammered into the earth on each side of the step took some effort. He managed it, however, and put them deep into the huge pocket of his pigskin apron, after which he carefully obliterated all trace of the holes, and even took the trouble to hide them under dead leaves picked up from the ground round about. Once that was done, he calmly brushed his leather-gloved hands together to get rid of the dust.

In the niche of the wayside chapel, behind the padlocked iron grille protecting it from thieves, the compassionate eyes of the china Christ with open arms were watching him with something akin to pity.

The clock tower in Barles struck three o'clock.

Pencenat was found wound around the trunk of a wild cherry tree, each half of the inert body lying down the slope, in the way that the remains of old dogs are sometimes found.

No suspicious marks were found even on his ankles or instep, because the heavy boots the local people wore gave very good protection.

'Broken neck,' the doctor said matter-of-factly.

On the other hand, they did find the flask of brandy two thirds empty at the foot of the slope where it had rolled. 'Probably in an advanced state of inebriation,' the autopsy revealed.

In addition, the plain sealed envelope was extracted with tweezers from a cushion of yellow grass in the gutter, and sent for the usual tests.

The only fingerprints on it were those of the deceased. When at last it could be opened, a piece of music manuscript was taken out, on which someone had carefully copied or traced words, which therefore could not be analysed: *The measure you give will be the measure you get.*

The paper, the ink, the envelope, the prints, everything was the same as the two identical letters discovered at the homes of Mademoiselle Véronique Champourcieux and Madame Ambroisine Larchet.

No need to look any further. Especially as a pair of boots exactly matching the footprints found in the houses of the two cousins were discovered sitting in their usual place in the shed in Pencenat's garden. The same number of nails were missing in the same places.

Laviolette and Judge Chabrand went up to Barles for the funeral.

'What do you make of it,' the judge asked, 'as one who know this region well?'

'Let's wait . . .' Laviolette replied.

'What? For another murder?' the judge replied sharply.

Mightily comforted by Rose's support, which was largely unnecessary, Prudence faced misfortune with admirable fortitude. As the funeral people had not been able to decide the evening before between the grave that had already been dug for the purpose and the tomb that would have to be reopened, Prudence immediately indicated the family vault, her vault. She gave instructions that Pencenat should be put into it so that he could wait for her there as long as possible. She wanted to have him in her grasp for all eternity to punish him for having been a mere man.

As no one seriously believed that Pencenat was a murderer, there were so many people at the funeral that most of them had to follow the burial from over the wall. Behind the grim-faced widow and some vague relations came a swaying line of old men and women. The card-players arrived in a bunch: the captain, the mushroom-hunter and the schoolteacher. They all had the inscrutable look of people whom it's better not to question.

It was in the chance movements of this milling crowd that Laviolette thought for a moment that once again he recognised in someone certain features of the ancestor's portrait that had intrigued him so much in the summerhouse. But how could he be sure? By the time he had alerted Chabrand to the fact, the man had vanished, either behind other people or, as it rained for the burial, under an umbrella, or more simply, perhaps, behind himself. For a face is nothing but a kaleidoscope in which the various hereditary pieces that make up the puzzle are in turn clear or vague, mixed in clever combinations, superimposed, and also changed by the mobility of facial expression. All it needs is a ray of light from some other source, and with each change, what you thought you saw has already disappeared. Even when he knew the whole story, Laviolette never again found the person that the oval portrait reminded him of.

To compensate for so much rain and sadness, Laviolette went to visit Félicie Battarel in her den. The postmistress had a certain charm despite her size. Her round face in particular was lit up by the beautiful blue eyes of a romantic schoolgirl untouched by life.

So that he could look at her to his heart's content, he ordered an assortment of stamps, which she took some time to find. He stood there enjoying the sight while she was doing this. Like most fat women, she was all pink flesh and dimples. It did seem to him, however, that the postmistress's hands were trembling a little as she leafed through the stamp book, and that she was redder in the face than he had observed the first time. He sensed some unusual agitation that he wanted to lay to rest.

'Don't worry,' he said in a kindly voice, 'I'm not from the police.'

'Ah? You haven't come to question me then?'

'No, not at all. I've come to admire you. You know that . . .'

'Oh! . . . I'm not very admirable, you know. I've been hiding something.'

'It must be delightful,' he whispered with a smile.

'It's him!' she blurted out like a confession.

'Who do you mean?'

'Pencenat. He *is* the murderer. No one believes it, but I know. It's him. He came to post his letters. He bought the stamps from me. I took the letters from the box as soon as he left. I had a good look at them. It's him!'

She collapsed into her chair with her hand across her chest, vainly trying to encompass the volume of her breasts.

'Phew!' she breathed. 'So much for confidentiality. It was killing me. I had to get it off my conscience to someone, so it may as well be you, as you seem a really nice person.'

Laviolette was about to assure her that he could do even more when he saw her come to life and bloom like a dahlia as she looked past him. It was a lively, light, bright smile that suddenly lit up her face; a smile that spoke more eloquently than words. Magne, the tall bus-driver, had just come in with a ringing hello. He was thin, lean, with piercing eyes and an annoying moustache. He had that spontaneous, cheeky humour that makes women laugh and tend to think that 'with him it won't lead to anything'. What was more, he seemed to like overabundant curves too. And he was under thirty. Laviolette conceded defeat with a rather heavy heart.

Pretending that he knew the 'love butcher' Grimaude had spoken so much about, he went off there to hide his disappointment. The butcher was a soft, fat man with a round brown face, but whose sad eyes seemed to contain a whole lost landscape.

Over a quail in caul stuffed with juniper berries and an acceptable bottle of red, they talked with great affection about black pudding and pork brawn in words redolent of the whirling dead leaves of autumns past.

But this rustic feast did not lift Laviolette's melancholy. The memory of the very large postmistress, no sooner found than lost, prevented him from savouring the simple things of life. Gloomier sights, he thought, were more suited to the minor bereavement he had just suffered.

He made enquiries about the farm where the Melliflores had come from. It was high up in the hills, but the walk would do him good. The rain had stopped and the sky had cleared.

'Are there any Melliflores still up there?' he asked.

He was told that no, the two brothers who had lived there as joint owners had not been able to agree on repairing the roof. One night it fell in on both of them, taking a part of the wall with it, killing one and injuring the other who, once he had recovered, went into the old people's home.

'And who owns it now?'

'The bank, the Crédit Agricole, like nearly all of the rest of us!' he was informed.

He went up there all the same. This place was totally suited to his mood. It was a large, forbidding ruin taken over by elder trees. Their knotty branches with white muscles had broken out through the windows, and from a distance seemed to be waving at anyone thinking of approaching. The broken joists formed a St Andrew's cross, which raised its threatening but impotent arms to the sky.

A vineyard bristled with vines three metres high, sending out shoots like tentacles, choking the worm-eaten plum trees. Great canes dotted with red berries from the wild rose bushes pierced this charnel house of vegetation, striking an oddly cheerful note in the decaying vineyard.

At the foot of three dying poplars left to the mercy of woodpeckers, a fountain was still flowing strong and clear but benefiting no one. A barrel had been left to swell in the water. It was still there, drifting from one side of the basin to the other on the lazy current.

Laviolette went through the crumbling doorway; someone had stolen the lintel. A few old beehives sat on sharp cornices, put there perhaps in the hope that they would repopulate and abandoned when they did not.

The room where Laviolette looked at the sky through the broken joists must have originally been a kitchen. A piece of the floor was visible at the foot of the rubble spewed forth as far as the entrance by a stairwell buried under the ruins. Within the outside wall you could still see the outline of a wash place with slots to slide in the washboards. There had once been women in those ruins. Women who sometimes had the misfortune of bearing two children when only one could scarcely eke out a living.

This wash place was the only sign of life. That was all there was after so much attention to inheritance, so much crude avarice.

'Unto dust thou shalt return.' This consoling thought, so well illustrated by the ruins, perfectly suited Laviolette's state of mind as he stood gazing at the sky darkening with the approach of evening and the light of the late October day playing with the old amber of the crumbling walls.

He thought of Dr Pardigon and the doctor's father who had stepped through that doorway. They had brought help or indicated that there was no help available to people who only ever called them when it was too late. He thought of Gaétan Melliflore, who had become a postman and then a town crier, and who had turned up in Pardigon's waiting room one day to tell him that he had found a fortune in the cartload of old things that his dying brother had sent to him.

Laviolette looked all round the walls. Through the broken windows and doorway, he gazed at the surrounding land returned to nature and the pasture invaded by thistles; the alluvial sand on the slopes washed away by erosion; the broom flourishing on the fields where crops had been sown; the sudden collapse of the levels towards the ravines and the Bès, tearing away great chunks of arable land; the woods of stunted, overexploited oaks. What possible treasure could this relentless poverty ever have concealed, produced or retained?

Laviolette's eyes lingered on the black wall where the chimney flue had been half destroyed. At the top of the open mitre, in the shelter of a cornice from the ceiling, a piece of the hood still remained attached; and still nailed to that was a rectangle of cardboard, no doubt following the old country practice of blocking up the flue for the summer.

Without knowing why, Laviolette was intrigued by this relic, which was highlighted in the slanting rays of the setting sun skimming over the ruined walls. He followed the light and was able to identify it. It was a post-office calendar, on which he was even able to make out the year in a corner of the blackened card: 1912.

He paused to think for a few moments. He thought back to when he went to The Cedars with Chabrand and discovered the collection of

166

calendars in the attic. Of course there was nothing that would lead him to suppose that this was the missing one, for even in those far-off days, the annual output was an assortment of several subjects. Chance should not be discounted nonetheless. Laviolette had enough experience of the tricks it could play.

Sweating and panting, he piled up all the stones and rubble he could in front of the broken chimney hood. His precarious heap crumbled beneath him the first time he tried to climb it, landing him on his behind among the scattered debris. But this hardly stopped him at all. Using a joist that he wedged against a pile of several flat tiles, he finally managed to haul himself up to the calendar, which he tore off the wall. He then hurried outside with it.

The dusk was still light enough under the trees beside the fountain for him to see that there was a printed picture. However, years and years in a smoky atmosphere had tarred the calendar so much that the illustration was indecipherable. Laviolette lifted it up to the rays of the setting sun, but to no avail. All he could make out under the dark varnish and fly specks were the ridges of a kind of off-centre triangle against a neutral background. It was impossible to tell what was inside it or around it.

Laviolette hurried through the valleys like a young man full of hope, with his calendar under his arm. He was imagining all kinds of practical ways of cleaning it without destroying the picture. Once in Digne, he'd be thinking about it all night. He had completely forgotten the voluminous Félicie and her bus-driver with his sharp moustache.

The death of Émile Pencenat didn't cause much of a stir among the people of Barles. On the very night of his funeral, after a few exchanges of 'Do you think we should?', Prudence and Rose were in each other's arms again. What's more, the earthy spice that the Grim Reaper sprinkles on people in his wake was heavy in the air between them. Through the departed, who didn't count for much in himself, the rustle of his funereal charms had whispered alluringly close to the receptive ears of these two simple people. And so that night they made love with the frenzy of castaways, which always characterises the love between couples who have just felt death whistling over them.

Even Monsieur Régulus's game on Wednesdays and Saturdays was not particularly disturbed by Pencenat's passing, as the 'love butcher' also liked old schools, dusty yards, playgrounds with chestnut trees where at night the east wind can be heard sweeping the brown leaves across the ground. Amongst other things, he had coveted a place with the privileged few who played cards with the schoolteacher. At Pencenat's funeral, he did what was necessary to get himself invited.

'Well, why not?' Monsieur Régulus said. 'It's Wednesday evening. Is it Wednesday today? Then tonight, if you like.'

'Do you think we should?'

'In the *ancien régime*,' the teacher replied, 'the living immediately replaced the dead, and a moment later the dance began again. In full mourning, I grant you, but to the lively rhythm of a rigadoon! Besides, it will be paying homage to Pencenat. If one of us had died, Pencenat wouldn't have wanted to miss his Wednesday game because of that. Gentlemen,' he added, seeing them looking a little embarrassed although in complete agreement on the principle involved, 'gentlemen, that's the way it is. As Montaigne said, "Wherever there are humans, there are human frailties." Now you surely don't think you're wiser than Montaigne? Like it or not, we have to get used to accepting ourselves for what we are. I did long ago. And so, till this evening.'

All three nevertheless felt a slight repugnance in making room for this new partner. He always had a suspect trace of fat and pink meat around the square fingernails at the end of his short fingers, which disgusted the three ascetic, thrifty men. He did make a good impression, however, by refusing the ritual glass of walnut wine as too generous a mark of friendship.

'Later, if I deserve it,' he said humbly.

'Later, did you say?' Régulus exclaimed. 'You'll do me the pleasure of drinking with us. And right now. Gentlemen! To peace in heaven – if it exists – for our friend who had his cross to bear on this earth. Bottoms up! Please don't leave a third of it in your glass as you usually do.'

It had just occurred to him that he always poured this third back into the flagon, and that the muddy liquid contained a little of the dead man's saliva. Of course Pencenat wasn't suffering from any disease. He had simply had an accident. It gave Régulus a strange feeling all the same to think that he was ingesting a dead man's saliva. The flagon should therefore be finished in the shortest possible time.

On that same evening Monsieur Fondère caught Captain Combaluzier by the sleeve of his jacket once the butcher had left them, after vainly inviting them to come and sample something.

'Stay with me,' he said softly, 'and we'll go part of the way together. I've something better for you.'

'Well? Have you found out our host's secret? Thanks to my binoculars?' the captain said caustically.

Fondère gave a little chuckle with his chin down in his coat collar.

'Much better, my friend! Much better! Those navy binoculars are marvellous. With them you're right on top of the object in question.'

'Well then? Please tell me what it's all about. What's this hoard our schoolteacher's hiding?'

Fondère pursed his lips.

'Nothing of any note: books that he reads avidly.'

'Books? He keeps books under lock and key?'

'Yes, indeed. Books, albums, diaries. How would I know what they are? But I can assure you that they keep him enthralled for hours on end.'

'Books!' the captain groaned. 'That's no great help to you. That's no great find, no matter how precious they are.'

'Probably,' Fondère admitted quite happily. 'And I would go so far as to say that judging by the flushed face of our teacher when he's absorbed in them, they can hardly be anything but dirty books.'

'Bah!' the captain exclaimed in disgust. 'And so, in your opinion, nothing that can be traded for hard cash?'

'Oh, no. Nothing at all, in my opinion.'

'But Fondère, you still seem to have been quite elated over the last few days for someone who's come back empty-handed.'

'But I didn't say that. On the contrary. I told you that thanks to your binoculars, I'd found something much better.'

He automatically looked behind him down the road bordered with nettles, to make sure that they had not been followed or watched.

'Keep this to yourself . . .' he whispered. 'I don't think Pencenat died a natural death.'

He surveyed the landscape of fields and wet hedges either side of the road. He even looked suspiciously at the path of a gust of wind across the wild oats in a fallow field. He was as attentive as a hare for any untoward sound coming from one of the little bridges over an irrigation channel.

'I saw a sapper!' he whispered.

Combaluzier stopped in his tracks while Fondère kept going.

'You saw what?'

'A sapper, I tell you! A man dressed as a soldier of the Old Guard in Napoleon's Grande Armée, with the gaiters, the pigskin apron and the fur cap. The lot!'

'But where, when did you see it?'

'One night recently. The very night our Pencenat met his death. After the schoolteacher put his light out and I hadn't seen anything interesting, I was idly looking at the village through the binoculars. And I saw him down there under the street lamp at the public weighbridge.'

'And what was he doing?'

'He was walking, heading for the steps up to the cemetery, and Pencenat was found down below the foot of those very stairs.'

'It's incredible!'

'Isn't it? In fact that's just what I said to myself. I stayed watching for maybe an hour, hunched in my chair, my feet freezing cold, thinking, weighing up the pros and cons, not believing my eyes. Then suddenly I saw him again, at the same spot, this time front on. He was coming back. According to the papers, it was the same time that Pencenat broke his neck.'

'But did you recognise this person?'

'Just wait here a moment,' Fondère, avoiding the question. 'I'll give your binoculars back to you. I don't need them any more. All I need is to piece my thoughts together.'

They had reached his house, where pieces of plaster were falling off the damp walls and a dead wisteria dangling from the collapsed arbour clicked with every gust of wind. Fondère hurried in and returned again almost immediately, holding out the old purple case to his companion.

'There you are. And thank you. You did me a real service, so I've decided to repay you.'

'You promised to show me a few of the spots where you find your morels.'

'It's not time for that yet. And besides, they're no longer in season. Instead I'll show you my helvella spot right away.'

'What's that?'

'Mushrooms, my friend! Better than morels. And there's lots of them at the moment. Well . . . lots of them if you know where to look. They smell like truffles, and what's more, they're aphrodisiac. Two birds with one stone, eh? The little hunchback, who knows them well, will certainly show you how very grateful she'd be to get some.'

'But where do you find them?'

'Cross the Bès at the Bouscarles' ford. The path continues on the other side. Follow it for about eight hundred metres up to the slag heap from the old lime kiln. Then . . . Here! I've done you a rough sketch with all the details.'

'Thanks,' Combaluzier said. 'But you still haven't told me who . . .'

Fondère put a finger to his lips.

'Everything leads me to believe that I'm on track to make some cash.'

'Do you know what I think, Fondère? I think we should get out of here straight away. Untie the longboat and let the ship spring a leak. Believe me, a place where someone disguises himself as a sapper at two in the morning should be given a wide berth. Especially in our case. Believe me, Fondère, despite the talents of our antecedents, we're out of our class here.'

'Are you really thinking of doing that? Quite apart from the cash,

I'm having the time of my life at the moment. Nothing's been any fun for the last twenty years or so, Combaluzier.'

He disappeared into his dilapidated dwelling, shutting the door again as best he could, but it always stuck against the floor and never closed properly.

And so everything would have returned to normal in Barles if the mushroom season had not been unusually long. At that time Monsieur Fondère happened to prepare a good panful of entolomas and, not being able to finish them all, kept some aside, intending to make an omelette with them later. He put them into his old refrigerator under an upturned plate. He made the omelette the following day, and had it for his supper.

Once they are cooked, there is nothing to distinguish the edible entoloma from its poisonous livid cousin, which is not generally fatal, according to the encyclopedias, although they are divided on the question. But here we have a person showing the wear and tear of a bad life, penalised now and again by several years in prison and regrettable excesses; a person whose red-veined nose indicates that his liver is in a woeful state. Such a person can be the exception that allows the use of the vague adverb: *generally*. Nevertheless, according to those who have cautiously tasted it, the *entoloma lividum* is much tastier than the ordinary species, which should have alerted as discerning a connoisseur as Monsieur Fondère.

As for any other explanations . . . Who knows? An unfortunate mistake? Or perhaps on the evening when Fondère told Combaluzier about the ghostly sapper, was someone lying in the wild oats which seemed to move for a moment? Was someone spying on them behind the little bridge over the irrigation channel where Fondère thought he heard a noise?

In this case, perhaps it was an uneven door, left that way through lack of money to get it planed down, and which had to be pushed and pulled a bit to open. A short but fatal absence from the house, promptly put to good use by someone who knew that Monsieur Fondère was in the habit of going to Grimaude's at certain times. It doesn't take much time after all to exchange a plate of edible mushrooms for others that are considered extremely poisonous. Apart from that, the profound solitude and deserted streets of Barles at night would have been enough to guarantee the anonymity of a cautious killer. Quite often the only thing needed to kill efficiently and without making waves is just a little imagination.

Conjecture aside, it was the postman with a registered parcel to be signed for who found Monsieur Fondère lying dead in his own vomit, jamming the door. He must have thrown himself at it to shout for help, but probably didn't have the strength to pull it towards him.

They said he had died the right death. They said that in the end the poor mean wretch had been punished by his besetting sin. In any case, he was not much mourned. Now other people would be able to eat their rightful share of mushrooms when the season arrived. Of course they wouldn't have killed him for that, but since someone else had taken it upon himself, they were not going to put on sackcloth and ashes for so little. No one seriously believed that Monsieur Fondère had made a mistake. Besides, statistics plainly contradicted that explanation: in Barles one inhabitant dies every four or five years, and here were two dying one after the other within a week. The field was wide open for any number of theories.

This second death so close to the first took everyone so much by surprise that it only then dawned on them that the cemetery was full; there was not a single plot left in the general area. The authorities cast their eyes on Pencenat's grave, which was still open and under construction. When a respectful request was made, Prudence agreed to have Monsieur Fondère laid to rest there. Having the grave her late husband had so carefully prepared occupied by an intruder was another good trick to play on him.

'A murderer is always present at his victim's funeral.' The whole of Barles understood the meaning of that saying, just by estimating the number of gendarmes who had invaded the territory. And so there wasn't a single inhabitant who missed the burial. Even Grimaude closed the café and walked there, pushing Françoise in front of her.

Also noticed among the crowd was a very elegantly dressed middle-aged couple who came from Seyne or further afield; anyway, as far as the morel-hunter had gone to get his modest pension when he was alive.

There have always been strange people in this strange region. The man, who was dressed with old-world elegance as if he had stepped out of a nineteenth-century engraving, was wearing a double-breasted frock coat, buttoned boots and a jabot tie. As for the woman, she was in beige silk stockings and court shoes, her supple waist enclosed in a bottle-green riding skirt of a material that had not been made for seventy-five years or so. Her prettily faded face with its pointed chin and pink complexion was partly hidden under a large wide-brimmed hat trimmed with honeysuckle flowers.

A suitably sad expression clouded the faces of these two people, but they could not suppress the occasional happy glance at each other, and their eyes sparkled with pleasure at the fine weather.

Prudence, who noticed everything and made a point of visiting the grave of her dead husband every day, reported that she had seen the couple again the day after the funeral.

'I had the impression,' she said, 'that they were inspecting the grave itself very closely, as if they feared it might not be sealed properly. Well . . . that's the way it seemed to me . . .'

Big Magne also saw them again at the mule fair in Seyne, choosing an animal.

'They were transformed,' he said. 'Younger . . . years younger. A whole lot younger. But this time they were really dressed up. I mean, dressed in modern clothes. No suggestion here of having got their clothes out of the attic. There was only one thing: he was smoking a cigar with a band around it, and this band – I saw it clearly, I was close by – this band . . . you don't see it these days. I'd seen a cigar like it when I was little in a box I was given to play with, to keep me quiet when my grandfather died.'

That's what Big Magne the bus-driver said at the schoolmaster's card game where he had been accepted as the fourth player after

Monsieur Fondère's death. He spent two nights a week in big Félicie's bed but, for the sake of propriety, she would not let him in before midnight, and so he had found this convenient way of killing time until then.

'Go on! When your grandfather died!' exclaimed the 'love butcher'. 'You'll be having us believe that this couple is from the last century. Are you going a bit crazy, or what?'

Big Magne laid his hand over his heart.

'I'm just saying what I know. I'm telling you what I saw. Don't ask me, and don't try to make me go into the whys and wherefores. I haven't a clue. I have no imagination. But since you've tackled me on the subject, I will say that on the day of the funeral, that couple smelled of dried lavender.'

'Go on! Dried lavender?'

Big Magne thumped an ace of diamonds down on the table, though he was sure it wouldn't win the trick.

'Exactly!' he insisted. 'Dried lavender. As if they'd been stored in a wardrobe.'

He snapped the cards in his hand together, then licked his thumb to fan them out. A furtive glance confirmed with pleasure that his companions were hanging on his words.

'Or in a coffin!' he said in a lugubrious voice to put fear into them.

He stared defiantly at the 'love butcher' with the indecisive face who was beginning to weaken.

'Say what you like,' Magne went on. 'Everyone could see those two on the day of the funeral, and everyone could see that, dressed up in those clothes, they could almost have come out of the 1900 Exhibition, behind Armand Fallières.'

'Come on! Now you're really raving.'

'What about it?' the teacher exclaimed impatiently, after listening to them arguing. 'What about it? What's so peculiar? What's so strange? There are certain things that travel through the ages, travel through the night, without the average person even being aware of it. You make me laugh! What do you know? What can you swear to? Only to your easily deluded senses. Now I ask you: was it really your neighbour Alartéus you greeted a while ago in the dusk? Or was it the ghost of his grand-father angrily tapping his cane against the stones on the sunken road? Are you sure, you men of little understanding, that there aren't some-times slippages of time, either backwards or forwards, that happen without warning? At full speed? Just for one lightning moment?'

'Those were the words he flung in our faces! Point blank! It was enough to make your blood run cold,' Big Magne, an ordinary bus-driver, told his friends one night when there was a storm in the mountains.

'Anyway,' the butcher began, 'as far as I'm concerned, I can guarantee to you that I have good eyesight and that . . .'

'No! You can't guarantee anything at all. What can you be sure of, you poor ignoramus? I ask you, what can you boast of?'

Big Magne's ace of diamonds had been followed by Combaluzier's ten. With an aggressive sweep of his arm, the teacher now trumped the ace with a seven.

He looked around the table and gave his fellow card-players one of his relentless scrutinising stares.

'If you'd correctly sized up the weird things that have happened in the past, you'd never get over it. Sometimes fate only needs to do an about-turn to flatten you completely.'

At that moment an infernal din was heard above their heads, as if a piano had been dropped from on high. They instinctively ducked, the captain most of all.

It was the first avalanche of the year, which had just collapsed into the corridors of the Estrop, from almost three thousand metres up. The noise it made had been forced down the Bès valley as through a horn. It was the mountain's way of protesting against snow that was too early for it to hold.

The captain stared at his three companions. They all had the nervous look of hares at the opening of the hunting season. They all had the same tight lips as their ancestors, through remembering and keeping too many secrets for the whole of their lives.

He left them, his shoulders hunched in his old jacket. Sea water had bucketed down for decades on that jacket, which was as saturated with salt as its owner. Combaluzier was a man who had countless times been lucky that death was not hungry at that particular moment. But he had never felt death so close or so active as in the peaceful silence of this valley.

'I'll have to get out of Barles,' he thought. 'The sea's not far enough away . . .'

X

THE CHESTNUT TREES IN THE OLD PEOPLE'S HOME WERE LOSING their last leaves on the morning when Laviolette walked up to the end of the path to meet Dr Pardigon. He was there, ensconced on the green bench in a haze of pipe smoke. His face had the wry look of a man who doesn't give a damn and doesn't bother to hide it.

'Well now,' the doctor said sourly. 'I didn't think you'd be back to see me.'

'Why? Do I look like a person who'd be happy with half a story?'

'No, but . . . It's all over now, isn't it? I read it in the paper. According to them, the murderer himself died.'

'Yes, someone died,' Laviolette muttered. 'But whether he was the murderer or not . . .'

'Anyway, those two mean creatures have had a lucky escape.'

'Who are you talking about?'

'Why, the last two. The two remaining women. Firstly Véronique's sister and then Ambroisine's niece.'

Laviolette thought about what the old man had said for a few moments.

'What makes you think that they were in danger too?'

'According to the paper, the victims had received a letter saying: *The measure you give will be the measure you get.*'

'Yes. What about it?'

'What about it? I think that as far as giving bad measure is concerned, there's no one in the whole of Digne and for miles around so capable of it as those Melliflores.'

He blew out a puff of smoke and, as usual, accompanied his words by eloquently waving his pipe about in the air to express how complex the whole question was.

'For as far back as you can go,' he said with a sigh.

'Exactly. Let's talk about that. The other day you said to me, "We'll get a hold on this thing by the middle." I'd really like you to tell me the other half of the story today.'

'Well, well! You have a good memory in spite of the cigarettes.'

'And so do you, in spite of the pipe.'

'Excuse me! It's not the same thing. It's the paper, not the tobacco, that affects the memory.'

Laviolette made no comment on Dr Pardigon's somewhat rash assertion.

'There's one thing that gave me food for thought,' the old man said, getting back to the subject. 'It's the portrait you showed me the other day. Ah, that one! He was a true Melliflore: obstinate, obtuse, obsessed by his own rights. When I thought about it, I realised that without any doubt, the chain of grievances started with him. I did say to you the other day to remind me to tell you about it . . . It won't be of any use to you, but since you like the past . . .'

'I'm going to be honest with you,' Laviolette said. 'I'm not with the police, I'm not with the gendarmes. I don't work things out pragmatically. I don't try to pursue only what's palpable. You talk to me about ashes of the past? That's fine. I'm quite at home with things you can't touch or see. And I'll tell you another thing. I don't think that the murderer is dead. No motive has been found for the man who died. And you don't kill two people without a genuine motive, don't you agree?'

'But you don't discover the truth either with stories that are more than a hundred years old,' the old man replied. 'Because that man . . .

that man whose portrait hung in the summerhouse lived more than a century ago. That places his story somewhere in the 1860s. What relevance does it have today?'

'You may be right. But he did have a story.'

'Oh, yes. If you're talking stories, he had one all right. He was obstinate, obtuse and obsessed by his own rights. I could add vindictive to that. At least that's the way my father described him. Because . . . of course everything I know about him comes from what my father told me. I wasn't born then. Unfortunately this man was a younger brother, and there was only one gun up there in Barles, in what they called "Horse-Choker Farm", because that was the only kind of grass that grew there.'

'I know. I went there myself.'

'I'm talking about things that happened in the time of Napoleon III!'

'That doesn't matter. The farm couldn't have been poorer than it is today.'

'Exactly! The fascinating thing about the Melliflore family was their poverty and their way of fighting it with avarice. And also the way they casually held the great benefits of the Revolution to be null and void . . .

'At that time, this younger brother was about twenty. His father dies. They are both there at his bedside, he and his older brother. As soon as the father breathes his last, the young one gets off his chair and closes the old man's eyes, to be quite sure that he's gone. While he's still standing over the bed, and without turning round, he says to his elder brother, "You're not going to treat me the way he treated his brother. You're not sending me to look after the sheep in La Crau like a servant. We'll share. Besides, that's the law."

'But when he turned to face him, he found his elder brother armed with the only gun in the house, which he had already taken down as a precaution. "You're going to clear off, that's what you're going to do," the elder told him. "Nature's law! If you don't like it, you can blame him." And he pointed to the body on the bed. "He's the one who pleasured himself begetting you, the bastard! I've had to go without Francette for five years now; since the boy was born. He should have done the

180

same." That was what he said, and a whole lot of other reasons . . . He stood there watching his brother pack up his bundle, pointing the barrel of the gun between his shoulder blades, actually touching his back.

'Who knows where he ended up, you'll no doubt be thinking. Well, it just so happens that I do know. Because . . . in our part of the world, he wasn't the last person to be poor. Take my father, for example. He was poor despite his degree. At that time, you know, doctors didn't make a big income. My father had me at forty-three. He couldn't afford a son any earlier, he was so short of money.

'There was already a doctor here, and that was too much for the small amount of treatment the people would seek . . . So, what did my father do? He'd heard about a place up in the mountains that had never had a doctor. Abriès it was called. Ah, Abriès! I haven't been there for about forty years. And yet it's a wonderful place. A superb place! A place with water, and trees. A place where you can hear the sounds of silence.'

'What was your father going to do in Abriès?'

'Earn his daily bread. And that's not just a figure of speech. It wasn't to buy a new pair of shoes, a suit, and even less to build. No. It was literally to earn his daily bread. To earn his living by the sweat of his brow.

'Just imagine that when he arrived, he had nowhere to live. He shared the presbytery with the parish priest. When there was a snowstorm, they often left together on the only mule they had. The priest guided the animal and my father carried the crucifix on the end of its stick over his shoulder like a lance. One would give the last treatment, and the other the last rites . . . "Ah, what a sight we must have been," my father used to tell me, "both of us on the exhausted mule, which must have been twenty years old and asleep on its feet. Luckily both of us were so thin, the priest and myself, that we wouldn't have weighed a hundred kilos between us."'

Laviolette watched the old man as he lived his story by imitating the poor creature's trot on the park bench, even though the mule must have been dead for well over a hundred years. The nicotine in his pipe stem was making an unpleasant gurgling sound like a waste pipe, and the bowl had just gone out for lack of tobacco. But the old man didn't take any notice. He was sucking on air. He no longer needed any external stimulus, as he was so irresistibly drawn into the depths of those lost years, still able to see their life, colour and movement with such clarity.

'It was there that one night he met the Melliflore from Barles who had been thrown off the farm by his brother. Oh yes, he met him,' the old man continued, 'but under sad circumstances. Just imagine it! A farce by torchlight on a snowy night. Ten men shouting down the trenches – which was what the streets of Abriès become in January – and chasing another with pitchforks, fully intending to kill him. This other man starts banging frantically on the door of the presbytery, and my father comes downstairs in his shirtsleeves to let him in. The other man, who's frightened out of his wits, is also in his shirtsleeves with his trousers barely done up. "Hide me!" he cries in a strangled voice. "Don't put on the light! Shut the door quickly! Hurry! They want to kill me!"

'He was clutching his back. He'd been hit in the backside by one of the pitchforks. Fortunately it was a wooden fork for turning hay, but all the same, wielded with the fury you can imagine, it must still have hurt. My father sees to him as best he can with arnica and ointment, and as he's doing this, asks for some kind of explanation. "How did this happen?" he asks. "Why do they want to kill you?" "I was with the Girauds' niece in the barn," he says. "The barn door won't close properly. The uncle wasn't sleeping well. Marguerite must have let out one cry too many . . ."

'Just at that moment the priest arrives and crosses himself on hearing those words. But there was no time to be lost with recriminations. There were about ten of them down below, trying to break the door down with the handles of their pitchforks. The priest sticks his head out of the attic window. He says what's needed, in their language, by rubbing their noses in their own filth; by telling them, for example, that the reason why they are so up in arms against the other man is not so much for the thing in itself, but mostly because they all would have liked to do the same with Marguerite. "All of us?" they protest. "Absolutely! All of you! Even the uncle!" "Oh!" they say. "Oh!" "There's no *Oh!* about it," the priest replies. "And besides, Dr Pardigon is treating the man. We don't know if he'll pull through. The doctor says he may have tetanus."'

The old man interrupts his own story to give a gentle laugh.

'He was fond of women, that priest, my father used to claim. And if you remember that the whole scene takes place in Abriès in the middle of winter, and that all these people who came rushing when they heard the uncle yelling have hardly had time to pull on their trousers, you'll understand that standing there with both feet in the snow, they feel some contrition as they listen to the priest. "All right," they say, "all right. We'll go. But we'd better not find him in Abriès tomorrow morning. Otherwise we'll soak him in the fountain until he's stiff. A word to the wise is enough." And off they go, because that's all they can do if they don't want to die of pneumonia.'

'Did your father often tell you stories like that one?' Laviolette asked quietly.

'No. Not often,' Pardigon admitted, giving it some thought. 'But he told that one about ten times, in preference to so many others he was full of. Why? Well, because he used to say that it was one of the great regrets of his life. And you'll soon see why . . .'

But Laviolette had to wait. This time Dr Pardigon had accumulated so much nicotine saliva in the back of his throat that he had to spend some time getting rid of it. Then he just had to refill his pipe and light it to revive his energy.

'The great regret of his life,' he continued at last. 'He explained it to me so many times . . . This Melliflore trembled, his teeth chattered; he was a thoroughly frightened man.

'"I'll have to go," he said. "I can't even go back to my attic to get my few belongings. The uncle's watching out for me, for sure. What you said was right, Monsieur le Curé. He wants Marguerite for himself. In spite of his four children. In spite of his sick wife. He was prevailed on to take her when she was four. Her parents died trying to save their livestock from a fire in the barn. He took her in out of charity."

"'Do you love her?" my father asked. "Yes, of course I love her." "Well? Why don't you just marry her?" "That's right," the priest added. "Leave the uncle to me. We'll make a respectful request, but if need be, I'll really mortify him with his own depravity!"

'But Melliflore from Barles took three steps backwards. "Retreated right to the wall," my father used to say. He cried, "No! No!" as if he'd suddenly seen a rattlesnake rear its head in what was being proposed. He was three times more frightened than before, though not by the same thing. "No! No!" he begged. "She has nothing and neither have I. Not even a roof over our heads. What would we live on? And anyway, I don't want any children. No thank you! I've found out the hard way what it is to be surplus to requirements." "But people would help you." "No. People don't help here. They're too poor. And anyone who wanted to help me would quickly be pulled into line. In case you've forgotten it, her uncle is also the mayor. And you don't know the power of a mayor around here. They gave him the power of life and death over them all, and he took it without any humming and hawing!" "Oh, really," my father said, not taking it seriously, as he believed in the power of the republic.

'And he gave all sorts of reasons to encourage Melliflore to stay. But the young man tossed and turned all night like a wild boar in a pen. He wrung his hands. "What can I do? I have no land in Barles any more; here I can't even sleep with a girl without almost getting killed . . . So? What can I do?" And he looked out of the window where the snow had begun falling again.

"'I can't even leave. I haven't any snow shoes. I only have what I stand up in." "Where are you thinking of going?" the priest asked. "I'll go down to Marseilles. Last week the pedlar told me that there was some disreputable ship leaving to trade birds on the Adamastor coast. It seems that they'll take anyone, and of course you'll have to be willing to do anything . . . But what does that matter to me? If I stay here, the uncle is sure to get me one way or another, so . . ."

'In the end they gave in to his point of view. He left before sunrise with the lantern for the dead which the priest gave him, the moth-eaten cloak worn by the shepherd in the live nativity scene, and my father's snow shoes . . . And also with five francs for the coach from Briançon to Marseilles, which the priest and my father had got together by searching their pockets. "I'd have done better to throw those five francs away," my father would say bitterly. "I'd have done better to tie the boy to the bedpost, despite the mayor's power."

'And yet both of them, the priest and my father, would come to know the full extent of the mayor's power a few months later, when the fine weather returned. It was a morning at the end of May when there was some warmth in the air for the first time. You could hear the Guil rumbling as it carried along the stones from the avalanches that fell into its stream higher up, much higher up under the terraces of Mount Viso.

'Now the presbytery was down below at the end of the village, near the road that leads out to the rest of the world. We hear the hurried footsteps of a crowd coming down the street. A happy crowd? No . . . not exactly happy, my father used to say, searching for the right word. A crowd of something like a hundred people, which was enormous for Abriès. The noise they were making under our windows was a joyful noise. A serenely jubilant crowd was the way he used to describe it. Yes . . . sure of its rights, its conscience clear . . .

'They lean out of the window, my father and the priest, and what do they see? At the head, the mayor wearing his sash of office, and behind him, head down, the offending body: the niece Marguerite, who had been kept under lock and key until then, and who was now showing a bump of about six months. This disaster was no doubt the work of Melliflore from Barles. The girl followed her uncle, her bundle of possessions in her hand. And behind them was the whole of Abriès, coming to witness the execution. For, given the poverty of the region, this mayor had taken sole responsibility for its protection. And, making sure he was in charge, while he was at it he also gave himself the right to make souls conform to a blameless code of conduct, which helped to retain property and share it among the fewest mouths possible.

'In short, the mayor of Abriès had thrown the girl out on to the Basses-

Terres road with nothing but her bundle and her big belly! He had cast her out from the community like a leper. Had he sent her to her death? Of course not! On the contrary, he had waited for the fine weather so that he would have a completely untroubled conscience. Perhaps he had even provided her with a few coins, as he wasn't a thoroughly bad man. What he wanted to do above all was to make an example of her. Let people know that in Abriès, girls should not forget themselves.'

The old man stopped for a moment and sat up straight.

'There were some people in those days,' he added, 'with tough, resolute characters, I can tell you.'

He shook his head sadly.

'But my father, my father was too uncompromising to get rich. He says to the priest, "You're surely not going to let them do that, are you? You have Christ to back you up, and they're afraid of Christ." The priest spread his arms helplessly. "I also have the bishop," he says. "He's closer, and he'll be rapping me over the knuckles, in Christ's name what's more. I'll even have to plan my sermon to illustrate this sad event with some words from the Gospel," he replies with a wan smile.

'"Just a moment!" my father says. "I don't have a bishop!" Down he goes and stands in front of the uncle-mayor. "You don't deserve the bread you eat! Aren't you ashamed? What about your conscience? Doesn't it tell you you're doing something wrong? Don't you know that if God acts consistently, the next time you set foot in the church, it will come down on your head? And on yours too!"

'He gestured around at all the men, and especially the women who were there to witness the banishment. All those who had come as if to the circus, and who stayed until the girl had disappeared across the small plain, not missing a single tear she shed. Oh no, they weren't hostile. They didn't shout at her . . . They just gloated quietly, individually, for their own personal reasons. It was as if they were saying, "And what then? It would be the end: you could do what you like with your belly! What reward would we respectable women have left?"

'I should mention that there were more women than men in that crowd. The men, apart from the old ones, had nearly all ducked out on the pretext of having work to do. In these circumstances, the men are not anxious to see a big belly. They're all aware that in such a case, they could well have been responsible for it, and kept a low profile under the suspicious gaze of their lawfully wedded wives. For a while at least, the scandal was no joke to them . . . Because an unwanted child, you know, is such a disaster in a poor community.

'What's more, do you think that dispenser of justice in mayor's clothing is put off when my father grabs him by the lapels? Not on your life! He looks him dead in the eye and says, "Dr Pardigon, if you promise me here and now to provide for her bastard until it comes of age, I'll call my niece back and leave her in your care!"

'That's what the mayor of Abriès said point blank to my father that day. And you doubted that he'd remember it? You doubted that he'd tell me, ten times over, what happened in Abriès on that day more than a hundred years ago?'

'Heaven forbid!' Laviolette exclaimed, responding to the doctor's vehemence.

'What's more,' the old man went on sadly, 'that was the day my father chose to be poor for ever. That was the day he decided to leave the Queyras region, where he had begun to make a niche for himself. Because he had become well liked and started to have patients who consulted him out of charity, to give him money! And there were some amongst them who should have come earlier. In short, they said to him, but to no avail, "Stay! We're not all like that. We know girls who got pregnant and who stayed here with no trouble. Why are you taking everything so seriously?" But it was no use. He told me that he saw Christ's stigmata just looking at them going about their daily lives.

'He left, and came back here where there was already a doctor, who was not happy to see him arrive on the scene. My father bought a mule – at so much a month, and more! – and it's thanks to that animal that he was able to live. With the mule, he was able to do all the deep valleys; places where the other doctor wouldn't go. He went to places that you'd never imagine: to Archail, Draix, Mariaud, Auzet, Bellaffaire.'

'And Barles?' Laviolette asked, interrupting him.

The old man shot him a sideways look.

'Yes. To Barles, naturally. But if you don't show a bit of patience, you'll get me muddled and I won't be able to tell you anything more.'

He slashed a line through the dust at the foot of the bench with his cane to emphasise that *anything*.

'Of course the only thing that interests you is the story of the Melliflores, and you want to know whether my father ever came across the one from Abriès again. Well yes, he did. But before that, he also treated the one in Barles, the one who had made his brother take to the road. It was through him that my father first had any news.

'The elder brother was at death's door at forty, and despite what he had told his younger brother, he had done the same stupid thing as his father: he had also had two children. He knew that he was on his deathbed, because those two were already eyeing the only gun in the house.

'The man in the bed was writhing like a worm from the pain, but also from the effects of a curse. He told my father between groans, "My brother has bewitched me! He's cast a spell on me for sure. Just think how easy that is for him to do, down there somewhere deep in Africa. It's full of sorcerers, so they say. He sends me threatening letters. Venomous letters. He tells me that I'll keep. That he'll come back . . . I'm sure he will. I know he's the one who's killing me!"

'"That wasn't necessary, the poor mean wretch!" my father used to say. He died without any extra help, from tuberculosis of the bowel. Yes, it was widespread in those parts at the time, because people drank any kind of water.'

He spat on the ground in front of him to express his scorn for those who died in the old days because they couldn't even choose their water properly.

'And when he did come back,' Laviolette asked, 'did he at least try to have his rights recognised by his nephews?'

'For heaven's sake! You must think I'm a clairvoyant. I'm just telling you what my father used to say to me. That and no more. When he came back! When he came back!' he complained.

'Mind you . . .' he continued hesitantly and a little less definitely than before. 'Mind you, at that time quite a few people around here did disappear in the hills and dales. There were isolated roads, you know, with long, silent stretches between the rare appearances of a carter. People on foot rushed along them panting as if the devil was at their heels. Even pedlars galloped through without stopping. And they knotted their few coins in a handkerchief so that jingling money wouldn't attract anyone's attention and they could get past without making a noise. I can tell you, for example, that people didn't beat the bush on the embankments by the side of these roads, despite the fact that some of it was full of game and well known to hunters. These men were careful not to loose their dogs there for fear that they might flush out something other than game.

'I can also tell you about bodies in there that have disintegrated among the loose stones over fifty years or so. In the end the wind peels the bones bare, the frost breaks them up, and the pounding rain eventually makes holes in them like soft stone. The skulls especially become fossilised and dull, just like the stones all around them. Children occasionally find someone – I'm talking of fifteen or twenty years ago, when I was still in practice. They think they've found prehistoric remains, when it might simply be one of their great-great-grandfathers who got into a fight with a neighbour on the edge of a holly-oak wood. When all's said and done, it doesn't take long in families . . .'

'Are you trying to tell me in so many words,' Laviolette sighed while the old man caught his breath, 'that one fine day that Melliflore disappeared without trace? But before then, your father had seen him again, hadn't he?'

'Yes,' Pardigon admitted, 'yes, he saw him again. That was a piece of information that I might have kept for later, but since the subject has come up . . . So, my father comes back to the Digne region, and slowly his kindness and unselfishness get through to people. He finds better lodgings and, to save on the mule, he opens a practice – a practice! – in Blégiers or Prads, I can't remember which. Yes! It was in Prads, because all he had found in Blégiers was a little room so damp that all his patients caught their death of cold.

'It was there that one day he saw someone arriving who was so thin

189

and stooped that he looked as if he been carrying a cartload of stones on his shoulders for weeks. That's how my father described him. And then, even before my father asked what he could do for him, he puts down five francs in a line on the corner of the table. "Wait a moment!" my father exclaims. "I haven't treated you yet, and it won't be as much as that anyway." "I owe it to you," the man says. "Don't you recognise me?" "No," says my father.

'But at that moment he does recognise him. It was the man from Abriès. The wildness of the ocean had battered his face for more than five years and disfigured it. No longer the fair-skinned man he had been in Abriès, he was now very dark. To tell the truth, my father used to say, the ocean had nothing to do with it. He had simply caught a form of tropical dermatitis that makes your skin like parchment and your features as frozen as a mummy's. As a result, he could no longer laugh or cry. It was the face of desolation itself.

'"I'm sorry," the man says to my father. "I'd have liked to give you interest as well, but I can't. I'm still in almost the same situation as I was then. You know . . . I waited three years for a boat to get back here . . . from that cape . . . Adamastor . . . I told you about. It had another name, but the Portuguese I was with never called it anything but that. Three years . . . as a docker or whatever was needed. You don't save anything out of that . . ." "Just a moment," my father says. "Do you know that you have a child?"

'"Oh yes, I know." "Well?" "Well, he's up there in Mariaud." "Well? Aren't you going to fetch him?" "Fetch him? Where would we go? What would we do? Up there he's being given food and shelter. With me it would be life on the open road, cold feet, leaky roofs. Do you think I could be so selfish?" "But he's your son!" my father says. "Yes, he is, but there's no use in him ever knowing that." "Just a moment!" my father says. "What about his mother?" "She's dead. Otherwise I'd have taken up with her again. I'd have tried . . ."'

'Just a moment!' Laviolette requested. 'You mentioned Mariaud without any explanation. What's the significance of Mariaud? I know that it's a little village, but . . .'

'At that time there was a convent of Poor Clares in Mariaud, up there in the fresh air, which was something of a retreat for girls of good family who had had what used to be called "an offspring of sin". Now these convents always needed servants to look after the girls, and given the fact that the rich were not the only ones to sin, it was a useful arrangement . . .

'In short, getting back to the man from Abriès, as he turns to leave, my father tries to put the five francs back into his hand, but the man backs away, waves his hands, and says, "You need it more than I do!"

'My father suddenly has a thought and says to him, "Wait a moment! Do you know what they called that child?" "Yes, they baptised him Clare Rogations. Rogations because he was born on that day, and Clare because that was the name of their order." "Clare? For a boy?" "What can you expect? They don't know anything else!"

'And off he goes. And my father kept the five francs. There were times when he needed that money, but he never touched it. There were also times when he had a franc or two that he didn't strictly need, so he put it in the kitty. Then he invested it to earn some interest. You know that savings banks didn't exist at that time. He told me proudly that when Clare Rogations left for military service – he signed up for seven years – my father had the pleasure of sending him a postal order for forty francs! "And that," my father said, "was the last I heard of him."'

'And his father, the man in Abriès who originally came from Barles?' Laviolette asked.

'I heard nothing more of him either. A little while ago I mentioned the sunken roads and the dark thickets . . . There are quite a few of them around Barles. My father had twice gone back there to see the nephews, who had stayed together for a while after their father died because they were only sixteen and twelve. One of them was the Gaétan Melliflore who became a postman and then town crier – the one who married the Rosans' daughter.

'In short, one day my father asked them if their uncle had come to see them by any chance. "What uncle? And why come to see us?" That was their reply, my father said, but at the same time both of them shot a furtive glance at the gun hanging above the hood over the fireplace. In situations like this, there are some almost imperceptible spontaneous movements that are as revealing as the most emotional confession. You just have to know how to interpret them . . .'

The old man sighed.

'That's the way it was . . . Are you with me? These thickets where no one will let their hunting dogs loose . . . Corrosive weather that crushes everything in its path like a millstone . . . So there are men who have never even been buried when they died.'

He gazed into the distance at the chestnut trees that a wide swathe of wind had just stripped of their leaves in a single sweep, revealing the bare structure of the branches.

'I'm still wondering,' he said, 'why the stories of these wretched people fascinate you so much.'

'Because . . .' Laviolette replied. 'I'll explain it to you, since you know how to keep a secret: I have a conviction that the source of all these murders lies in the past.'

'Oh!' Pardigon laughed. 'A personal conviction! That doesn't count for much in court.'

'I've twice come across someone who has the same battered head as the portrait I showed you the other day. Oh, it hit me in a flash, I grant you. And after that, nothing. I peer into everyone's face, but it's no good; it's finished. The resemblance has gone. Do you think that's so unusual?'

'You know . . . there are loads of battered heads and faces around here. We fell out of our nurses' arms when we were little. Sometimes we came into the world with heads like sugar cubes. It was the midwife who tried to put us back into shape, when she thought of it, and she didn't do a wonderful job.'

'Yes, but when the bumps and hollows are identical, surely heredity must come into it?'

'Indeed. You'll have found some descendant of the Melliflores from Barles.'

'No. They're all dead. I've made enquiries. There were two bachelor brothers left. One day the roof fell in on them. One was killed on the spot and the other died ten years ago at the old people's home in Manosque. No. As far as this family is concerned, apart from the two women who have been murdered, I don't see . . .'

'Pardon me! You're forgetting their sisters. There's Véronique's elder sister Violaine.'

'Ah, yes,' Laviolette exclaimed. 'I know *her*.'

The old man took his pipe out of his mouth and looked him up and down.

'You know her? You mean surely that you've met her? Because as far as knowing her goes, even I don't, and I brought her into the world.'

'I must say she does seem rather eccentric.'

The old man shook his head for a good fifteen seconds before replying to this opinion.

'Eccentric? You mean that her head has every one of the bumps that the Melliflore character had acquired through the generations in their clashes with the back streets of Barles. I could see that she was already a grasping little thing before she was ten years old . . . going to the Sisters of the Trinity and trampling on the dolls that her mother was giving to the children of the poor.'

'So she's Véronique's sister then?'

'Yes, the sister of Véronique Champourcieux. The elder daughter of the tanner Champourcieux. He, by the way, didn't count for much in his own household. The gene for domination, the hereditary character came down through the Melliflore women. Not much to say about this Violaine. She was kept on a tight rein for all sorts of strange reasons. She was rather inclined to hysteria and flights of fancy; much like all the girls at that time, forcibly chaste until they were about twenty . . .'

He shrugged his shoulders in a gesture of resignation.

'I treated them both with laudanum. What else could I do? I couldn't go up to the parents and baldly tell them to their faces, "She needs to make love."'

'No,' Laviolette conceded, 'you couldn't do that.'

'In short, there's not much to tell about this girl Violaine until she meets the Maillards' son . . .'

The old man pondered for a few seconds as he drew on his pipe. He was looking into the distance over the tall trees at the russet oak groves outlining the top of the cliffs behind Les Dourbes.

'Way beyond there,' he said at last, 'is a hell of a place you can scarcely imagine, called Chanolles or Chavailles, I can't remember now. A place where the Bléone has broken three bridges over its knee, as if the river didn't want us to go and see what happens there. And that's only since I was born.

'At that time one of the Maillards from Thorame-Haute had settled there. This Maillard had inherited a sawmill on the banks of the Chanolette and, on his own initiative, had installed a small hydro-electric power generator when he arrived somewhere around 1895. He was ahead of his time. He sold the surplus electricity to the neighbouring villages, who looked on him as an industrialist. All very well!

'But . . . it's one thing to set yourself up where there's a supply of energy on your doorstep; but raising a family there is another thing altogether. He fathered a son, but a poor, weak specimen. He was a child who'd grown up in the shade: a tall, thin, pale string bean, stooped and with a pigeon chest. Oh dear! For fully ten years I told his parents to put him out in the sunshine, otherwise he wouldn't have more than three years to live. Unfortunately, he lasted a lot longer than that.'

He shook his head as he recalled the story of this child with the pigeon chest.

'Fate often calls on things from very far away . . . One day this child with the fragile constitution witnesses a frightening scene: his father's four workmen come right into the dining room to demand a little more money for their twelve hours of work per day. They come in with their boots covered in sawdust, their jumpers frayed, their trousers without braces crumpled around their ankles.

'What a sight for a protected child brought up in the shade. It leaves a lasting impression on him. Especially as his father pushes him gently into the bedroom and locks the door, telling him not to be frightened as he is there to protect him, no doubt to teach him never to expect anything good from workers. (One can't be a boss without being involved in a certain amount of treachery, otherwise one goes bankrupt.) This very attentive father was naturally unaware that by talking to him in that way, he was preparing him for an early grave.

In short! When this child is seventeen, he is taken to see Italy, the Leaning Tower of Pisa, the monumental railway station in Milan, the masterpiece of the regime. And what does he see? He-men marching, self-assured, looking to the future; the unemployed brought to heel at last and applying themselves to their work in sparkling clean streets; flags everywhere proudly flapping in the wind; uniforms from the best tailor; fabulous boots. Perfect order! He comes back transformed. He told me himself, and confessed to me that from the time of that trip until he could show it openly, he had worn a shoulder belt under his jacket, as others might wear a hair shirt.

'Ah! The leather belt across the chest has such sexual appeal for girls. In those old-fashioned days when Freud's theories were still only applied in America, brutality was often mistaken for virility. That's exactly what happened with Violaine Champourcieux. When she saw young Maillard, so clean and tidy, looking so uncompromising and rich, it was love at first sight. And yet he was a man with a willy like a semi-colon, if you see what I mean. And more skin than prick! I know what I'm talking about. I examined him more than ten times, and couldn't believe my eyes.'

He spat a long jet of saliva stained with nicotine into the dust, to express his scorn.

'But what defence is there against a leather shoulder strap? He was twelve years older than she but didn't look it, being so pale and thin. And snobbish with it. He insisted that she be seen playing tennis and skiing. He bought her an enormously long white car so that she would do him credit.'

'She still has it . . .' Laviolette murmured.

'That doesn't surprise me. Melliflore women never wear anything out. The wedding took place with great ceremony. Two honourable wealthy families were joining their children in marriage; but nonetheless with a settlement under which husband and wife administered their separate properties. Because . . . Violaine's mother may well have played the harp while gazing soulfully into the distance, but she was still both a descendant of the Melliflores and the granddaughter of Rosemonde Rosans, milliners from mother to daughter. She had both feet on the ground, and they were size nines!

'"You love him, he loves you, all right! You get married, fine! But you have this, this and this! Plus considerable expectations: from Uncle Albert, who is leaving you everything, and your godmother Chabottes, who's so fond of you. So, we'll draw up a contract. It won't hurt anyone and won't stop you loving each other."

'She was farsighted, was mother Champourcieux! However, love is selfless in the beginning. No sooner has the mother gone out of the notary's office than the two of them sit down again, hand in hand, and both leave everything to the last surviving partner. Are you following me?'

'Oh yes, indeed,' Laviolette said.

'Right! I'll tell it to you as quickly as I can, because meal time is approaching and I'm starving. Well now, at that time war is imminent, is declared, and turns out as you well know. The time has come for the Maillards' son to wear his shoulder belt on the outside, put on boots like the ones he admired so much in Italy, and swap his felt hat for a cocky beret with a conqueror's insignia. He still has a pigeon chest, but he hides it under a black shirt.

'All that lasts a certain amount of time, as you well know: elite then defeat. One fine day the moment of reckoning comes. At three in the morning, ten men descend on Chavailles, shouting and yelling, armed to the teeth as if they were about to attack four battalions. They are also wearing shoulder belts and illegible armbands. They drag Maillard out of bed in his nightshirt. It's the Liberation! They slap him round the face as they give him the news, then fire a bullet into his head.

'Oh, I'm not saying that he didn't deserve it. Because . . . he had the execution of ten Resistance men on his conscience, plus some Jews he had betrayed to the barbarians. In short, they tore his body limb from limb with four cars – so that he would be easier to handle. After that they cut him into cubes, as if to make a casserole or an osso bucco. They sawed the bones with a metal saw. And then, finally, they took the protective grille off the pressure pipeline above the factory, and dropped him into it piece by piece. And they did this work with religious care, the care of men who are believers and who hope that, wherever he may be, that desolate soul is present as his flesh is broken up.'

'Why?' Laviolette asked with surprise.

'Why? According to Violaine, they explained it to her as they spat in her face, before disappearing for ever and becoming ordinary people like you and me once more. They told her that they did it so that his bitch of a wife couldn't kiss a single piece of his body. Her love for him had become well known, or imagined, and punishing her for this love probably seemed to them an act of great purification, if not patriotism. They had tied her to the bedpost with the chain from the well. They shaved her head, of course, but also her body hair, so that when she was found, she was completely hairless . . . But note this. No one had raped her.'

'Why?' Laviolette asked again.

'Ah! Why? That's the question the state prosecutor asked. Because . . . that's not the way it happened. The prosecutor cursed with impotent rage, for if Maillard had been brought in for judgement, apart from any jail sentence, he would have been deprived of citizenship rights and all his property would have been confiscated. And if you've been following what I'm saying, you'll know that, for as long as their joint estate lasted, his property was also his wife's. An ordinary murder and the need to make the fewest waves possible surrounding this distressing episode ruined all the fine judicial set-up whereby the state would have profited . . .

'Well . . . People wondered, quite naturally, whether the Liberation wasn't being used as an excuse for everything . . . Because the ten wild men with the illegible armbands – and try to find a witness on 26 August 1944 at three in the morning in the wilds of Chavailles! – well, it was never possible to identify a single one of these ten dispensers of justice. The widow had conveniently fainted on the spot and remembered only one thing: they all smelled strongly of pastis.'

The old man halted in the course of his story, as if the weight of his words bore down on him more and more heavily as he went on. Not long ago he was serene and at peace with the world; now lines of suffering creased his eyelids.

'Ah, what a story!' he sighed. 'And I can even add a highlight. I'm a decent man, as you say, but can you believe that it was I who brought that consumptive fascist torturer into the world, and also the ten jerks who made mincemeat of him with the turbo-alternator? Not to mention that Violaine,' he added, 'who probably had him executed to save the inheritance! Me! Yes, me! I'd have held up these bouncing babies in my hands, announcing "It's a boy!" or "It's a girl!" And everyone was ecstatic. Do you understand anything about providence? I certainly don't.'

'Oh!' Laviolette groaned. 'Oh!' It was his turn to wave his arms in the air. 'What about it? You're crazy to think like that. Whatever kind of man you bring into the world, those characteristics are his lot from the beginning. So . . . whether it's him or one of the others . . .'

The old man was staggered. He took his pipe out of his mouth and stared at his companion.

'Ah! You really believe that, do you?'

'Yes. In the end, that's what I've come to believe.'

'Right. Well then, what are we two doing here?'

'We do the best we can with what we've got,' Laviolette said grudgingly. 'As far as I'm concerned, that doesn't keep me awake at night. So? This family? Is that the end of the story?'

The old man didn't reply immediately. He was listening to the vague sounds coming from the house. He was interested in other old men who were getting up from seats nearby and tapping their canes on the ground.

'You still can't hear the dinner bell?' he asked.

'No,' Laviolette replied, 'there's still a good quarter of an hour to go.'

'They're always late,' grumbled Pardigon. 'Particularly when there's braised beef and polenta. Well now . . . what were you saying?'

'I was asking you whether you'd finished telling me about the family.'

'Almost. However . . . Ambroisine Larchet, who has just died so suddenly, she also had a sister, like her cousin Véronique. They only had girls in that family, as you'll have noticed. She was a flighty one. Now that I think of it, I brought her into the world too. A feather-brained blonde with a turned-up nose and a come-hither look in her eye that drove the men wild. She married an aristocrat. Some fellow who had a castle – a castle! Over in Esclangon . . .'

'That's where my mother comes from,' Laviolette said.

'Really? Oh dear, I'm afraid I can't congratulate you on that. As for the wretched chateau, it was called Malefiance!* Not a very promising name.'

'Indeed . . .' Laviolette agreed.

'Anyway, this nobleman, when he received his allowance – no one knew where it came from – he took a return ticket to Nice and went to gamble it all at the casino. He met Ambroisine's sister on the Digne–Nice train. It was love at first sight. He talked to her about living dangerously. Her father had just died and she immediately demanded her share. And it was a packet, I can tell you! Ambroisine and her sister quarrelled for good and all. They never saw each other again.

'She and the nobleman tried everything at Malefiance: they raised horses, hares, quail, pigeons, bees and even mink. That finished them off. They had managed to turn a large fortune into a very small one. To cut a long story short, they both killed themselves, from poverty, one evening as they were coming out of the casino in Menton, where they'd lost their last shirt. They had the good taste to get run over by a man who was driving at a hundred kilometres an hour, drunk as a lord. She died immediately and he followed three days later. That meant that their daughter . . .'

'They had a daughter?'

'Yes. In spite of it all. She's up there in Malefiance, squandering the insurance money. And the only thing she raises is tramps and vagabonds. The house is always chock full of them. The poor girl!'

* *Malefiance* means doing harm or evil.

'Why do you call her a poor girl?'

'Because it's a shame to die so young. Do you realise that she must be only twenty years old.'

'All the more reason not to die.'

'She'll die all right,' the old man insisted. 'Like Violaine up there in Chavailles; like Ambroisine Larchet and Véronique Champourcieux who are already dead; and for the same reason.'

'And you know why, I suppose?' Laviolette said, with a mocking edge to his voice.

Dr Pardigon shook his head.

'No,' he said. 'But I think I know by whom.'

Laviolette sprang to his feet.

'You should have told me that in the first place.'

'Sh! It's the bell this time, I'm sure.'

'No.'

'Yes it is! Listen. There it goes for the second time.'

He got up from the seat, turned away from Laviolette and made his escape, striding up the path with his cane vigorously prodding the ground in front of him. The idea of keeping Laviolette in suspense had just come to his capricious mind, which had its prankster as well as its serious side. Laviolette followed him, walking in front of him, around him, trying to make him stop.

'Come now! Really! You can't leave me like this! The end of your story involves someone's death. Don't you realise that?'

'Of course. But tomorrow's another day.'

'Tomorrow?' Laviolette asked in despair.

'That's what I said. Tomorrow. What's so strange about tomorrow?'

He stopped suddenly and faced Laviolette.

'You're not the first person I've told this story to. And he was patient enough to wait. For twenty days I made him wait. You've scarcely had ten days.'

'You've already told this story to someone?' Laviolette exclaimed, astounded at what the old man had just said.

'Yes, and with all the details.'

'When was that?'

'During the summer.'

'But to whom?' Laviolette asked, almost shouting.

Standing near the steps ringing the little bell, the woman on duty frowned, thinking that someone was manhandling her charge. She was ready to fly to the aid of the home's mascot, who was fully expected to one day celebrate his hundredth birthday.

'Tomorrow! Tomorrow!' Pardigon exclaimed, with a little skip to the side.

'That's shut him up a bit,' the old doctor thought. He was delighted to have had that effect on the calm man he didn't altogether like.

Laviolette rushed over to Chabrand's office. There he found the judge with his chin in his hand, playing with the string he was probably going to tie around the file marked *The Pencenat Case*, lying open in front of him. Laviolette, who was quite out of breath, collapsed into the chair usually reserved for the accused.

'There's a man who knows!' he announced out of the blue.

Taking no notice of the time – the judge was about to set off for the boarding house where he had his meals – Laviolette gave a succinct account of his conversation with Pardigon, quickly skipping over the parts that he wanted to keep to himself.

'You'll have to call him in immediately,' he said in conclusion.

Chabrand raised his arms to the heavens.

'What nonsense! He has nothing to do with it. He hasn't witnessed a thing. He told you stories with the most recent going back at least fifty years. He's probably gaga. After all, he's well into his nineties. And the oldest man in Digne to boot. We'll just make ourselves look ridiculous, if not worse. What do you expect me to do with this so-called new lead?'

'Prevent a murder. Maybe two . . .'

But the judge wouldn't be persuaded. He slapped the open dossier before him, unable to decide whether to file it or not.

'May I also point out,' he said, 'that the enquiry found Pencenat guilty, and consequently all legal proceedings have ended.'

'Except if proof to the contrary is presented to you tomorrow.'

'All right then. Tomorrow. I can live with tomorrow. Tomorrow the old boy will tell all. And then, if there are grounds, we'll look into it.'

But no. No one looked into it. Tomorrow. It's a word many of us mortals bandy about with amazing unconcern, which is all the more thoughtless when one is approaching a hundred years of age.

November is the month when people over sixty fall thick and fast. They are human autumn leaves.

Precisely the morning after the day that 'tomorrow' was mentioned, the woman on duty went into Dr Pardigon's bedroom to open the curtains, and found him lying on his side facing the wall with the bedclothes still tucked up around his neck. There had been no fit, no convulsive movement; he had died the death we all envy. As they say, he passed away peacefully in his sleep.

When Laviolette began walking up the path under the chestnut trees, full of expectation, the van from the funeral parlour drove past him. They were coming to take measurements for the coffin.

He took wry pleasure in going to give the judge the bad news in person. He did, however, spare him any mention of his 'tomorrow'.

'In any case,' muttered Chabrand, who remembered it very well, 'the law could never have moved as quickly as death.'

The Pencenat case file was still on the desk. Chabrand quickly tied up the string that was still lying on top of it, and put the file away in a drawer, which he slapped shut again.

'I think you can delete that name,' Laviolette said.

They looked at each other uneasily.

XI

THE MAN WAS WRITING, WRAPPED IN A DARK RED DRESSING gown with the seat almost threadbare with wear. He squirmed from time to time, making his cane chair creak as if he were sitting on something prickly.

He was writing slowly and ponderously. Occasionally, when his mind wandered, he would spend a few seconds doodling triangles in the margin of his notebook. He even went as far as writing a saying that he had read some time in the past in a book he could no longer remember: *If triangles had gods, they would give them three sides.* But he very quickly and carefully crossed out these words so that they could no longer be read, as if the fact of having written them, even for himself alone, threw too much light on the very heart of his secret.

Sometimes he stopped with his pen poised above the page, listening to the noise of the wind swirling through Barles and the countryside around it. This lively wind which wound around the Blayeul and danced in swirls on the eddies of the Bès was anything but soothing.

The man whose back was bent over his writing listened anxiously to that noise, as if it had some fatal import for him.

'I probably started putting this down on paper to delay for as long as possible what the wind is telling me to do,' he wrote. 'I remember, it was one night in autumn. Despite my intentions, at that time I was still an ordinary man like anyone else. I had a passion, but I thought it was harmless.

'Oh, why did I take it into my head last summer to change the wall-paper in my bedroom? I'd put up with it for so many years. Why did I discover the sealed-up cupboard underneath it and, inside that, the jumble of notes with evidence in which an idle soul like me had described the genealogy of a family, simply to establish the persistence of birthright by tacit agreement in our remote valleys? An undertaking that death probably prevented him from completing . . . ?

'And, going on that and a few suspicions highlighted by chance in those notes, why did I suddenly develop a passionate interest in my own past, which in turn opened my own Pandora's box? And above all, why did I seek out the Dr Pardigon who was mentioned in the notes, and why did he, without omitting a single detail, tell me the whole story of the Melliflores, which a priori didn't concern me?

'After that, I haunted the valleys that branch out around the Bléone on my moped, and in the end I found out, as one always finds out precisely when one shouldn't.

'Hence, I've done what all dreamers do. The word "treasure", and so many details that Dr Pardigon – who is infernally long-winded – described to me about the postman Melliflore, wouldn't leave my mind, making me think, convincing me. Convincing me first of all that if the treasure existed, it belonged to me. Convincing me next that, if need be, I had the right to recover it. And above all, in the course of so many sleepless nights, to wonder what it could be . . .

'What kind of thing could two miserly men have transported in "a cart-load of old stuff", to use Dr Pardigon's expression, which would escape their vigilance, as it had already been very carefully sifted by their avarice?

'There was another question, just as disturbing: how could this treasure, revealed to Dr Pardigon by Gaétan Melliflore, have stayed slumbering through successive inheritance of these Melliflores, hidden from all by the ancestor who did not even want to share it with his descendants? A man who preferred to let it slumber for ever and disappear in the mists of time? If that was the case, where could it be hiding?'

The man stopped writing and threw his pen down on to his notebook in frustration. He raised his hand to his mouth and began scraping his fingernails against his teeth as he tried to make sense of difficult thoughts.

He had turned his attention to a picture he had taken from the pile of papers and propped up against the pot of chamomile tea. It was an old sepia postcard of a man wearing a fur cap and pigskin apron like a sapper of Napoleon's Grande Armée. A short, puny individual, of sunken form, deep-set eyes and a hostile gaze, whose whole personality was summed up in a thick handlebar moustache that hid the lower part of his face. The photo, dated 1919, had the heading: *Colourful Occupations: The Town Crier of Digne.*

The man picked up the old card, raised it to the lamp, looked at it from all angles as if it could reveal some secret, put it down again with a sigh and began writing again.

'I have nothing but intuition to guide me. It's only because my atavistic avarice can guess where another miser might hide his treasure that I could also imagine what kind of thing it might be. I have been so scornful of intuition and premonition; so-called psychic phenomena have always made me feel deeply uneasy, when they haven't sent me into a rage. Now here I am forced to rely on them almost entirely in the most important event in my life.'

The man crossed out these last words and wrote instead, 'In the only event in my life.'

He gave a start. Down below, near the storeroom he used as a wood-shed, someone was knocking urgently. There a door opened on to a field of rye grass with no path through it. He listened. The knocking became louder, stopped and started again several times. The man listened for a moment longer, holding his breath and sitting perfectly still. But now all that could be heard was the wind blowing over the Bès whistling through the trees. The man gave a deep sigh and shook his head.

'I can't even interrupt the flow of my thoughts to take part in the simplest of pleasures. I know that this mad search, which consumes me heart and soul, taking the place of love, children, joy of living, brings me down to the level of a madman. Since it began I have been struggling in the toils of a terrible doubt.

'Have I built up a fantasy? I *think* I'm right on the first point, thanks to the discovery I made in Madame Ambroisine Larchet's attic. But on the second? The most important? How can I check? My two attempts have ended in failure. Have I the strength to continue? Have I really come to the right conclusions? If it wasn't the case, all my victims would have died for nothing . . . That thought weighs heavily on me. I live in a continual state of anxiety and – dare I write it? – remorse.

'I'm not a murderer. For someone who has already caused the deaths of four people, that's a nice thing to say. No! I'm not a murderer. The fact that I have no weapon proves it. Each time I use what comes to hand. Can you call that old rusty bayonet a weapon? Or the well cover? Even less the ball of string I used to trip that old fool Pencenat, who really believed he could make me pay for the columns on his grave!

'Yes, I know. I'm fairly clever. I wore gloves for all the rather delicate operations involved. I disguise myself to do the deed and later resume my usual appearance. And thanks to the old uniform in Mademoiselle Champourcieux's attic, I also thought – wrongly, I'm afraid – that I would strike terror into my victims so that they would hand over their property without my being forced to overcome their resistance. But apparently their strength of character and determination equal my own.

'Here I am at the turning point of my story. I can stop and return to my calm, ordinary life, since Pencenat's fingerprints, like the letter he was holding when he died, seem to have been more or less enough for the law to decide that he committed the two murders, and if nothing new comes to light, it will stop there.

'But I'm like a player who has only two cards left to turn over: unsuccessful so far, I can't give up the idea of searching the houses of the two last inheritors for the legacy they shared. If the secret exists, it's with one or other of those two women. But . . . will there be even one who won't defend her property though it could cost her life? Oh! I shouldn't have warned them. I shouldn't have started them thinking. But I was asking for so little; hardly more than a memory. How could I have doubted that their greed would not allow them to give or sell me the little I asked for? After all, it's as natural in them as it is in me.

'Once again I'll have to defend myself against their stubborn determination. And that is what frightens me the most. For I am afraid. I'm a man who is as scared as a hunted hare. Causing death goes against my whole character (I even rescue insects that have fallen on their backs), against my whole philosophy, against all the battles that I fought in my youth and also, I must confess, against my natural cowardice . . .

'I'll never be able to put the pieces of my shattered integrity together again. With each step I take from now on, I'll only sink further into shame and self-disgust. My integrity was already something I could never take for granted, never achieve without a struggle. My gifts of money, my acts of charity, my fairness, my indulgence for the failings of others, my composure were only ever achieved grudgingly at first and then through strict discipline.

'I was never enough on my guard. I thought I was invulnerable. Why must fate have overwhelmingly weighted the scales with stakes so hugely disproportionate to a poor wretch's powers of resistance? Is it simply for the pleasure of seeing me go against my better judgement, lose control and loathe myself? To see me wipe out with one act a whole lifetime of probity, silent resignation and, I must add though it sounds a little pompous, in my own small way, of fighting for the common good?

'And yet in the beginning my obsession seemed so harmless! But vanity finds its way into everything, and when the stakes become worth it, pride also comes to the fore, leaving you no choice of weapons to defend yourself.

'I scarcely dare write down the futility of the motive that makes me act, and yet . . . Just imagine some lonely or unhappy person, whose only consolation is his artistic sense, because all the other goods of this world are forbidden him; imagine him in a situation where he can possess for himself alone and for ever, with minimum effort, let us say

Peter Breughel's *The Numbering at Bethlehem*. Would this man hesitate to get rid of any obstacles that prevent him from having it? And I say Breughel, but it could just as easily be the *Mona Lisa*, if his taste were more popular than mine, or Picasso's *Guernica*, if his heart were more easily moved.

'I ask you this question, you the person who will open the cupboard and read this when I'm dead, because that is exactly what will happen. I'm about to own personally, for myself alone, something as precious as a Breughel the Elder. Here in this backwater of Barles, I, wretched and needy, approaching old age, definitely not good-looking: mediocre, as ordinary and commonplace as an alley cat, I shall be one of the great, not simply one of the haves of this world but one of the owners of this world. Every evening I shall sit down at this table and enjoy the thrill of well-being that possession brings, when for the whole of my life I have never owned anything of value.'

The man bending over his notebook remained lost in thought, analysing the lines he had just written for a few minutes more. He had been vainly trying to justify his acts and put back together the remnants of his life, which had been broken up and thrown into a bag like lottery tickets. He would never more be able to pull anything out that would let him see himself with any confidence or any pleasure.

The noise of the wind outside seemed to be inviting him to use it as a cover once more, but he tried not to listen. He tried again to struggle against that part of himself that swept away all inconvenient objections and left nothing but the object of his desire glittering and gleaming at the end of a nightmare tunnel.

Not that this was the first time in his life he had desired something belonging to someone else, or to God, and desired it in vain, precisely because he had always resisted the means of obtaining what he wanted. Then it was always things that could be used or turned into money, such as desires of the flesh, banknotes, houses, gardens, social advantage.

Now the thing in question was a miserable possession which, if described, would be laughed at by most reasonable people. If he got it, if it existed, he could only ever be with it alone, enjoy it alone. The way he acquired it would prevent him from mentioning it to anyone, sharing it with a friend or making a mortal enemy mad with envy.

This lonely man then realised that if the sincerity of what he had entrusted to the notebook did not extend to his deepest thoughts, at least the words could help him to formulate them clearly and directly, without humming and hawing. Then something prompted him to pick up his pen again, almost in spite of himself, and write:

'Don't beat about the bush. The truth is that you have always more or less had the desire to kill, probably inherited from an unexpressed atavistic revolt in your ancestors. But you had never before found such a good reason to put it into action.'

This confession was too much to confront. The man carefully crossed it out until it was completely illegible. He put the sepia postcard inside the notebook and slapped it shut with something akin to anger.

He stood up, then gathered together all the contents of the file scattered about on the table. The two doors creaked confidentially as he opened the recently discovered cupboard. He put his papers on one of the shelves. Then he took out a musty, odd-shaped parcel which smelled of gun flint.

He listened to the inviting call of the wind. He unrolled the strange old sapper's uniform put together long ago by Melliflore the postman. After whitening his face in front of the wardrobe mirror in the bedroom, he attached the enormous moustache to his upper lip, making himself look unrecognisable, fearsome and vaguely unreal.

Apart from the wind that mewed around the isolated house, the only sign of life in the whole of Barles was the man dressed as a sapper.

When he opened the door on to the night, the man looked past the shed and saw a sallow moon rising in an overcast sky. He had forgotten to check the time, but from the position of the stars, he reckoned that it must be well past two o'clock in the morning.

The moped was leaning against cages where rabbits were sitting up on their hind legs, hoping that this unusual visit meant extra food. The man in the shadows looked at them and said a few words, as he always did when he came to feed them. He was sorry to leave the confines of his ordinary life, which the smell of the rabbit cages made him sorely miss already.

The old moped was cantankerous and difficult to get going. A good deal of patience, skill and even strength were needed, but it always started evenually, taking the man wherever he wanted to go.

He got on and let it warm up for a few minutes. His eyes strayed further down the valley to the fallow land with its waving grass. The high wall of the shed hid the willow groves, although he could hear them whispering, and even the wind-swept, bare grazing land around the looming Blayeul.

He thought to himself, 'Would I have been different without Barles, without this valley, without this isolation? Would what is happening to me have happened?' But he no longer had a notebook to receive these bitter thoughts, and it was only because he had already got on to his bike that he kept moving. This was helped by the fact that when he came out of the shed, the wind blew joyfully at his back for the whole length of the dirt track, bowling him along like a dead leaf until he reached the tarmac road.

He went through part of the sleeping village, with its shutters tightly closed and not one light shining for those still awake, except for the lamp posts illuminating empty streets. He entered the gorges towards Verdaches. A few dogs barked behind their fences as he went by. The sound of the waters flowing in the Bès covered the noise of the moped. He passed fountains, barns and hamlets. A few murmurs from carelessly closed stables greeted him as he rode through Verdaches. When he reached the Seyne turn-off, he took the right fork. The smell of the pines and the damp fields rising in tiers on the slopes came to meet him.

He was surprised how easily he went up the steep ascent of the pass. As if the wind that had pushed him along in the gorges had turned with him at his command, as if it was carrying him, as if the machine itself was superfluous and the man could just as well have done without it, since the wind was with him.

High above in the moonlight dimmed by the clouds, above the battalions of pines in formation supporting the pillars of the mountain, shone the granite of the Estrop. Solidified streams of sparkling frozen water ran down it, waiting, hoping for snow.

It was there before his eyes for some time, and more than the familiar smell of the rabbits, this pure and noble alpine scene almost made him change his mind and go back. It too had been part of his blameless past. Now it was part of everything he no longer had the right to love.

But the wind was too favourable; it made everything too easy. The man knew that if he turned back, he would only do it another time. He had tried, he had controlled himself several times, but never for long. He knew that some day he would give way again to the overwhelming lure of what he stood to gain. He also knew that the law, which always has the last word, would eventually tighten its net around him, that he could not beat it, that all his schemes could only postpone the inevitable, that he would certainly get himself caught if things dragged on for too long. There was no time to lose.

He went over the pass and down into the valley. When he emerged from the pine forests, the whole of the La Javie region was spread out before him. Despite the wind and the moon, a mass of clouds hung over his head like a charcoal-coloured lid. The village lights and the halo of Digne in the distance cut through this dark cover at forest level, and under its baleful shadow the irrigation canals and the ruined farms still gleamed in the moonlight.

The man on the moped was going through La Javie when two o'clock struck in the bell tower under the chestnut trees. He passed a moving shadow: it was a baker's apprentice in his vest washing croissant baking trays under one of the spouts in the fountain. Absorbed in his work, he did not even glance at the man passing by so late at night.

The smell of bread was carried thought the open bakery door further along on the other side of the street, and drifted on the air for more than a hundred metres down the road. This was another thing that might persuade the person to go back to his quiet life. He was still aware of it around him when he took the ill-defined road, half-track, half-stream, that lead to Chavailles. But the wind was so fair that he already felt the presence of that valley where he hoped he might discover his life's illusory goal at last.

What could La Bléone be whispering as it flowed over its stony bed, brushing the side of the road?

'The world would be such a beautiful place, were it not for the people in it.'

XII

THE PREVIOUS AFTERNOON, VIOLAINE MAILLARD HAD GONE HOME at about four o'clock. The forests on the Cheval Blanc, skimmed by the November sun at midday, were already returning to the long night of the north face, where from October to March all the wildfowl retreated hastily to lower ground, to places that were more dangerous but also benefited from more sunlight. As a result, silence settled heavily beneath the black pine forests, and the whole base of the mountain they surrounded echoed eerily like the corridors in a deserted house.

The forest petered out at the edge of the large clearing where the Maillard ancestors had built their sawmill, their turbine and their house.

Violaine got out of her car with her arms full of flowers. Today it was a long sheaf of red gladioli, out of season, very expensive, and ostentatiously carried from the florist to the car parked some distance away, so that the whole of Digne could admire them. This was a ritual that she had been performing once a month for more than fifteen years on the date that her husband had been put through the mill turbine.

From the following year, once she had regained her senses, Violaine kept strict observance of this terrible event every month of her life by getting blind drunk and passing out across her bed, where she could still be found the next morning. She also commemorated it by putting flowers on his grave. Sometimes it was a palm, sometimes a large exotic plant, but always in a brilliant colour that showed up under the cellophane, so that the whole of Digne would remember seeing her pass by.

Violaine believed that this brazen drunkenness and profusion of priceless flowers were not too great a price to pay to highlight the necessity of mourning. As a grasping, cautious Melliflore, she was compelled to continue her grief well beyond the prescribed limits, so that all the rumours which had circulated then would have time to die down and disappear completely. Of course many of the witnesses had died in the last fifteen years. Unfortunately some still remained, and until the world was rid of them, it was imperative, according to Violaine, not to slacken her efforts.

That particular evening she was coming back from Thouard, where she had gone to fetch the object that was causing her so much anxiety. She had a team of half a dozen woodcutters in Thouard, who worked amongst other places in a beech forest she had inherited. They were burly lads and none too bright, like Greek heroes; tough customers and touchy on the subject of honour, about which they had very strict views. Thanks to them, Violaine did not suffer from sensual deprivation. Every week she would call one of them, who came up to the villa for two nights in great secrecy.

But men drink, and when they have drunk, secrets spill out of them like wine from a burst barrel. One day the Forestry Department warden rang Violaine in a state, telling her that there was a lot of wild shouting coming from the overexcited woodsmen's house.

She dashed into her Delage and drove as fast as it would go, at the risk of leaving the gears strewn on the roadway. They were at axes drawn. She separated them with a whip, lined them up naked at attention like lions in a circus. She undressed as well. She told them that none of them was any better than the others, and that she would prove it to them there and then.

These two days and two nights without food or drink, performing in front of each other on their mattresses fanned out like beech leaves, were a world-changing experience for them. Previously, when she had been alone with one of them, she had released a few cries; here, with all of them, she resisted them without a tremor, without a sigh. After this they were never jealous of each other again, and obediently took their turn.

Thus avarice can be of use on any occasion. It allows one to grasp everything without a second thought. The notary who took her virginity immediately after she was widowed gallantly, if somewhat crudely, complimented her on it. 'Violaine,' he said, 'there's not much flesh on your bones, but it's pulled as tightly as purse strings, around an incandescent suction machine.'

The memory of it made her laugh out loud. She leaped out of the enormous car with her legs raised, even though no one could see them. Still with not much flesh on her bones, she triumphantly bore the sheaf of red gladioli.

She was reassured to know that the securely tied parcel was safe on the back seat. Despite their axes, their broad shoulders and their stamina, equalled only by their stupidity, she did not think that these forces of nature could pose any real obstacle to the extraordinary correspondent who had been exhorting her for months to hand over her property. She shook her head. No. Definitely not. He was capable of killing the whole six of them to get it from them. That would be the last straw! You don't come across six burly, dim-witted woodsmen every day.

As always happened when she came back, even after a short absence, Violaine's enthusiasm was curbed by the sight of the environment in which she lived. The bare, flat area of aggregate from La Chanolette on which the buildings stood looked as if the forest to the north of the Cheval Blanc mountain had disgorged the deposit and left it there. It was like a pale crescent-shaped gash across the echoing valley. No grass had grown on it for a hundred years. The wind in the mountain above it could be heard through the constant roaring of the water, like the wailing of a desolate animal.

The person who decided one day that he could easily found a dynasty there must have been singularly lacking in imagination. The whole place spoke of heart-rending poverty, down to the rust camouflaged by the horsetails growing on pools of clay that oozed slowly but continuously towards the valley floor; down to the yarrow growing on the gneiss rock that had burst and scattered along the irrigation channels. Erosion was everywhere, around the banks of the Chanolette and as far as the old moraine spewed out from the Lachen pass. It was palpable, active, almost visible and audible to the naked ear and eye.

In the disused power station, rust flaked under the glass, bricks in the hastily constructed walls broke one by one, eaten by the winter ice, then quietly crumbled during the night. The factory itself was being racked by the movement of the erosion.

In the dilapidated sawmill, its feeders ripped out, an elder tree had sprung up out of the sawdust. The wood lathe was still in position between two gates. A twenty-ton larch tree clamped to its carriage was slowly rotting away.

What catastrophe could suddenly have brought the work to a stand-still and frozen it in time? The day after Maillard's execution, the fright-ened workers had disbanded, leaving everything just as it was, for fear of being associated with their boss. They had tried later to work the mill for themselves, but Violaine refused. The power plant, the chalet, the sawmill were all part of the mausoleum; she insisted that every-thing remain in the same state as it had been on that hot August night in 1944.

Thanks to the passion the widow had inspired in a big shot, and which she had immediately shared, though in great secrecy and not for long, she had been able to buy the power plant back from the state. This was the only example at that time, and she was the only one to know about it. Not that she didn't pay more than it was worth with a bundle of shares that Maillard had left in the bank safe under Violaine's name.

It should also be noted that none of these shares were in German or even French companies. They were all English. Which just goes to prove that Maillard was as equivocal a creature as anyone else, since he had given his life for an ideal that was incompatible with the one that decided his choice of share portfolio.

The big shot allowed Violaine to extract all the necessary authorisations and signatures from him during the course of delightful intimate evenings. And it all happened without prejudice to the state he represented, and no one was sorry to be rid of that unpleasant reminder of a heroic moment. People in high places were actually grateful to her for doing it. Particularly as the plant was very old and the civil engineering works on the feeder canal were on the verge of collapse. The pressure pipeline was nothing but rust. The unfortunate turbine itself dated from the beginning of the century and was still without its jets – and that says everything. It had been badly blocked by the ill-digested bones of its former owner. The chambers would have had to be cleaned, splinter by splinter, which would have provided the journalists with far too many sensational photos.

The chalet was new. Well, it was scarcely thirty years old at the time this story took place. Young Maillard had pulled down the family home to erect in its place a smaller version of the sanctuary where his god lived and breathed, over there in the Bavarian Alps.

It occupied the best spot on the platform; in other words, it saw the winter sun for two hours a day. Geraniums that Violaine had long ago allowed to die used to spill over the Tyrolean window boxes on all the balconies, even the very small one on the attic. You fully expected to see one of those cuckoos that gaily tell the hours burst through the tiny double doors on the attic, like the shutters on a Swiss clock.

The brightly coloured façade, the pretty inn curtains at the windows, the hearts cut out of the wooden shutters, the carved roses at the edges of the roof; the tables on the terrace in the summer, indicating relaxed evenings with friends, which had never taken place, down to the unrecognisable remnants of a flag that used to gaily flap in the breeze: all that tried to give the impression of perfect happiness, serenely acquired with God's blessing.

But, apart from the site of Chavailles, which seemed to spew out this intruder in disgust, the chalet itself looked artificially dressed up in all that forced brightness. Something aggressively harsh in its proportions, which they had not been able to soften, frightened even the birds. None ever came and perched on the balconies or the roof. Only the magpies sometimes looked down on it from the highest branches of the elder tree, but only from afar and in a sizeable group. And even then it was always to give those sharp, frightened squawks that indicate imminent danger.

The house had been built quickly only three years before the war to welcome Maillard's little fiancée, and there had never been time since to treat the wood and protect it against predators. As a result they lived there surrounded by the incessant noise of the wood-eaters. All that beautiful soft new wood was eaten by mites and borers as if an army of bit-braces were drilling holes for long screw pulls.

Anyone but Violaine would never have endured it. But she took a certain pleasure in that enormous amount of teeth-grinding, which never troubled her tranquil nights. No, if she paused every time she came back there, it was because the sound of the car door closing reminded her instantly of the August day in 1944 when she came home from secretly consulting the notary who later became her lover. He had told her, speaking close to her ear, what could await her having a husband in the militia. She could find herself with nothing overnight, at the mercy of public charity, if she didn't sort it out. She could still hear his cold voice saying, 'A word to the wise is enough!'

'Sorting it out' had not involved long deliberation between herself and her conscience. She had the means. A simple telephone call had done it; just a minute's conversation to inform the invisible person on the other end of the line, and once the receiver had been put down again, she had looked at her completely clean hands without a tremor.

Violaine gave a modest smile at the thought as she walked towards the house. Her mind was at ease despite being perfectly self-aware. There are people like that who can know remorse but feel no embarrassment, fear or anxiety of any kind; people who make no judgement on what lies in the depths of their soul, which they nevertheless know intimately, and who calmly enjoy the good things of life without ever being haunted by their acts.

You just had to watch Violaine Maillard's light step as she made her way towards the house to be convinced of that fact. Her slight figure walked quickly, lightly, slim legs in high heels, her bag bouncing against her thin flanks. She was almost hidden behind the symbolic offering she was carrying in her arms: the huge, expensive sheaf of red gladioli enveloped in crackling cellophane.

Nevertheless, the sad sound that is the lamentation of the world for mortal sins flowed down and around her from the corridors of the mountain she defied with such a lack of concern. But who hears it? Who listens to it? The evening that was beginning to fall on the depths of Chavailles was nothing less than balmy. Now and then the pale top of the Cheval Blanc above its dark forests appeared through the long banners of mist. At the moment when Violaine shut the car door, the wind rising in the west brought a burst of children's voices coming from a school far off in the valley.

Violaine nimbly climbed the few steps leading to the terrace and the front door of the chalet. She put the flowers down on a garden table, rummaged about in her bag, took out the bunch of keys and opened the door.

'My darling!'

Every time the mites and borers heard this cry, they were so startled they all stopped gnawing at once. That usually lasted one or two seconds, then, breaking the sudden unbearable silence, they began feeding as before.

'If you could only see what I've brought you, my darling. You were so keen on flowers, I guarantee you'll be happy with them. And you were so keen on my being conspicuous; if you only know the price I paid for that!'

She gave another spontaneous laugh.

The living room crammed with useless objects was a cemetery of successive inheritances that their owners could never part with. It contained three sideboards, three tables, two sewing machines, a large number of chairs and armchairs lined up against the walls as around a dance floor. Five or six chandeliers hung from the joists, most of them not connected. The chimney in the cold fireplace bristled with a number of trammel hooks that had been hung closely together, more or less side by side.

Every day the golden snow the borers extracted from their holes settled on all these objects as well as the impressive collection of *The French Hunter* magazine, complete for the last eighty years. It took the two women who came in from La Javie to do housework most of every morning to remove it.

A full-length photo portrait of the victim of Chavailles stood on a gilt plaster credenza: he had the long, seductive face of a charmer from the 1920s, straight hair carefully slicked back with a parting on the side. His slim body was clothed in a tight-fitting puppet uniform: half officer, half gang leader, with riding breeches and leather gaiters that emphasised his bandy legs.

'Well, my darling? We seem to be looking rather glum this evening.'

The housekeepers claimed that Violaine talked to herself. Nothing was further from the truth. But when someone has lived as a couple for years, continually mulling over the reasons why there was never love between them, the habit is established, and the death of one partner does not put an end to that strangely courteous contradiction. The only difference is that the survivor usually keeps the terms of the dialogue to him- or herself. Some people with very strong personalities, however, still keep on talking.

Although she came to love him in the end, as one comes to love opium, Violaine had never completely got over having always been alone throughout her life, whether as a little girl, a wife, a widow or a lover. That state never ceased to surprise her. The fact that this loneliness could have stemmed from her innate inability to communicate with others because of her avarice was something that she naturally wouldn't be aware of.

'Come on, my darling! Don't look like that.'

She had spontaneously picked up the portrait to plant a kiss on the head through the glass protecting it.

'Yes, I know! It's another of those anniversaries of your death. But still, after all this time, it shouldn't affect you any more.'

She put the photo back on the credenza and opened the door of one of the sideboards. She felt inside and withdrew a bottle, then took down from the dresser a silver christening cup some godmother must have given a baby, intended for pure water. Violaine filled it two thirds full and downed the contents in one gulp.

'Whew! That's better!'

It was her first glass of the day. How many more would she have to empty to be convincingly drunk? She had too good a capacity for alcohol. It was essential for the two cleaning women to find her in the morning dead drunk on the living-room divan, with the portrait of her deceased husband clasped to her bosom and the bottle of vodka lying on the floor in front of the radio blaring away.

In the beginning she would get drunk on anything at all, then it was gin, but since she discovered vodka, she could drink in all confidence. She was as fresh the day after the monthly commemorations as if she had been drinking water.

She sank on to the divan, facing the credenza, and put the bottle down at her feet. The portrait had lost nothing of its haughty look.

'Come on, my darling! Stop looking at me like a judge. Hardly appropriate for you, with at least ten deaths on your conscience. Come on! Come on! Be a bit more natural with me . . . You know very well I'm never troubled by metaphysical anxiety.'

She gave a childish laugh at the idea going through her mind.

'I've cultivated a face that never blushes,' she repeated to herself.

She stood up, turned her back on the portrait, poured herself another cup, began to drink, tasting it this time, then came back and sat again facing the picture.

'Good Lord, my darling! What a bore you are. How could I have admired you for so long? Oh yes, I know. I've certainly made up for it since. That's easy for you to say. But do you have any idea what it is to be faithful to a man who has never touched you? Faithful. For seven years. And after all that, would you think it was right for me to end up with nothing because of your stupidity? You surely wouldn't have wanted that!'

She gave a start. The clock in the passage struck six rapidly, as if it wanted to silence her. Violaine realised that she was in the dark. She leaped up to the switch, hurried out of the room to turn on the lights in the passage, the stairs, the floors above and the terrace. She came back startled and out of breath. What had made her rush like that? Normally she would let the dark surround her for a while in silence before banishing it with floods of light.

When she came back to it, the merciless portrait looked no more kindly than it had before.

'Oh, I know very well what you reproach me with. Yes, it's true. I made love again this afternoon. But it was so little really.'

She burst out laughing.

'In the car. In a hurry. Have you ever made love in a car? Oh, that's right. You've never made love anywhere. What's that? Did I cry out? Of course I did! My mother told me to. But you could have kept on trying all the same. No? You couldn't? Are you trying to tell me that you could never have done it? Still, that's not the only thing. Didn't you have hands? A mouth? Here . . . I'll tell you a secret . . .'

She sank her nose into the cup as if she were sitting in front of a real person and was embarrassed by what she was about to confess to him. She gazed at the liquid she was swirling around, seemingly to keep her eyes lowered.

She said quietly, 'Of course you won't tell it to anyone, but sometimes you know, when I'm with a lover, I wonder whether it's not the hands and the mouth that I really prefer . . .'

She swallowed the rest of her glass in one gulp, then stood up and walked past the photo, which she touched lightly with one finger.

'You see,' she said. 'You could have tried.'

She began to walk towards the door, but then remembered that the air outside might not be good for the sheaf of hot-house gladioli that she had left on the terrace. She stopped in her tracks, struck by an idea that had suddenly come to her. She slowly turned towards the portrait.

'That's strange . . .' she said. 'I have the impression that I've never said so much about it before. What's got into me this evening, telling you everything like that?'

She poured herself another half-cup of vodka, but didn't sit down again to drink it. She was not talking any more. She was slightly breathless. A golden dust that spilled from the panels in the ceiling was caught in the beams of light around the two illuminated chandeliers. The grinding of the wood-borers sounded like a weathervane turning.

Violane impatiently plunged her hand inside the front of her blouse, as if she had been resisting the gesture for some time. She took out from her bra the piece of rough paper that had been irritating her breasts since she received it that morning in the mail. She unfolded it quickly. For perhaps the tenth time she reread the maxim that had been so skilfully written, the maxim that her sister and her cousin had also received before they died, according to the newspaper.

The measure you give will be the measure you get.

She angrily crumpled it into a ball, threw it on the ground, stamped on it, spat on it then, on second thoughts, she picked it up again, smoothed it out and put it back where it had been. She opened the door wide. The cellophane around the bouquet was crackling softly in the breeze. Night had not yet fallen completely. Down near Digne where the valley narrowed, a vaguely aquamarine colour still held the last fading gleams of daylight. At the edge of the clearing, the forests on the slope of the Cheval Blanc scarcely trembled in a light wind that had still not gathered its forces.

Violaine took the flowers out of the cellophane and held them in her arms. She went down the steps from the terrace. With her elegantly arched back and provocative gait, she proudly crossed the open ground where the gravel crunched beneath her heels.

She had told herself for years to get a workman to come and grease the hinges on the huge door of the power plant. Every time she opened it, she had to brace the whole weight of her small backside against it for two minutes, emerging exhausted from the confrontation. This time was no exception and she made the same vow as she struggled with the iron frame. Half the glass panes were missing from the door, as from the rest of the windows in the building. She picked up the flowers she had put down on the ground during this exercise, and walked resolutely into the gloom.

There had not been any light in the electricity plant for a long time. The small amount of daylight still remaining lingered on the strange shapes of the metal objects strewn over the ground or reaching up to the roof. They were dark obstacles in Violaine's path, but she knew them well and even noticed unexpected debris that the plant had shed since the last time she had been there.

Holding her bouquet in front of her, she turned and went around the cast-iron pillars holding up the framework, deftly avoiding the dynamo in its wire cage.

A huge greenish object, four times as tall as she was, rose up in the half-light. It was a kind of giant snail with a complex smell still hovering around it: a mixture of heavy-duty oil, asphalt, aggregate, tartar, and above all, rust.

That was Roland Maillard's tomb. That rudimentary turbine dating from the beginning of the century, which the dead man's antecedents had so lovingly maintained. A tall dark vase in front of it still held the remains of a bouquet of agapanthus, last month's offering. Violaine had had a picture of the dead man sealed on to a marble base next to the turbine. It was the same as the one she kept on the credenza in the drawing room. She pulled the dead flowers out of the funerary urn, tipped the smelly water on to the ground and filled it again with a watering can always left there for the purpose.

Then, with practised hands, she arranged the gladioli in an elegant rising shape like a fountain. She stepped back to judge how it looked. The outline of the flowers became blurred in the dim light like everything else, but their vibrant colour still stood out in the dark.

Violaine observed the overall effect with satisfaction.

The vodka had scarcely begun to affect her senses.

Yet she couldn't make up her mind to leave that strange, fascinating tomb. She looked at the curved top of the turbine where she knew there was a name cast into the metal, a name in huge letters, a symbol of pride and efficiency: BERGER. What good were they now, that new cast-steel god, that new protecting cross in spiral form that would withstand the wear of a thousand centuries? What was that mausoleum where no one after her would place flowers or even remember that it hid a grave?

She burst out laughing, but discreetly as one should at a grave, even though it was made of steel.

This commemorative ceremony usually took Violaine just a few minutes to perform. It was only done to feed the curiosity of the two cleaning ladies, who would come the following day to make sure that the bouquet was as ostentatious as usual, and then go off to spread the news.

But today she lingered, for no good reason that she could see. She vaguely made out the tortured shapes of the scrap iron, and could almost hear the rust crumbling. A large openwork mass extended up two thirds the height of the glassed section. Sixty years ago it was a staircase with iron steps, only used for surveillance, and therefore without a guard rail. Well, not entirely: at about every five steps there was a vertical metal tube on each side, probably meant to be welded to a chain, but after due consideration, the owners must have found it too expensive for the purpose.

This staircase served the travelling crane and the surveillance footbridge that went around the enclosure where the ancient transformers slept.

Violaine stood lost in thought for some time in front of what she could still see of the steps that disappeared into the shadows. She finally turned and slowly made her way out. A slight haze in her head began to come between her and the real world.

She came back towards the chalet, went in slamming the door behind her, took a fresh bottle of vodka from the sideboard, opened it and turned up the volume on the radio as far as it would go. It was jazz music, and what she liked best was to shake her own resonance chamber with the dull thuds of the drum kit and the blaring of the saxophones.

She stretched out on the divan and gazed at the ceiling. She no longer spoke to the portrait. She no longer even looked at him. His stern, blasé stare had no effect.

La lombarde, the east wind, was beginning to rise in the isolated valley. When this wind lows like a heifer down there in Chavailles, no one is usually out of doors to hear it. It's a wind to wring your heart, to make people and animals want to huddle together. It whispers the pointlessness of living in the ears of the wretched. It encircles the Cheval Blanc and the Couar. The large dry meadows on the summits that long for snow to cover their bareness are beaten like carpets. It turns, zigzags, it staggers – at least that is the impression it produces on those listening. They say it comes from Italy, but those who say so are becoming fewer and fewer, because they are old men and their ranks are thinning.

It's a wind that must have been invented by a poet. One particular night he was no doubt the only one out of doors to identify it. Meanwhile, despite the scepticism of the experts, it blows by whatever name people call it.

It also seems to carry smells. Smells from near and far, smells that are sometimes not even of this time, but are held within its ethereal body from gale to gale and century to century. Whiffs of noble decay, from those years when the aroma of chanterelle mushrooms being cooked used to waft in the streets around houses that kept a good table. Sometimes they are even smells from forgotten balls, old-fashioned weddings in the church square bathed in the scent of narcissus, where the blushing newly-weds have long ago crumbled to dust. On its way it has swept up what remained of these faded odours from the ruins of deserted villages, and stored them in its whirlwinds. On certain nights *la lombarde* serves them up again at the edges of the forests between the Estrop and the Cheval Blanc, to make them nostalgic. Sometimes it will even bathe the Blayeul, which overlooks Barles on one side and La Javie on the other. But it likes most of all to lurk in the depths of Chavailles, especially around the old Maillard sawmill. So much human sweat for nothing, since the ruins are all that remain; since the only person there is the tiny woman, who once again has forgotten her washing on the line, where the bras and panties fill out, thanks to *la lombarde*, in curves they never clothed.

Look. The moon has risen over the valley now. It joins the wind. Over there on the banks of the Chanolette, there is only one sign of life: the chalet with all its windows lit up, as if a party was in full swing. But there's no party going on. The poor woman has fallen asleep on the sofa, her head heavy with vodka. Now that she is lying there defenceless, you can see that she is starting to look her age.

The bottle of alcohol lies half-full at her feet. The empty silver cup has gently tipped over on the carpet. Last of all, Violaine had grabbed the man's portrait from the sideboard and clasped it to her bosom to complete her image as the inconsolable widow. The photo is beginning to slip out of her limp hands. The radio belts out blues continuously but the volume seems to be decreasing. Suddenly the music stops. There is some mumbling and crackling, then nothing.

The night advances. Over the pale waters of the Bléone and the little Chanolette, only the intermittent sound of erosion breaks the continuous surge of the wind flowing in harmony with the rumble of current, before disappearing into the forests. The moon is almost at its zenith; its journey across the sky is long at that time of year.

Violaine is still asleep, her mouth slack and half-open.

It was the silence that woke Violaine. A nerve was beating dully against her forehead, spreading across the aching arch of her eyebrows. A siren sounded in her right ear, distant but piercing. That was the only drawback with vodka. She was surprised. She usually slept undisturbed. Even on these trying commemoration days, despite the amount of alcohol consumed, she managed to sleep her eight hours undisturbed by a dream or even a start, though she was fully clothed and still wearing her shoes.

'I forgot to put new batteries in the radio . . .' she said aloud.

That was the silence: the radio had stopped. But no, it was something more subtle than that. Outside the wind was blowing and the river was rumbling, but that made no difference to the silence around her, the only silence that really counted, the one that directly communicated its alarm to Violaine's dulled senses. She clicked her tongue two or three times. She had not been asleep long enough for the effects of her drinking to wear off. And it was hard to think with the irrational euphoria that made her see everything through rose-coloured glasses, in spite of herself.

Suddenly she sat upright, gasping in surprise. She looked up to the ceiling. The borers in the beams and floors had all stopped, as if they had the power to be on their guard, as if a threat had alerted them.

In all the time she had been living there, the wood-borers had never stopped their noise for more than a minute. All the events in her life, its pleasures and pains, had taken place against the background noise of these predators patiently occupied in turning the chalet back into sawdust.

She shivered and quickly got to her feet. The photo fell to the ground face down, as if it were annoyed. She picked it up, raised it to eye level, and gazed at it through her alcoholic haze.

'It couldn't happen, could it, my darling? If someone had walked in front of you, you'd know it. There'd be some sign of it on your face, wouldn't there? You wouldn't leave me with no warning.'

For the first time in her life since she had been gazing at the mystery of that picture, it seemed to her that the inscrutable portrait now had the suggestion of a mocking smile, and the smile stayed there.

She threw the picture against the dresser, where it smashed to the sound of shattering glass.

'Bastard! I knew you'd win in the end!'

A strange sensation crept into Violaine's mind through the vodka fumes. She felt something like gentle encouragement from an intangible person who was guiding her, holding her by the hand, wanting to take her away to a place where it wouldn't be so bad after all.

'No!' she shouted. 'No! No! No!'

She stamped her foot on the carpet like a temperamental child. She poured herself a full cup of vodka. The neck of the bottle clinked repeatedly against the silver rim. She downed the drink in one go. She listened. The silence was just as profound. It was still a presence, like a real person, dense, emphasised by the sound of the wind and water outside.

To keep the insatiable appetite of the wood mites at bay like that, the unknown enemy must have been watching and waiting, wandering anywhere, observing everything; perhaps there was more than one; perhaps it wasn't human.

Violaine let out a shrill laugh.

Perhaps he was up there in her bedroom, among the tastefully erotic perfumes and lingerie she liked to wear to add spice to her nights of love. Perhaps he was lying naked between her sheets, waiting for her, but what kind of loathsome nudity would he reveal?

She shook herself. The vodka was beginning to have its effect. This usually happened when she was sound asleep. But here she was, swaying but still standing, trying hopelessly to collect her thoughts, and feeling terror slowly emerging from the intoxication.

Suddenly she let out a terrible cry. She clapped her hand to her mouth as if she had seen something unbearable. She had just remembered that the object she had fetched from Thouard and her woodsmen was still on the back seat of the Delage. She rushed outside.

She caught the full strength of *la lombarde*, which almost knocked her over. Combined with the alcohol fumes, it relieved Violaine of the little judgement she still retained. She reeled, then clutched the wooden post holding up the eaves. It took her more than a minute to catch her breath and suppress the desire to vomit, which had overcome her as soon as she had gone out of the door. She hesitated for quite a while at the top of the steps. Normally she skipped down, but tonight they seemed like an impossible obstacle. She risked it nonetheless, clutching the rail with both hands, and taking two steps to go down each level like an old woman. The car was not far away, but as she left the porch, it looked to her like a distant promised land. But she had to reach it. She couldn't leave the parcel on the back seat at the mercy of the person who already had announced his presence.

Buffeted by the wind, she stumbled and twirled like a marionette. It whipped her face and made her lungs work overtime, while the accumulated effect of the alcohol overwhelmed her brain, paralysing her reflexes and depriving her of coherent thought.

She collapsed across the hood of the car with her arms out in front of her and her cheek against the cold metal. Her short skirt was pulled up, revealing the top of her thighs, which the playful wind began to caress.

'I'm going to die!' she breathed.

Her heart was in her mouth, her legs were like jelly, her brain had given up and a migraine was jabbing at her forehead. A single thought remained in her disorientated mind: it was the parcel, there, less than three metres away, on the back seat. All she had to do was stand up again, take a few steps, open the car door and grab it. It took her three minutes to try and think, focus, and summon up some will power before she could do anything.

She struggled vainly with the back door handle, damaging her fingernails in the process, before noticing that it was locked from the inside. She opened the front door and leaned over the seat. The parcel was very high and wide, and before she knew it Violaine found herself wedged on top of it with her arms flailing. After floundering around she finally fell in a heap in the back, feeling dizzy, her nose pressed against the green leather, which still held traces of a twenty-year-old perfume.

The scent made her laugh idiotically. That very afternoon, she remembered, her nose had been buried in the fragrant leather. She had been making love with a frenzy heightened by the awkward position she was in. But was it really she? And where was it? And with whom? Her laugh ended with a giggle and a burp. Her hand relaxed and inadvertently hit the large parcel she had forgotten once again. That caused a dull rumbling sound which made her jump, and restored her presence of mind for a moment. She took hold of the package, but then she had to push the door open. She tried unsuccessfully several times, falling back on to the seat with each attempt. Finally she found herself standing upright with her arms closed around the cumbersome parcel.

She took a while gathering the few wits she still had to understand what was happening before her eyes. Teetering and swaying on legs planted well apart, she blinked repeatedly as she stared, bemused, at the sight in front of her.

Neither the wind nor the mountain noises had ceased their duet. The shape of the gorge had become blurred, but the shadows that emphasised it and the clear sky outlining the crests surrounded the clearing where the moonlight was concentrated.

There it stood, the machine that so astonished Violaine, right in the middle of the moonlit open space halfway between the electric power plant and the chalet.

When she saw it, she sank back against the mudguard of her tourer, still determinedly clutching her precious parcel. She gave a burst of laughter despite the anxious look in her eyes, for although she felt the anxiety, she was also a happy drunk. The contrast between the very real threat she could still grasp and the mindless optimism she owed to the vodka was a ghastly sensation.

The machine that made her laugh was set arrogantly on the gravel, not far from the drying area. It was dirty, decrepit, leaning slightly to one side on its stand; the rear red light was smashed and the mudguard twisted in an old fall. She could see in the moonlight that it was leaking oil. It was a moped.

Violaine looked at it without really taking it in, trying to gather the thoughts that this strange object inspired. She turned her head towards the chalet, where the flag was snapping in the wind, where all the windows, all the corridors and all the balconies were lit up *a giorno* from top to bottom. Seen from there, the chalet looked enormous and ready to crush her.

Then a shadow loomed up behind one of the first-floor windows, blocking out the light. It moved about clumsily, stopping frequently. It hesitated as it began moving again. It went from one window to another with the same heavy, wandering steps. Its silhouette suddenly obscured a small balcony, lit only from inside the house. It vanished for some time before reappearing again at last on the ground floor, behind the picture windows of the drawing room where Violaine had been sleeping.

'He's searching . . .' she whispered.

Her eyes came back to the very distinct moped resting on its stand like an animal in a nightmare. Something strange had happened behind the machine, over in the drying yard. Violaine had the impression that her clothes were beckoning to her. Suddenly she understood: only half the garments she had pegged on the lines that morning were still there. Her blouses and the sleeves of her dressing gown were waving sadly to her in the wind. All the rest – the various panties, bras, tights and lace garter belts – had been stolen. Violaine realised that their disappearance was her death sentence. She couldn't string two thoughts together, and yet the truth burst into her mind with great clarity, already formulated in a sentence she said softly out loud: 'He wants to make it look like a sadist's crime . . .'

She shivered as she finally understood the whole situation: the shadow behind the windows, the moped on its stand, her underwear now in a pile somewhere, soiled and crumpled by who knows what hands, the bulky parcel in her arms. Her life would be played out with the scattered pieces of this chess game.

If the man with the moped had known that the object he coveted had been lying unguarded for hours on the back seat of the car, he could have quietly taken it and left the way he had come. But as he was the mere instrument of fate, no intuitive feeling or sudden thought had come to him when he must have brushed past the tourer.

Violaine let out a helpless moan. Her faculties were clouded by alcohol. There was no hope of sobering up under a cold shower since she couldn't go into her own house. Involuntary little bursts of idiotic laughter shook her from time to time like sobs.

Yet she knew that there was a solution, and the idea exasperated her as she desperately tried to work it out. She knew that she had a way of avoiding her fate. The car? Given the inebriated state she was in, she would crash into the first ditch. The intruder prowling around the house could just come and get her.

She searched as you do in a dream, when looking for something you know you haven't lost in real life.

'The gun!'

She almost shouted the word. She quickly put the parcel down on the side of the bonnet and, without taking her hands off the bodywork holding her up, dragged herself to the back of the car. It took her three attempts to raise the boot lid. Would she ever get it open? It still contained the same objects that were there five years ago when she was mistress of the notary (now dead). He had insisted on introducing her to hunting because he loved women in riding boots who had a slight musky scent of the forest floor.

She still had a double-barrelled gun in its luxury case, a Henry game bag that he had given her and a well-stocked cartridge pouch. All that lay peacefully in the depths of the car, waiting for the right occasion. Well, the occasion had arrived. But Violaine wondered anxiously whether she would be clear-headed enough to do everything necessary to arm herself.

It took her several minutes with shaking hands and chattering teeth to take the gun from its case, put it all together, and slip a cartridge in each barrel. She was puffing and panting like an old man, and burping from a constant feeling of nausea. Despite her drunken state, she was aware that the last cupful had been the *coup de grâce*, and added to that, she had never gone out into the cold valley air at night before.

She was torn between fear, determination and the irresistible temptation to forget everything and go dipping her feet in the river. At the same time she felt impotent rage against her own stupidity. She slammed the boot lid closed as hard as she could. Her angry gesture prompted the package balanced on the edge of the bonnet to fall off with a boom that sounded something like a gong. This rumbling rose in the air right up to the tips of the northern forests. A night bird on the top of a spruce slowly took flight and glided across the moon for a few moments above the rushing water and the sawmill.

Violaine clapped her hands to her ears. Over in the chalet, the silhouette prowling from room to room stopped suddenly in front of a casement window and stayed there.

Violaine instinctively rushed forward to rescue her property, falling on her knees in front of it. The gun she had clumsily put around her neck bumped heavily against her, and the strap cut into her tendons. She stayed prostrate for more than a minute, with her arms around the recalcitrant package that was giving her so much trouble. On all fours, one knee after the other, she painfully levered her body, light though it was, from the ground. The alcohol which deadened her reflexes made it seem three times heavier.

She began to walk: one step, two steps, her eyes never leaving the silhouette of the person who must surely be watching her bathed in the moonlight. Attacking him in the house seemed a crazy idea. He could wait for her anywhere, in one of the many nooks and crannies, at the bend of a corridor, under a staircase, behind a door. He had got the better of Ambroisine and Véronique, who hadn't come down in the last shower, and who were also perfectly lucid.

A gun is all very well, but you have to aim it. God, how many years was it since she'd last used one? Besides . . . she didn't always see a single target; sometimes it divided. She saw two men, two windows, two chalets. It didn't last long, but it kept happening.

Moving like a sleepwalker, with the gun swaying around her neck like a shackle, Violaine began crossing the open ground, making for the electricity plant. An idea was trying to impose itself on her drunken euphoria.

'Set a trap for him . . .' she mumbled.

She was quite sure that he would pursue her until he had taken her cumbersome parcel from her. She could, of course, just put it down there on the ground and make her escape to save her life. But this idea didn't even occur to her: the Melliflore atavism was there to prevent it. She preferred to settle things with her gun.

She kept moving without looking in the direction of the chalet. She tried to walk straight, saying to herself that it was all over if he guessed she was drunk. But the plant over there seemed as far away to her as the Italian border. The open ground began to look as vast as a desert to be crossed. The sudden thought that the intruder might rush out of the house and catch her there in that empty space where she would never have the strength to run helped her make a desperate spurt. She collapsed breathless at the heavy iron door. She pushed herself against it, opened it and heaved it closed again. This effort left her exhausted.

La lombarde was whining in the struts of the shed above her head. Through the methylene blue that had been daubed over the glass during the war, the moonlight almost at its zenith fell straight down on to Maillard's tomb and the red gladioli that decorated it. A hundred metres above the plant, sweeping along the dry canal, *la lombarde* also disappeared into the empty pressure pipeline which ended here under the chambers of the turbine. As it emerged through this opening, it gave a sombre, muted moan of pain.

Violaine froze for a moment when she heard this strange sound. She had the impression that Maillard was calling her to tell her about his hell and put her on her guard against the one awaiting her. She stumbled back from the monstrous steel mass, her eyes bulging out of her head. It was the only moment in her life when repentance tried to reach her through that voice. She strained to see the eyes of the portrait, which must be seeking hers from the shadows cast by the gladioli. But the moonlight was shining too vertically and the picture was dark. It was vaguely possible to make out the head of a man but not his features. She was still sure that he was looking at her in a different way. For a second, just one, a feeling of compassion went through her befuddled senses and almost threw her.

But she really had drunk too much. Her body felt very heavy. And also she was too preoccupied with the parcel, which she was determined to keep for herself come what may. She sensed that footsteps were approaching outside in the wind. She straightened her back.

The object that she had just put down at the foot of the tomb was easy to see in the moonlight. It was gift-wrapped in Christmas paper that gleamed softly, reflecting the various rays of light. The gold ribbon was artistically tied in an ornate bow that sat on top like a big shell. It was a parcel intended to excite envy and fire the imagination.

The trap had been set. Violaine backed away, gun in hand. She slowly turned to face the stairs going up towards the travelling crane. They looked very steep. The absence of a rail made her shiver, but that was where she had to take up her position. She climbed the steep steps on all fours, gripping the vertical iron pipes originally intended to hold the safety chain whenever she could. Her intoxication seemed to be lifting a little, only to be replaced by a pervasive dizziness which made her feel sick. She reached the gangway on her knees, now encrusted with iron filings picked up on the way. Her stockings were in tatters, her shoes scuffed, and the red polish on her nails had been chipped in the course of her struggles.

She crouched down behind the winch drum and tried to aim the gun, but she trembled so violently that the steel hit against the iron, ringing out like a warning.

The tangled cables above and around her hung in spirals among the struts of the transformers, forming odd garlands which sometimes framed gently waving spider webs. Swaying in the draughts from the broken glass panels, the huge green glass insulators on the ends of their rusty brackets sparkled in the moonlight like chandeliers.

Violaine listened intently to the silence as she held up the butt of her hunting rifle, careful not to look down into the twelve-metre drop below. She tried to aim at the package in the shadow of the gladioli. Their red colour, which was still visible, made an ideal target. But the trembling of her body and the uncontrollable hiccups gripping her diaphragm prevented her from concentrating. The barrel of her gun shook as much as she did.

Suddenly she heard the door opening, and he came in. He had been so much in her thoughts through all the days since he had declared himself, and she had imagined him in so many guises, that she expected to be confronted with a gigantic enemy. But the person who had just pushed open the iron door of the power plant – with as much difficulty as she – and appeared like a Chinese shadow embossed against the moonlight was nothing but a ridiculous little man.

He came in slowly. He made a lot of noise. He must have been wearing working boots, for they clattered on the cement floor. He halted in front of the flowers and stood looking at them for a good minute.

Violaine had decided to fire at him when he leaned over to pick up the parcel. He would make the easiest target bending over. Of course the light from the moon would hardly be enough for her to take good aim, but the crimson gladioli would serve as a target. She knew her trembling would badly affect her precision, but she thought that the lead shot would scatter and wound her adversary, then all she would have to do was go down and finish him off at point-blank range.

What on earth was he doing? He was not bending down. He was standing there stiffly in front of the gladioli as if at attention. Violaine couldn't see his face, since his back was to the light, but his whole stance was that of someone deep in thought. No, he was definitely not going to bend down. He began to walk again, over the floor strewn with debris of various kinds. He stopped and thought for a few seconds at the foot of the iron staircase. It seemed to Violaine that he was looking up apprehensively, then slowly, step by step, he began to climb.

The sound of his noisy tread on the metal revived echoes that had not been heard for a long time in the power plant. They were the steps of a workman, a labourer. As though in a dream, Violaine watched his progress in the changing half-light that one moment made him look obese and the next stick thin. She knew she mustn't let him come nearer than a certain distance if she didn't want to miss him, and yet she couldn't make the decision to press the trigger.

Then he stopped and crouched down, mumbling something for more than a minute between two of the vertical posts spaced out along the staircase. At last he stood up and turned around. He went down again. Violaine, stunned, lowered the barrel of her gun. She had just realised that all that time he had been climbing the stairs, she had seen him double. And the stairs themselves had looked extraordinarily high and wide, as at the opera.

He was going down. He came to the bottom of the steps and walked over to the Christmas present. He reached out for it.

Violaine fired. She fired blind, wildly, without consciously aiming. The report caused a hail of broken glass falling from the vertical door frame to echo around the building. Rusty steel fragments showered down around the turbine, the dynamo and the metal of the transformers, slicing through the gladioli on their way down. The man had fallen forwards over the package, which he seemed to be covering with his body.

Violaine rushed down the stairs, brandishing the gun. The shot had cut through her intoxication. She was in a hurry to finish off the intruder. She was no longer afraid. She went down eight steps, unsteady on her high heels and still teetering a little from the lingering alcohol fumes.

At the ninth she caught her foot on something which made her lose her balance. There was still a ten-metre drop beneath her. She screamed as she fell headlong into it. The steel framework of the turbine tomb stopped her fall. The large head of a bolt made a deep indentation in her forehead. Her dislocated body fell between the sheaf of gladioli and the portrait of the dead man with the inscrutable face.

Then the intruder stood up again. It wasn't known, ever – for he hadn't the time on this earth to share his secret with anyone – if he had willingly shown himself or if he was sure that Violaine would miss him because he had come across so many empty bottles in the chalet. As far as one could judge later from the character of the man, it does seem that in this case he took a calculated risk, and it wasn't there that fate awaited him.

Whatever the reason, it was only then that he picked up the parcel, for he had pretended to fall dead not on it but beside it, for fear of damaging what was inside.

He laboriously climbed the stairs to remove the simple killing device which he had already tried out once with such success. He went down again. He gave a sigh as he passed Violaine's body buried under the gladioli.

He went out on to the open space in front of the power plant. He walked to his moped and carefully secured his trophy, which let out a dull vibration with each movement. His backfiring machine started up and moved off. The Delage shone ghostly pale in the moonlight. He gave it a wide berth as he drove past, avoiding any contact.

In the clearing the chalet was lit up as if at the end of a party. Now there was nothing but the eternal sound of the wind, the forests and the stream. A natural peace once more descended on this deserted place that men had disturbed for a brief moment in time.

XIII

IN THE MORNING THE CLEANING WOMEN, WHO WERE QUITE familiar with the monthly ritual, were alarmed to discover the portrait of the dead man with its frame broken against the dresser, two empty bottles of vodka and the silver cup hidden under the cushions.

The fact that all the lights were on did not surprise them. She was in the habit of indulging in this excess of illumination. But usually after these celebrations they found the lady of the house lying on her stomach on the untidy divan with her arms hanging limply and her head buried under two pillows with moon-faced pierrots on them.

One would take her by the feet, the other by the shoulders, and carry her to the bed with much moaning and commiseration for her undying love. They did it in case she might have been able to hear them. As for the rest, their religion had been formed long ago, like that of all the inhabitants of Digne and valleys.

They made a great clamour with their piercing voices up and down the floors of the chalet. They became very anxious when they saw that the washing which had been hung out had not even been taken down. They hurried over to the power-plant-cum-tomb, discovered the body among the gladioli, and rushed straight over on their mopeds to the gendarmes in La Javie.

The familiar note so carefully written on music manuscript paper was found stuck in the victim's bra. (Everyone racked their brains to work out why she kept it in that particular place.) The envelope was not found, but the paper, the words and the handwriting indicated murder. After intensive questioning, the woodsmen spilt the beans. Yes, their employer had indeed come to their camp the previous evening to pick up a package. They described its appearance from the outside, but even when threatened, all they could say was that when it was knocked while being moved, a curious sound came out of it.

After that the whole machinery of the law and the accompanying journalists descended on Barles in force. The inhabitants felt very uneasy.

Captain Combaluzier made himself as inconspicuous as possible in case the police might dig up his past. Just before the thaw, he had shown Françoise the places Fondère had told him about where the special helvella mushrooms grew. He had been expecting his reward, but Françoise was still putting him off. She hadn't really been serious when she made that promise, thinking that Fondère would never reveal his secrets, and now that she had her back to the wall, she baulked at the idea. The very sight of the captain with his scaly skin and his sunken ears like a dead herring revolted her.

She already had enough to do coping with her current commitments. To avoid being noticed by the gendarmes, when she went to see the schoolteacher every Sunday evening she had to take off her ankle bracelet with the little bells. It was her good luck charm and she always felt anxious when she took it off. She also had to go by the ford and the path behind the school. Coming home, she groped her way through the gate in the wall by the dungheap. Furthermore, she put up with all these constraints through habit rather than desire.

Her orgasm was limited to a brief jolt accompanied by a donkey bray. It was over and forgotten in no time, and not repeated. There was no point in her bothering to undress, as she was eager to get back into her own warm bed and her dreams of who knows what else.

She secretly envied that inhabitant of Barles who had created such an interesting life for himself by enlivening it with a few murders. If she had known him, she would have offered herself to him, so that she could hear him describe his adventures. In the mean time, she just had to imagine them. Not that she had much free time to indulge her fantasies. The days were exhausting lately. The café was never empty, Sundays and weekdays alike. Her mother, Grimaude, kept a strict eye on her, and a kick in the behind awaited any slackness on her part.

The large postmistress worried so much about Big Magne that she had lost four kilos. The police had their eye on him, as he had at one time shared Ambroisine's bed and, a little later and very sporadically, Violaine's also.

Prudence and Rose suffered through this invasion of all kinds of suspicious investigators. They could only see each other hastily and briefly, like the most unfortunate heterosexuals.

There was no one or nothing, down to the primary schoolteacher's peaceful game of cards, that was not disturbed at least twice by the unexpected, if cordial, arrival of the gendarmes.

The weather was magnificent around the Bès, the Blayeul and the Montagne de Chine. Barles shone in the sun like a village on a post-office calendar. The river waters ran so clear that on one occasion at least, a furtive fisherman with no line (the season was closed) was noticed one evening in waders, waterproof hat down over his ears, lingering around the ford. But who would be paying any attention to a man fishing?

It was also a beautiful day like that when Captain Combaluzier nearly drowned in the river. Thanks to his navy binoculars and some mentions Fondère had made to him before he died, for the last few days he had taken up Fondère's favourite pastime, and thought he had some sound views on the various murders that spread gloom over the region. He was preoccupied with timidly trying to work out how he could turn them to some profit. Unfortunately, on certain nights there was too much moonlight in the prism of the binoculars trained on a certain object, which revealed their presence to the person being spied upon.

It was two days afterwards that a stone in the ford, which had always been perfectly stable, slipped when the captain trod on it. He was chasing mischievous Françoise, who escaped his clutches by nimbly jumping several stones at a time with all the grace of her unique walk, cleaving the air like the bow of a ship. Because of this particular way of moving, with one shoulder leading the rest of her body, she had one buttock much more rounded than the other, a charming imperfection the captain was mad about.

Was it carelessness? Was it clumsiness? Françoise in her daisy-print dress was already on the other bank and disappearing around the bend in the path, her laughter ringing in the afternoon air. The captain was left there alone. His head had just missed a big dihedron of sharp rock sticking out of the foam. There he was, floundering in eighty centimetres of raging water, struggling against the current, having all the trouble in the world getting a foothold again some fifty metres downstream from the ford. The absurdity of his situation then struck him in all its horror: he, Combaluzier, who had extricated himself so many times from the clutches of the sea, which was intent on drowning him, in danger of ending here deep in the mountains, drowned in eighty centimetres of water, freezing I'll grant you, but fresh water! It was enough to make fate laugh. And in fact, Combaluzier laughed the whole way from the river bed of the Bès to his Anglo-Norman house, a harsh, convulsive laugh interrupted by the incessant chattering of his false teeth, emphasising the shivers running through his body.

No! Crime really didn't pay in these valleys: poor Fondère was the dead example of that. He should be content with all his little sources of income, so dearly earned, and not take on those who were cleverer than he. Not many people were capable of patiently prising a stone loose from the ford, knowing that at this time of the year there was only one person who used it to get across to the thickets on the other side. The captain had been warned, and henceforth he left his navy binoculars hanging on their nail.

As his mother used to say on the subject of minding one's own business, 'If you don't get yourself into anything, you don't have to get yourself out of anything.' That would be his guiding light from now on.

Thanks to which he died peacefully in Barles many years later, warm and dry in his bed where, unfortunately, he was never able to entice Françoise.

That autumn Pencenat's tomb received more visits than a saint's. People also took notice of Fondère's, which poor wretched Pencenat had dug for his own use. No one, however, noticed the horizontal slot in the gate through which the whole thing had been set in motion, and since Pencenat was dead, its secret was now known to only one person in the world.

But even the most shocked reactions die down quickly in these deep valleys where eternal mystery is inherent in the geology and geography of the place, as well as in the physical appearance, the character and the habitual silence of the cautious inhabitants. A fortnight of unsettled, warning weather saw the last dead leaves drop to the ground. The schoolchildren began to appear wearing hats, and when the blanket of low cloud parted one fine evening, there was the Estrop looking like a ghost with three heads. The summit of the Blayeul itself had a little snow slashed in places by squalls of wind. Nothing is more conducive to calming passions than the warning shots of winter. Added to that, as far as the visitors had been able to ascertain, there was nothing to be gained or discovered in Barles.

Soon only the two hundred and twenty inhabitants were left. The police still kept an eye on them, of course, but it was sporadic and half-hearted. The columns of smoke from the chimneys either drifted towards each other and entwined or avoided each other and went in opposite directions. For there were affinities and hostilities between chimneys which came less from the way the wind was blowing than from the determination of the inhabitants, who wanted either unity or confrontation. In the fading light of the short evenings, people would follow the smoke rising from the chimneys in swirls that were arrogantly mistrustful or lasciviously amorous.

You would see slow-moving figures in vegetable gardens stuffing stalks of celery and chard into tubes of old newspapers; hollowing out trenches at the back of sheds for carrot and leek seedlings; putting up straw-filled sacks to block out the small windows where the potatoes were stored. One eye was always trained on the Montagne de Chine, where winter would strike first, but this was done furtively to avoid being called romantic.

From the *charcuterie* came the pervasive aroma of sausages wrapped in caul fat, which the 'love butcher' was smoking, his eyes watering from the smouldering dead leaves which he prevented from catching fire by beating them with a spade. His work had been very much held up by all the goings-on in the village, and so he was working overtime.

People who are thus occupied in preparing for the special occasions of winter do not tend to be particularly afraid or disturbed because, according to stories going around, there might be a murderer in their midst. The story itself was fascinating. People talked about it at the evening meal. But they refrained from making any predictions, at least at the beginning. For indeed the memory of traps laid for people in the gorges in the old days, in which a number of their ancestors were more than likely involved, made it impossible to accuse anyone. No one was qualified.

All the more so because the Melliflore descendants who were so much talked about were something like a local version of the family of the Atrides.* For generations people had been used to seeing misfortune strike them, just to cleanse them of their sins; and those who had no more to reproach themselves with than most thought philosophically that while it happened to the Melliflores, it wouldn't happen to them. This explains why, apart from Grimaude, who had an old grudge against fate, nobody even thought of locking a door. In Barles, people had trusted in the Almighty for as long as anyone could remember.

Oh, of course . . . Lately some had had their sleep interrupted by the discreet backfiring of a moped going past in the night.

The thought might have come to them that it was always heard on one of the nights when those bad acts had been committed against the same Melliflore descendants. They could also have calculated the large

---

* In Greek mythology, the Atrides were the descendants of Atreus, king of Mycenae, notably Agamemnon and Menelaus.

number of people who used that kind of transport. A rapid review of the character of each, given his heredity – which was easy because everyone knew each other – allowed the search to be quickly narrowed down to two or three suspects, and then to one – unfortunately never the same. It depended on which family you belonged to. The case was discussed, but only silently in hearts and minds, for everyone now had all the details to put the gendarmes on the right track.

And yet nothing was said. Without prior agreement of any kind being necessary. Talking would bring a whole lot of unpleasantness that keeping quiet would certainly avoid. All those throughout the world who have, at some time, said something at the wrong moment will easily understand this. People also kept silent with impunity as they knew where the murders had been committed: on the outskirts of Digne and down in Chavailles, late at night. In those calm and peaceful places, no living soul could or should have met another.

When things happen without witnesses, and the perpetrator is careful – and there was every reason in the world to think he was – crime does pay. Of course that's a figure of speech, for sometimes you have to look at the results of the events after many years. The locals were in a good position to know that fate is rarely as blind as justice. All that goes to show that by saying nothing, they risked nothing. And yet it wasn't for all those very good reasons that they stayed silent.

They said nothing because although it may not have been so important to know *who*, it was, on the other hand, terribly important to work out *why*. They could let their imaginations take off like fireworks. Everything led them to believe, and glaring examples had shown them, that if the guilty person was arrested, the whole wonderful structure of their theories would be ruined.

In the heavy hands of the law, the truth of the matter was likely to disappear, dissolve, vanish; it would be reduced to shreds, dissected by both prosecution and defence, until all that was left was one of those banal, trivial, prosaic motives which, it seems, make human nature act; in short, a motive that would disillusion the thirst for the supernatural.

The villagers believed that a murder committed by one of them could only be done for a really extraordinary reason, a desperate situation, dark as the curtains of rock in the gorges, and worthy of being embroidered on Ariosto's tapestries.

They said nothing. May God never forgive them, for there would not have been another murder to mourn in the depths of the valleys if they had spoken.

When a very bitter and disillusioned Judge Chabrand went to Popocatepetl, he found no light behind the large French windows, where Laviolette usually took his ease.

He had to go up the nearby stone steps, call very loudly, with no result, then go into the large entrance hall that recalled so many bad memories. A ray of light was coming from one room. He walked over to it and found a cold, unwelcoming kitchen, with a high ceiling. It was more than five metres long and only three wide.

A bent old woman was muttering as she worked away at opening several tins. Fourteen cats with their tails in the air were waiting more or less patiently at her feet for their share.

The judge introduced himself without a greeting, and in a brusque voice asked for Laviolette. But when he asked her how it was that she didn't know where her employer was, as his car was in the drive, Chabassut, who was sour by nature, replied with as much ill-temper as he.

'How would I know? I don't live in his pocket. Don't you know by now that he's eccentric? You've been seeing each other regularly for long enough. Get the gendarmes to look for him if it's as urgent as that.'

The judge was already at the end of the drive, his carrick coat flapping in the night wind. He was alone, downcast, and with a miserable feeling of being abandoned by God, to the extent that his imagination could conceive of such a thing.

Unrest was brewing among the official bodies at the law courts: the public prosecutor and his deputy needed a culprit. Certain people were going about spreading panic. If this slaughter continued the way it was going, there wouldn't be a single presentable woman left. And no one could give a reasonable guarantee that it would stop at the Melliflore family. The tea rooms and dances were already less frequented. Lawyers found that certain well-advanced divorce proceedings unexpectedly fell through, as freedom suddenly appeared quite daunting and unappealing to women who, once separated, would be on their own.

Social life in general was affected by it: 'No, no! You're not going to the Rotary meeting tonight. If you do, I'll go and see young Carbonnier. He's been hanging around me for three weeks now, and he'll be delighted. You don't imagine that I'd stay here alone in this great empty house until midnight, do you?'

The trouble with this whole story was that the leading citizens in particular were worried, especially those who were lucky enough to live in one of those huge family mansions with spacious attics, where so many suspect nooks and crannies could be hiding anything, and so many secrets lay undisturbed.

'And everyone knows,' Judge Chabrand said to himself wryly, wrapping himself in his carrick coat, 'that some of them are the kind of people whose demanding telephone calls to any official body have the most influence.'

He moved through the grounds at Popocatepetl like one of Verlaine's shades, but there was no ghost at his side to make him remember that there had been a time in the past when hope still existed.

'They can sort it out for themselves!' Laviolette thought, accompanying his reflections with a careless wave of the arm as if he was throwing salt over his shoulder. 'Anyway, I don't really know any more about it than they do.'

This plural 'they' included Judge Chabrand, whose sarcastic comments he preferred to avoid, as well as the chief at the gendarmerie, whom he had bumped into the other day. The chief had replied to his greeting with a simple salute, whereas he usually shook him warmly by the hand. There was no one, down to the present superintendent, who, coming across him at the corner of a street, hadn't deliberately turned his back on him and slapped himself on the forehead as if he had forgotten something that obliged him to immediately turn back on his tracks.

'They can get out of the bloody mess on their own!' Laviolette thought more bluntly. 'You'd think they were a bunch of grocers faced with a rival competitor. Anyway, if you don't get into anything, you don't have to get out of anything.'

Well then? Why had he scrapped his old apple-green Vedette? Why had he betrayed her by hiring this Swedish tank that swayed like a cargo ship in a heavy swell if he only intended going for a drive to get some fresh air? Why had he zoomed off – not like him at all – and on to the Hautes-Alpes road?

The truth was that in the course of these murders, an indefinable feeling of unease had come over him; a certain profile of the murderer was taking shape in his mind. He felt intuitively that a bizarre similarity of character identified him with this unknown person, and the basic reason, he believed, why he had ignominiously dropped Judge Chabrand was because he was beginning to feel oddly drawn towards this murderer.

At first he said to himself, 'He's a poor soul like me.'

'A poor soul! Don't make me laugh! A poor soul who coldly does in three poor women and two other poor souls. He's hardly such a poor thing as all that!'

'That's not what I said. Listen to what I'm saying. I'm trying to make you understand that you have to search among poor souls.'

'They're all poor in Barles.'

'To start with, I didn't promise you that he was in Barles. Next, I'm not playing dumb to find out something. It's not that kind of poor I mean.'

'No, of course not. You're talking about the poor in spirit. You're talking about an emotional wasteland. You're talking about the determining role of frustrating antecedents. I can see what you're trying to do. You want me to get landed with a psychological analysis of all the people involved. You know I'm not the right person for that.'

'I know that you won't listen! That you're so sarcastic about psychological analysis simply because you're lazy!'

'In any case, I'm taking no further interest in that story. If you don't get into anything, you don't have to get out of anything!'

'Ah, yes. Well then, what the hell are you doing here?'

Laviolette was suddenly aware of the distance and direction he had travelled almost automatically since he left. His internal conversation had absorbed him so much that he thought he had chosen any old route. It was only at that precise moment that his eyes registered the landscape. He had just turned on his indicator to signal a right-hand turn. In a flash, the Pelvoux range on his left had been superseded by a copse of beech trees. The scaly grey walls of the Mont-Dauphin fort gleamed faintly under a sickly sun. Further down, the clear waters of the Guil disappeared into the already dirty waters of the Durance.

The contour of the road immediately straightened up again. Everything here was waiting for the imminent arrival of winter, which had not yet made its harsh presence felt. Vast ossuaries of larches stripped of their needles spread over the cliff sides. The slopes bristled with rotting tree trunks sticking out of huge open graves dug out by ancient storms. Sometimes an avalanche had pushed them all into a heap at the end of a clearing. As far as the eye could see, there was scarcely a cheerful prospect along these ravines.

Laviolette went through the last village of any substance, all its sun-loving balconies soaking up the warmth. But it was prepared for winter. There were overflowing stacks of newly cut wood under porches and stairs. Any that were only half full had men busily chopping and sawing rhythmically in front of them.

There were still three big sweeping turns that took him up more than two hundred metres. Going round a bend, he saw Le Pelvoux in front of him for the last time, then he was back in the shadows. The darkest road in France was trying to thread its way through the Le Queyras coomb. 'Trying to' were the words that came to mind when you entered it. You always felt that nothing was certain after the next turn, the next little bridge, the next narrow pass. Laviolette had to sound his horn all the time. Tunnel exits spat down huge drops of water which burst against his windscreen.

It was the land of shadows, the land of weeping, oozing moisture, and at each turn of that difficult road, Laviolette felt he would come across the ghost of the unknown young woman, sent away from the place where she was born by her uncle more than a hundred years ago.

She was no doubt a strong girl, probably blonde, standing on big solid feet in men's boots, because that was what she needed for walking. Was she pregnant enough for it to show already? Probably, according to Dr Pardigon's story. Anyhow, Laviolette imagined her with head held high. Proud? Perhaps not. But humbly neat and clean, wearing a head-scarf, with her bundle over her shoulder on the end of a stick. Anyhow, she was keenly aware of the mean treatment she had just received, and calling on the angels for justice.

'She was pregnant with a Melliflore from Barles,' Laviolette said to himself. 'In 1860 or 1861 . . . What was happening in the world in those years? Nothing as usual. The French were making money. The poor were silent. There was no one in that coomb to take that girl's hand and tell her that God existed in spite of everything.'

The fact that this solid man with the prominent eyes found himself driving though that countryside was also one of those strange things one impatiently tries to get out of one's mind to avoid compromising with the mystery of the world. All because of the girl who died long ago, but who was there at every turn, young, open-faced, striking sparks from the cobblestones with her hobnailed boots.

Laviolette stopped at a parking bay in the darkest stretch of the coomb to listen to the voice of the Guil. Not one vehicle passed while he was rolling a cigarette. He was alone with the current flowing five hundred metres below, wondering what he was doing there. He was even tempted to go back, but the defenceless girl whose ghost was still there on that road urged him on in spite of himself. A determination to find out a truth that doesn't concern you is a bad fault to have. Laviolette had it to the nth degree. The story told by old Dr Pardigon, who died too soon, guided him on this road into the past. There was no doubt that the mystery taking place today in Digne had its origin there, at the birthplace of that quiet girl.

'She was pregnant with a Melliflore,' he thought. 'And even if he was born in state care, and even if he and his descendants – if he had any – never bore that name, he was nevertheless a Melliflore, with all that implies . . .'

'That's irrelevant to the case you're working on.'

'How would you know what's relevant and what's not? Weren't you taught at school that you have to check all hypotheses, even the strangest? I don't necessarily subscribe to these wild suppositions, but I'm checking them out. That's what I'm doing. I have every right to do that, don't I?'

He came out into the Abriès basin towards midday. The flat grasslands were empty. The cattle had gone back to their barns. The open air was so vast that the Guil hidden in the undulations could no longer be heard. The mountains all around glistened with free-flowing but silent water, being so far away. They offered the black depths of their snow-hungry scree to the sun, but it was not strong enough to throw light on them.

At the bottom of the ring of mountains, under the welcome protection of the wing of a church, stood the houses of Abriès. A channelled water-course separated them as they jostled each other, each one trying to catch more sun than its neighbours.

Over on the mountainside, bare except for flat grass, a chapel with dazzling whitewashed walls stood beneath bare poplars. On the dry road which dominated it, a few crooked wayside chapels sat on the slopes basking in the sun. They were unsteady on their bases and from a distance looked like kennels.

There was a swarthy man working in front of all that whiteness. He had made several small piles of burning leaves, which sent their smoke rising gently straight up into the air. He watched over them all, leaning on what appeared to be a rake.

Laviolette parked his car in a Highways Department area. There was a nip in the air although it was midday. He thought that a little air from a fire wouldn't go amiss, and besides, the chapel and the dark man seemed interesting. He walked across country to the path, which he climbed, puffing slightly as he went.

The fires were unattended. The man had disappeared. He could be heard through the wide-open door of the church, where he was moving furniture. Laviolette walked into the dim light inside. The man was struggling with a worm-eaten pew that he was trying to put on top of another, so that he could sweep underneath it.

'Can I give you a hand?' Laviolette asked.

'Why of course!' the man replied. 'And if you have a spare moment, you can even help me with the others.'

'I have as many moments as it needs,' Laviolette said, taking hold of the other end of the pew.

'That's fine,' said the man.

He was wearing blue drill pants and a hand-knitted jumper with a metal crucifix pinned to it. He was young, sturdy. He had strong shoulders and a round head.

'In the old days,' he said, breathing hard, 'there were excessively devout women who were criticised because their faith was too ostentatious and seemed suspect. But at seven in the morning on the dot they were there, with a brush and a bucket of cold water, floor cloth in hand, ready to make the house of the Lord presentable.'

He grabbed a broom and energetically began to sweep the flagstones now exposed.

'Now,' he added, 'all the zealots of France and Navarre have gone to clean in Heaven. The only faithful left are fervent, earnest women, but they've become as idle as hermits.'

He had already almost reached the door. He gathered the rubbish, which he went to throw on the fire. Laviolette did not follow him, staying to look at the inside of the church. In the centre, like a kind of grotto, there was scarcely enough room for thirty parishioners. The interior church structure was like the hull of an upturned boat; as if he had walked into an upside-down Noah's ark. It had tenons and mortises roughly cut with an axe, and embedded geometric roses, the emblem of the high valleys. The enormous black beams seemed to have been brought from a fire that did not want them. That was what was important, not space for the faithful: these tree trunks were rough-hewn five hundred years ago and the clumsy cuts could still be seen. They had been soaked with so much accumulated sweat that it was impossible for God not to heed those in their great need who had poured it out.

A ray of sunlight pouring through the plain round window played on this framework, slanting across the end of a beam resting on a black granite corbel. A word appeared, carved into the deeply scarred, cracked wood: *Give*, Laviolette read.

The priest arrived back with his shovel and broom.

'But,' he was saying, 'we have to do some tidying up. This chapel is used only once a year, a few days before Christmas, to ask Jesus to turn his attention to our need for snow, because no snow, no ski season!'

'Of course . . .' Laviolette said. 'Are you the Abriès parish priest?'

'Yes, and of a few other places with similar needs.'

'In any event, you have a wonderful chapel here. A good place for solitary prayer.

'If you feel like it . . .'

Laviolette thought of introducing himself, but it seemed to him that the priest, who was stoking one of the fires, couldn't care less about knowing his name.

'To him,' he said to himself, 'I'm just one wandering soul among so many others.'

'Next spring,' the priest said, 'all around here will be a symphony of gold. When winter is over, everything you see now that is bare will become a huge field of primroses and daffodils. They even grow between the roofing tiles. You should come and see it!'

He moved off once again in the direction of the pews to continue cleaning. Laviolette followed him, talking as he went.

'Tell me . . . I see that you have an inscription engraved on the beams, but I can only read the first word . . .'

'An inscription?'

The priest seemed surprised at this remark, as he hadn't looked at the old carved letters for a long time.

'Oh yes,' he said. 'It goes all around the nave on the beams. It's hard to see because there's not much light. Besides, it's interrupted after every group of three words by a symbolic scene of the crucifixion.'

'What does it say?'

'*Give good measure, for the measure you give will be the measure you get.*'

As he recited these words from the Gospel, the priest had unconsciously adopted a preacher's intonation, and the echo of his voice hung for a moment high up in the vault.

Laviolette sank down heavily in one of the pews.

'It's a fine inscription,' he said, hardly thinking.

'A fine inscription and a fine eternal truth. You'll find the same one in the village church. It must have taken a lot of time and patience. Every letter was made in the local forge – I still have them in the sacristy – about three hundred years ago. Then they were heated red-hot and pressed into the larch wood one by one, just as criminals used to be branded on the shoulder.'

'A good image . . .' Laviolette said.

'That's because . . . the inhabitants of this region are very particular where justice is concerned.'

Laviolette nodded his head and murmured, 'I know . . .'

Once again he could see the ghostly presence of the pregnant girl who had passed through these valleys; the girl an implacable uncle had banished from the region scarcely a hundred years ago.

'I'd like you to show me the presbytery. Oh, not the inside, of course . . . No. Only from outside: the doors . . . the windows . . . The way it faces the last street, where the road leads out towards the south . . .'

'Ah, no,' the priest said. 'You're referring to the old one. It was so rundown it collapsed sometime in the 1920s. They rebuilt it nearer the church, where it got more sunlight . . .'

He thought for a moment as he looked at Laviolette.

'It's strange that you should ask me that,' he said slowly, 'because . . .

last summer a man came here and made the same request, in almost the same words.'

'What did he look like?'

The priest opened his arms wide, signifying that he didn't know.

'How could I remember? So many people come here. It was in the church, where a volunteer was showing people around. I was there to see that nothing was taken. He came over to me in the half-light and said . . . Well, he said the same thing as you . . .'

'It must have been my brother,' Laviolette said. 'We're both retracing memories. He wouldn't look like this, by any chance?'

Like a magician drawing a rabbit out of a hat, he whipped out of his wallet a postcard-sized copy of the portrait in the summerhouse.

The priest took the card and gazed at it for some time. He shook his head and gave it back to Laviolette.

'How could I tell? Inside the church . . . a group of something like twelve people. All I can tell you is that he looked less old-fashioned than your photo. Firstly, as far as I can recall, he was wearing glasses. And he had a thick handlebar moustache, while your person is clean-shaven. But . . . now that I come to think of it, and since you've made me look back . . . I had a strange impression . . . that the moustache was false.'

'The glasses too, you can be sure of that . . .' Laviolette sighed. 'But those bumps there. Those bumps, and the hollows on his forehead and head, and the ears that stick out? It's fairly characteristic, wouldn't you say?'

He shoved another photo under the priest's nose, as if he were insisting on selling it to him. But the young man shook his head.

'No! No! How could I tell? A church, the dim light. And so many people . . . Besides, by the time I saw him out in the sunlight, he had put his hat on again.'

'What build was he?'

'Neither tall nor short enough for it to be noted.'

'Did he . . . notice the inscription?'

'Everyone notices it, and some even whisper it. Why not your *brother*?'

He gave Laviolette a piercing look.

'But,' he said, 'come to think of it, what are you looking for? I don't believe this story about a brother. I've never seen a single man, not one, do you understand me, who goes round with a photo of his brother in his wallet, unless he was killed in the war.'

Laviolette gave another sigh.

'You're right,' he replied, 'not to believe . . . It's a much grimmer story than a brother who died in the war.'

'My poor man, what are you carrying round in that head of yours? This might be the right time to tell me about it.'

Laviolette put a finger to his lips, and began backing away.

'I'll come back in the spring,' he said, 'when the primroses are growing on the roof tiles. For my own pleasure. I'll tell you everything then. Well . . . I'll tell you . . . I'll tell you if I know . . .'

He turned away from the priest with a little farewell wave of his hand. He walked over to his car and started the engine. Before reaching the road, he looked back at the chapel in his rear-view mirror. The priest had not moved. Leaning on his broom, he watched Laviolette leave.

He got back to Popocatepetl at one o'clock in the morning, with his long scarf trailing on the ground. He parked his Swedish car under a cedar. As he closed the car door, he had the feeling that someone was looking at him. He turned round. It was the headlights of his apple-green Vedette. They were not switched on, but they still seemed to be reproaching him like a wife who catches her old husband coming home after visiting his mistress.

'Come on!' he muttered, stroking its hood as he passed. 'Don't carry on like that! We're both old now. We have to accept it . . .'

He went in through the door that was always ajar, intending to go straight to his den. But that was reckoning without the cats. They came running from all directions: down the main staircase, up from the cellar, in behind him from the garden, some of them cajoling, others resentful. They surrounded him, pushed him, dragged him, forming a chain leading straight to the kitchen, all of them meowing desperately.

They were telling him that once again Chabassut had forgotten to feed them, that they had been starving since the night before last, and that they were at death's door. It was a trick that never failed to get the right result from Laviolette. Although Chabassut wrote in large letters on the notepad: *The cats were fed as usual at their normal mealtime*, Laviolette would turn the notepad to the wall and begin attacking tins from the pantry with the opener. Which he did once again on that particular night.

At last he was able to collapse in front of his cold hearth and pour himself something strong. As usual Chabassut had placed his mail on the low table in front of his armchair. Laviolette flicked a lazy finger through it. He never expected anything that would have him eagerly ripping the envelopes open. Glowing advertisements – *Open this now. You're a winner* – could wait until tomorrow to be thrown on the fire without even being read. As for the rest . . . Laviolette cast a vague glance at two periodicals in wrappers, which he lifted up from the table. They were hiding a large cardboard envelope with this simple company name at the top: *Oberthur Rennes*. Laviolette grabbed it and more ripped it apart than opened it. A pile of photos fell out on to the carpet, with a short letter which said:

Dear Sir,

In reply to your detailed request, which entailed considerable research through our press proofs and archives, we are pleased to send you the photos of the subjects on the post-office calendars printed here for the year 1912.

We are naturally unable to give you the originals, but we hope that these faithful colour reproductions in the same size and format, for which you will find the bill enclosed, will allow you to complete your enquiries.

A prompt settlement of your account would be appreciated.

Yours faithfully, etc.

Laviolette could hardly wait to gather up the large photos scattered on the floor. One of them immediately caught his eye. He got up and literally ran to the dreadful mess he had the nerve to call his desk. He searched about for a long time, muttering, complaining, groaning. At last he pulled out the illegible calendar he had taken from the stove pipe in the ruins of the Melliflore farm. He brought it over to the lamp. Good Lord! So that's what it was! The perfect colour photo showed him the real subject of the almost indecipherable piece of cardboard. He couldn't stop gazing at it; he was in raptures.

He still did not know the identity of the man who had murdered the three Melliflore women inheritors, but on the other hand he now knew *why* they had been killed. Well . . . he thought he knew.

XIV

LAVIOLETTE HAD WALKED ALL AROUND DIGNE IN A FESTIVE MOOD.
He had been bumped into by pretty women who couldn't see anyone
because their arms were laden with presents. He had chosen complicated games in shop windows for imaginary nephews. He had admired
the fir trees lit up on the esplanade. He had sat in the rotunda listening
to the wind, which replaced the now nonexistent band.

He had gone home at peace with himself to distribute Christmas
presents among the fourteen cats and five chickens. This was done
without Chabassut's knowledge, as she would most certainly have
lectured him about the starving people in six continents and his out-
rageous selfishness, of which, by the way, he was well aware.

The fire was flaming in the hearth. A lively fire with dancing blue
flames. A fire of choice wood, that gives the best colours as they burn.

Laviolette would sacrifice a dozen logs when he needed to be happy.
He was about to open the volume of Proust, *Le côté de Guermantes*,
where he had left off the previous evening. A bottle of Chambertin,
which had been breathing for two hours, was there waiting to be slowly
savoured in the huge crystal glass sitting on the low table.

Someone knocked on the glass pane. It was Judge Chabrand, who
entered without greeting him.

'I came looking for you last week,' he said severely, 'but you weren't here.'

'That would be right. I was in Abriès and elsewhere.'

'Really . . . You take very little interest in what happens to me.'

'Tell me then. What on earth is happening to you?'

'I'm caught in a stranglehold between the public prosecutors and the councillors who want heads to roll. You can't imagine the fuss that all these murders have caused! Of course, you couldn't care less. You're on holiday. In Abriès. Meanwhile, all this is killing me.'

'But you look marvellous.'

Under his legendary carrick coat, the judge's long, thin frame was clothed in a charcoal-grey suit complemented by a crimson bow tie. In place of a reply, he took a card from his pocket and held it out to Laviolette. The words were clumsily typed on an old machine. It stated:

Pénélope des Ormes
Invites you to a night of dancing she is organising for her 20th birthday on 24 December. Cold supper; no alcohol. Donation for expenses 20 francs.

Chateau de Malefiance
Esclangon

Laviolette let out a long whistle.

'The Chateau de Malefiance!' he said.

'Yes. Do you remember? That old man who told you so many tales from the nineteenth century . . . He mentioned the fourth Melliflore inheritor; at least that's what you reported to me. Well, there you are, it's her, Pénélope des Ormes! Of course no one uses that name. She's called Isabelle,[*] because of her cream-coloured underwear – when she wears any, if you get my drift.'

---

[*]The word 'isabelle' in French can be an adjective meaning cream or off-white. It comes from a breed of Arabian horses that Queen Isabella of Castille loved, horses that were more beige than white – hence the colour.

Chabrand had sat down, but now he stood up again and began to walk up and down the big room, gesticulating as he talked.

'We protect her – as much as we can, since she throws empty tin cans at gendarmes. Just think: she's the last surviving member of the family. Inheritances from her aunts and cousins will rain down on her as a house of cards falls on the last one standing.'

'My word!' Laviolette exclaimed.

'Oh yes, I know. It's not my role, but I have an intuition.'

'You?'

'Yes, me! You've lectured me for long enough about yours. Now it's my turn.'

He placed his hand on his chest.

'The wind has risen. Everything has been quiet for several weeks, since Violaine Maillard was murdered. And tonight Pénélope, the last survivor, is giving a dance. What better opportunity could there be than a dance to quietly bump someone off, something our killer does so well?'

'And a dance at Maleffiance!' Laviolette pointed out. 'That's not an intuition, it's reasoning. But . . . how the devil did you come by that invitation?'

Chabrand looked away, stopped waving his arms about and seemed suddenly contrite.

'I . . .' he began. 'I met this Pénélope . . . in . . . in a nightclub . . .'

He had trouble getting the word out. He slipped his index finger between his neck and the collar of his shirt, he was so embarrassed to admit something he considered irresponsible to Laviolette.

'Oh, it was only once,' he went on. 'Because . . . occasionally . . . well, I go dancing.'

'You go dancing?'

'Yes, I do. I go dancing. What's surprising about that at my age?'

'Oh, nothing. Heaven forbid! Well then, have a good dance,' he added, extending his hand.

Chabrand shook his head.

'I should have been pleased if you'd accompany me,' he said. 'Because

'. . . this invitation can only mean one of two things: it's either a challenge, or an appeal for help.'

'Me? But I don't go dancing.'

'If you pay your twenty francs, I think you'll be accepted whether you do or not.'

He sat down opposite Laviolette and looked him in the face, through his glasses.

'You're not telling me everything,' he said accusingly. 'You've never told me everything. Today even less than before, since you're no longer obliged to. You're ducking out of it. You look as though you've lost interest in these dead women. And do you want to know what I really think? You feel more and more drawn to the murderer. You excuse him, you understand him. One only has to see the haughty way your cats take advantage of you to realise how far you'll extend the limits of charity.'

Laviolette shook his head.

'That's not quite true,' he said. 'First of all, I don't know him.'

'Well, let me be still more precise. You don't know him, agreed. But you've built up a picture of him.'

He pointed an accusing finger at Laviolette's chest.

'You've filled his heart and mind with the overflow from your own. In short, he's as like you as a brother. That's why you've been lying low for the last ten days.'

They stared intently at each other for a few seconds.

'So what?' Laviolette retorted. 'Do you expect me to fall on my knees and beg your forgiveness?'

'I expect you to get involved!'

To the left of the big door with the glass panels stood a café coat rack with several hooks. Chabrand went over to it and took down Laviolette's hat, overcoat and long muffler. He came back and held open the coat. Laviolette got up with a sigh and gave the Chambertin and the book with its faded illustration a look of resignation and regret.

'It'll be your fault if I catch my death of cold,' he said.

'The weather is so mild you'd think it was spring,' Chabrand assured him. 'And there's a delightful breeze, just the kind you like.'

It was true. The temperature outside was like the month of April, and the wind Chabrand had praised was a sea breeze that brought rain. As soon as Laviolette put his nose outside, he stopped short.

'You call that a delightful breeze? Wait a moment while I get my brolly.'

He dashed back into his den and came out again with a huge blue umbrella under his arm.

'We'll look ridiculous with that!' muttered Chabrand.

He gave his bow tie a pat. That vulgar umbrella might serve the purpose for some shepherd way up in the mountains, but it seemed to him to clash with his elegant attire.

'It's better to be ridiculous than soaked to the skin. Look what's coming. Just look at the sky!'

'I can't see a thing.'

'Exactly . . . No matter what the weather, you can still normally see the tops of the trees. Today, not a thing! So, if you don't mind, I'll take my brolly.'

It was indeed a warning sky. Way over on the southern horizon, in the eye of the evil triangle formed by Barrême, Saint-André and Castellane, a thunderbolt close to the trees would sometimes burst out into the dark night.

Laviolette automatically went towards his old apple-green Vedette. Chabrand caught his arm.

'No, no!' he said. 'Given your weather forecast, if you don't mind we'll take mine. It'll be safer.'

Laviolette regretfully complied. Nevertheless, he seemed to hear a sneer behind him coming from his own car. He turned round. No doubt it must have come from some cat contemplating under the chassis. A short while later, in the thick of the events which made that night unforgettable, Laviolette would remember that sneer apparently coming from the rejected car's snout.

'Your 1936 model Citroën Traction Avant isn't exactly young either,' he sighed, flopping into the sagging seat.

'It's a collector's item,' Chabrand explained proudly. 'It was used on

Gestapo business and straight afterwards by the patriots in their exploits.'

'That's what I said. It's not exactly young.'

'It doesn't like the damp much, I'll give you that, but once I've got her going, I can do what I like with her.'

He fiddled with the starter and the choke, and then coaxed the accelerator pedal for a good minute. Laviolette hoped that it wouldn't start and that they would be forced to take his car. But the engine suddenly came to life in a cloud of petrol fumes.

They drove past houses where the windows were lit up with candelabras and Christmas trees. People dressed to the nines bustled in the street, hopping from one party to the next.

Chabrand gave an inward sigh. The pockets of his suit jacket held five or six invitations to parties where there would be more women than men: divorcees on the make and widows from car accidents. He preferred to attribute the impetus for this evening to the fact that the Melliflore mystery appealed to his imagination, and above all to the sadistic need to drive Laviolette into a corner. He suspected him of trying to bury the case rather than helping him to clear it up, and to be in tacit complicity with the presumed killer.

'That vixen Isabelle,' he muttered, 'she's playing games; now she will, now she won't. She summons her lovers by telephone in the middle of the night, and when they arrive full of hope, she asks them what the hell they're doing there. She's painted hazy spirals that go from royal purple through rose pink to heraldic green. I think she's smoking grass . . .'

The car had left Digne. They had passed the Bailey bridge over the Bléone. All that could be seen in the pencil of light from the headlamps was the road ahead and the red glow of a few smelly fires from a rubbish dump. Soon they were alone with the Bès, which kept its distance in the middle of a bed that was too wide for it.

'Her lovers!' Chabrand said scornfully. 'Young tramps who also smoke grass. That must make them half impotent, which also explains why she's half mad.'

'You do at least have a torch in this rattletrap, don't you?' Laviolette asked out of the blue.

'Of course I do.'

'Good. So do I.'

'You're very anxious. Does the rain frighten you?'

Laviolette shook his head slowly.

'You can laugh,' he said. 'I can't even make out the tops of the mountains on the right. I've just seen an aspen in front of me flapping about in a very strange way. As if it wanted to escape from the earth. And if you could stop for a moment, you'd hear a noise like a hunting horn echoing in the valley. It's the sea wind. If my senses serve me right, we're in for a spectacular show: a storm on the twenty-fourth of December.'

'How did you acquire so many of these useless bits of knowledge?'

'My mother came from here. And as for the usefulness of my knowledge, wait until tomorrow before you make fun of it.'

The headlights suddenly lit up a signpost on a lopsided mound indicating Esclangon. But there was nothing behind the name. On the washed-out banks of the ragged stream stood a few straggling dilapidated houses. They were ugly: badly finished, without plaster, and damaged. Old mechanical shovels, half-tracks bought from army surplus, bulldozers from the war in the Pacific lay at odd angles rusting away, stuck there for ever. They were already submerged up to the tracks in piled-up alluvium. In a hundred years they would no longer be visible. In a thousand year the archaeologists would find nothing but porous rusty dross, which would be difficult to explain. The earth and its waterways are greedy for civilisations to swallow up and digest.

Was that the whole of Esclangon: relics of failure that cost too much to remove? But no, there was a path. It was definitely not a road, more a kind of track, barely half metalled, leading straight between two enormous slopes of scree, and looking as if it might peter out at any moment. Chabrand drove his old rattletrap on to it without hesitation and at a fair speed.

'Well done!' exclaimed Laviolette. 'You seem to know the place well.'

'Yes . . .' Chabrand replied. 'I've been here already, not that it did me any good . . . Once!' he added. 'No more. But that was more than enough.'

'At two in the morning, no doubt? And probably summoned by telephone?'

'Probably,' Chabrand admitted. 'And, as I explained to you, I went away empty-handed . . .'

Despite saying that he had been there before, he nearly missed a track on the right with deep ruts worn in the rocky ground. The chassis of the car hit hard against a nodule of limestone. Chabrand had to resign himself to going into a lower gear and driving slowly.

They passed a post with a makeshift letterbox; above it was nailed a sign made out of a rough plank of wood from a packing case. It said *Mâlefiance*. Showing his ignorance, the writer had adorned the *a* with a circumflex accent.

In daylight the site of the Malefiance property was quite charming. On the north side, it opened on to a kilometre of pasture for thin sheep and furrows for growing spelt. This was the least infertile land in the Bès valley.

Over a thousand years, those who had conquered this land had done so by piling up pyramids of pebbles like victory monuments at the end of every hedgerow. Some were ten metres high. The level of the fields between the low walls had gone down more than a metre because of the stones that had been cleared way. These bare lands rose towards the north against the endless sky. The only things that marked any boundary up there were a few poplars. Usually they waved happily in the wind, but crows in their branches gave them a funereal look. A spring of warm water bubbled up at their feet.

Built across the valley on an alluvial cone which had been dry for the last thousand years, the chateau could not be distinguished from the rock base until one was up close to it, as the colour and material were so similar. It was bare. There was no tree or hedge to soften its appearance. It was stone on stone.

The façade was like a sinister face with a sabre gash. Lightning had slashed the stone, putting a large crack in the rows of tiles under the edge of the roof, breaking a main wall to the height of one floor, and causing a diagonal fissure in the millstone of a mullion window. All that was some time ago. Since then this grimace had become a permanent feature on the façade of the chateau like a hare lip on the face of a child.

Thus it appeared, broad-faced and ill-favoured, in the headlights that lit it up from the bottom to the top, because of the steep road leading up to it. The path finished in a cul-de-sac at the wide flight of weedy steps leading directly to an esplanade with a crumbling balustrade.

The two men got out of the car, closing their doors at the same time.

It was very dark. A dull, indistinct rumbling sound could be heard in the depths of the dense shadows.

'Do you hear that?' Chabrand asked. 'You were right. There's a storm brewing.'

'Quiet!' Laviolette said.

He listened.

'No, it's not the storm,' he said. 'Not yet.'

'What do you think it is then?'

'Someone's beating a drum . . .' Laviolette replied, as if talking to himself.

'Beating a drum?' Chabrand repeated after him, absolutely amazed.

'Furiously!'

He tried three times to turn on his torch, but the button didn't always connect. With his muffler flying, he nimbly climbed the steps at the end of the path. Chabrand was close on his heels when he came out on to a terrace with rounded paving stones, lit up by garlands of coloured electric lights on a Christmas tree standing under the lightning gash that disfigured the chateau.

Around its green tub, a tangled mass of motorcycles decked with party plumes and good-luck squirrels' tails gleamed in the light around the stairs like a burning bush ready for the sacrifice. A nauseating smell of hot motor oil rose up around this machine graveyard.

The façade of the chateau was completely in the dark. There was no light from the windows apart from the reflection of an occasional flash of lightning skimming the hills down between Barrême and Saint-André. It seemed very far away from where they were.

'Come on!' Laviolette said. 'It's coming from over there.'

He was pointing down from the main house to a large building with an apse, which must have been used as a chapel in the old days. There was a dim, dull light showing behind two windows with Gothic arches. The entrance was through a low arched doorway on a level with the terrace. Rays of light also filtered through between the dislodged oak panels.

The rumbling sound of the drum could be heard through that door. Laviolette pushed it wide open, the judge following close behind. A dreadful cacophony hit them like an avalanche and made them reel. It was the din of piston engines running without oil in their cylinders. The scream of white-hot steel rose and fell, imitating a heartbeat; the whole thing was blaring out of four loudspeakers, their diaphragms trembling with the volume.

Two saxes, a cornet, a trumpet and an extraordinarily unimaginative rhythm section tried to embroider on this painful leitmotif. All to drown out the wildly beating drum.

That was what they heard, and this is what they saw: as soon as they entered, which was straight into the gallery, they were faced with a lot of wooden pikes stuck in an umbrella stand. Nearly all of the sticks had lost their masks, but three or four of them still held charming pasteboard calves' heads with stalks of parsley in their nostrils.

Watching over this livestock was a sullen-looking girl, otherwise blonde and quite pretty, dressed in an Indian dancer's tunic, which showed that she was completely naked underneath. She was holding some sort of blue tickets and gazing enviously at the scene below the gallery in the body of the church.

It was indeed a former chapel. The Gothic arches and Romanesque pillars bore witness to that. But the more or less happy combination of these two styles expressing the strength of popular faith had been openly challenged by a mad painter who had illuminated them with

268

labyrinthine colours of royal purple and heraldic green, as the judge called them. These arabesques included snails, ammonites, half-unrolled streamers, mother-in-law's tongues, intricately interwoven question marks, sometimes in erotic poses, especially around the pillars.

Down below, a strange, unreal crowd moved around to their own rhythm. It was indescribable. In the whole assembly, comprising at least sixty people, there was not one real head.

Most of the dancers camouflaged themselves behind the pathetic calves' faces, but there were also others moving from person to person: two or three war widows were swaying about in transparent black veils, and a remarkable trophy of Louis XVI's head in a bran basket stood out higher than the others, with its wig and little plait on each side, the Bourbon nose and the good-natured face.

Apart from what the masks covered, all these creatures were naked from top to toe, or at least sometimes from waist to toe. To the left of the sullen girl stood three or four café coat stands tied together. Clothes were piled up on them, dangling from them or lying on the floor of the gallery. It all smelled terrible, like the sweat from rowing galley slaves. Under the smoke at the back, the remains of a country buffet beginning to go stale languished on trestle tables across what used to be the choir.

A few scarves had ends trailing in bowls. Butts from the thin end of hand-made cigarettes were drowning in cups of coffee or lying dangerously close to the last petits fours. Everything was sticky because of the soft drinks and fruit juice, the only drinks consumed by the people there. On the other hand, the smell of cheap grass was heavy in the air, that smell which is more repulsive than death and decomposition for anyone who is not a user.

The judge looked down on the weird crowd. He listened to the ear-splitting din like a connoisseur aesthete.

'It's canned music!' he pronounced contemptuously. 'Supermarket music!'

Nevertheless, as he watched the movement of the dancers on the floor, he also began to let himself go to the erotic rhythm of bodies nonchalantly enticing each other. He took two gliding steps forward and back, extending his long hands in a swimming motion on each side of his hips, undulating his thin behind, obscenely thrusting his pelvis at some imaginary partner.

The girl in the green Indian tunic took off the judge's carrick coat before extending her hand, curtly demanding her due.

'Hand over your twenty francs!'

They complied. She vigorously got Laviolette out of his coat and scarf, took off his hat and pushed one of the remaining disguises over his head and down to his shoulders.

Chabrand was already about to go downstairs and mingle with the dancers.

'Do you know where we are?' Laviolette asked him, almost shouting.

'No doubt in the asylum!' the judge replied jokingly as he continued dancing about on his own.

'That goes without saying, but all that aside, something's not right here . . .'

'Something's a sight here!' Chabrand sniggered.

He turned round to check whether his companion was suitably impressed by his wit. It was the first and last time in his life that Laviolette heard the judge roar with laughter. Chabrand had suddenly seen how hilarious Laviolette looked: this stocky man, always in overcoat and muffler, now topped off with a charming sign for a high-class butcher instead of a face.

Trying to hide his annoyance, Laviolette took the ticket girl to task.

'What are you waiting for to stick one on him too? What's all this favoured treatment?'

'I was going to do it . . .' she sighed, unconcerned, 'but he's so handsome that I wanted to look at him for a while longer.'

Pressing her warm navel against the judge's hip, she reached up on tiptoe and put the obligatory disguise on him too, but gently, as if she regretted having to do it.

'Perfect!' Laviolette exclaimed. It was his turn to suppress a strong urge to laugh.

'Well now, are you in the right mood to listen to me now?'

Laviolette made an effort to speak with the worried voice that justified his sudden misgivings, but it was difficult with the calf's head on his shoulders, muffling the sounds. Chabrand had been no less surprised than Laviolette when he heard himself laugh, and he now felt humiliated by it. Fortunately the spectacle of what was going on all around them excused him from asking himself too many questions. The atmosphere not only attracted but captivated him. All those supple naked bodies, both men and women, stimulated his libido and made him lose his head.

He especially wanted to reach the goddess standing alone and scarcely moving on the flagstones almost in the centre of the chapel, surrounded at a distance like a queen bee by the adoring dancers who wound their way around her.

She was a girl of probably barely twenty. A hussar's frogged jacket fitted tightly over her breasts, but she was naked from the navel down to the thighs clad in tight phosphorescent green boots. Long green gloves with flared tops, also phosphorescent, covered her forearms to the elbow. Resting on her well-balanced shoulders was the grotesque pasteboard head of a mental defective who looked as if she had been pressed through the mill of too small a pelvis at birth. It was a sad, yellow, oblong face with drooping eyes, like those the African storytellers describe.

Below the fitted jacket and above the tight green boots that seemed to catch all the spotlights, her softly rounded belly undulated lasciviously. It was emphasised by a triangle of blonde hairs in tightly knitted little curls like chain mail, as dazzling and eye-catching as a Christmas tree.

Sometimes, however, this promise of delight was hidden by the town-crier's drum the girl had hanging from a strap around her neck, as her green hands drummed wildly.

'It's Isabelle!' the judge whispered. 'I recognised that hair. I've never seen more adorable pubes. Nor more unusual. Nor more inviting.'

Yet a fierce determination seemed to emanate from that body under the idiot's head, which was in stark contrast to the assemblage of limp creatures around her; a desperate determination, a mixture of terror and defiance. This was expressed by the way the drumsticks tirelessly rose and fell, striking the vellum, sounding the frantic beat that communicated its waves of panic to the figures of the dance, which had difficulty maintaining their own rhythm.

Sometimes a man would move away from the crowd towards the lone girl, who kept herself carefully isolated in her magic circle. He would weave his way around her, miming his advances. As if gravely offended by this sight, she would suddenly turn her pasteboard head away from him. If he insisted, the menacing drumsticks would make a movement like a nutcracker towards the boy's penis, whereupon he would bow out apologetically and turn his attentions to some more accessible female calf's head. Then the relentless drumming would start up once again.

Laviolette put his hand on the judge's shoulder.

'Wake up!' he said. 'It's a curious thing we've come upon . . .'

'Everything is always curious!' Chabrand replied, still in a state of euphoria.

'No, but . . . I mean here . . . Can you recall all the people in the "Dinner of Heads"?,[*] he suddenly asked out of the blue.

'Yes, of course,' Chabrand replied without giving it the slightest thought.

'No, listen. Do you even know what I'm talking about?'

'By Prévert,' Chabrand complained. 'It's strange. People of your age always think they're the only ones who know the classics.'

'That's fine. All right then, off you go. Describe them to me.'

'Oh!' Chabrand said. 'Ooh!'

He waved his long arms about his calf's head to express the impossible task being asked of him.

'That's just what I thought. You've forgotten everything . . .' Laviolette muttered. 'Now *I* recite that masterpiece to myself several

[*] A poem by the Surrealist poet Jacques Prévert, 'An Attempt to Describe a Dinner of Heads in Paris-France', in which people have their heads completely covered by masks of various kinds. The war widow, the head of Louis XVI and 'charming calves' faces' are among the characters included.

times a year, and I'll be damned if I've ever come across a sapper from the Grande Armée with buttoned gaiters, handlebar moustache and pigskin apron . . .'

'Certainly not,' Chabrand said. 'Where can you see one here?'

'Over there beside the platform with the four musicians. Between the buffet and the north pillar of the nave. The man who isn't in disguise, who isn't naked. Who's not much younger than me. That man discreetly swaying his hips with all the grace of a dancing bear. That man who looks like . . .'

He stopped short. When he had reported Dr Pardigon's stories to the judge, he had left out the description of the disguise Gaétan Melliflore, the grandfather of the three victims, put on when he went out on his rounds as town crier. Laviolette had thought it an insignificant detail. On that night, as it happened, the man he described was wearing that very same old uniform.

The man in question only had eyes for the green goddess with the African idol's mask, and only for her navel. He made no attempt to approach her. But Laviolette suddenly had the impression that the girl's mask was also turned towards the odd-looking sapper. It seemed to him that she too only had eyes for him. It seemed to him there was even more to it than that: it was for him and him alone that she was beating the drum so furiously. He had the clear impression of witnessing that kind of morbid buzz a fly makes as it dances in front of the spider's web that will soon ensnare it.

He could sense the strands of a strange eroticism being woven between these two curious expressions of human eccentricity. Were they both under the influence of drugs?

He had to find out immediately, and above all he had to get to that man, stop him, and pull off his fur cap. Then he could see if perchance he had those bumps and hollows which were so evident in the summerhouse portrait, and which Laviolette thought he had briefly seen again on some occasion last month in a person who lived in Barles.

He was about to ask Chabrand to follow him, but the ticket girl, leaving her post, unceremoniously pushed him out of the way and went

273

down the wooden steps before he could. She turned the judge around to face her, pressed herself against him, amorously kissed his calf's nose and dragged him towards the platform where the musicians were trying to be heard in all the noise.

Laviolette knew that was the end of any help from Chabrand. He could only count on himself now, and that was dubious, for down below a girl suddenly emerged from the smoky crowd and trotted over to the buffet.

She had a wide back, a short neck and exceedingly plump arms, but it was all smooth pink flesh in full bloom, carried with pride and joy, because she was young. Like the parts, the whole was perfectly harmonious, precisely distributed, as light and smooth as a bronze goddess imagined by Maillol. She was wearing the head of a war widow with a veil that floated down to her waist, her only item of clothing.

In the swell of her walking, Laviolette from afar could see the surging of the sea. He had as little power of resistance in her wake as wise Ulysses in the green waves where the sirens sang. Laviolette, however, was not lashed to the tiller. He was irresistibly drawn towards this profusion of naked flesh. Relieved of his older man's heaviness, released from his normal reserve, he even tried a few dance steps he thought he had forgotten ages ago; relieved above all – and he would never forgive himself for the rest of his life – of the alarm he had felt when he saw that man disguised as a sapper indulging in the luxury of being as grey as death in the midst of all that shimmering colour.

If Laviolette rushed forward through the couples on the dance floor, it was with the express wish of turning the stranger towards him and tearing off his disguise. But half his good intentions were now corrupted by the other imperative desire: to lay hands on the buxom 'widow'. The confusion in his conscience was powerfully encouraged by the fact that the two people concerned were almost side by side. Going towards one was going towards the other. All he had to do was to let himself be deluded; to believe that he was acting for the right reason while in fact he was acting for the wrong one.

It was not that Laviolette asked much of luck or chance, but still . . .

Who knows whether his old head, so well camouflaged under his mask, might not have hidden him from himself as well as from others? Who knows whether the big girl might not agree, through nonchalance, apathy or indifference, to let him take her in his arms and join one of those obscene dances? If he succeeded, it would be a complete Christmas Eve. A mortal who is obsessed by that kind of hope can hardly reason sensibly.

As he reached the bottom of the stairs to try and make his way between the contorting couples panting from their ludicrous exertions, a fleeting shaft of light streaked across the stained-glass windows, and for a moment a solemn boom of thunder drowned out the din of the instruments.

Laviolette paid no attention to it, such was his state of mind.

He was now almost halfway towards his promised land, sometimes obscured by couples who drew apart at arm's length then suddenly came back together again. He thought he recognised Judge Chabrand, still encircled by his ticket girl, from a calf's head held more arrogantly than the others. He was about to call him, but changed his mind. He crossed the empty space where the girl with the blonde pubic hair was beating her drum, with her false head still turned in the direction of the grey sapper.

There were two or three more streaks of lightning across the stained-glass windows, which for a moment merged the colours of all the lights. They were followed by thunder, which this time did not overpower the noise inside. It seemed, nevertheless, that a new, continuous sound had joined it and blended it into one.

Laviolette had managed to avoid all obstacles, and the buffet on its trestles was now only two or three metres away. The girl standing in front of it was leaning forward in an amazing attitude, trying to reach a plate of cream puffs at the back. She grabbed one, then raised the pasteboard widow's head that covered her own, revealing a little full-moon face with a turned-up nose and more than a hint of sulky, bored sensuality. Laviolette found it utterly charming.

She was within arm's length, but so was the lugubrious sapper, who kept his fascinated eyes trained on the green goddess who seemed to defy him with great waves of drum rolls. With a rational man's last effort, Laviolette reached out his arm to pull off the stranger's fur cap, but jostled by a couple dancing backwards, he missed. The girl with the round face turned towards him. As if for a joke, she mischievously smeared his calf's face with the rest of the cream puff she was eating.

Then a blinding flash dazzled the guests, followed immediately by a sound like material being violently ripped. The spotlights, the fairy lights, the electric candles flickered, frayed into purple filaments and went out altogether. The sound system gave a drawn-out moan from the last micro-groove on the record being laboriously ploughed; then died. The poor rhythm section, the saxes and the cornet, unable to read their music, tried to improvise, then foundered ingloriously.

All that was left was the imperturbable, wildly beating drum. Now that it was alone and holding a dialogue with the formidable claps of thunder which shook the windows and the deluge of hailstones which were a reminder how close the *clues* and the Bès were, it seemed to beat more loudly, more furiously, like a challenge or a grim invitation. The sound of the drum was insistent, incoherent and dominating, as if it wanted everyone to know where it was in the total darkness, pierced only by the flashes of the storm.

The solitary goddess in her halo of green, suddenly lit up when the lightning blazed, still did not move from her spot. She kept hitting the drum with a furious rhythm.

Laviolette, however, emboldened by the darkness, was still trying to grope his way towards the girl who had fascinated him so much. He took a step forward. At that moment someone brushed past him, someone with the characteristic smell of chamomile tea. A flash of recognition went through his mind, dispelling the extravagant thoughts that had taken possession of it.

Suddenly he understood everything. He took his torch out of his pocket to locate the sapper. He didn't need it. Lightning once again lit up the scene.

The man was no longer there. Laviolette turned on his torch, but the batteries must have been almost finished. All he could get out of them was a light so dim that it was useless.

'Chabrand!' Laviolette shouted.

There was a note of panic in his voice. He had a sudden intimation that something terrible was going to happen in his presence. There was another streak of lightning. He saw the sapper from the back walking slowly towards the girl in green. He dashed forward, tripped over a couple who had decided to make love in the dark, and collapsed heavily on to the stone floor. His calf's head hit the ground and rolled off.

At that moment the drum beats stopped abruptly. In the darkness rent intermittently by lightning and the silence by thunder, a powerful surge like a cattle stampede threw the couples against each other as they groped their way in a wild, disorderly flight. They rushed for the door, and were pushed up against it, but as it opened towards the inside, a great deal of shouting was heard before they could move back far enough to open it. They found themselves faced with a wall of hailstones as big as cherries. Anguished screams and cries rose here and there from the crowd of people falling over each other, clinging together or frantically pushing someone away.

That kind of panic wasn't natural. The darkness and sudden silence, the noise of the storm outside and the deluge of hailstones could have added to it, but it must have been caused by something extraordinary in the first place.

Laviolette was thinking this flat on his back (he hadn't had the time to get up again) while people trampled on him, stumbled over him or kicked him in the ribs. Someone fell astride his head. He felt a weight spread over his head and chest, which he identified as a woman's body. But it wasn't the fat girl. He was no longer thinking of her anyway; when one is struggling to breathe, eroticism loses its charms. Laviolette dug his fists into the pliant flesh, which brought a piercing scream, and with a powerful heave managed to throw her off as far as he could.

'Chabrand!' he shouted once again.

But the judge must have been otherwise occupied, or else the combined din of the cries, the shouting, the noise of the thunder and hail, and the backfiring of motorbikes starting up must have prevented him from hearing.

Laviolette shouldered aside two people who were trying to get dressed again. He waded through a sea of bodies which had collapsed and were vainly trying to get up and make their escape, for the effects of the grass had slowed both their movements and the working of their brains.

Thanks to the lightning, he finally reached the goddess. She was lying dead on the flagstones like a marble statue, untouched by the crowd. Her blue eyes, which were wide open, still seemed to have a flicker of life when they reflected the lightning. She had been strangled by an ordinary piece of washing line roughly twisted into a rope and tightened around her neck with a wooden garden peg that usually has string wound on it. This rudimentary garrotte had loosened and hung like a necklace around the dead girl's neck. Her carnival head was broken beside her. She lay in the dust right in the middle of a spilt bowl of bulgur wheat salad. In the general panic that had followed the discovery of the body, the buffet on trestles had been knocked over and the plates of food trampled underfoot were strewn over the stone floor in a horrible slush. The only things floating on the surface were the drumsticks, which only a few minutes ago had been beating the vellum for all they were worth.

The drum itself, with the strap that had emphasised the pretty girl's hips all evening, was now nowhere to be seen.

'Chabrand!' Laviolette called out.

'No need to shout so loudly. I'm here.'

And indeed there he was, also leaning over the beautiful half-naked body, which was still as attractive in death as it had been in life.

'What a pity,' he sighed.

'Come on!' Laviolette said. 'Now I know who it is!'

'You know?'

'Yes. Well . . . I think I know. The murderer has only a five-minute head start on us. Everything leads me to think that he's on a moped. We must catch up with him, for if we don't, there'll be nothing for it but to throw ourselves into the river. Because it's unpardonable of us. Do you understand?'

He repeated, 'Unpardonable! Unpardonable!'

His hands were flailing the air in front of him as he went up the stairs lit by the sporadic lightning flashes. Chabrand followed as best he could. He could only see out of one eye as his glasses had fallen off in the confusion, and when he had found them again, one of the lenses was broken.

'Wait a moment!' he called out. 'At least let me get my coat.'

The carrick coat lay among the smashed heads – calves, widows, admirals, clay pipes – all trampled by fifty pairs of shoes that had wiped their soles on them. That was nothing compared to Laviolette's hat, which had been flattened under the wide-open door.

They both picked up their items of clothing with that automatic dusting-down gesture, a comic expression of their profound wish to get back to the stability of lost order.

It was not to be, yet. Outside, the lightning was continuously streaking down between the closely packed spears of torrential rain, emphasising its striking depth and density.

'Where's the umbrella?' the judge asked.

'In the car,' Laviolette replied quickly. 'And your torch?'

'In the car,' Chabrand answered laconically.

They dashed out. When the storm stopped lighting up the night, they were suddenly stopped in their tracks by total darkness. Sometimes it caught them with one foot in the air, on the terrace or on the wide steps. But it didn't last long, as Malefiance seemed to have been chosen a long time ago as a place where storms gather. During the minute it took for the two men to reach the car in pouring rain, the lightning twice struck deep into the split in the façade of the chateau, filling it with a blue plume which lit up the black walls, as if it were a long-awaited reunion.

The two men's coats were as heavy as lead by the time they sank on to their seats in the car.

'Where are we going?' the judge asked, almost shouting.

He wiped his face like a diver coming out of the water. The pouring rain that had half blinded him was beating loudly on the bodywork of the car. It sounded like a waterfall.

'In the direction of Barles. Did you doubt it?' Laviolette replied, just as loudly.

Chabrand shook his head.

'Nothing is more like a moped than another moped . . .'

He pulled the starter, which refused to respond, for fully thirty seconds.

'We'll recognise that one. That's not what's worrying me,' Laviolette added, staring anxiously at the red light on the dashboard.

'How?' Chabrand asked, trying the starter once more.

'Even if he's taken off his disguise,' Laviolette said, looking more and more anxious, 'he'll be carrying a drum on his luggage rack. That's what he came to get.'

'A drum!' Chabrand said between clenched teeth. 'What an idea!'

The car suspension shuddered like a ship hitting a reef. It was simply the temperamental engine suddenly deciding to get going.

'Yes indeed, a drum,' Laviolette muttered. 'And pray heaven we find it.'

The *clue* rose up before them, shooting out flashes of lightning as the deep waters of the river spewed out under the bridge. Long shafts of lightning forced their way through the narrow parts of the canyon. On that particular night, it was as if the Last Judgement had chosen that insignificant fissure in that insignificant region as an illustration of what mortals might expect.

But Laviolette and Chabrand were not the only ones to have ventured into the place. The car headlights and the flashes of the storm intermittently picked out the red light of a reflector in the dark more than a hundred metres ahead of them.

'We've got him!' cried Laviolette. 'Go a bit faster!'

But the road at the end of the *clue* was also covered with little white-flecked waves of water, as if a stray flock of sheep was hurrying down it. That made visibility even more difficult. And it was there, on the other side of the last bridge, in the gravel of a soft shoulder on the road, that the car died on them. Without his glasses, Chabrand misjudged the turn, and the right front wheel sank deep into the water-logged verge. The engine suddenly cut out. Chabrand pulled on the starter so much that he almost ripped out the cable. No response.

'That's all we needed!' Laviolette groaned.

Despite the combined efforts of the storm, he imagined he could again hear the sneer of revenge from his old car, which he thought he had already heard early in the evening when the judge had scornfully rejected it.

He took his blue umbrella and thrust open the car door.

'Where are you going?' Chabrand shouted.

'To Barles. That's where he's going.'

'But you're on foot!'

'Can't be helped. I'll do what I can. That'll teach me!'

'I'm coming with you!'

Chabrand got out of the car after him, and huddled under the blue umbrella, half bent over.

'You hold it.' Laviolette said. 'You're taller.'

They were now at the mercy of the storm, which was circling above the *clue*. It seemed to have found its home port, its haven, the spot where it could shamelessly frolic to its heart's content. It lit up the land-scape in great bursts, right to the top of the Blayeul and the fallen rocks of the Montagne de Chine. It made the waterfalls iridescent as they cut through the layers of the vertical schists above the narrows. Its deaf-ening noise bounced from one sheer wall of the *clue* to the other. It was impossible to tell which flash of lightning caused which clap of thunder, they came in such quick succession.

The storm kept shafting spears down on the large chocolate-coloured dragon which, amazingly enough, turned out to be the river. It was too big for its bed, and the Bès scraped its sides along the strik-ingly curved banks, which were almost cylindrical, with something that sounded like harsh groans of pain. The two men were offered an example of erosion at its most violent and mysterious. The lightning pursued them relentlessly, now here, now there, behind them or in front of them, as if it were sure it would nail them sometime or other. By its intermittent light, they could also see the wretched little man with his fur cap and gaiters straining to push his moped with its flooded motor less than a hundred metres away in the middle of the *clue*.

'Look! He's on foot too!'

Laviolette rushed forward beyond the shelter of the umbrella.

'Where are you going?' Chabrand shouted after him.

'It's obvious where I'm going!'

'But what if he's armed?'

'Armed!' Laviolette said scornfully. 'With what? He's only a poor wretch of a man.'

'What the hell! Let him go if he wants to,' Chabrand said to himself.

Even the most steadfast person will become afraid of lightning when it persists with such malevolence, and this was the case here. Chabrand was rooted to the spot with fear. The fact was he realised that he definitely loved life, and its most recent manifestation filled him with respect. Deep in his heart – the last part of him that was still warm and dry – he had the memory of the ticket girl who had besieged him and with whom he had hoped to see out a joyful Christmas Eve. Good Lord! That was scarcely an hour ago! Now, instead of that, here he was in this whirling maelstrom, a pure example of madness that made human madness look positively harmless. Here he was with this fellow Laviolette, who was not afraid of death simply because he was old. It looked magnificent all right, but it could be fatal nonetheless.

The older man kept going, in water up to his ankles. He charged ahead, the lightning whizzing at his back. What kind of God could this man have conceived, to give him such calmness in the face of danger?

'Curiosity!' Laviolette would have replied if he had heard the judge's question. For it was that, and that alone, which spurred him on. The insistent fury of the storm frightened him as much as it did Chabrand, but he was driven by the need to know.

Not much more than fifty metres ahead of him, the person in the sapper costume was pushing his moped. Soaked to the skin and dripping wet, in the flashes of lightning he looked more and more like a mangy alley cat.

'A murderer!' Laviolette whispered, and his mouth filled with rainwater.

The man was now almost within reach. With just a bit more effort he'd be able to seize him by the collar, turn him round and know. He'd know at last!

Only thirty metres, only twenty to go, in the flashing golden light of the storm, in the infernal clamour of the Bès being hurled, squeezed and ripped through the narrow part of the canyon.

Laviolette was puffing like a grampus in his effort to catch up to the man. He streamed with rain and rippled with lights from the incessant electric flashes.

Suddenly he was stopped in his tracks by the sight in front of him.

'I thought it was you,' Chabrand said to him later.

Despite the doubts of those listening to him when he was telling what happened, Laviolette insisted that he only saw the flash of lightning *afterwards*. To tell the truth, he though it was a feat of human memory to be able to separate two visions that were so close or perhaps even simultaneous. But the fact existed: what he saw *first* was the little man becoming incandescent, like a metal rod turning red-hot. His legs parted, his arms rose up to the sky above his head, as if he were crying for mercy. For a fraction of a second, Laviolette thought that the lightning was going to snatch the sapper from the earth and never return him.

It was only then that he saw the flash. It had four violet forks that crackled as they fastened themselves around the projections in the walls of the *clue*, where they braced themselves, wove their way along two chimneys, sucked down by the draught of air, then joined in an almost transparent blue line from which the little man was suspended like a puppet on a string.

The whole thing disappeared in a weak, almost confidential rumble of thunder, which made no impression on the roaring of the river.

The little man fell in a broken heap on the ground; the moped toppled over on to the submerged road.

'Chabrand!' Laviolette shouted. 'The drum!'

'What about the drum?' Chabrand protested, catching up with him.

'The drum! Go after it, for God's sake! Can't you see that it's rolling! We're done for if the drum gets away from us!'

It was true. The drum had bounced quite a distance from the moped. It rolled, it reeled, it floated, borne away on the little white waves on the road. It was about to be swallowed up in the river through one of the slits placed twenty metres apart in the wall along the bank of the Bès.

Chabrand let go of the umbrella, immediately threw himself along the ground and caught the drum like a rugby player.

'Get it out of the wet!' Laviolette ordered. 'Put it under your carrick!'

He leaned over the body and gazed at it in the light from the storm. Chabrand came and stood next to him, loaded down with the drum and the umbrella, which he had also rescued. They stared at each other in the flashes of lightning. They looked like boxers after a match.

'Do you have your torch?' Laviolette asked.

'Yes. Get it out of my pocket. I can't let go of the drum.'

Laviolette turned on the torch and trained it on the face of the corpse, which he could not see properly with only intermittent flashes of light.

The lightning had turned the face into a block of anthracite shining black in the stark beam of the torch. The enormous handlebar moustache that had adorned it not long before had gone up in smoke.

The fur cap had vanished. Now it was easy to see the hollows, bumps and planes that nature had used to sculpt this particular face. The face as such no longer existed, but its disappearance had revealed the origin of the elements that had been borrowed from elsewhere. Well before the birth of that body, the same pieces of this jigsaw had already been used – apart from a few details – to make the subject of the portrait that hung over the fireplace in the summerhouse at The Cedars.

At the same time as he rediscovered that analogy, which he refused to call an exact resemblance, Laviolette remembered an unpleasant scene he had witnessed in Barles that autumn. It was a fire of dead leaves that someone was poking with a fork; someone who calmly picked up a rat trap full of wriggling field mice and threw it into the flames.

He bent over the gnarled rootstock that had been a man. Around the tendons on his neck, now sculpted in black, shone a heavy watch chain which the fickle lightning had left intact. On the end of this chain dangled a large turnip watch, on which the moving second hand showed that it had not even been damaged by the electric shock. It hung next to a bunch of keys carefully fastened with a pin.

Laviolette gently picked up the keys, which he detached. He turned over the watch. It was engraved with two entwined initials: an A and an R.

'Adamastor . . .' he murmured. 'Good Lord! I should have thought of that . . .'

'What did you say?' Chabrand asked.

'Come on,' Laviolette said, 'we're going to Barles.'

'But how? The car won't start.'

'On foot. Given the state we're in, all we can do is walk if we don't want to catch our deaths. Hold the umbrella. We're off.'

At that moment a nasty bolt of lightning, as round as a billiard ball, hit the winding waters of the Bès. Chabrand jumped and began to shiver.

'Our death of cold!' the judge specified.

Laviolette patted him on the shoulder.

'Don't worry,' he said. 'There was one chance in a million and it's already happened.'

He pointed to the body.

'Come on, let's go. There's no more danger. Anyway, it can't be more unhealthy further on than it is here. And keep a good hold on the drum. Remember that without it, we have no chance of understanding anything about this mystery.'

XV

THE TWO MEN SOAKED TO THE SKIN UNDER THE BIG BLUE umbrella were a pitiful sight as they made their way through the darkness in the gorge. They were frozen, exhausted and desperate. The umbrella scarcely protected them from all the water coming almost horizontally straight at them, and going up their noses as they breathed.

The storm gave them no quarter during the two kilometres they had to travel. It harried them from behind with sly sparks of lightning, which sometimes zigzagged on the ground around their feet. The torrential rain never let up. Deafened by the sound of the thunder and the roaring of the Bès, they even gave up speaking to each other.

Going through the Barles tunnel afforded them some relief. The electricity had not gone off in the village, which gave them hope. However, the storm was still raging. It had reduced the awning above Grimaude's terrace to tatters. The lightning tried to strike the Christmas tree in the tub with its twinkling red and green lights, which the citizens of Barles had set up between the war memorial and the public weighbridge.

'You do know where you're going, I hope?' Chabrand asked in a listless voice.

Laviolette nodded his head without replying.

Barles was sleeping the sleep of the just. For two hundred and nineteen inhabitants out of two hundred and twenty, this Christmas Eve would have been very uneventful; nothing more than the memory of a huge storm that had beaten the ground all night while they listened to it tucked up in bed, enjoying the dry scent of lavender on the freshly changed sheets.

All that could be heard when the thunder ceased was the sad neighing of a horse in a stable. Because of the comings and goings involved in the preparations for midnight parties, someone had forgotten to put it out to graze.

Huddled under the almost useless umbrella, the two survivors of the storm walked for another two hundred metres, then Laviolette stopped short. Chabrand, holding the brolly (Laviolette had taken the drum, which he was carrying as best he could under his open coat), took two steps more and left his companion in the rain. It was easing off, however. The storm's angry rumblings became less and less aggressive. The lightning withdrew to the middle of the sky, concentrating on shooting blinding paths of light down the slopes of the Blayeul or into the gullies of the Estrop, showing the depths of new snow with each flash.

Chabrand turned round and looked up. He saw an iron grille fence with the gate ajar, surmounted by a faded flag dripping wet like a floor cloth, slashed by hail and tattered by wind and rain. He saw a courtyard beyond, where another Christmas tree with lights was standing, but smaller than the municipal one. At the back, a very dark, high covered playground echoed with the sound of the Bès and the last bursts of the storm.

Through the window on one of the upper floors in the building a light shone peacefully under the net of green beads that served as a lampshade.

'The school?' Chabrand asked, not understanding.

Laviolette just pushed open the creaking gate and crossed the yard. His shoes trod on the scattered remains of a fire of dead leaves, which must always have been burned on that spot. The black marks on the ground were still visible despite bad weather and the trampling of children's feet during hundreds of playtimes. The man whose black corpse was now being washed by rain deep in the *clues* had stood on this spot in October, calmly holding a rat trap in his hand.

Laviolette went up the three steps in front of the corridor leading to the classroom. There was a coat rack along the wall at children's height. A few scarves or balaclavas still hung there next to a schoolbag, although it was holiday time.

A long flight of stairs led to a small landing and a closed grey door. Laviolette climbed it laboriously. At each step the cumbersome drum hit the railing and gave a dull rumble. Chabrand had closed the big umbrella and hung it on the coat rack, where it blithely dripped away on the floor. He also dragged himself up the stairs.

'Hold that for me,' Laviolette said, putting the drum into his arms.

He felt around in the bottom of his pocket for the bunch of keys he had taken from the watch chain on the dead man's chest. The door had two locks: one ordinary lock, probably the original, and the other with a bolt, obviously a later addition. They were both double-locked.

'All this is quite illegal, you know,' Chabrand pointed out.

'You're right, absolutely. But do you want to know the answer immediately, yes or no? The legal investigations have been dropped. But if it's going to worry you . . .'

He was already putting the keys back in his pocket.

'No! No! Open it . . . We'll see about that.'

Chabrand went in behind Laviolette. The pleasant atmosphere of the warm, spacious kitchen welcomed them, as it would have its owner, if by chance he had come back. There was a neat row of spice pots lined up according to size above the hood of the blocked-up fireplace. They watched over the tidy scene below. In front of the fireplace, the kitchen range which had recently been polished with emery cloth crackled away quietly. The master of the house must have stoked it up to capacity before leaving on his moped for a few hours. On the top of the range, an earthenware kettle was talking to itself with a gentle hiss. Next to it was an ordinary saucepan in which fully opened chamomile flowers were macerating.

Over on the dresser, next to a set of liqueur glasses, a little basket of counters and a game of piquet in its box stood on a baize cloth for cards. The round table covered with a waxed tablecloth was otherwise quite bare. The ceiling lamp with its bead shade at half height shed a green light over it.

'Right!' said Laviolette. 'The first thing to do is to stoke up the stove.'

He took hold of the hook to shake the ash through the grate, after which he lifted the catch and put in two logs from the basket. He turned the damper as far as it would go, then opened the stove door.

'The second thing,' he said, 'is to get undressed.'

He had placed four chairs with their backs to the range, and quickly began to remove his clothes, which he spread out over them.

'Well? What are you waiting for?' he muttered from inside the jersey he was pulling over his head. 'Are you afraid I might ravish you?'

Chabrand gave a weak shrug of the shoulders and also began to undress. Laviolette was already down to his long johns and flannel vest of that grey colour they all have, even when new; no one knows why. Chabrand was wearing wide half-length boxer shorts, and his cotton vest seemed very clean. He stood there like a plucked rooster, looking strangely vulnerable because of his spectacles with one lens missing.

'Put your back to the stove!' Laviolette barked. 'Your bones are nearer the skin than mine. And you're more reserved by nature. That makes you more shivery.'

He made him sit down.

'Goodness, you're trembling!'

Laviolette walked behind him and began to rub his back vigorously.

'Not from cold,' Chabrand said through chattering teeth. 'I can't deal with death as easily as you,' he said without bitterness.

'It's just a question of familiarity . . .' Laviolette replied philosophically. Let's see now . . . The third thing is to get something strong into us . .'

With his head in the dresser, he searched around and came up with a bottle. He raised it to the light while placing two of the liqueur glasses on the tablecloth. He looked at the school exercise-book label on the bottle, then read it aloud.

'*The remainder of a cheap armagnac given to me in 1949 by a student who had just passed his elementary certificate.* Bravo! That's just what we need!'

He pushed a full glass towards Chabrand and watched him put it to his lips. The judge gave an awful wince.

'Are you all right?' Laviolette asked.

Chabrand pursed his lips.

'More or less . . .'

Outside, Barles was blanketed in silence. The storm had died down. Rain dripped slowly from the bare trees in the school yard.

The two men sat under the light staring at the drum placed squarely between them on the tablecloth. It was an ordinary old town drum with dirty skin around the only clean spot where the drumsticks always hit. It was faded blue, white and red, like a child's toy from days of old.

'It must be about sixty centimetres in diameter,' Laviolette calculated. 'It or its brother could have fitted into that puzzling square parcel you thought was in Ambroisine Larchet's attic . . .'

He was looking absent-mindedly at the bunch of keys he was tossing in his hand. There was one in particular, smooth and clean, a little worn by a certain kind of use, as if it had often been handled in preference to the others.

Laviolette stood up. There was a half-open door to the left of the fireplace. He went over and pushed it open. He found himself in a dark place with closed shutters, which smelled of cold, freshly laundered linen. He switched on the light. It revealed an austere room, the bedroom of a poor wretch of a man. There was nothing personal on display, not even a book. It was entirely filled by a huge wooden Louis-Philippe bed, solid, squat, unattractive, and by a fifty-year-old wardrobe with a mirror. On the dark bedside table was an ancient photo of a woman with her hair pulled back in a bun, neat but not stylish. It was a woman of the valleys. The photo had been taken when she was still young and in her prime, but one could sense that it would not be long before her harsh, spare beauty would become like a rose hip.

Laviolette gazed at it for some time. She bore the same stigmata of a hard life, the same bone structure and the general skull shape as the portrait discovered in the summerhouse, but in the female version. She also had the same clear-headed look of those who expect nothing good to come from existence or their fellow men: a look of a person always anticipating misfortune.

The photo was in a modern frame between two sheets of glass. Laviolette turned it over. On the back was an inscription in rather faded purple ink: *My mother when I was five years old*. The room apparently contained no admission of weakness other than the photo and its inscription.

Over on the other side of the windows, however, there was a tall cupboard set in the wall. One could only just make out the double doors behind the cheap wallpaper.

Laviolette went over to it. There was a hole in the wallpaper, a keyhole which could also hardly be seen as it was just a cut in the paper. Laviolette chose what he thought was the appropriate key from the chain. It turned easily in the smooth-working lock. The cupboard door opened with hardly any noise. The cupboard itself was almost empty. Although neatly protected by blue paper used for covering books, three shelves out of four held nothing but a mousetrap baited with Gruyère on each.

Only the lowest shelf was filled. It held the following articles: two diaries with old, discoloured edges that had often been leafed through; a cheap, *Le Pratique*-brand exercise book; a post-office calendar; two fat volumes in a fine binding of padded green cordovan leather, which must have been very expensive. The cupboard smelled of both quality leather and chamomile tea.

The shelves went down to the floor and in the dark space something gleamed faintly in the shadows. At first sight it could have been taken for brightly coloured children's toys.

'Chabrand!' Laviolette called. 'Just come and look at this!'

The judge arrived, dragging his feet.

'Look!' said Laviolette.

He was pointing to the dark bottom of the cupboard. There was something sinister about that brightly coloured jumble of things that smelled of wet horse harnesses.

'In Bluebeard's castle,' Laviolette said, 'the cupboards held as many dresses as he had committed murders. Here it's drums.'

'Drums?' Chabrand exclaimed. 'But . . . they've all been slit open!'

Laviolette nodded.

'Exactly,' he said. 'Come!'

He had removed all the documents from the lower shelf. He thumped them down on the table next to the one drum still intact, which they had brought with them.

Chabrand sat in front of the kitchen range. He snatched the bottle and poured himself a full glass, which he began to sip without much attention, but with a hint of pleasure nonetheless.

'We'll know at last,' Laviolette said, pushing his own glass towards the bottle, so that Chabrand would not forget to pour him one as well.

He held the volume to the light. It was obviously handmade, and someone had written on it these words in free, elegant copperplate:

Monograph of Barles, by Léon Martin
Primary Schoolteacher
1930

Laviolette thrust the book under Chabrand's nose. It was a kind of register.

'To begin with,' he said, 'we'll never know why this Léon Martin, schoolteacher in Barles in 1930, left these two volumes here; why he didn't take them with him when he changed schools or retired.'

'Perhaps he died first,' Chabrand suggested. 'In any case, what does it have to do with what we're looking for?'

'I've told you from the beginning that I'm sure the key to this story has its roots in the past. It wasn't by chance that I looked for walking encyclopedias of memories. And it was scarcely by chance that I came upon Dr Pardigon . . .'

He opened the book in which a man had meticulously noted down all the items of general information that could interest a studious pupil about his region, and leafed through it slowly.

'You can be sure that the seeds of all these crimes are in here. It may be something insignificant, something perfectly harmless . . .'

He turned the pages one by one, admiring the care that had been taken with their presentation: the headings underlined in black, blue or violet ink; the dropped initials in red copperplate capital letters at the beginning of each chapter. Suddenly he stopped short at a particular page.

'Well, no!' he exclaimed. 'Not as harmless as all that . . . Here! Read it for yourself.'

He handed the open book to the judge.

'I can only read with one eye,' Chabrand said sadly, 'and it's not my best one.'

'I'll have to read you the main points of it all, as we'll find the key to the mystery somewhere in this hotch-potch.'

'Please . . .'

The armagnac that Chabrand was warming in his cupped hand was beginning to make him more sociable. Laviolette began to read.

'*A typical example of the old right of the eldest son to inherit, which persists in our remote valleys: the Melliflores. There was a family, locality Horse-Choker Farm, where it was traditional for the younger sons to leave the region without anything of value. This custom, raised to the status of a right in violation of the law, did not always occur without incident.*

'*Talking to old inhabitants of the region, we have discovered an example of our assertion. Towards the middle of the nineteenth century, in 1860 to be exact, a Melliflore younger son refused to yield to his elder brother, who sent him off with gunshots.*

'*This young man went to Abriès in the Hautes-Alpes, which he was made to leave in disgrace for having taken advantage of a local girl. The claim was even made to me that the girl was also excluded from the community for having been about to give birth to an illegitimate child.*

'*The man then took a ship to South Africa. He kept writing to his brother*

from there, reproaching him for his attitude and heaping curses on him.
He did come back, however. He did not give up. As his brother had died
in the mean time, he went to his nephews and claimed his due. We lose
track of him around the 1870s. There was a rumour that he had joined
the Foreign Legion. At the time, this institution was a convenient cover
for a certain number of awkward disappearances, which the families only
half-heartedly asked to be investigated. I have never been able to find out
anything certain about the rumour.

'*I wanted to report this rather trivial anecdote here, despite its insignifi-*
cance in the history of Barles, to illustrate that the benefits of the Revolution
had sometimes still not been understood sixty years on.'

Laviolette snapped the book shut.

'I won't read you any more, as the passage I've just quoted is the
only one that was underlined by the present schoolteacher, now
deceased. We can therefore deduce that it was the only thing that interested him in this monograph . . .'

'You already spoke to me about that story on the evening you came
and asked me to listen to this Dr Pardigon, and I sent you packing. Do
you remember?'

Chabrand stood up and began to walk around the table, unconsciously wringing his hands.

'Do you think that we could have avoided two murders if I'd agreed?'

Standing there in his baggy underpants, which emphasised his
extreme thinness, he was at once solemn, pitiful and ridiculous,
tormented by doubt and a kind of remorse.

'Of course not,' Laviolette replied. 'Don't think that way. There was
no question of it. That evening, no one could have got Dr Pardigon
away from his mothering nurses, who watched over him like a treasure.
And the next day he was dead. So . . .'

'Of course. So . . .' Chabrand sighed, stretching his cold hands out
above the range.

But for a long time to come, despite the fact that death had struck
too soon, you can be sure this 'if I had' would haunt the judge's nights,
prone as he was to mull over things and scrupulously take account of

the mistakes he may have made. And besides, he could still see the body of the girl he had desired so much, dead but still pink, and the vision of that waste of flesh would not soon leave his memory.

'Sit down again!' Laviolette growled. 'You're making me dizzy, having to look up at you walking round.'

He held out the exercise book, which looked so unremarkable under its pink cover.

'Do you want to know what's at the bottom of this whole affair, yes or no? It's in there! Now, listen to what's written on the label: *The Diary of a Poor Wretch.*'

'It sounds as if you're the one who wrote it,' Chabrand said sarcastically. 'It's your favourite expression for the murderer.'

'Be open-minded,' Laviolette said. 'And listen.'

He drank a little armagnac, smacked his lips and began to read.

'*My name is Alcide Régulus. It is enough to say that I am the descendant of an abandoned child, for in the old days new-born babies left at convent doors were given these odd names by the sisters at the convent gate. I was born at Archail.*

'*Until last summer, I had no history of any kind, neither bad nor good. I was a primary schoolteacher with a good record, respected in his village, and I led a peaceful existence, enlivened by one or two hobbies.*

'*My life sank into disarray because of two equally insignificant events: the first took place last summer and the second a century ago, in 1861.*

'*Last summer I took it into my head to change the wallpaper in my bedroom, which I had valiantly put up with since I arrived in Barles fifteen years ago. It was then that I discovered the existence of a cupboard covered over by successive layers of wallpaper applied by some of my predecessors. Inside it I found the monograph of Barles, written by a certain Léon Martin. Amongst other things, this man told the story of a family called Melliflore, who still carried on the right of the eldest to inherit.*

'*I became interested in the life of the younger son, who had lived in Abriès, fathered a child there, left for Africa, came back, and then disappeared. I was probably guided by that diabolical mystery which determines all our acts.*

'I won't give all the details of my research, the time I spent on it, or how I came to be certain that he was my great-great-grandfather.

'Léon Martin's monograph referred to information passed on to him by a certain Dr Pardigon. I knew that this medical practitioner was still alive, although very old. Last summer he told me the story of the Melliflores with an incredible wealth of detail. He revealed to me, amongst other things, the existence of the treasure that Grandfather Melliflore had supposedly discovered in an inheritance his brother had passed on to him.

'When one has a receptive mind, it can embroider infinitely on any subject. Who can deny that a lost treasure always shines its brightest in the imagination of a poor wretch of a man?

'For lack of a better explanation, I could no doubt say that. But no one will ever rid me of the idea that this treasure had a certain magnetic charge (or something else?) that allowed it to come into my mind, in a way, to call me . . .'

'Strange pathos!' Chabrand interrupted coldly. 'Strange pathos for a teacher who should only argue from results.'

'He was a man,' Laviolette said, trying to account for an event that defied analysis. 'If you get down to the problem one day, you'll understand that it invariably entails a certain amount of trial and error. Shall I go on?'

'I was about to ask you.'

'I said,' Laviolette read, 'that I was sure I was descended from this Melliflore who went to Africa. Searching through my family papers (they are in the left-hand drawer in the dresser), I discovered a contract of sale for a house in Draix, and that my great-grandfather, a farrier, was called Rogations. That was the name Dr Pardigon gave me when speaking about the foundling left with the Poor Clare sisters in Mariaud. Since it was a made-up name, there can't be two of them.

'Until then, the Melliflores had been content to rob the younger sons of their property. From that day on, they also robbed them of their family name. As for me, I learned at the same time that my ancestors, both paternal and maternal, came from foundlings. And yet I was a direct descendant of the Melliflores of Barles.

296

'You will find included a family tree I have drawn up with all the dates, all the concordances of births and deaths, proving without doubt what I have claimed.'

After he had read these words, Laviolette shook the exercise book over the table. A large sheet of handmade paper folded in four to fit the format of the book fell out of it, and also a sepia postcard, which Laviolette picked up. He looked at it carefully and held it out across the table to Chabrand.

'In spite of having only one eye,' he said, 'you can certainly see that!'

'Yes. It's a man . . . But . . . it's the body we left behind in the *clues*, isn't it?'

'No. It's the original. The photo is dated 1919. You can't read the caption, but this is what it says: *Colourful Occupations: The Town Crier of Digne.*

'He's carrying a drum,' Chabrand pointed out, 'an identical drum to the one in front of us.'

Laviolette took back the postcard and turned it over.

'I'll read you what's written on the back, in the same violet ink as we found in the exercise book: *The only town crier remaining in Digne at the time, and that was because he had offered his services at a reduced price, was Gaétan Melliflore. I found out that the authorities replaced the drum every five years, and that he kept the old ones. As he worked in this capacity for eighteen years, that made four drums in all, which must have been shared out equally between his two daughters – as was all his property – since he died intestate.'

Chabrand shook his head.

'It's not getting any clearer at all,' he groaned. 'In fact it seems to be getting more and more obscure . . .'

'We'll never know how he came by this postcard,' Laviolette admitted. 'All the same, it does prove how meticulous and precise his research was. Shall I continue?'

'*If I had not been on the lookout, because of my hobby,*' Laviolette went on, '*I could never have imagined what this treasure might be, and it is here that I can speak of fate's hand in the game, for if Dr Pardigon's story had fallen on other ears than mine, it would* never *have had any conse-quences. And no one else, for a very different reason, could have discov-ered the likely place where the old miser would have hidden his find.*

'*When you think that the two daughters never found it, if I can rely on what Dr Pardigon said. When you think (and you will understand why it was easier* for me *to identify the problem) that it had escaped the uncle who gave away the cartload of useless old wares, his sons who delivered them, the inheritors, especially the girls, who were not only greedy but also vigilant, and on the lookout for an extra sou that the other one might get in her share. Under these conditions, how could it remain unknown to all of them?* Only because of its very nature. The only precise clue was the words Gaétan Melliflore said in the presence of Dr Pardigon: "What it is to be ignorant!"

'*It was one night, one windy night when I had to get up to fasten the shutter in the kitchen, which was banging against the wall; it was just when I was leaning outside with my face being whipped by the cold night air; it was at that precise moment that I knew for sure, and not from any process of reasoning: the uncle (that is to say my great-great-grandfather) had sent his curses to his brother for more than a year from a place that Dr Pardigon called Adamastor . . .*'

'Adamastor!' Chabrand exclaimed. 'That's the word you said a while ago when you leaned over the body.'

'That's true. Pardigon used that word to me too when he talked about the place where the outlaw of 1861 had spent a year's exile. Adamastor. Probably because some connections were not working very well in his brain. For example, he could never say what instrument Gaétan Melliflore used to make people gather round him when he was town crier. In this instance he was confusing a precise geographical name with more or less vague literary recollections . . . because Adamastor doesn't exist anywhere in the world. Adamastor is . . . but I'll tell you about that later.'

'Go to the devil!' Chabrand muttered.

Laviolette continued reading unperturbed.

'*If I was not mistaken, the treasure discovered by Gaétan Melliflore* must be so small that he could keep it on his person all the time. But as he did not want to leave it to his legitimate heirs, his daughters (or to anyone else for that matter), who would necessarily find it in his clothing when he died, what other possibility remained?

'The idea of the drums came to me from the subjective phenomenon called intuition, and from the power of my reasoning. Both had received long training from my having to discover the hiding places where my sly pupils hid incriminating or forbidden objects. This is an exercise in which I have always excelled.

'It was then that I wrote to my cousins, and I have every right to call them such, to ask them to sell me the drums, using the pretext that I was a collector. I never received any reply . . . Then the very nature of the treasure, which I guessed, began to drive me mad . . .

'I went prowling around the easily accessible attics of the Champourcieux tannery and The Cedars villa. (Some doors were always open there.) But I couldn't find the drums. The two women had put them in a safe place or else they moved them from one place to another. On the other hand, I did discover the collection of calendars that belonged to their grandfather, the postman. That's where I came across an illustration of the 1912 calendar, which was a revelation, for the grandfather had circled it in black, and in the margin under the dates had written these two words: "That's it!"'

'I must stop you there!' the judge exclaimed. 'There's something wrong somewhere. If your murderer wrote to the two heiresses, asking them to sell him the drums, that should have made them suspicious, since they knew that there was a treasure their grandfather had hidden, and which had never been found. At the very least, they should have looked inside them themselves to check.'

'As they're dead, they can't answer that question. One could conjecture, however, that if they didn't, it was firstly because they didn't confide in each other, and consequently they couldn't know that the other inheritors had received the same proposition. It remained a simple request that didn't need an answer.'

'But afterwards? When they received the threatening letter we found in each of their houses? They must have suspected that there was some-thing fishy going on.'

'Now then. First of all their well-known avarice did not allow them to damage something that had cost money. They also knew that there were four drums shared among the four women. If one of them contained the treasure, the three others were obviously empty. I think that their pride made them prefer not to know, so that they would have no regrets. They were content to fiercely defend their own property. Perhaps if they'd had the time, they might have eventually opened up their drums. Who knows what goes on in a miser's head?'

He thought for a moment, then added, 'Then again, how do you know that they hadn't been opened? A drum can be taken apart, if one has time. The murderer ripped them open because he was impatient . . . Shall I go on?'

Though not entirely convinced, the judge nodded and mumbled his agreement.

'But,' Laviolette read, '*when fate has decided that you will lose respect for yourself, you can look surprised at its tricks as much as you like. As unbelievable as its actions may seem – to you who are forever referring to the sacrosanct estimates of probability – fate is there, it taunts you, it pulls out of its cheap magician's hat an event that you would never think has anything to do with you. And this event took place well over a hundred years ago, in the year 1861, 12,000 kilometres from here, on the shores of the Indian Ocean (which the doctor called Adamastor because he remembered* The Lusiads *by Camões,* * *but he had forgotten his geography). That circumstance does not make it any less real or less tragic.*

'*What could seem more unremarkable, however, than a poor soul who goes into a tobacconist's (or its equivalent, as there have always been shops that sell writing materials and stamps all over the world) to buy notepaper,*

* The poem *Os Lusíadas* (1572) by Luis de Camões gives a fantastical interpretation of the jour-neys of Vasco da Gama. Adamastor is a mythical beast of rock, a symbol of the desolation of Africa and the forces of nature the Portuguese navigators had to overcome. The classic work of Portuguese literature.

a penholder and some violet ink? Well! It was nevertheless this most insignificant of events that made me a murderer . . .'

Laviolette stopped speaking. He continued reading in silence for a few moments more, turning the pages then skimming them, before closing the exercise book again and putting it back on the table.

'That's it,' he said. 'From there on, the diary doesn't relate facts any more, only pages of soul-searching, and I'll spare you that. It's a debate between a man and his conscience. The laments of the one when the other comes back from one of his sorties. The highs and lows, and also the repetitions, the redundancies of a mind going round in circles. In the calm atmosphere of your study, when you have the use of both eyes again, you can study page by page the descent into hell of an honest man.'

He stopped talking and pulled the drum towards him, jealously closing his arms around it. He looked slightly mischievously at Chabrand over the top of this bulky object.

'As for the rest,' he said, 'the drum will reveal that.'

He stood up, looking large in his long johns and flannel vest. He went over to his clothes steaming over the backs of chairs. He searched through the pockets, muttering under his breath about his untidiness.

He came back with a folding knife in his hand.

'Thanks to my old Glandières,' he said, 'if this drum has it in him, he'll tell us right now!'

He opened the knife and secured the ferrule. He pointed it at Chabrand to emphasise the importance of his words.

'Because,' he said, 'there's one chance in two that the teacher's deductions were wrong; one chance in two that the Melliflores' treasure was hidden somewhere else; one chance in two, I'll admit, that one of the women inheritors opened one of the drums and took it out; in short, one chance in two that all these murders were committed for nothing!'

He gave a wide sweep of his arm holding the knife to encompass the whole atmosphere of the tranquil room where they were sitting.

'Try to picture it!' he said. 'Try to imagine! Leave your rigid persona as bogey of the Republic for a moment and turn your attention to suffering humanity. You see . . .'

He lowered his voice as if some ghost could be listening attentively.

'He's a poor wretch of a man,' he said. 'I can see him, as if I were present, each time he comes back here. He comes up the stairs full of hope. The drum he brings with him bangs against the banister on the stairs as this one did. He comes in. He locks the door. He puts the drum down on this table. He rips it open. Nothing! It's empty! And this happens three times. Isn't that enough to unhinge his mind?'

'It was unhinged before that. You don't kill all those people for such a doubtful benefit, or if you do, you're mad.'

'If this one is also empty,' Laviolette said, pointing to the drum, 'you're free to draw that conclusion. But if that's the case, and you want to know what it possibly *could have* contained, you'll just have to take my word for it.'

'Because, of course, you know!' Chabrand exclaimed, with more than a hint of sarcasm.

'Do you remember the calendar that was missing from the collection in Ambroisine Larchet's attic?'

'Naturally. The teacher took it. He mentions it in that exercise book.'

'Yes, but I've found its twin. The same. It was blocking the flue in the ruins of the Melliflore farm. It was illegible except for the date. But I had the idea of writing to the printer – the same firm has been printing these calendars for ever. They sent me a facsimile of the whole 1912 range.'

'Since it was illegible, you couldn't know whether the one that was stolen was the same as the one at the farm.'

'No, I didn't know. And I really can't boast: I had no intuition about it, not a glimmer. I was looking, that's all. I was prompted by those words of Gaétan Melliflore: "What it is to be ignorant!" Why then wasn't *he* ignorant? Well, it was simply due to the fact that he was an avid collector. One day he found himself looking at the original of what he had seen on the illustration of the 1912 calendar, and he recognised it. And here's that very calendar!'

He waved it theatrically in front of him.

'You're showing me the wrong side!' Chabrand complained.

'I'm keeping some ammunition in reserve in case the drum is empty . . .'

He sank the blade of the knife into the skin, which gave a sound like a little squeak of pain. He slowly began cutting out the white leather around the rim, as if opening a tin. It took some effort

'If this knife wasn't a Glandières,' he said, 'I'd never be able to do it.'

He gave a sigh of relief and took his time closing the knife again. Chabrand had risen from his chair and was staring at the scrap of old hide still separating him from the truth. The two men's heads almost met above the instrument. Laviolette delicately lifted up the piece of hide. The underside of the skin looked pale, just like new.

The cavity was empty. All that came out was a musty old smell that soon disappeared in the air.

The two men fell back on to their respective chairs, stunned and disappointed.

'You have a curious way of concluding your demonstrations,' the judge said sternly.

Laviolette shot him a reproachful look. He put his arms around the empty drum again like a sulky child whose offered toy has been rejected. He almost laid his face on it. He began to feel it all over, hold it up to the light, smell it, peer at its seams and joins, and at the parts that kept it circular and rigid.

The judge followed this with sympathy for his perseverance.

'I notice,' Laviolette said tentatively, 'that the ring around the drum holding the bottom skin in place isn't in one piece like the one on top. Someone has tinkered with it. It's possible that . . .'

He tapped various parts of the remaining skin with his index finger. It gave a dull thud. He put his ear against it like a deaf musician trying to catch the sounds it produced. After a while he put the drum back on the table with a sigh, but the other way up. He picked up his knife and opened it again, giving Chabrand a furtive look.

'It's possible that . . .'

With infinite caution, he inserted the point of the knife into the leather, but did not sink the whole blade into it. When he had pierced the skin, he lowered the handle parallel to the edge of the drum to avoid cutting vertically. He put his hand in as soon as he had made an opening big enough. As he began to pull back the piece of hide towards him, Chabrand, who was looking on fascinated, noticed that another pale skin was appearing under the first. Once again the two heads almost met.

As Laviolette folded back the top skin above the second new intact one, an object appeared which was soon completely visible. It was a plain brown envelope without any writing or any particular marking.

'So he wasn't mistaken . . .'

Laviolette spoke softly as if the man lying broken in the *clues* of the Bès could still hear him. He picked up the flat envelope with great care. It was light and unsealed. He lifted up the flap. Inside was a single sheet of paper of that smoky colour typical of things that have aged for a long time. It was not folded in four, but in the intricate way used in the old days to achieve the required format, before envelopes were commonly used by the poor. It must have been closed with a seal originally, but had then been opened and since those early days had lain there for whoever wanted to read it. Laviolette unfolded it carefully. The ink used to write it was almost faded. He held the paper up to the light. He ran his eyes over it first, under the eager gaze of Chabrand, who finally could contain himself no longer.

'Well, for God's sake! Are you going to read me what it says?'

Laviolette began, speaking softly as if apologising for revealing these painful words.

Tuesday, 24 October 1861

Brother by no means dear; loveless, worthless brother. I have been such a long time here in the Cape, which for me is of bad, very bad hope. I am under this overcast sky, this endless overcast sky. I am here on the end of the jetty, no use to anyone. In front of me, stretching for 10,000 kilometres all the way to the South Pole, is this sea, this nasty, ugly ocean of frighteningly dark water. And I who like only the land . . . Six months. I have been waiting here

*for six months. When I sail on that ocean, it will be on a boat
that is as worm-eaten as Grandmother's bread trough at home . . .
Your home, that is . . . Who knows when I will arrive? Who
knows if I will arrive? I think of Barles. That is the only place
where I was happy . . . I would have looked after the sheep in the
sunshine. For just a crust of bread . . . What would I have cost
you? I hope, I wish that one day you will suffer what I am
suffering now.*

*When I was in Abriès, I went into a church one day and this is
what I read on the beams:* Give good measure, for the measure
you give will be the measure you get. *This is for you who gave
me such unfair measure: may the days meted out to you, your
children and all your descendants be as bad as those you meted
out to me. This is my only wish for you.*

Amen.

Laviolette was quiet for a moment, then gave a sigh.

'And it's not even signed. He knew that his Christian name itself, his
name, no longer meant anything to those who would receive that
letter . . .'

'Very well!' Chabrand exclaimed. 'So is that all there is? So? What
does that have to do with the treasure? How does it explain all those
murders?'

Laviolette put the letter back in the envelope without a word, and
laid it down on the table.

'There,' he said, 'you'll have to make a little effort. Hold the docu-
ment up to your good eye and take a close look at it, please.'

Chabrand did as he was asked. He managed to make out and read
aloud the address that had been written in now faded ink:

*Monsieur Rosarius Melliflore, Horse-Choker Farm, Barles, Department
of the Basses-Alpes, France.*

He gave Laviolette an enquiring look.

'Well,' he said. 'What else?'

'Above it! Above the address! What do you see?'

'I can see five triangles. Probably postage stamps. What's surprising about that? The postal service had been in existence since 1849.'

'*O sancta simplicitas!*' Laviolette exclaimed. 'To think that you've been taught so many things and not taught so many others!'

He picked up the ordinary piece of greyish paper lying on the table, and waved it under the judge's nose.

'Don't you know,' he said, 'that if right now word got around that here in Barles there's a letter with those five stamps, thousands of people would descend on us to snatch them up for a huge amount of money, or perhaps even kill us for them? They'd come from everywhere: the US, Japan, Russia, the Arab Emirates, and who knows where else?'

He pointed his finger at the letter and tapped it peremptorily to emphasise his words, being careful not to touch the stamps.

'What you have before you is one of the rarest stamps in the world. I'm not an expert, but I've done some research. Give me your attention for a moment longer. The Colony of the Cape of Good Hope was a British dominion, which Dr Pardigon confused with Adamastor, the Giant of the Rocks. In 1853 it issued two triangular stamps with an upright anchor watermark: one was the fourpence red, and the other the one-penny blue. These stamps were printed in England. Are you following me?'

'Perfectly,' Chabrand said.

'Well, here's where the destinies of the four Melliflore descendants, Pencenat, Monsieur Fondère and the poor devil lying in the rain in the Barles *clues* come together . . . Listen carefully! And for your edification, just marvel at what fate can devise so long in advance.

'Well now, in 1861, a coach is carrying a package of these stamps to be loaded on to a frigate. (I hope you admire how well-informed I am). This coach breaks an axle between Battersea and Southampton. By the time the repairs are done or the vehicles are changed, the sailing ship has departed and the stamps are left behind. Are you still with me?'

'Yes, yes . . .' Chabrand sighed.

'Good! So now the Cape Colony is short of stamps. What does the colonial government do? It decides to print a series itself. But there are two drawbacks: firstly it doesn't have the same materials as the home country – only laid paper without the original anchor watermark; secondly they make a cock-up of the colour. The woodblocks are mixed up, and some sheets are printed with colour errors. The one penny that shold be blue comes out red, and the fourpence that should be red becomes blue. In addition to that, the two series will be rapidly withdrawn and destroyed: just the time it takes to realise the mistake and send the current printing from England.'

Laviolette paused for a moment, then continued.

'That explains to you why, in today's market, each of the five unremarkable stamps stuck on this letter – two penny reds and three fourpenny blues – is worth three hundred thousand of our francs apiece!'

'You're joking!' Chabrand exclaimed.

Laviolette shook his head.

'And that's just the catalogue price. You'd get much more from a knowledgeable, keen collector because the stamps are in perfect condition. Remember when Lord Curzon's inheritance was sold . . .'

'It's ludicrous!' Chabrand said, interrupting him.

'The ludicrous thing,' Laviolette said, 'was that precisely that year and during those months, the Melliflore brother from Barles should be exiled in that particular spot in the world, waiting for a boat to take him home and spending his time writing letters full of curses to his brother. Who knows how many of those letters the brother must have thrown out or burned? And how many others were lost in those times when the post was in its infancy? Will we ever know by what miracle and what lucky escapes that one arrived at the farm? Just think of it: twelve thousand kilometres!'

With a dramatic gesture he produced the 1912 post-office calendar which Monsieur Régulus had discovered in The Cedars villa. This time he presented it right way up.

'Look at it carefully,' he said. 'These are enlarged facsimiles of the two stamps: one red and the other blue. If Gaétan Melliflore hadn't had this calendar right in front of him, he would never have been able to discover how valuable they were. That's what he meant by his remark: "What it is to be ignorant!" Look at the two words he wrote on the top of the calendar: *That's it!*, and don't forget the exclamation mark.'

He took a deep breath.

'Five examples of two of the rarest stamps in the world! Can't you imagine that someone could kill for them?'

'I'm not a philatelist. I don't understand obsessive people,' the judge said haughtily. 'In my opinion, those murders were committed by a madman. It's as simple as that.'

'And in my opinion,' Laviolette said, 'they were committed by a poet, a man of imagination. Those stamps were that wretched country teacher's golden fleece. And besides, he certainly didn't go after them for their market value.'

He leafed through the two albums bound in padded cordovan leather. Everything a poor wretch of a man had been able to afford in the pursuit of his passion during the whole of his life was there inside them, sorted, grouped, impeccably set out and annotated. You could see how he had spent the best times of his life with these decorative pages of brightly coloured stamps. A hint of chamomile still lingered in his precious albums.

Laviolette stopped and stared. In the middle of the black pages with so much in them, there was a completely empty one, recently added and numbered as an extra page. A label in the left-hand corner explained in copperplate writing why it was empty:

Fourpence Blue (1861 issue)

In the centre of the page a tiny triangle had been meticulously drawn to scale, ready to receive the marvel the schoolteacher hoped to find.

'He was only looking for one,' Laviolette murmured. 'How could he have suspected anything more than that?'

He turned away from the table to expose the reverse side of his overcoat to the heat of the well-stoked kitchen range.

'I can't help thinking,' he said, 'of that burnt body in the rain . . . and that when fate has once decided you'll be a loser, you can show as much competence, intuition, lack of scruples, duplicity, or cruelty as you like. There's nothing you can do about it. Despite the crimes you wouldn't hesitate to commit, fate will make you a figure of mockery . . . In the end, if it hasn't got you by other means, it'll thrust a bolt of lightning into your head, and you can say goodbye to everything. That's your lot.'

'You look as if you regret its verdict.'

'I'd have liked . . .' Laviolette began. 'But you wouldn't understand. He didn't even see the stamps, the poor wretch! We did, and we couldn't give a damn. We who see these things for what they are: miserable bits of paper! And we're the ones who can gaze at them with not a tremor of excitement!'

He stopped talking. He was holding the envelope and fingering it nervously.

'Chabrand!' he said suddenly. 'Are you up to understanding what I'm going to say to you?'

Chabrand just looked at him with eyebrows raised.

'Yes,' Laviolette went on. 'It's an idea that's come into my mind because I've just estimated the fortune that these little things represent. What's going to happen now? This letter will moulder away in a glass case in a museum until some mad super-wealthy philatelist pays crooks to steal it for his private collection. Just look at it! It's even easier to hide than a diamond.'

'It's absurd,' the judge said.

'Exactly! You should . . . well, you could . . . slip that in your wallet and trade it anywhere in the whole wide world. You're young, you can dream up some great, urgent needs. With this, you can have everything! The Bermudas, Tahiti, the hula girls, the birds of the Galapagos, you name it. We burn the exercise book with the teacher's story. We even burn the biography. As for the rest, you can count on me to find a plausible explanation for everything. The drum was empty. Who would understand? Who would know? Especially now that investigations have been dropped. Everyone will think as you do: Monsieur Régulus was mad!'

He held the letter out across the table.

'I'd just like to see you live,' he said.

The judge seized the square of paper in which an exile had poured out his curse in a wail of pain and longing for his lost homeland. He looked at it in silence for a moment, shaking his head. He returned Laviolette's long, piercing look with a mocking smile that may also have contained a hint of affection. He finally put the letter down on the table, murmuring almost to himself:

'That's right. But that would mean that I could never live here again.'

He stood up, a little embarrassed by what else he had to say. He turned away from Laviolette to fetch his trousers, which must have been dry by now, and added:

'You know that Digne is the only place in the world I love. It's the only place where I can live.'

This confession of faith brought four tiny tears to Laviolette's eyes, which he could not suppress. He almost put his hand on the judge's and told him, 'Me too.'

He walked over to the stove to hide his emotion. Without thinking, he shook the damper, opened the door and threw another log on fire.

'What are you doing?' Chabrand said. 'We must find a telephone and inform the gendarmes about this whole crazy business.'

Laviolette nodded. He put on his trousers. The judge was already adjusting his bow tie, which made him look a completely different man.

They heard the plane trees rustling in the school yard. The storm had disperse far off to the west. A salmon-coloured dawn was rising in a wave above the Blayeul.

Standing out against that sky, which would slowly reveal a fine Christmas Day, the ruins of the Melliflore farm could now be seen from the window, high up on a foothill of the mountain. Two narrow pieces of wall still stood arrogantly pointing upwards from the rubble, like discreet fingers placed over the secret they had harboured.

Down below towards the south, the narrow gap of the *clues* opened a stingy section of its labyrinth to the radiant light, which would never penetrate to the bottom.

The resounding joy of that winter morning seemed to express the great relief of all the elements that had resolutely shunned the truth throughout the whole of this long story, the unabashed dissembling of the inhabitants, the cover of darkness, the solitude of night. Barles was delighted that just one corner of the veil covering all its mysteries had scarcely been lifted.

'The wind is rising . . .' the judge said.

Laviolette was thinking of his cats. He was also thinking with some regret of the big girl at Malefiance whom he could perhaps have held tight in his arms, if it were not for this night which had been so eventful and full of surprises. And he thought again of the bottle of Chambertin – not unrelated – which he had opened and never tasted the evening before, and which had been sitting ever since next to his book opened at the unfinished page. These two objects on the coffee table must tell each other curious tales of solitary men.

All these lost opportunities gave Laviolette enough feelings of regret for him to complete the judge's remark with his favourite quotation:[*]

'"We must choose life",' he said.

[*] 'Le vent se lève! . . . Il faut tenter de vivre!' ('The wind is rising! . . . We must try to live!'), from the poem by Paul Valéry, 'Le cimetière marin' ('The Cemetery by the Sea').

BY PIERRE MAGNAN
ALSO AVAILABLE FROM VINTAGE